GRIP

(GRIP TRILOGY BOOK 2)

KENNEDY RYAN

GRIP TRILOGY BOOK #2

Read the Full *Grip* Trilogy!
FREE in Kindle Unlimited!

Box Set in KU:
All (3) books
US: https://amzn.to/2Gh3Rrs
Worldwide: http://mybook.to/TheGripBoxSet

FLOW (Grip #1)
GRIP (Grip #2)
STILL (Grip #3)

*Audiobooks available for all 3 titles.
Check Audible Escape to listen FREE with subscription!

COPYRIGHT

Grip
Copyright (c) Kennedy Ryan, 2017

Cover Art:
Najla Qamber
Qamber Designs

Cover Photos:
Sarah Zimmerman Photo

Editing:
Angela Smith, Word Whisperer

Proofreading/Copyediting:
Ashley Williams, AW Editing
Paige Maroney Smith

AUTHOR'S NOTE

I'm so excited to share Grip and Bristol's story with you. This is a really special journey that encompasses not only a timeless love story, but also touches on some of the most pressing issues of our time. I wrote these books a few years ago, and hoped issues like police brutality would be less relevant by now. Unfortunately, they are more pressing than ever.

When I decided to do a box set and new covers for the Grip Trilogy, I also decided to revisit the conversations around social justice to ensure I had clearly articulated what my characters believe and where they stand. Bristol and Grip's story has not changed. It is as I originally dreamt and penned it, but with a few word choice changes for clarity. Doing an update through Amazon should deliver the most current changes to readers' devices.

Readers tell me all the time how this journey has touched them. To every person who has ever reached out, expressed how this story affected you, just know that *you* impacted me, and I'm so grateful Grip & Bristol's journey brought us together!

Thank you for reading!

ALSO BY KENNEDY RYAN

The SOUL Trilogy

Want Rhyson's story?

Two musicians chase their dreams

and catch feelings!

Dive into the Soul Trilogy!

(Rhyson + Kai)

(FREE in Kindle Unlimited)

My Soul to Keep (Soul 1)*

Down to My Soul (Soul 2)*

Refrain (Soul 3)

Audiobooks Available in Audible Escape!

ALL THE KING'S MEN WORLD

Love stories spanning decades, political intrigue, obsessive passion. If you
loved the TV show *SCANDAL*, this series is for you!

The Kingmaker (Duet Book 1: Lennix + Maxim)

FREE in KU!

Ebook, Audio & Paperback

mybook.to/TheKingmakerKindle

The Rebel King (Duet Book 2: Lennix + Maxim)

FREE in KU!

Ebook, Audio & Paperback

mybook.to/RebelKingKindle

Queen Move (Standalone Couple: Kimba + Ezra)

https://geni.us/QueenMovePlatforms

The Killer & The Queen

(Standalone Novella - Grim + Noelani)

Coming Soon!

(co-written with Sierra Simone)

www.subscribepage.com/TKandTQ

HOOPS Series

(Interconnected Standalone Stories set in the explosive world of professional basketball!)

LONG SHOT (A HOOPS Novel)

Iris + August's Story

Ebook, Audio & Paperback:

https://kennedyryanwrites.com/long-shot/

BLOCK SHOT (A HOOPS Novel)

Banner + Jared's Story

Ebook, Audio & Paperback

http://kennedyryanwrites.com/block-shot/

HOOK SHOT (A HOOPS Novel)

Lotus + Kenan's Story

Ebook, Audio & Paperback

http://kennedyryanwrites.com/hook-shot/

HOOPS Holiday (A HOOPS Novella)

Avery + Decker's Story

http://kennedyryanwrites.com/hoops-holiday/

Order Signed Paperbacks

THE BENNETT SERIES

When You Are Mine (Bennett 1)

Loving You Always (Bennett 2)

Be Mine Forever (Bennett 3)

Until I'm Yours (Bennett 4)

"You are the perfect verse over a tight beat."
–Brown Sugar

PROLOGUE

EIGHT YEARS AGO, After Spring Break—New York

I FEEL LIKE A FOOL.

Like those foolish girls who fall for the tricks of beautiful men. Men who keep women on the side. Men who cheat and don't think twice about lying. I'm usually an excellent judge of character, but I was blinded by a charismatic smile and gorgeous body. By a brilliant mind and a silver tongue. So starved for attention, I mistook Grip's attention for kindness. Something I could count on. Something I could believe in. I forgot I can only count on myself. Only believe in myself. But now I remember. His girlfriend screaming on the front lawn jarred my memory.

"Cheating asshole," I mutter, rolling my mammoth Louis Vuitton suitcase through the front door of my parents' New York home.

My classes at Columbia don't start back up for another two days, so I'll hang here until I have to be back in the city. My apartment is cold and lonely. I glance around our foyer, checker-boarded with black-and-white tiles, and up the wide staircase. This crypt of a house is pretty cold and lonely, too. After the last week in LA, surrounded by Rhyson's friends, I feel the isolation more profoundly.

At least there's an elevator here. Because dragging this huge suit-case up the steps is not my idea of fun after a five-hour flight. I'm headed around the corner to the elevator when a sound above draws my eyes up the stairs again.

A moan?

I listen more closely, despite my suspicion that I shouldn't.

Grunting and cries of what sounds like intense pleasure.

"Well, well, well." I laugh despite the crappy day I've had. "At least somebody's getting some, even though it's my parents. Ew."

I'm not actually disgusted. I think I'm . . . happy. Happy that after all these years of thinking my parents didn't even want or love each other, they thought I wouldn't be home and are upstairs happily fucking in their glorious middle age. I'd always assumed their marriage was more of a business partnership than anything else, with Rhyson and me the two-for-one requisite heirs of a powerful arranged alliance. But it seems they do want each other. It makes my heart just a little lighter.

That's saying something considering I stayed in the bathroom crying until the flight attendant forced me out for takeoff. Over that . . .chocolate charm lothario. That cheat. That . . . liar. My eyes are still a little puffy, a situation I need to remedy before Mother's sharp glance starts probing. I'll already have to endure an interrogation about how Rhyson is doing in Los Angeles. They haven't seen my twin brother since that fateful day in court when he emancipated. They've talked to him even less than I have over the last few years.

"Oh, God! Yes. Yes!"

They're getting louder and more fervent. Okay, this is getting awkward. They obviously don't think anyone else is home, or they wouldn't be quite so uninhibited. I'll just slip into my room and come out later.

Someone walks through the front door behind me just as the elevator opens. Maybe Bertie, our housekeeper?

It's my mother. Oh my God.

Every auburn hair in place, her face as smooth and lineless as it has been the last twenty-one years. She sets her Celine bag on the table by the front door.

"Bristol, welcome home." She walks forward, her gait even and confident, so similar to mine it's like watching myself move. She air kisses, an insubstantial affection that falls short of my cheek. "I want to hear all about your trip, of course."

"Of course."

I mentally scramble for a way to get her out before the couple upstairs starts grunting and moaning again. Is it Dad? I can't even convince myself that my father is not upstairs fucking another woman. There's no other logical explanation.

"Mother, I want to tell you everything." I leave my suitcase by the elevator and walk to the front door. "Let's go grab coffee. That little place up the street. Pano's?"

"Coffee?" Mother has a way of injecting tiny amounts of scorn into just about anything, including the little laugh she offers at my suggestion. "You just got here. I just walked in the door. Why would we—"

"Fuck, yes!" The exclamation comes from upstairs.

Mother freezes and whatever drops of scorn she was poised to deliver congeal on her painted lips. Her eyes slowly climb the staircase before they return to meet mine. She looks as self-assured as she ever has, but there's a film over her eyes as fragile as blown glass.

"Mother, we could—"

"It's fine, Bristol." She nods to the suitcase by the elevator. "Take your bags upstairs and we'll talk at dinner about your trip to see your brother."

"But, Mother, we should—"

"Bristol, my God! Can't you just listen for once? Can't you just for once do exactly what I ask you to do and not make my life any harder?"

It isn't true. It isn't fair. I haven't made her life harder. Not ever. I've accepted the nannies who raised me when she and my father took Rhyson on the road. I lay on the couches of New York's finest therapists when Mother abdicated walking me through my "issues" as a child. I was an honor student. When she asked me to do the stupid debutante thing with the sons and daughters of all her Upper Eastside friends, I did it. I'm in an Ivy League college, like she wanted. If anything, I've bent over backward, pretzeled myself to please her when I could.

I turn to leave, but a door upstairs flies open, and a blonde girl, maybe a year or two older than I am, rockets down the hall. Nina Algier, a brilliant flute player and one of my parents' clients, stops and stares at us over the railing above, hair wild, eyes wide and horrified. Tall and coltish, she's a rising star in the Boston Symphony Orchestra. She looks back over her shoulder as my father joins her there.

Rhyson and I share his dark coloring, taking only Mother's gray eyes. He looks so much like Rhyson and Uncle Grady, handsome, distinguished, with just a little gray at the temples. His eyes flick to me before moving on. I never feel like I even register for him. I'm not musical; therefore, I'm worthless. That is how it's always felt. The hardness in his eyes softens just a bit when he sees my mother, maybe with remorse. I've never seen my father sorry for anything, so I wouldn't recognize it on him.

"Angela," he says so softly that his voice barely reaches us by the door. "You're home."

I bounce a look between my father and my mother and Nina Algier, certain that I'm in an alternative universe. That's all? That's fucking all he has to say?

Nina, who has been as still as an ice sculpture to that point, galvanizes into action, rushing down the stairs. Her white silk blouse is half-buttoned and hanging from the waistband of her skirt, and there's a flush painted on her cheeks when she cannons past us. She smells of my father's cologne.

"I'm sorry, Mrs. Gray," she mumbles, avoiding our eyes and fumbling with the door handle until it finally opens and she springs free.

"Go to your room, Bristol," my mother says, her voice the same low, even tone it's always been. "We'll talk about your trip later."

I'm torn between railing on my father, comforting my mother, and getting the hell out of here. I take door number three.

Or rather I take the elevator. As soon as I step off and start toward my bedroom, I hear their raised voices. Their anger, their contention, it was a sound I had never heard before that moment. Not even when Rhyson sued to emancipate did they present anything other than a united front. A cold front, but always united. My parents aren't prone to displays of affection or expressions of love, so I never expect the emotion that rises from downstairs before I hear the front door slam.

Damn this day. It has ravaged me.

I flop onto my bed and close my eyes. My room, which has been empty for months, is cold. New York is cold. It was only last night that I waded nearly naked into the waves, a hedonist seeking my pleasure with a beautiful man I thought I knew in no time. Even after only a handful of days, I thought I knew. How he got close enough to break my heart so quickly, I'm not sure, but I know it is not whole. Maybe I fell for the possibility of him. The idea that there was actually someone out there who saw me, flaws and all, and would accept me. "Got" me. That must be it. And yet, I can already feel those places around my heart that I stiffened and starched to forget him . . . softening. Giving some quarter and asking me if I shouldn't let him explain. If maybe he does deserve that second chance.

"Weak bitch." I'm the only one in the room to hear the admonishment. I'm the only one who needs to.

Exhaustion must have demanded her due, because I don't even recall falling asleep. When I wake, the room is darker and colder. I'm not in LA, the land of sand and sun. It's still New York, and it's still cold, and maybe that's as it should be. I slip out of the wrinkled clothes I flew and slept in and put on leggings and a Columbia sweatshirt before padding down the stairs in search of food. Surely Bertie made something for me.

I'm in the kitchen, foraging between the pantry and the fridge, when I hear the weeping. I drop a drumstick on the counter and follow that sorrowful sound. Seeing your mother cry for the first time is always hard for a child. I don't know that it's any easier because I'm twenty-one years old. I can't recall ever seeing her tears, not this way. Not sprawled on the living room floor surrounded by shattered glass and spilled liquor.

"Mother, let me help you." I reach for her, but she wrenches away.

"Leave." A broken sob drowns the word. "God, why can't you just leave me alone like everyone else does?"

Her words are always sharp, but I think she sharpens them to their finest point for me. And they always find their mark, bull's-eye in my heart.

"Get up." I grab her arm despite her efforts to keep it from me. "There's glass everywhere."

"Bertie will get it," she slurs.

I look more closely and realize she's drunk. Totally, sloppy drunk. I loop her arm over my shoulder, half-dragging her to the couch where I prop her up. Her head droops to the side, and I see the tracks of tears in her usually flawless makeup.

"Mother, he isn't worth this." I keep my voice soft but try to sound convincing.

"How would you know?" The words roll around in her mouth, a soup of consonants and vowels. "You have no idea."

"I know that if a man cheats once, he'll do it again."

"Once?" A bitter laugh cracks her face open. "You think this was the first time? Oh, God. I've lost count. There's the ghosts of a hundred Nina Algiers in our bed."

"Then leave him." I take a seat beside her, grabbing her hand to urge her. "You're stronger than this."

"No." She says the word sadly, quietly, helplessly. "I'm not."

When she looks at me, I see that it isn't just the decanter that's shattered all over the floor. My mother is shattered, and there are shards of glass, decades old, in her eyes.

"I love him," she whispers. "He'll have to leave me, because I love him, and I don't know how to stop. I don't know how to let go."

The strongest woman I know? Tough as nails negotiator? The enemy you never want to face, leveled by love?

"I can't believe you tolerate it, Mother."

"Oh, spare me, Bristol." Her disgust and anger trip over each other to get to me. "You'll be here one day if you're not careful. In this same spot, with this same broken heart."

"You're wrong." Something in my heart whispers that she's right, but I can't acknowledge it. I won't.

She sits up from her drunken slump and looks me right in the eyes with sudden clarity.

"You are just like me, maybe worse," she says. "You need too much. And you'll love too much, too, if you're not careful. I fell in love with the wrong man a long time ago, and people like you and me, we don't know how to stop."

"Stop saying I'm like that." The words throb in my throat before I can release them.

"I don't have to say it." She drags herself up and over to the bar, grabbing another bottle and pouring herself a drink. "You already know it's true."

Even knowing all that Grip has done, there is still some part of me that wants it to all be a cruel joke so I can forgive him. Give him that second chance. Maybe she's right. Maybe I am like her. But if I am, I'm learning her lesson here, today. She loves the wrong man so hard that even when he hurts her, she can't turn it off.

If that's how we love, then it's better to never start.

G<small>RIP</small>

. . .

S_{IX} Y_{EARS} A_{GO}, After Graduation—Los Angeles

B_{Y THE TIME} I _{ARRIVE}, Bristol's welcome party is in full swing. Maybe that's best. Maybe it will make things less awkward. We haven't seen each other in two years. When she wouldn't answer my calls or text messages, or even confirm she received the book of Neruda poems I mailed to her, as hard as it was, I had to let it go. I messed up, and she shut me out. I told myself I'd try again when she finished college and moved here to LA. Rhys and Bristol kept in touch and made progress over the last two years. Now, she's here to do what she said she would—manage Rhyson's music career.

I've entered Grady's house more times than I can count, but I've never felt nervous crossing this threshold. Like can't-eat-need-a-drink nervous. And there hasn't been anyone to really talk to about this. I know Bristol didn't tell Rhys what happened between us, and I took my cue from her. How we resolve this is our business, no on else's. I hope once we get this shit sorted, once she understands, we can see if there's anything left of what we started two years ago. If it's even worth trying. It wasn't long enough to be love. It's too deep, and I'm too old for a crush. It's too raw for infatuation. I may not be able to put a name to it, but it didn't vacate the premises when Bristol left. I can't evict it.

The living room is packed, crowded with people I don't think Bristol knows. They're our friends, and all they know is that Rhyson's sister is moving to LA. I walk in on some joke already punch lined because everyone is laughing. I slip in, wanting to go unnoticed. Jimmi immediately makes that impossible.

"Grip!" She unfolds herself from the cross-legged pose on the floor and throws herself at me. "I wondered where you were."

I squeeze Jimmi but look over her shoulder and directly into Bristol's silvery eyes. Only for a second before she looks away and dives back into a conversation as if I don't exist. But that second tells me a lot. It'll take more than an apology to fix things between us. She looked right through me as if I wasn't there. As if she wished I weren't.

She looks even better than before. Her hair is shorter and sits just above her shoulders instead of down her back. Her face looks leaner, like something chiseled all the illusions away from the soft flesh and striking bones, sharpening her. Black jeans, high-heeled boots, and a silk blouse that leaves her arms and shoulders bare and ties behind her neck. She had a high shine before, but now there's something more polished about her. The sophistication gleams even brighter. It could have been that big-time internship she got with Sound Management in New York. Or maybe she just grew up.

"Dude." Rhyson stands, too, coming to dap me up and grin. "How'd the session go?"

"Good." My eyes stray to Bristol, who is still in deep conversation with a small group of people. "We knocked out both verses in no time."

"Nice." Rhyson glances at his phone and grimaces. "I'm still waiting on that call from the label."

"For real?" I reassure him with a grin, though I know I can't unknot his stomach or calm his nerves while he waits to hear back from the record label considering signing him. "They'll call."

Rhyson's finally ready to perform again, but he's going back in as a contemporary artist instead of a classical pianist.

After a few minutes, I work my way over to the circle of conversation Bristol is embroiled in. I even take an empty spot on the couch facing her, restricting myself to a few furtive glances, though I'd rather stare.

"So, Bris," Luke, our friend from high school says. "What are you gonna do while you wait for Rhyson to make it big?"

"I'm not sure I'm 'waiting' for him to make it big." Bristol's laugh is husky and assured. "I think it'll be my job to ensure he makes it big."

She rakes her hair, cut into its stylish bob, back from her face. "But I'm doing some stuff with Sound Management's LA office while we work toward our goals." She goes to take a sip of her white wine, only to find it empty. "I'll be back. I'm grabbing a refill."

She doesn't acknowledge me, but stands and heads toward the kitchen. I could let this go. She's sending me clear signals. It's unlikely she wants to take up where we left off in the ocean that night, but my whole life has been a series of unlikelies.

I swing the kitchen door open soundlessly. I'm glad Grady oils his hinges because I get a moment to study Bristol before she realizes I'm there and that she isn't alone. She leans into Grady's kitchen counter, arms stretched to the side, both palms laid flat on the surface. Her wine glass sits empty beside a full bottle of white. She drops her head forward and expels a heavy breath. The ease she projected out there drops away. I know an escape when I see one. If she's running from me, I'll have to disappoint her.

"Hey."

I drop that one word in the quiet kitchen, and she jumps as if it were the report of a bullet. She rounds on me, and for just a second, everything about her whispers vulnerable. The wide, troubled eyes. The tremulous line of her full lips. An uncertain frown. She tucks it all away so quickly, you'd miss it if you weren't watching. One thing I got really good at the last time Bristol visited, was watching her.

"Hi." She picks up the bottle of wine, her excuse for leaving the room, and pours herself a glass.

"Salut." She lifts her glass and starts to walk past me.

I grab her elbow before she makes it to the door. Her eyes zip-line from my hand on her arm to my face.

"Did you need something, Grip?"

She raises both brows, disdain on her face. When she told me she had been one of those high-class New York debutantes, I couldn't reconcile that with who I met: the approachable girl with the easy laugh and curious eyes. I see it now in the frosty look she gives me. It's designed to put me off, but it'll take more than that.

"Did you get the book I sent you?" I ask, not letting her go, waiting for her to jerk away. She doesn't. She wants me to think our skin-to-skin contact doesn't affect her the way it affects me, but her pulse is a hummingbird flapping at the base of her throat with rapid wings. Pink washes over her cheeks. Her pupils swallow the silver in her eyes.

"The poems?" she asks calmly. "Yes."

"And?"

"Thank you." Her lashes drop. "I brought it back for you."

"No, I wanted you to have it. You never returned my calls or text messages. I emailed you. I—"

"I didn't see the point," she interrupts. She tugs at her arm to gently extricate herself and walks back over to the counter, putting a safe distance between us.

"You didn't see the . . ." I check my frustration. This is, after all, my fault. I'm the one who didn't tell her the whole truth. "I think we *were* the point, Bris."

"Then I'm glad I didn't waste my time or yours because there is no us." She looks me in the eyes, but I think it's only to prove she can. "You lied to me."

"Not really." I risk a few steps closer until I'm leaning against the counter beside her. "I was trying to figure out how to break things off with Tessa for a few weeks."

"You aren't still together?" she asks nonchalantly.

"Wasn't my kid." I suck my teeth and release a short breath, exasperated. "That's what I'm trying to tell you. If you'd just listen—"

"Listen?" she cuts in, showing a spark of anger. "To what? You cobble together some technicalities and semantics to disguise the truth?"

I prefer this, the honesty of her anger over that frigid, fake indifference.

"I should have told you," I admit softly, pouring all my regrets into the gaze we hold. "I was looking for the right time."

"The right time was somewhere between the airport and that Ferris wheel." She curves her lips into a fraudulent smile. "But that's okay. It doesn't matter now. It's worked out for the best."

"It isn't worked out. I tried to get in touch. You never responded." "Nothing to say." She lifts one slim shoulder, perfectly executing carelessness. "It's behind us now, and we can have a fresh start." Is she saying . . .

"You mean—"

"As friends, yes." She looks at me pointedly. "Look, I'm on a whole new coast and starting my new job. Figuring out where I'll live. Getting Rhyson's career off the ground. There's a lot of things I need to focus on. What might have been between us if you hadn't lied isn't one of them. Let's forget all the other stuff."

I roll back the sleeve of my denim shirt, showing her the black watch I wear every day. The cheap watch she won for me on a priceless night.

"Does that look like I've forgotten, Bristol?"

Surprise flits across her face before she cements it back into her designated expression.

"Look, we'll both be in Rhyson's life," she says with her eyes on the floor. "You trying to make that week something it really wasn't will only make things awkward."

"I'm not trying to make it something." My voice scolds and pleads. "It was something, and you know it."

"I know you lied to me." Her voice is flat, eyes steady. "And the only thing left for us is friendship."

Her face softens, and a smile warms her eyes for a moment.

"I actually think we could be good friends," she says. "Who else is gonna teach me remedial hip-hop?"

I can't bring myself to smile at her lighthearted comment. She's offering me crumbs when I want the whole loaf. I want so much more than she's willing to give me. If I'm honest, I want more than I deserve. Doesn't make me want it any less. We only had a week together, but the conversation, the connection—I never had it with anyone else before or since. It is real, and real is so rare, you can't ignore it when you find it. You don't give up on it.

The kitchen door swings open, and Rhyson rushes in, his face alight with excitement, his phone pressed to his chest.

"It's them," he whispers to Bristol. "It's the label about the deal." "Oh my God!" Bristol waves him over to the kitchen table and he lays his phone down on the table, putting it on speaker.

"Hey, I'm back." Rhyson glances at his sister, their identical eyes locked. "You're on speaker with my manager Bristol."

I half-listen as they start preliminary talks for what will be the foundation of Rhyson's first record deal. I know later on I'll be thrilled for him. Right now, though, as I glance at the cheap rubber watch on my wrist and remember that night at the carnival, the kiss when our hearts wheeled with the stars, I'm sad. And I can't help but think the watch is a perfect symbol.

Because I'll be biding my time.

CHAPTER 1

PRESENT DAY

THERE ARE DAYS you want to just start over because it feels like every hour takes you into a deeper level of hell.

And there are days you wake up already scraping the very bottom of the pit, unable to claw your way up the fiery walls.

This week has pretty much alternated between the latter and the former. Today, I'm trapped in some purgatory between the two.

No matter how I look at it, this week's been hell.

"Sarah." I barely raise my voice, but I know my assistant hears through the open door connecting our offices.

At first, I managed everything for Rhyson's music career by myself. He translated his fame as a classical piano prodigy into a modern rock sound that made him one of the biggest stars in the music world. Now, in addition to managing Rhyson and helping with Prodigy, the record label he recently launched, I also manage the other acts on our fledgling label and our friend Jimmi, who isn't actually signed to Prodigy. Rhyson and I recognized once I took on those additional responsibilities, I would need help. We've made astounding progress in just a few years.

The things you can do when you have no personal life. "Yeah, boss." Sarah appears at the door. "You need me?"

I thought I was in hell. Sarah looks like hell trampled her face. She isn't so much standing as allowing the doorframe to prop her up. "Sarah, I hope we've reached that point in our relationship where I can tell you when you look like shit." Sarah nods weakly.

"Good." I grimace and gesture for her to sit down in the chair across from my desk. "Because you look like shit."

"I probably look worse than I feel." Sarah settles carefully into the cream-colored leather chair.

"Let's hope so." I glance back down at the multiplying mound of papers on my desk. "I'm sorry you're not feeling well. I'll make this quick so you can go home, but are you well enough to tell me what the hell is going on in Denver?"

"Denver?" Sarah blinks slowly back at me. I cling to my patience. I really do, and I remind myself she isn't feeling well.

"Yeah. Denver. They have snow and mountains and the Broncos." "Did something go wrong for the guys?" She frowns with pain-dulled eyes. "Everything was set up at the venue."

"Yeah, well, I just got off the phone with Danny from the band, and he says everything's screwed up. There are several items from the equipment list missing."

"I sent their rider two months ago." Sarah shakes her head, confusion drawing her brows together. "I spoke to Elle, our contact at the club, last week, and she confirmed everything."

"Have you talked to Morris?" I ask of the road manager who's supposed to be handling things. I tap my nails on the edge of my desk, but stop immediately. My mother does that. There are enough naturally occurring similarities between my mother and me. I don't need to cultivate more.

"No, but I'll call him right now." She pulls her phone from her pocket and dials, looking at me while she waits. "It's ringing."

"That's usually how it works. When things go really well, he actually picks up. Something he hasn't done for the last hour I've been calling him."

I don't mean to sound like a bitch, but Rhyson handpicked Kilimanjaro, and they're an incredible band. They could have signed with any number of huge labels, but they chose us. They don't have a studio album out yet and are still considered "underground." This tour is building a grass roots fan base for their first release.

Prodigy may be small and just starting, but my brother's reputation is on the line. So is mine.

"Hey, Morris," Sarah says, forcing a smile he isn't here to appreciate. "How're things going?"

How're things going?

I just told her they're going to shit. I need to get to the bottom of it, not find out if he's enjoying his day.

"Give me the phone," I whisper-shout, extending my hand.

"I've got it," she mouths, nodding as if that's supposed to reassure me. "Uh huh. That's great, Morris. Look, the band called and said things weren't quite what we'd asked for."

She listens for a second, finally biting her lip and clenching her eyes closed.

"I see." Her sigh sounds a little too resigned to me. "Well, I guess it is what it is. Not sure what can be done about that since we're not there and the show is tonight."

The hell.

"Give me that phone, Sarah." This time I look at her sternly enough so she knows it isn't optional. She reluctantly passes it to me.

"Morris, it's Bristol."

"Hey, Bristol." Nervousness creeps into his voice.

"What's this about things not being what they should be for the band out there? Their rider is very clear, and Elle signed off on everything."

"Yeah, I think there were a few things they wanted equipment-wise that we were told would be available that aren't."

"Then Elle needs to fix that."

"I've tried to talk to her but haven't gotten any movement yet." His shaky laugh from the other end irritates me. "She's one tough cookie, that one."

"Hmmmm. Okay, well, I'll call her right now, and if that cookie doesn't want to get crumbled, she better give my guys every damn thing in the rider."

There's a short pause after my statement. "Good luck," Morris finally replies.

"By the way, Morris." I pause until I'm sure I have his full attention. "If I have to do your job and mine, one of us is redundant. The next time I send you out as road manager, I expect you to manage. If you can't, I'll find someone who isn't intimidated by a small-town club owner."

I don't wait for a response. What can he say to that? I hate incompetence. I haven't had trouble out of Morris before, but this is strike one. I use Sarah's phone to call Elle so she won't see me coming.

"Sarah, hey," Elle answers after the third ring, sounding bored and distracted. "If you're calling about that outrageous rider, I'll tell you what I told Morris. Take what you get. The show is tonight, and we don't have time to get all the equipment they're asking for. They'll be fine with what we have."

"Not Sarah, Elle. It's Bristol."

"Bristol, hey." I can practically hear her sit up and take notice. "Well, you heard what I was just saying then."

"Oh, I heard you. Now you hear me."

I lean forward, planting my fist on my desk to support my weight. "There's a contract between you and me, lady. One you signed.

Not fulfilling those terms places you in breach." I pause before resuming. "Is that clear?"

"I can't possibly find those mics they want in a day, Bristol."

"I didn't expect you to, which is why you've had the rider for months. You assured us that was more than ample time to secure the guys' equipment preferences."

"Well, I was wrong."

"Did you even try?"

I know she won't admit that she didn't try, but she needs to know that I don't believe she did.

"Elle, I don't give excuses, and I don't accept them. Make it happen or you'll be hearing from my lawyer."

"This is ridiculous!" she screeches from the other end.

"What's ridiculous is that this conversation even needs to happen." I smack my lips together in disbelief. "You actually think I'll fall for that? Waiting until the last minute and then shrugging all c'est la vie when you don't have time to fulfill the terms?"

"No, I—"

"You will find that equipment," I cut in. "I don't care if you find it up your ass. Just clean it before you give it to my band."

I end the call before I threaten to come out there myself. Then I'd have to actually follow through, and after being in hell all week, the last place I want to be is Denver. I got enough snow living in New York most of my life.

"Thanks." I hand Sarah's phone back to her.

"You're so badass," she whispers with her hand pressed to her stomach.

"Only when I have to be."

She barely lifts a knowing brow.

"Okay, yeah. Kind of all the time, but you know people make me, right?"

Sarah lets out a low groan and squeezes her eyelids closed.

"What is it?" I walk around the desk and press the back of my hand to her forehead. "You don't have a fever."

"No, I have a period," she responds listlessly.

"Ohhhhhh." I sit on the edge of the desk, studying her pretty face, which is twisting with discomfort. "Bad month?"

"Do the words 'red wedding' mean anything to you?"

I grin at her *Game of Thrones* reference, and she slits one eye open and offers an anemic smile.

"Go home." I gesture at the daunting pile of papers that seem to be metastasizing on the desk behind me. "Believe me. I can attest to the fact that the work isn't going anywhere. I've been trying to get rid of it all week with no luck."

"Really?" She sits up from her slumped position, one hand open on her forehead, the other at her belly. "You sure you'll be okay without me?"

"Yeah. I'll probably just follow up with the band and make sure Elle came through."

I don't mention the dozen other things I need to do that have made this week hell because she might feel bad.

"Okay." She stands gingerly and is making her way toward the door. "I'll just close out this one last email and be out."

"Sounds good."

My cell rings, and I glance down to see who it is. Will Silas. A fellow manager.

"Will, hi. What's up?"

"Bristol, hey. Nothing much. I wanted to talk about tomorrow night."

"What about it?" I walk back to my desk and sift through a few contracts I printed and started marking up. "The venue is all set. I spoke with them earlier. Sound check is at seven. Everything else is in the email I sent."

"Yeah, the email you sent at two o'clock this morning." He chuckles, a note of admiration in his voice. "When do you sleep, girl?"

"When all the work is done." I give a little laugh and check my impatience. I really need to look at these contracts. "So if we're all set for tomorrow's performance, what can I do for you?"

There's a pause on the other end screaming Will's reluctance. "Uh, Qwest has a special request," he says after a few seconds more of screaming quiet.

"Okay. Let's hear it."

"I know you have that reporter Meryl scheduled to talk with Qwest and Grip after the show."

Grip's upcoming album is Prodigy's first release. Even though *Grip* will be his first solo project, his popularity has grown through features on other artists' singles, all of which went platinum. He built a sterling reputation as a writer and producer over the years, along with hugely popular underground mixtapes. Now an artist in his own right, there's nothing like him out there. He has *it*, and brings *it* to everything he does. His current single "Queen" featuring Qwest, currently sits at number one, and the album hasn't even dropped.

"Yeah. *Legit* is doing that in-depth piece on Grip," I tell Will. "And I agreed to a chat with the two of them before she flies back to New York the next day."

"Yeah, she has, um, some other things she'd like to do after the show."

This time the pause is mine. The reluctance is mine. Qwest doesn't have some things she'd like to do after the show. She has someone she'd like to do after the show.

Grip.

"Oh, yeah?" I drop the contract and run my hand over the back of my neck where the tension always seems to gather. "Like what?"

"She was thinking she and Grip could hang out after the show. They haven't seen each other since they wrapped on the 'Queen' video a month ago. So . . ."

Pairing Grip with Qwest, the hottest female rapper on the scene right now, was sheer brilliance. I wish I could take credit for it, but Qwest approached us about working with him.

"So . . ." I pick up where Will left off, waiting for him to voice the request.

"Could we cancel the chat with the reporter so Qwest and Grip can go out after the show?"

I swallow the big no that lodges in my throat. It's true that Meryl will be irritated if we cancel. She'll be shadowing Grip for the next few weeks leading up to the album release writing this piece. I don't want to start our working relationship not delivering the one-two punch of Qwest and Grip together. But, if I'm honest, that isn't the only reason I want to refuse Qwest's request to spend time with Grip.

I clear my throat before responding.

"Um, let me see what I can do, Will. I can't make any promises, but I'll try. I don't want to alienate this reporter. This piece she's doing is great exposure for Grip's album."

"I get that, but you know how Qwest is." Will laughs, probably to keep from crying, because Qwest is a handful. "If we make her do the interview, she'll probably say some outrageous shit and ruin it anyway."

Irritation prickles under my skin. Qwest is undeniably talented. And undeniably hot for Grip. I've seen it for myself. She practically engraved an invitation for Grip to screw her at the "Queen" video shoot. For her to put her libido above a commitment is highly unprofessional, but then, it *is* Grip. She wouldn't be the first woman I've seen lose all sense of decency where he's concerned.

"If I can't get them out of the interview without potentially damaging this piece," I say, stiffening my words just enough. "Then I'll expect your artist to be where I need her to be when I need her to be and to conduct herself professionally. If you can't control Qwest, don't make me do it."

"That won't be necessary." Will's tone stiffens a little, too. "It shouldn't be that big a deal. Promise the reporter something else. Something bigger."

"Like what?"

"Like what if she goes with us next month? She'd get Qwest and Grip performing in Dubai. The optics alone will be a great add to her story."

Damn. Wish I'd thought of that, too. Grip and Qwest are giving a sweet sixteen concert for the daughter of one of Dubai's ruling families.

"That's a great idea." My tone still makes no promises. "I'll pitch it to Meryl and get back to you."

"Sounds good. See you at sound check."

With a million things clamoring for my attention, demanding

action, I stand still at my desk for a full minute, staring unseeingly at the work waiting for me.

Qwest and Grip.

They're perfect for each other. Not only that, but it would be good for business. Their fans would eat up a romance between them. They'd be the king and queen of hip-hop. All the ideas spin through my head of how to maximize on a relationship between my artist and Will's. I could spin a street fairy tale of it. It's what Qwest wants. It's what everyone would want.

But I'm the one thing I know without a shadow of a doubt Grip wants. Over the years, we've managed to become friends. Really good friends actually, and I was thrilled when he finally agreed to let me manage his career. But that's all. Grip has made it clear he wants more, but that's all I can give, and that's all we'll be.

So if you won't have him, Qwest can.

That little voice of conscience and reason whispers to me every once in a while. Depending on the circumstance, sometimes I listen. Sometimes I ignore. I know this time I should listen.

Sarah's groan from the outer office pulls me from minutes of contemplation I can't afford. Despite all the work I've already done, I still have so much to do.

"You're still here?" I call out, walking to the door.

I fight back an ill-timed smile when I see a Hershey's bar, a Costco-sized bottle of Midol, and a legion of tampons spilled on the floor from Sarah's purse. It's like a Menstrual Survival Kit.

"Yes." Sarah sighs, pressing two fingers to her temple. "I forgot about an errand I'm supposed to run. Ugh. I just wanna crawl between the sheets and die for a little while."

"Let me handle it." Another thing I can't afford. Doing other people's jobs, but it feels like I've been doing that all day. All week. "You sure?" Doubt pinches Sarah's pained expression even more. "I know you have a ton to do."

"As you can see by the state of my desk," I say, pointing a thumb over my shoulder toward my office. "Work isn't going anywhere. Anything I don't finish today, will still be there tomorrow."

"Oh, good." She blows out a relieved breath. "Let me get Grip's bag."

"Let you get what?" Tiny thrills of panic and anticipation alternate through me. "Grip's bag? What do you mean?"

"He left his bag here earlier today when he met with Rhyson." She bends to gather the spilled items from the floor, shoveling them into her purse. "He needs it tonight, and I told him I'd drop it off on my way home."

Apparently, I'm back at the lowest level of hell. After a week like I've had, the last thing I need is Grip being all . . . Grip. He'll ask me out. I'll refuse. He'll try to kiss me. I'll evade. I'll leave, and he'll go screw some random girl, thereby proving I was right not to give him a chance.

It's what we do.

We've been playing this game that isn't a game for years. One day, he'll realize I mean it when I say there isn't a chance in . . . well, hell, that it'll ever happen between us.

"I need to give you the code for his loft. He texted it to me." Sarah pulls out her phone, scrolling through messages. "He says he misses the bell all the time. So just use the code and go right in because he'll probably have the music up or be in the shower."

Grip in the shower. My mind paints vivid pictures that involve Grip's powerful body, rivulets of water, and not much else. I may not want a relationship, but I'm not blind or dead south of the waist. My heart, though, last time I checked, was north of my belt. I don't let anyone near that thing. If I let Grip in, the compass goes out the window. North or south wouldn't matter. No territory would be off-limits with him. I see Grip all the time. Here at the label offices. In the studio. At shows and appearances. But alone. At his house. Freshly showered. And me vulnerable, and let's face it—horny, is a disaster waiting to happen. A disaster I've managed to avoid for a long time.

"Maybe he'll be fine without the bag tonight. I mean . . ." I falter, embarrassed at how husky my voice sounds, though Sarah would never guess it's because of the shower scene playing in my head. "It can't be that urgent."

Disappointment and resignation flicker across Sarah's face, but she covers it quickly.

"Don't worry about it." She pulls the purse on her shoulder and reaches under her desk to retrieve a black leather backpack I recognize as Grip's.

"He offered to come get it, but I said I'd bring it. I'll do it."

Guilt burns in my chest. Sarah lives around the corner. She'd really be going out of her way to take the bag to Grip. I, on the other hand, pass his exit on my way home. I really wish I was as much of a bitch as people think I am.

"Gimme." I flick my fingers for her to hand the bag to me. "I got it. You go home, dope yourself up with Midol and chocolate, and I'll see you tomorrow."

"You sure?" Relief slumps her shoulders and brightens her eyes.

"Of course." I take the bag and shoo her out the door. "Go." "You're the best boss ever." Sarah makes her way carefully toward the door like lady parts might fall out if she walks any faster.

"Yeah, yeah. Whatever." I manage a grin. "Remember this when I have you working till midnight next week."

Once she's gone and the office is quiet and it's just me and my never-ending pile of tasks, I get back to work. I can barely focus, though, with that bag sitting in the corner mocking me. Daring me. Taunting me.

I keep working until the angle of the sun through the window behind me shifts from shine to shadow, the only indication I have of how long I've been at it. Other than the growl of my stomach.

I touch the home button on my phone to check the time.

"Shit." I drop my head into my hands and blow fatigue out through my nose. "Food, Bristol. Food should have happened hours ago."

Sarah usually makes sure I eat. She's becoming invaluable to me in ways I didn't anticipate. Mostly personal ways. Slipping me food. Ordering my favorite coffee blend that I can only ever find online. Putting up with my bitching when things don't go my way. Being a friend. Generally, I only allow myself so many of those. Her continued proximity has me bending that rule.

The problem of proximity. It's exactly why, despite my working with Grip as closely as I do now as his manager, I still find ways to keep my distance. If anyone could make me bend and forget the rules, it's Grip. He doesn't know that, though, and I need to keep it that way.

It's getting darker in the office now, not quite sunset. The dimming light camouflages the bag tucked into the corner, but I know it's there, and it's time for me to deal with it.

And the man who owns it.

CHAPTER 2

HE'S COME A long way.

When I first met Grip, he lived in a one-room hovel and subsisted on two-for-the-price-of-one street tacos. His pride wouldn't allow him to ask my brother for much help financially, and Rhyson respected him too much to force the issue. So Grip was sweeping floors in exchange for studio time, deejaying in clubs all over LA, writing for other artists. He paid his dues pursuing his dreams. As I pull into the underground parking lot of the exclusive loft complex where he lives now, I can't help but think he's finally getting paid back.

Even though Sarah said I should use the code and go right in, I can't make myself do it. In the lobby, I press the button to ring his place, waiting for a response over the intercom that never comes. With a heavy sigh, I shift his bag on my shoulder and punch in the code that opens the cage-like elevator that will take me to the top floor.

It's all very industrial and modern, an old warehouse renovated into upscale loft apartments. A rolling garage door of sorts faces me as soon as I step off the elevator. The blare of nineties hip-hop bleeds through the concrete walls. I pull out my phone again to check the instructions Sarah sent. Once I punch in the code, the door rolls up, and high-decibel Tupac gushes out like water from a cracked dam. The first night Grip and I met, we talked about Tupac. I barely knew any of his music. I barely knew anything about hip-hop. Raised in a family of classical music aficionados, I'm still not a huge fan, though ironically, I'm managing one of its rising stars.

The loft consists of a large, open space with high ceilings, red brick walls, and exposed rafters. Pillows pepper an L-shaped sectional the color of molasses. The thick slab of wood serving as a coffee table is flanked on another side by a latte colored backless couch. Four barstools line up along the strip of matte steel converted into a countertop separating the living area from the kitchen. A set of rail-less steps float up to the second floor, where a length of walkway leads to a closed door. Grip's bedroom, I presume. Vinyl albums fill decorative mahogany crates stacked and lining the wall housing the fireplace. A multi-shelved arch is built into another wall and holds dozens and dozens of books. Grip is nothing if not well-read.

A beautiful brown leather journal on the coffee table catches my eye. I gave him that three birthdays ago. I walk over to brush my fingers over the supple leather. He says some of the best lyrics he's ever written were conceived between those sheets.

"Nosy bitches get shot."

The words are followed by the click of a gun being cocked. My heart slams against my rib cage when I see the girl standing just a few feet away in the open door of a bathroom, eyes and hand steady over the gun aimed at me.

"Don't shoot." My hands fly up automatically. "I'm a friend of Grip's."

"Not one I ever met."

She's a pretty girl. Her unblemished skin glows, smooth and richly colored mocha. No makeup that I detect. Her hair is cropped close to her head and worn with its natural texture. A plaid shirt hangs large over baggy jeans and Chucks. Big brown eyes, almost doe-like and framed by long, curly lashes, never leave my face. They lend her an air of innocence belied by the 9mm aimed at my heart.

"Jade." Grip's voice drops from above. He stands at the walkway rail, looking down at us. "Put that damn gun up."

"Some stranger rolling up in the house," Jade says, lowering the weapon. "I didn't know."

For a moment, I forget about the gun trained on my torso. With the arresting picture Grip makes, T-shirt looped at his neck and hanging over his bare chest, he's more dangerous than the armed girl in front of me. A stack of abdominal muscles trails down to the indentations carved into his hips. Drops of water bead the smooth slope of his shoulders and the arms splattered with vibrant ink. Belt-less dark wash jeans hang low on the lean hips. I lift my eyes to his face, a dazzling arrangement of jet-colored brows and bold bones balanced with lips so sculpted you would never guess how soft they are.

I don't have to guess. I remember.

"Your hair," I gasp. Gone are the dreadlocks he's been growing the last few years. There's barely any hair at all it's cut so short, just a subtle dark wave shadowing his scalp.

He runs a hand over his head, a wry grin tipping one corner of his mouth.

"Just something different." He exchanges a look with the girl holding the gun at her side. "Jade cut the locs out for me."

"Jade?" I drag my eyes from his face to hers. "As in your cousin Jade?"

Her eyes shift to mine, adding another question about me to her gaze.

"Yeah." Grip slips the T-shirt over his head and starts down the steps. "Good memory."

Jade and I watch each other warily. Grip told me they grew up together in Compton. He also told me about a dark day on a play-ground when an officer went too far while searching her, crossed a line of innocence. Knowing that, my heart softens some, even though she's still giving me the same hard look.

Eyeing Jade, focused on her, I took my eyes off Grip. Now he stands right in front of me, looms over me. I'm usually braced for the raw sexuality that clings to him, so strong my knees have been known to go weak. But him being so near and looking so much like the guy I met eight years ago, before the dreadlocks. Before the underground mixtapes and concerts and record deals. Before his fame. The start of a beautiful friendship. Anything else we could have been ended almost before it started.

Almost.

"So, Bris, to what do I owe this pleasure?" Grip grabs a remote from the table and silences Tupac. In the abrupt quiet, his eyes make a slow voyage down my body, his perusal pouring over me like hot oil. The silk romper I wore to the office today suddenly feels too short as he takes in my legs. Even though the sleeves reach the elbow, my forearms prickle with goose bumps under his stare. By the time his eyes reach my breasts, my nipples are tight and beaded in the silky cage of my bra. His eyes linger there before lifting and roving over my face.

He knows.

Even though I ignore this awareness that always seethes between us, no matter how much I pretend it isn't there, he knows. Even with Jade standing just two feet away, his proximity, his nearness and heat, cloister us in false intimacy.

"Um, Sarah was sick so I'm just bringing . . ." I don't bother finishing the sentence. My voice is unnaturally husky. My breath, abridged. I just hold up his backpack as explanation.

"Oh, yeah," he says. "Thank you."

He takes the bag by the strap, his fingers deliberately touching mine. I glance from where our fingers mingle to the face that looks even more handsome with barely any hair framing it. He looks so much like the guy who picked me up from LAX when I visited for spring break years ago. Nothing has changed, and everything is different now. He looked at me that day the way he's looking at me now, as if I were some new mystery he wanted to lose himself in solving. Conversely, he looks at me like he knows my every secret.

Jade clears her throat before speaking, snapping the moment between Grip and me.

"Man, I hope you ain't trying to bring her home to your mama." Jade's eyes follow the same head-to-toe journey Grip's took over me, but derision weights her look at every stop. "You know Aunt Mittie would have a fit if you start shit with some white bitch."

"Bitch?" I have a low give-a-fuck threshold, and she just crossed it. "You've called me bitch twice, and you don't even know me. Or did we meet and I forgot you already? I see how that could happen."

"Bristol." Grip chuckles down at me, the warmth that probably made Jade suspicious in the first place evident in his eyes. "She does still have a gun."

I glance from the firearm at Jade's side to the smirk on her pretty face, feeling bold now that I know who she is and bolder still now that Grip is close enough to hide behind if necessary. He'd never let anyone hurt me. Except himself. I'm pretty sure Grip could crush me without noticing.

"Jade, ease up," he says. "She's Rhyson's sister."

"And Grip's manager," I add. "You and your Aunt Mittie can rest easy. There's nothing going on between us."

I feel Grip's eyes on me when I say there's nothing between us. I won't give him the satisfaction of looking, of letting him mock the defenses I wrap around myself to guard against anything that could develop. They've held this long, and I have no plans of yielding any time soon.

"Your manager, huh?" Jade studies me again, as unimpressed as the first time. "I see."

"You need to be thinking less about me and more about you. About what I said." Grip hooks an elbow around her neck and kisses her forehead. "Come to the studio next week. Lay some tracks."

Jade stiffens under his arm, observing him with narrowed eyes. Grip also told me their relationship wasn't as close after that day at the playground.

"Hmmm. We'll see." She pulls away and walks over to grab an

Oakland Raiders cap from the countertop. "I'm out. Some of us still gotta actually work to make them ends meet."

Grip is one of the hardest working artists I know. He's what they call a studio rat. He's behind the board and in the booth every chance he gets. Not to mention the appearances, writing for other artists, photo shoots. Indignation rises up in me on his behalf. Before I can mount my defense, he's diffused it with a grin aimed at his cousin.

"Whatever, J." He tweaks her nose, his affection for her obvious and, from my perspective, inexplicable. "Just come to the studio. Maybe it'll keep you out of trouble."

"I am trouble," she bounces back with a sassy grin. "I'll think about it." She looks to me, raising her eyebrows like she's waiting for me to say something.

"Nice meeting you," I offer in her expectant silence. Even in the face of rude bullshit, the manners instilled in me are flawless. She ignores my comment and brushes past me and out the door.

"I'm gonna walk J out." Grip takes my wrist gently between his fingers. "Could you wait a second? I have questions about the email you sent last night."

I see right through this ploy. He knows that without a good reason to stay, I'd be right behind him and on that elevator. Except I've been in hell all week. Working myself to the bone for longer than I can remember. There's tightness across my shoulders, noosed around my neck, trapped in the fists balled at my side. I just want to unfurl, and as much as he makes me tense, there's no one else I can relax with the way I can with Grip. So, against the better judgment I've exercised for years, I stay.

When he comes back, the two takeout bags he's holding release tantalizing scents into the air. I'm settled onto the huge comfortable sectional taking up so much of the living room. I could fall asleep right here if I weren't so hungry. Starvation has eroded my sense of self-preservation, and as much as I dreaded coming here to see him, I dread going home to my empty cottage even more.

"Ran into the delivery guy." He raises the bags and gives me a measured look, like he knows I could bolt at any moment. "You hungry?"

"I could eat," I understate while the lining of my stomach feasts on itself.

"Empanadas?" He smiles because he knows they're my weakness. One of my many weaknesses.

"Baked or fried?" I ask, as if I'm particular.

"Which do you want it to be?" he parries.

"Fried."

"Then they're fried." He hooks the bag handles over one wrist and grabs plates from the cabinet with his free hand. "Come on."

In utter laziness, I watch him cross the large space to a door in the far corner.

"Make yourself useful and grab me a beer from the fridge and whatever you want to drink." He looks over his shoulder at me expectantly. "I can't carry you and the food up to the roof, Bristol."

"The roof?" I groan my exhaustion and settle deeper into the cushions.

"Oh, sorry." He pauses, concern sketching a frown on his face. "Is it too high?"

I have a selective fear of heights. Put me in a little bucket in the air on a ride that could plunge me to my death, I'm chop suey. But sitting safely on the roof, I should be fine. I do not, however, need him reminding me of our night on that Ferris wheel. Not tonight when I'm already feeling weak.

"No, the roof isn't too high," I answer. "It's too far away. I'm tired."

"Well, food's going up and so will you if you want some," he says, disappearing through the door.

Sigh.

I grab a beer for him and a bottle of Pinot Gris for me. If I were alone, I wouldn't bother with the glass I pull from the rack. It has been a straight-from-the-bottle day . . . week . . . month. But I'll save that for the privacy of my own home. And it'll probably be vodka, my self-numb-er of choice.

Damn these shoes. I've got a thing for heels. Even wearing the romper, I'm still sporting three-inch Jimmy Choos. By the time I make my way up the winding stairs to the roof, I want to toss the shoes off the building despite how much they cost.

The second I step through the door to the roof, I forget about my shoes, my empty stomach. I even forget the empanadas for a moment. We're just high enough to see the city's skyline in the distance, set ablaze by the horizon's last hurrah before sunset. There's no fear, and the view takes my breath. For just a second, the sheer scope of the sky makes all the problems that followed me home from the office seem small in comparison.

"This is gorgeous," I whisper, taking the last few steps to the center of the roof.

"Yeah, I can't take credit for the view or this setup. The decorator did it." Grip eyes his rooftop retreat with a pleased smile. "I don't get up here as much as I'd like, but every once in a while to eat or write."

I can see how it would be the perfect place to write. Padded benches tuck into the far corner, and slate-colored cushions rest against the brick wall. Four low, square tables stand in the center with candles of various sizes and shapes strategically dotted on them.

Grip sets the bags on one of the tables and walks to the wall to turn a few knobs. Soft music fills the air around me, and strands of fairy-tale lights now glimmer over our heads. It's all very romantic.

"You know this is just two friends eating dinner, right?" I flop onto the padded bench and put down our drinks.

"I do know that." The innocent expression is the only thing that doesn't look right on Grip's face. "But if you need to remind yourself, I understand."

I make sure he sees me rolling my eyes before tearing open the bags of precious fried dough.

Correction. Baked.

"You said these were fried," I complain around a bite of empanada.

"My bad." He stretches his brows up and takes a leisurely sip of his beer. "That's your second one, though, right? I guess you barely notice the difference when you inhale them."

"Very funny." I actually do laugh and polish off another one.

"Well, so much for leftovers." He leans back against the cushion beside me until mere inches separate our shoulders.

"You shouldn't have invited me to stay if you wanted leftovers."

"I think your company's a fair trade."

Our eyes connect across the small slice of charged space separating us. I sit up from my slouch, inserting a few much-needed inches between us.

"You mentioned needing to talk about the email I sent." My business-like tone clashes with the soft music and lighting, which is exactly what I need it to do.

"Yeah." He considers me for an extra moment, as if he may not allow me to steer our conversation into safer territory. "You mentioned that next Wednesday at three you have a sit-down scheduled with that reporter from *Legit*."

"I checked the shared calendar, and that block of time was free. Was I wrong?"

"It's my fault." He shoots me an apologetic look. "I forget to add personal stuff there sometimes. I'm talking to some students in my old neighborhood that day. Could we reschedule?"

Between my request to cancel tomorrow's interview for Qwest's would-be booty call, and nixing next Wednesday's sit down, Meryl won't be too happy with me.

"What if she tags along?" I sit up straighter, twisting to peer down at him. "She could see you talking to the students and then you guys could chat a few minutes maybe right there on the grounds. Get some local color shots."

"Local color?" A husky laugh passes over his lips. "There's four colors in Compton. Black, brown, red, and blue. In the wrong place at the wrong time, on the wrong street, any of those could get you killed. I don't know. And I don't want the talk exploited. Like headline shit. That isn't why I'm doing it."

"I know that. Of course it isn't. I'll make sure it isn't like that."

He glances up at me, wordlessly reading between lines.

"You'd be coming, too?" His voice is soft, but the look in his eyes is loud and clear. His eyes tell me he likes having me near. It makes my stomach bottom out like we're back up on that Ferris wheel, and if I'm not careful, I'll fall.

"Why not?" I give what I hope is a casual shrug, though it feels as stiff as my neck.

"You just haven't been around much lately." His eyes never leave my face, and I hope I drop my expressionless mask in place fast enough to keep him out.

"We connect every day." I look him straight in the face like it isn't hard to do. "So I don't know what you mean."

"We text, email, FaceTime, but we haven't seen each other much."

I rub at the knots in my neck, wishing a masseuse would magically appear.

"Are you tight?" His voice and eyes seem to simmer, both hot and steady.

The double entendre of that question is not lost on me. As little sex as I've had the last year . . . years, I'm probably as tight as a peephole, but he'll never know.

"It's just been a long few weeks."

"I know something that could relax you."

He bends over me, pressing me back into cushions. "Grip, what are you—"

"Relax," he interrupts with a laugh, stretching a few inches more to unscrew a jar sitting on the concrete pedestal beside my seat. He settles back into his space, freeing up my lungs to breathe again.

"My Uncle Jamal used to say if you can't have a good ho." He holds up a joint. "Have good dro."

"Have I mentioned that your uncle is a misogynist who subscribes to antiquated and archetypal notions of womanhood?"

"Yeah, more than once, but I'm pretty sure he was a pimp, so that makes sense."

What the what?

He says it as if he just told me his uncle was a fireman. "You mean like 'big pimpin', Jay-Z' kind of pimp?"

"No, like, 'bitch, go get my money on the corner' kind of pimp." A frown pleats Grip's expression. "By the time he came out west, no, but I think back in Chicago he may have been a pimp."

I'm having trouble processing this. I've met Grip's Uncle Jamal a few times, and he never struck me . . . maybe that is an unfortunate way to think of it considering he may have struck the women who worked for him . . . but he never struck me as a pimp.

"He's actually my great-uncle," Grip says. "My grandmother's brother. When she left Chicago to move out here in the seventies, he followed."

Grip shakes his head, blowing out a heavy sigh.

"The generation before him thought Chicago was the answer to Jim Crow, so they left the South. And then they thought the answer to poverty and crime was California and left Chicago," Grip says. "Always running. Stokely Carmichael said, 'Our grandfathers had to run, run, run. My generation's out of breath. We ain't running no more.'"

We have Grip's mother to thank for all the varied people he can quote.

"So your mother moved here for better opportunities?"

"My mother moved here because her mother moved them here." Grip considers me a few extra seconds before going on. "My grandmother was part of the Black Panther movement, which was huge in Southern Cali."

"What? I never knew that."

"It isn't exactly what I lead with when I meet someone." Grip laughs.

"Weren't they violent?" I ask carefully. "Like 'blowing up things' violent?"

"They were . . . complicated. They weren't perfect, by any means, but they were providing free lunch for kids in poor neighborhoods, tutoring students, teaching self-defense, doing a lot of good. That's what drew my grandmother to the movement."

"And your mother?"

"Ma definitely ain't a Panther." He chuckles. "But don't cross her because I wouldn't put it past her to blow shit up."

I have no plans to cross her.

He pulls a lighter from the pocket of his jeans, and I notice the black plastic watch on his strong wrist. I've never seen him without it since I won it at that carnival. I don't know what to think about that, so I don't let myself think about it.

"So you in or what?" he asks.

I drag my eyes from the plastic watch to the expectant expression on his face.

"You know I don't smoke weed."

"Oh, I'm giving it up, too." His sculpted lips stretch into a smart-ass smirk. "Next week. Come on. When was the last time you got high? Not high off contact, either."

"Columbia. Senior year. Finals." The memory of munching my way through my study sessions bubbles laughter from my chest. "I was lit through half my econ exam."

He leans into my shoulder, his deep laughter rumbling through me.

"Come on, Bristol," he cajoles, drawing on the joint, blowing a circle of smoke out, and then offering it to me. "It's legal in half the country now, ya know?"

"Medicinally."

"Well, it's all the way legal in Cali." White smoke halos his head, contrasting with the devilishly handsome face.

This is a bad idea. Even at my most vigilant, it's sometimes hard to stave off the attraction between Grip and me. If I'm . . . impaired . . . there's no telling what I'll give in to. But the string of tough days, the months of non-stop work getting the label off the ground, this hellish week—it all bombards me, and in a moment of weakness, I take one draw. And then another. And then another.

An indeterminate amount of time later, I'm feeling nice. Shoes off. Feet up. Hair down. High as a kite.

The wine conspires with the weed and my exhaustion to create a laid-back haze. My eyes keep closing, and my head keeps lolling onto Grip's shoulder. When I manage to crack my eyes open, he's watching me intently, alert. He's a creature who hides his weapons, lulling his prey into thinking he poses no danger. Maybe it's a survival mechanism he picked up from his childhood in a gang-infested war zone, camouflaging the threat, but he isn't hiding how dangerous he is now. The jet brows slant over eyes with the color and heat of melted caramel. His desire is a cloak, heavy on my shoulders, tight around my arms, hot on every part of me it touches.

He's such a beautiful man, his body a palette of precious metals—darkened gold, bronze, copper. I should remember that I'm not the only one who thinks so. If I took what that look offers, he would never be just mine. I'd have to share him. Not right away, maybe not the first time or the first year, but eventually. That's the way it is with men like him and women like me. I get it, but I don't have to choose it.

"I can't believe you cut your locs." Even to my ears it sounds like a diversion, nervous and chatty.

"Technically, I didn't." His steady eyes don't waver. "Jade did."

I follow the line of conversation like a lamp lighting my way out of a dark cave, hoping it will dispel the tension coiling around us.

"As many times as you've talked about Jade," I say. "I never envisioned our first meeting would be at gunpoint."

"She thought you broke in."

The corner of his mouth tips. I give him my "you're shitting" me look. "Yeah, because I look like such a criminal."

"Some of the worst criminals wear three-piece suits and have an Ivy League pedigree."

"Oh, you don't have to tell me. I grew up with half of them." I grimace and lean back, closing my eyes. "Just make sure I'm somewhere else if she ever does come by the studio."

"Bris, don't be sadity." His words and voice chide me.

"I don't even know what 'sadity' means, so I seriously doubt I'm being it."

"Sorry." His laugh rolls over me. "It means uppity. Stuck up. Jade's had it hard. Don't judge her."

"Me, judge her?" My eyes pop open, and I sit up, hand pressed to my chest and eyes stretched wide. "She's the one who called me a bitch before she even knew my name."

I lie back only to snap up into a sitting position again. "Oh, and again after she knew my name."

"She isn't the most polite, I give you that."

"And apparently, when I finally meet your mother it won't go any better."

That was the absolute wrong thing to say, and I don't examine what prompted me to say it. I've never actually met Grip's mother, but I know they're incredibly close. I never plan to be "the one" he takes home to Mama, but to think she would disapprove simply because I'm white is galling.

"My mom would adjust. She isn't narrow-minded, just . . ." Grip trails off, his long lashes dropping over clouded eyes. "You have to cut them both some slack. You can't imagine the things we experienced living where we grew up. I was lucky going to the School of the Arts. That was my exit. It could easily have been Jade. She just didn't apply. She's a better writer than I am."

"I doubt that," I mumble.

His gaze latches onto my face, narrowed and searching. "Why, 'cause she's hood? I'm hood, Bris."

"Maybe you are, but you never called me a bitch."

"At least not to your face." He doesn't even crack a smile.

Our eyes catch and hold. At the corners, my lips fight a smile. He stops holding his back around the same time I give in. Our laughter clears the air.

"And I didn't doubt Jade was better than you because she's hood or stupid." Eyes down, I circle the lip of the wine glass with one finger. "I doubt it because I've never met a better writer than you."

I inwardly slap myself. Why the ever-living hell do I keep saying things like this? As soon as things lighten, I say something stupid to let him know just how much he means to me. Must be the weed.

"You wanna know the real reason Jade didn't like you?"

Grip leans into me, pushing back my hair and rolling his still-icy beer bottle over my neck. I swallow, but don't dare look at him, hoping he'll drop it, but he doesn't.

"When you grow up on the streets, you don't just develop a sixth sense." He captures a lock of my hair and tests it between his fingers. "You have six, seven, eight, nine of 'em, because those instincts could be the difference between death or life. My mom and Jade have so many senses they almost know what you're thinking before you think it. And even though I've never told her, Jade only had to be in the room with us for a hot minute to know I want you."

I clench my eyes closed and pull in a stuttering breath, trapping my bottom lip between my teeth.

"Don't do this, Grip."

"Jade's right," he continues as if I hadn't spoken, hadn't asked him to stop. "My mom would flip if I brought a white girl home. If I brought you home. She knows I don't consider color when I date, but she'd love to see me with a woman who looks like her. You know better than most that we don't get to choose our family, but we still gotta love them."

I don't respond to that. He knows how contentious things have been between my brother and my parents. Beyond the headlines everyone else has seen, he knows how hard I've worked to reconcile them. I moved to LA to help Rhyson with his career, yes, but also to bridge the countrywide chasm between the two factions of my family.

"Like you, I'd do anything for my family." He comes in an inch closer, caressing under my chin and tilting it up with his index finger. "But if you'd ever give me a shot, I wouldn't give a fuck what anyone thought. I'd take you home to my mama."

I'm a little too high and a lot too horny for this conversation, for the stone-hard thigh pressing against me, for the heat coming off his body and smothering my resistance. I try to sit up, hoping it will clear my head so I can make my escape, but his hand presses gently into my chest, just above the swell of my breasts, compelling me back into the cushion. His lips hover over mine, and I will him to kiss me because I'll make the first move if he doesn't. After years of not moving, I have no idea how I'll explain that once the smoke clears.

Sometimes at night after the chaos dies, I think about our first kiss at the top of a Ferris wheel. Just like then, his lips start soft, brushing mine like wings in sweet sweeps, coaxing me open and delving into me. Sampling me, he groans into my mouth and chases my tongue. The rough palm of his hand cups my face, angling me so he can dive deeper. He doesn't come up for air, but keeps kissing me so deeply I can't breathe. He tastes so good, I'll choose him over air as long as I can. Why is it never like this with anyone else? I want it to be so bad, but it never is.

He releases my lips to scatter kisses down my neck. My back arches, and my nipples go tight. He knows that's my spot. After all this time, he still knows. My neck is so incredibly sensitive, a gateway to the rest of my body.

"You taste exactly the same." His words come on a labored breath in my ear. "Do you know how long it's been since I kissed you?"

Eight years.

"Eight years." He shakes his head, eyes riveting mine in light lent by candles and the moon. "And you taste exactly the same."

His words shiver through me, searching out my nerve endings and invading my bones. If I don't get out of here, we'll be fucking on the rooftop before I can draw another breath.

"I should go." I slide from under him, scooting down the couch as far as I can without falling off. "This is why I don't smoke weed."

I force a laugh, hoping he'll let me get away with it. I scoop my hair behind my ears and drop my chin to my chest. When I glance over at him, displeasure clumps his brows and tightens his mouth.

"It's not the weed, Bristol." His glance slices through the haze hanging in the air. "It's us. Don't pretend it isn't us."

"There is no us." My feet explore the floor, searching in the dark for my shoes. "You know that."

He puts a staying hand on my knee until I look at him.

"What I know is that neither of us has been in a serious relationship in years."

"That doesn't mean anything." I stand and slide my feet into the Jimmy Choos. "You haven't exactly been waiting around, have you?"

"Damn right I haven't been waiting around." He doesn't get up, but his firm hold on my wrist stops me from walking away. "I'm not Rhyson."

I look down at him, frowning my confusion. "What do you mean?"

"Remember when Kai put Rhyson in the friend zone?"

Of course I do. For a long time, my sister-in-law Kai denied the attraction between her and Rhyson.

"Yeah, so?"

"When Kai wasn't checking for Rhys, I assumed he had to be sleeping with other girls." Grip shrugs. "I mean, he and Kai were just friends. But, nope. He said he only wanted Kai and didn't sleep with anyone else."

"Then you're right." I tug at my wrist, but he holds on tight. "You're definitely not Rhyson."

"It was months, Bristol. She shut him out for months. Not years."

"I'm not shutting you out." I release a tired breath. "I'm living my life, and you're living yours."

"Right." He nods and turns his mouth down at the corners. "So, if you won't be with me, then I'll fuck whoever the hell I want. If you have a problem with that, you know what to do about it."

For a moment, our eyes tangle in the dimness. His words sink into my flesh like briars. Every word out of his mouth only proves that I'm right to get out of here. That I'm right not to give in. If I ever gave him a chance and he fucked around on me . . . I've seen what that looks like. It looks like a woman as strong as my mother reduced to pathetic, teary drunkenness.

"It's none of my business." I shift my eyes away from him and to the glittering city skyline just beyond the rooftop.

"It's none of your business until you say it is." I force myself to look back.

"Don't hold your breath, Grip." I say my next words with deliberation. "I mean, it's not like I'm sitting around saving it, either."

He pulls me forward, and I press my hand to the hardness of his chest so I don't fall into him. My knee supports me, pressed against his on the couch.

"Are you poking me?" One strong hand wraps around the back of my thigh, anger marking his expression. "Do you want to know if it bothers me when you fuck other guys?"

I just stare at him unblinkingly. He presses my leg, urging me forward until I'm fully on the couch, fully on him, one knee on either side of his legs, facing him. Straddling him.

"It makes me want to set the world on fire." His words come softly, but the truth roars in his eyes. "To think of you with them."

There haven't been nearly as many men as he probably assumes, but I don't reveal that. I can't offer him any relief.

"You wanna know what consoles me, though?" He looks up at me, calculation in his eyes. Before I can tell him I don't want to know, he goes on. "For one, I know when we're together, it'll only take once for me to fuck their memory out of you."

I shoot him an uncertain look. He sounds fierce enough to follow through on that threat right now. I manage to snatch my wrist from his grasp. I back off his lap, walking swiftly toward the steps that will take me back into his loft. I'm only a few steps down when he calls from the top.

"It also helps that I know how much it bothers you, too."

I freeze on the fourth step, my palm pressed to the wall.

"I don't know what you mean." The words echo in the narrow stairwell, sounding much more confident than I feel inside.

"The other women." He mock-sighs behind me like he's getting impatient. "Like I don't see it, Bris."

I know I should keep going, but I'm stuck on the stairs, afraid of what he has perceived. He slips past me and down onto the step below, his height still putting him eye level with me.

"You think I'm that oblivious?" He walks his fingers up my arm. "You always conveniently have somewhere to be when I'm with someone else."

"I'm busy." I study my shoes on the step, not looking up. "I have more to do with my life than hang around waiting for you to screw some groupie."

"And you watch me." He dips his head until he traps my eyes. "You watch me all the time. You can't keep your eyes off me any more than I can keep my eyes off you."

"You're delusional." I offer a hollow laugh. "Thanks for dinner."

I shove past him, squeezing between the stairwell wall and the taut muscles of his body.

"You don't want to know the third thing that consoles me?" he asks at my back.

"No," I fling over my shoulder. Only a few steps to go and I'll be in his loft and then out the door.

"They don't satisfy you." He plays the comment like a trump card. "Sexually, I mean."

My hand is on the knob to his loft, but I look up at him, anger overtaking the fear and confusion of the last few moments.

"Who the hell do you think you are?" I snap. "To presume you know anything about my sex life."

"Oh, but I do." He takes the few steps separating us until he's right in front of me, his hard body pressing me against the door. "Remember last year when you bought your cottage and invited us all over for dinner?"

I have no idea where he's going with this, but I can't pretend I'm not curious. I just stare at him, knowing he doesn't need my permission to go on.

"Everyone was playing cards, and then I left the room and was gone for a long time." He presses his forearm to the door behind me and over my head until our bodies are practically flush. "Remember?"

"You said my chili sent you to the bathroom," I say breathlessly.

I'm not a great cook and was surprised the chili turned out halfway decent. Grip was the only one who complained.

"I'm sorry about that." He grins at me, his eyes lighting with temporary mischief. "I lied. Your chili was pretty good. It really was.

No, I wasn't in the bathroom. I went to your bedroom. Ya know. To explore."

"My bedroom?" I can't believe him. "How dare you?"

"Desperate times call for desperate measures. I have no problem playing dirty. I welcome it actually. But I stumbled upon something in the drawer by your bed that was very telling."

There are two drawers in my bedside table. One holds journals and a few items that would tell him too much about my feelings. That drawer remains locked, so he wouldn't have seen what was inside. But the other drawer . . .

"I've never seen so many vibrators in one place." Grip's grin is half-teasing, half-cruel. "Residential, of course. You've got your own black market sex store in there."

My face heats, and I cannot even form words. Embarrassment chokes me.

"I figure anyone with that many vibrators can't be coming on the regular. With a guy, I mean," he clarifies unnecessarily.

"Stop it." I fire the words at him, so angry, so humiliated I want to slap him.

"It's okay." With gentle fingers he brushes the heavy hair back from my forehead. "I think I understand the problem. It isn't you. It's them."

I push away from the wall, only to be blocked and gently but firmly pressed back against the door.

"Guys, we can be so clumsy." He shakes his head and sighs. "You know? Quick. Selfish."

He trails fingers down my arm to link our fingers.

"See, I bet they start here," he whispers, slipping his hand between us until his fingers lightly drift across the space just below my belly where my thighs juncture. My panties soak with the promise of his fingers. My breath catches at the brief contact where I crave him most.

"When they should start . . ." His hand glides up and over my belly and between my breasts. Over the curve of my shoulder and neck until he reaches his destination. He finally taps my temple three times. "Here. They should start here and work their way down because your mind is your most erogenous zone, Bris. I look forward to making you come with my words alone."

I fumble with the knob behind my back until the door swings open. I take several steps into the apartment. I can think more clearly now that I'm away from that tower of muscle, bone, and heat standing pressed against me. The strong girl who has resisted him all these years is regaining her composure.

"Whatever you think you know about me," I yell, not bothering to turn around. "About my sex life, about anything—you have no idea."

I stride over to the couch and retrieve my bag, determined to get out of here with the hard shell still around my soft places. When I'm at the front door, I glance back, surprised to see Grip still in the stairwell where I left him, the door standing wide open. Our eyes clash one last time, and there's a coalition of sadness and frustration and want in his gaze. I can't afford to look too long, so I make a dash for the door, hoping against hope that he won't come after me.

I'm nearly at my car by the time I realize I'm perversely saddened he didn't follow.

CHAPTER 3

G~RIP~

I PROBABLY SHOULDN'T ᴴᴬⱽᴱ ᴷᴵˢˢᴱᴰ her.

Second thought, hell with that.

I'd do it again if given the opportunity. That's just it. There hasn't been an opportunity, no opening for years. And then all of a sudden last night, a crack. Something inside of Bristol opened just a fraction, but it was enough for me to explore and exploit. I would have explored and exploited all night if she had let me, but that space sealed shut almost immediately. Something shut her down. I don't know what holds Bristol back from making us . . . an us. It has to be more than what happened with Tessa.

I saw that crack in the wall she's used to keep me out. Maybe my Shawshank plan is working. Rhyson, Bristol's brother and my best friend, would appreciate that, movie geek that he is. In *Shawshank Redemption*, Andy hangs a poster on the wall in his prison cell. At night for years, he secretly chips at that wall until one day, he's made a hole big enough to crawl through and escape. That's me. Chipping away at that wall for years, and last night may have been a break-through.

Or not.

Because as Bristol walks down the hall of the Prodigy offices, headed straight for me, there's barely a flicker of recognition in her eyes, much less desire. She nods to me before carefully brushing past to enter the conference room for our meeting.

There are already a few people here, including Bristol's assistant Sarah. They chat as Bristol sets her iPad and phone on the table, her movements easy and graceful. She wears her hair in one of those complicated braid things it looks like you need a degree to do, the dark and coppery length tamed to rest on one shoulder. She's paired dark skinny jeans with her trademark stilettos and a slouchy shirt hangs off one shoulder.

The seat beside her is occupied, so I take the one across from her. She glances up, catching my eyes on her. The tiny frown pulling between her brows is the only indication she gives that she even knows I'm here.

"Let the party begin," Rhyson says from the door, wearing one of the ear-to-ear grins he seems to have all the time since he got married. The fact that Kai is also pregnant . . . well, let's just say it must hurt to smile that hard.

"You think you could tone down that smile, Rhys?" Max, Prodigy's head marketing guy and cynic-in-chief, asks. "It's too early for such joy."

Rhyson takes the seat at the head of the table, but his smile doesn't budge. Max just came through a nasty divorce, so he and Rhys are in very different places. So are we, for that matter. I won't lie. Seeing Rhyson settle down with someone who loves him the way Kai does and seeing them preparing for their first kid, it makes me wonder how close I am to any of that. I'm knocking on thirty years old. I'm in no hurry, though. My album drops in three weeks, and all my hard work is about to pay off. Is already paying off. Still, I'd like someone to share it with. Not just some groupie. A friend, a lover, a partner.

Bristol's head is lowered over an open folder. As hard as she works, as single-minded as she is about her job, you'd never guess family is everything to her. I've never met anyone who works harder than Bristol. She's ambitious, yes, but people don't realize what fuels it. She works hard for the people she cares about. I'm not even sure that Rhyson's career would have exploded the way it did without Bristol. She was the one who pushed him to get back to making his own music. When she and Rhyson were barely on speaking terms, she chose her degree based on his future and relocated from New York with no guarantees. She's sacrificed a lot over the last year building this record label not just for success, but out of love for her brother.

I always refused when she asked to manage me, too, because I didn't want to be just a job to her. I gave in a few months ago, hoping that working together so closely would force her to acknowledge the attraction, the connection between us. But she has somehow managed to keep me out, even as she propelled my career forward. I had success before she came onboard, but I know the unprecedented doors opening for me now are doors Bristol banged on and kicked in.

"Before we get started," Rhyson says, his grin now aimed at me and growing. "Marlon, dude, what the hell happened to your hair? Kitchen fire?"

He and my mom. The only ones who still call me Marlon. "Jokes." I nod, suppressing my grin. We pretty much bust each

other's balls every chance we get, a fifteen-year habit. "Nah. Just wanted something different."

When Jade came over last night, we started reminiscing about old times in the neighborhood where I grew up. Hard times. Thinking about how far I've come since then, how much has happened, made me even more excited for this next chapter. I feel something fresh happening inside of me, and I wanted the outside to reflect it.

"Well, you look about twelve." Rhyson ignores the middle finger I slowly slip into the air in his honor. "Okay, Bris. Tell us what we're doing."

Bristol flicks a glance my way before diving in. I think she's still adjusting to the new hair, or lack thereof. I am, too.

"Okay. Just to put us on the same page." Bristol looks down the table at everyone. "We're talking about the Target Exclusive."

I still can't believe it. Target approached us about an exclusive edition of *Grip*, my debut solo album. Usually reserved for the likes of Beyoncé and Taylor Swift, an opportunity like this is something we can't pass up. But we'll have to work our asses off to get it done in time. Fortunately, working my ass off is one of my specialties.

"They want three bonus tracks that will be exclusive to their stores." Bristol checks her notes before going on. "We need to choose the songs today. Rhys and Grip have several songs not included on the wide version of the album for us to consider. We have to move fast, though, because we'll need to re-master the tracks and get that version of the project pressed and shipped out as quickly as possible." "And how exactly did this happen again?" Max frowns at the folder in front of him. "Are we rushing? Committing to something we can't pull off well in time? I'm not sure about this."

Before I can tell Max to go suck his own dick, Bristol beats me to it . . . if not more tactfully.

"Max, I don't have time for you to punch holes in something because you didn't come up with it." She rests a fist on her hip and looks at him impatiently. "It's a freaking Target Exclusive for a debut album. What's there not to be sure about?"

"I do have legitimate concerns," he replies firmly. "It isn't that I didn't come up with it."

Bristol tilts her head and gives him a knowing look.

"Okay, maybe that's part of it," Max admits with a laugh. "But it's a lot to turn around in a tight time frame. Can we do it with excellence?"

"Max, I get your concerns." Bristol tosses her folder onto the conference room table. "But have you ever known me to commit to something we couldn't get done? I'm not saying it will be easy. Between this, the shows we have with Qwest over the next few weeks, the reporter trailing Grip for the story, and let's not forget a trip to Dubai thrown in the mix, I'll probably have a bald spot by the time this is all said and done."

There are smiles, snickers, various expressions of amusement from everyone at the conference table.

"But it'll be worth it." Bristol's eyes land on me. "*Grip* will be one of the best albums of the year, and we're damn well gonna treat it that way."

I knew she believed in me, but the sincere passion resonating from her is deeper than I even thought. I wish she'd direct some of that passion to me, instead of my work.

"And that starts with positioning it for the best possible opportunities." Bristol's eyes shift from mine and touch on each person at the table. "This is something we can't let get away. I promise you we can do it."

"I say let's go for it," Rhyson says.

And if he says it, we're going for it. Rhyson and Bristol often disagree loudly and vehemently, but when they agree, it's done.

"Well, that's settled." Bristol shares a brief smile with her brother but then snaps her fingers. "I almost forgot. Grip?"

She turns to me, and we look straight at each other. I barely catch the flash of vulnerable uncertainty before she shutters it.

"Yeah?" It's the first word I've spoken since the meeting officially started, even though it's all about my album. It isn't that I don't care about this stuff, but I'm much more interested in actually getting the music to listeners, for them to connect with what I created.

"Target wants you to film a spot next week." She taps the iPad, her eyes roaming over the screen. "They sent over a treatment for the commercial. I have it here somewhere."

"Lemme guess," I say. "There's lots of red and big dots."

"Smart ass." She shoots me her first natural smile of the morning. "I'll show you later. Let's listen to these tracks. My contact is waiting. Grip and Rhys, you guys walk us through our options."

Rhyson dips his head to defer to me. Right.

"So this first song," I say, pulling up the file sharing where we've stored the bonus tracks. "It's called 'Bruise.'"

There's so much I could say to set up this song. I tell them bits and pieces of it. How personal it is. How cathartic it was to write about the tension and fear that marked my relationship with cops growing up. Before black lives or blue was preceded by hashtags, the debate dividing our nation, divided my family. There's so much more I could say to make them know what this song means to me, but I don't say any of it. I just play the song and hope it speaks for me. And while it plays, I can't help but remember the day that inspired it.

CHAPTER 4

G<small>RIP</small>
 12 years old

"SEXUAL CHOCOLATE!"

I've lost count of how many times we've watched *Coming to America*. My cousin Jade, my boy Amir, and I know just about every line by heart. Every week, we watch this bootleg copy Ma bought at the barber shop, and not even the shadows of people's heads in the shots or the sometimes-unsteady camera work make Eddie Murphy as Randy Watson and his band Sexual Chocolate less funny.

"'That boy good,'" Amir quotes when Eddie Murphy does the infamous mic drop and leaves the stage.

"'Good and terrible,'" Jade and I finish the quote. We all crack up laughing like it's the first time.

"Y'all and this movie." Jade's older brother Chaz walks through the living room in his jeans, no shirt.

His body is like one of the graffiti walls off Largo Avenue, inked with five-pointed stars declaring his Bloods gang affiliation, "186" scrawled on his chest signifying the code for first-degree murder.

His other passion, the Raiders, vie for equal space on his arms and back. Ink stains every available inch of skin, but he left his face clear. Ma says thank God the boy is vain, otherwise he would have ruined that handsome face of his with tattoos. A teardrop or something.

Everyone says we look alike, Chaz and me. Ma and his father were brother and sister, but my uncle died before I was even born, so I never met him. Ma sometimes looks at Chaz with sad eyes and says if you've seen Chaz, you've seen his daddy. You've seen her brother.

"How many times y'all gon' watch this movie?" Chaz's bright smile flashes before he pulls his Raiders T-shirt over the muscular framework of his upper body. "If it ain't this, it's *Martin*."

"Wasssssup!" Amir, Jade, and I parrot Martin's signature phrase on cue, laughing while Chaz rolls his eyes.

"Y'all little niggas a trip." The pager on Chaz's hip beeps, and he plucks it off his waistband to read the message. I love that we made him laugh before we lost his attention.

Jade's other brother Greg is LAPD, but we don't trust cops, so they aren't our heroes. Chaz is our hero. He may be a gangbanger, and he slings, but he's cool. He always has the latest Jordans, the freshest clothes, and the sound system you hear before you see his car bouncing around the corner, hydraulics on point. His mom, my Aunt Celia, doesn't ask where the money comes from when he pays her rent every month. She turns a blind eye, but Ma won't take Chaz's money, no matter how tight it gets at our house.

"Shit," Chaz mutters, a frown puckering his eyebrows. He usually walks slowly so everyone can see his fresh kicks, to make it easy for what Ma calls "fast tail girls" to catch him, but he runs to the back of the house like someone's chasing him.

"What's up with Chaz?" I ask Jade.

"Mmm-hmm." Jade shrugs, her attention already back on *Coming to America*. "No telling. Trouble probably."

Chaz has been nothing but trouble for a long time. Like most kids, he thought he'd be a baller, get drafted one day. If it isn't rapping, it's sports. In the hood, those are a boy's dreams when anything seems possible. Most dreams don't last long on this block of rude awakenings.

Our three sets of eyes stretch wide at the sound of a helicopter overhead outside. The cops have been cracking down lately. Sometimes it feels like they've forgotten us here in Compton, like they give up on trying to regulate the violence and death we've become numb to. One minute, you're on the playground swinging, hanging on monkey bars, and the next you're dodging bullets. The cops come on their terms, usually when they're looking for somebody. That bird in the sky tells us they're looking for somebody. I don't say it, but Chaz's response to the pager and the helicopter that sounds like it's right on top of us has me wondering if this time they're looking for him.

"Amir." Ms. Bethany, Amir's mom, stands on our front porch, her usually pleasant face stern through the bars over the screen door. "Bring your narrow butt home right now."

"But, Ma." Amir gestures to the television. "We coming up on the barber shop scene where Eddie Murphy plays all the different characters."

"And I'm coming up on that butt if you don't get to that house like I told you." She sends a worried look up to the sky. "Go to the closet."

The three of us exchange glances. The violence has been so bad lately innocent people have been getting caught in the crossfire. Just last week one of our neighbors caught a stray bullet sitting in his kitchen. Drive-by. After that, Ma and Ms. Bethany told us we should go to the closets when we hear gunfire or even helicopters. Most times, those birds are looking for guys who run and shoot first, not caring where the bullets land until later.

"Hey, Bethany." Ma walks up the hall from the kitchen, drying her hands on a dishtowel. "Everything all right?"

"That bird." Ms. Bethany flips her head up toward the sky. "They looking for somebody."

She aims a careful glance at Jade, pausing before going on. "Word on the street's they're looking for Chaz."

Jade's troubled eyes meet mine. Chaz bounces between our houses sometimes. I'm not even sure Ma knows he's here.

"For Chaz?" Ma looks down the hall. "Chaz, you back there?"

The answering silence tells me he's gone. Probably snuck out through my bedroom window. My heart starts banging on my ribcage, dragging back and forth like on prison bars. My breath goes short. Mama says we have extra senses, things the streets teach us to survive. We smell danger. Feel trouble disrupting the air. In just seconds, an invisible hand is choking our whole block as that bird hovers, and none of us can breathe.

"Amir, I said come on." Fear adds a few lines around Ms.

Bethany's tight lips. "Now, boy." Amir drags himself to the door.

"I don't want to leave," he gripes. "Ain't fair."

"Fair?" Ms. Bethany pops his head with her palm. "Get your fair butt 'cross that street."

She glances over her shoulder at my mother. They watch out for each other. Amir eats at our table as much as I eat at theirs.

"Mittie, let me know if you hear anything about Chaz."

With that, she's gone, retreating into the house to seek shelter until what we all feel coming passes over. Ma grabs the remote and turns off the television, standing to block the screen. She points back down the hall to my bedroom where we hid the last few times.

"Get to the closet."

Before we can groan and complain like Amir did, a tall figure in uniform at the screen door distracts us. My cousin Greg takes after his mother. He and Jade share the same almond-shaped eyes and walnut complexion, where Chaz and I have skin like deep caramel, like Ma and her brother.

"Aunt Mittie, I need to come in." Greg's face is sober. He darts looks around our small living room, alert. "Hey, Jade. Marlon."

I flick my chin up like I see the older boys do, trying to be cool. Jade just stares at her brother. His decision to become a cop divided our family, and she doesn't know from one day to the next whose side she's on.

"To that closet," Ma repeats, her lips set in a line. She opens the door for Greg, not checking to make sure we obeyed. We walk down the hall but linger to eavesdrop as soon as we're out of sight.

"What's going on, Greg?" Ma finally allows the worry to seep into her voice now that she thinks we're out of earshot. "This about Chaz? They say y'all looking for him."

"Yes, ma'am." Greg's heavy sigh covers all the scrapes and trouble Chaz has been in leading up to today. "He's wanted for questioning in that shooting yesterday off Rosecrans."

"Shooting? The kid?"

"He was sixteen. He was a Crip, Aunt Mittie."

That's all he has to say. Between Crips and Bloods, color is the only offense needed.

"He ain't here." Ma's voice goes harder. "And your mama is working a double shift, so she ain't home yet. Greg, you look out for your brother now."

"Aunt Mittie, I've been trying, but he never listens to me. He's always tripped about me becoming a cop. A lot of folks here in the neighborhood did."

"I understand, Greg. You wanted to change things. I get that, but you know cops haven't made friends here. It'll take some time, but folks will come around."

A shot cracks the air beyond the front porch.

"Go!" Ma's voice becomes urgent. "If Chaz did what they think, he'll have to deal with the consequences. Just protect him, Greg. Just . . . for your mama. Okay?"

"I gotta go."

Jade and I slide down the wall, faces turned toward each other, connected by our fear and worry.

"What'd I say?" Ma stands in front of us, her eyes fired up with frustration. "Get in that closet. Now."

She points to my bedroom, looking from Jade to me.

"I know you're scared for Chaz, but be scared for yourself. A stray bullet could take you out. Now, get in there."

We stand and start down the hall. Ma grabs my elbow, pulling me around to face her. At twelve, I'm almost as tall as she is, but I'm straddling childhood and adolescence. Half the time I think I know best and don't need her. This is the other half of the time when I want my mama to hug me and tell me it will all be okay. That we'll all be okay.

"Remember what we talked about?" she asks softly. "You go in that closet and don't be scared."

"You can't make yourself not scared, Ma." I stuff my hands into the pockets of my jeans.

"That's true, but you can distract yourself. You're a sharp boy. You got a memory like an elephant. Recite some of them poems you're always reading in Ms. Shallowford's class. Sing a song. Say the Pledge of Allegiance. I don't care. Just don't leave that closet until I say so."

I nod and enter my room. Michael Jordan, NWA, Tupac, and the Oakland Raiders plaster my walls. Other than a small bed and dresser, that's all the decoration the room requires. Jade isn't in the closet. She's standing by the window Chaz must have left open when he snuck out.

"In the closet, Jade." I walk in, expecting her to follow. For a second, her face defies the order. She glances through the window and out to our front yard. Both her brothers are out there. On opposite sides of the law, but both at risk.

"There's nothing you can do." I make my voice certain like I hear Ma's even when she isn't sure at all. "Get in here."

As soon as Jade sits beside me in the tiny closet, the wail of approaching sirens splinters the air. Fear widens her eyes, and she clenches skinny arms around her legs. She presses her forehead to her knees and quietly cries. Jade is more sister than cousin to me. Nobody messes with me if she's around, and nobody messes with her if I have anything to say about it. Her tears, I can't take.

What Ma says is true. My head is like a vault. Poems, lyrics, all of it gets locked in my head. Ms. Shallowford's class is the only place I'm rewarded for remembering poems, for loving poetry. For writing my own. I do it only in class because I don't want to catch it from the other guys, but for Jade, whose hands tremble as the sirens come closer, I'll do it.

I start with the question that launches Langston Hughes' famous poem "Harlem," asking what happens to a dream deferred.

When I quote the line, when I ask the question, Jade lifts her head. I feel stupid. I usually do this alone. I'm usually in my bed when the sound of bullets rips through the air, and the words that calm and comfort me, I'm the only one who hears. But Jade's with me now, and I taste her fear. It's bitter like aspirin dissolving on my tongue as I continue, posing Hughes' questions about dried-up raisin dreams. Jade blinks at me, her tears slowing. She swipes at her running nose. Feet scamper past my open bedroom window, a chase underway. Angry voices bounce off the walls.

"Hands in the air!" Greg's voice reaches us in the closet. "Chaz, man stop. Come on. Put the gun down."

Jade's chest expands and contracts with breaths like she's about to hyperventilate, her eyes round as plates.

I continue with the lines of "Harlem," comparing the delayed dream to rotten meat and syrupy sweets. The words barely penetrate my mind, but they keep my heart from falling out of my chest.

I'm not sure if it helps Jade, but the words anchor me, give me something to focus on besides the chaos on the front yard. Besides the threat of violence chilling the air. I blink back tears, but Jade's flow freely down her cheeks.

"Chaz, no!" Panic and pain wrestle in Greg's words. "Don't make me do it!"

Pop!

It's a silly word for the sound a gun makes. Ms. Shallowford taught our class about onomatopoeia last week, but none of the sounds she used for gunfire seem right.

Pop! Crack! Bang!

If you've heard shots as many times as we have, if you live with it, you know the sound a gun makes when it's fired is a moan. The moan of a mother, a father, a daughter, or son losing someone they love. It's the sound Jade makes when she runs to my window, her eyes scanning the front yard for both of her brothers. We find them there together. Chaz's lifeless head rests in Greg's lap on the patch of grass. Greg's face crumples, the brows bent with pain, his mouth stretched wide on a wail. He's covered in the blood spurting life from his brother's chest.

Jade scurries through the window, rushing across the yard and hurling herself into the grief, pummeling Greg's shoulders, slapping his head, screaming obscenities. Ma jerks her off, pulls her back and into her arms, eyes full of pain locked on the blood-covered brothers. My Aunt Celia runs up the street and into the small crowd gathering. A cop restrains her, but you can't hold back a mother's anguish. We all watch Aunt Celia's face collapse, her eyebrows buckling over eyes streaming devastation. Her mouth, a gaping hole of torment. She strains, arms outstretched for her dying son, hands clawed to scratch the other. Sobs rack her body, and she is a world of pain.

"You killed my boy!" Aunt Celia's voice, a dirge, booms over the eerily still street. "I hate you! I hate you! I hate you, Greg!"

His mother's mournful litany bounces off Greg's head and shoulders as he cradles his brother, rocks him, imprisoned by his own guilt and pain.

I can't move. My shoes stick to the thin, cheap carpet in my bedroom. The smell of death invades my nose like an enemy, and my heart trills in my chest, hammering a rapid beat. My breath wheezes from my throat, and my head spins. I grasp for consciousness, searching for the words that calmed me moments ago. Moments before a bullet split our world right down the middle.

I mumble the final lines of "Harlem," even though I'm the only one listening, and I reach the same conclusion Hughes does.

So here in these streets, in my neighborhood, what happens to a dream deferred?

It explodes.

CHAPTER 5

G<small>RIP</small>

IT'S AS QUIET as a morgue when the song ends. I have no idea what the Prodigy team sitting around the table thinks. Verse one of "Bruise" is written from the perspective of a young black man, verse two from that of a cop. I'm the only black man in the room. As much as I love Rhyson, as close as we are, I'm not sure he can understand the indignity of being stopped for no reason by cops on the regular. Being forced to lie on the ground and get searched without explanation. Targeted. Profiled. Made to feel second-class. It isn't his experience, but all my life in my neighborhood, it was mine. I infused every line of that verse with the pain and frustration and resentment brimming over in my community. I hope I told Greg's story, too, my cousin who became a good cop. Who had to shoot his own brother and probably saved lives that day. I admire him as much as I admire anyone. Instead of running from the police force, he ran toward it and decided to do his part to make things better, though sometimes the system as it exists feels beyond repair.

"As much as I think it's a great social commentary," Max finally speaks first. "Are we sure this is what we want to bring up given how divided our nation is right now? I mean, will you be alienating half your listeners? I'm not sure it's the right song for the Target Exclusive."

I shrug like it doesn't bother me, but it does. Should I push? The song is special to me. I didn't even realize how much until now when it sounds like it might not make the cut.

"I agree with you, Max," Bristol says, her tone all business and brusque. "It isn't right for the Target Exclusive."

"I'm glad we can agree on something this morning," he says with a chuckle.

"It belongs on the wide version of *Grip*." Bristol has that defiant look she gets when she digs her heels in. "If it's on the Exclusive, fewer people will hear it, and everyone needs to hear that song."

She meets my eyes for a second before blinking away all softness.

"I agree," Rhyson says quietly.

My best friend and I stare at each other for moments elongated with the things we haven't talked as much about. We have so much in common—our passion for music, the video games we play, the books we read, our acerbic sense of humor—that we often haven't discussed the ways we're different. But the lyrics of "Bruise" paint a picture he's never seen up close.

"So what do we need to do to make that happen?" Bristol has shifted from any sentimentality she felt for the song to battle plan, figuring out how to make it happen at this late date.

Rhyson and I break down every step we must go through to get the song on the album in time. She doesn't blink, but Sarah scribbles frantically, jotting it all down.

"It'll happen." She looks at Rhyson and Max before her eyes land on me. "I promise I'll get it on there in time."

This is what I keep falling for over and over. Bristol is passionate and determined, one of those rare people who never accepts no for the ones she cares about. And whether or not she wants to admit it, she cares about me a hell of a lot.

We listen to three more songs. Bristol loves them all, but she likes everything I write. I'm not being conceited. I can't think of one song or poem I've ever shared with her that she didn't love.

"We need to nail this last song down." Rhyson glances at his watch. "And quick. Kai has an ultrasound today, and I'd much rather see my baby than go through eight more songs when we only need one."

He points to Bristol, his look only half playful. "You get no say this time, Bris."

"What?" She frowns and pushes out her bottom lip a little. "Why not?"

"Because you love everything Grip writes," he says matter-of-factly. "You're no help. We'll be here all day."

Her eyes flick to mine and then down to her iPad. She knows it's true. I've never been more certain of anything than I am that Bristol cares deeply about me. I wasn't guessing last night when I said she watches me. She does. I know she wants me, but a lot of girls do. None of them care about me the way Bristol does, though. The same bottomless devotion she has for her brother, for her few close friends —hell, even for her mother, who doesn't deserve it, she has for me. She hides it in friendship and excuses it with business, but every time I catch her looking, I know the truth.

"So I think I have the final song." Rhyson starts tapping the iPad in front of him until the first strains of the track fill the conference room. A song I never meant anyone to hear.

"Oh, not that one." I go into the shared folder, searching frantically for the file he's playing so I can shut it down. "Rhys, not that one. Let's not—"

"This one is the best option." Rhyson tilts his head, a look of consternation on his face. "Can we just hear it?"

I don't have to hear it. I know every word.

I FELL for her before the beat dropped. Between the verses and
  After rehearsal and
  In sixteen bars I was intoxicated

After sixteen bars, me and her was faded
Had our first kiss on a Ferris wheel
We was on top of the world.

I'M on top of the world (When I love her)
Top of the World (When I hate her)
Top of the world
(When I take her or leave her)
With her I'm on the top of the world

I ROLL her up tight in my blunt paper
Inhale her like smoke, in my lungs she's a vapor 'Cause she always on the run
Making me hunt, making me chase
Making me run like it's a race
Making me work like it's my job
Even when she bottom she come out on top
She be on top of the world

I'M on top of the world (When I love her)
Top of the World (When I hate her)
Top of the world
(When I take her or leave her)
With her I'm on the top of the world

AT THE LAST NOTE, Max starts a slow clap. Everyone around the table joins him. Everyone except Bristol, who stares blankly at the shiny conference room table.

Shit.

"I love it," Max says. "Rhyson, you're right. That's it. Man, the lyrics are so clever. It's infectious. Now that's a hit."

"And what's the song you're sampling?" Sarah asks. "Was it Prince?"

"Uh, yeah." I clear my throat. "'I Wanna Be Your Lover.'"

"As soon as I heard it," Rhyson says. "I knew it was the one. Maybe we should take this one to the wide release, too? Bristol, we should see—"

"If we're done," Bristol says abruptly, cutting off Rhyson's suggestion. "I need to get back to my office."

It goes quiet, and everyone stares at her, but she doesn't stop. She grabs her phone and walks quickly toward the door.

"Sarah," she tosses over her shoulder. "Could you go over that last item on the agenda?"

"Um, okay." Sarah's wide eyes scan the agenda Bristol left. "Here we are. Bristol wants to—"

"I gotta go, too." I push back my chair and stand. "Let me know if you need anything else."

Before anyone can stop me or ask questions, I'm out the door and racing up the hall to catch her before she leaves. I round the corner and come to a halt. Bristol leans against the wall, head down. I approach slowly, cautiously, like she'll run off if I startle her.

"Bris," I say softly once I'm right in front of her.

She stiffens, raising her lashes to reveal the accusation of her eyes.

"How could you?" she asks, her whisper knife-sharp.

"It was just for me." I grab the end of the braid hanging over her shoulder. "No one else was supposed—"

"But the song's about us." She jerks back, freeing her hair from my fingers. "About me. How dare you?"

"How dare I?" Now I'm pissed. "Those are my thoughts. My ideas. My music, Bristol. No one dictates how I express myself. Not even you."

"Even when those thoughts and ideas are about me?" She presses her eyes closed and flattens her palm to her forehead. "What happened then was private, and you've put us on display for anyone shopping at Target."

"I didn't mean to. I'd forgotten about that track until Rhyson started playing it." I squat until I'm eye level with her, even though she still doesn't look at me. I lift her chin until she has to. "It was for me, not anyone else. Music, writing—it's how I process what I'm feeling. Always has been. You know that. That's how I was feeling, what I was thinking, and I needed to get it out."

"How you were feeling." Now that she's looking at me, she isn't looking away, and her eyes sear me even before her words do. "You hate me? In the lyrics, you said when I hate her. That's how you feel?"

There's startled hurt in her eyes, but I won't lie to her.

"Maybe that day, that moment." I shake my head. "But no. I don't hate you. How you make me feel? I hate that sometimes."

"How do I make you feel?"

Alive. Tortured. Exhilarated. Hungry.

"Confused," I say instead. "Frustrated."

"What's so confusing about no?" She glances down at the shiny hardwood floor at our feet. "I've been telling you no for years. I mean it."

"What's confusing is that no matter what you say, I know what you feel."

"And you know this how?" She looks up, one imperious brow lifted. "A few kisses on the roof one night when I was high?"

All those walls are firmly erected. No gaps. No cracks. We're back at square one. Judging by the indifferent look on her face, we might even be pre-square one. Have I been fooling myself all these years?

But despite what my eyes tell me, my gut says she has no idea what to do with the way I make her feel. All my instincts tell me Bristol wants me, and fuck if I understand why she won't give us a chance. Maybe she suspects what I know for sure. If I ever get her, no way in hell I'm letting her go. That gap last night showed me what's behind that wall, and I want all of it.

She lures me closer without trying. Her scent, her warmth, her softness, her toughness entices me to lean into her. The feeling of last night, the want, rushes through me again. My hands find her waist, and I imprint my shape into hers against the wall.

"Grip, no." Her breath shivers over her lips, and she turns her head away from me.

"Why not?" I run my nose up and down her neck until she shudders under me. Her body is honest with me even when she hides the truth. I want her truth. I have to know.

She wriggles free, stepping away and pacing a tight circuit in the corridor.

"Bristol, about last night—"

"The other song, 'Bruise,'" she cuts in, stopping her pacing to face me. "It's fantastic."

Not-so-deft change of topic. I'm not sure if it was because she was genuinely interested in the song or afraid of what I would say next.

"Thank you." I slip a fist into my pocket and lean against the wall to watch her

"And your cousin Chaz who was shot by his brother, the cop." Her eyes fall to my left forearm where Chaz's name is inked into the skin. "They're Jade's brothers?"

"Yeah."

"I can't imagine what you described. When I think about that happening, you getting stopped like that over and over again . . ."

Bristol bites into her bottom lip. She turns her head to stare at me, sadness saturating her eyes. "Can you just tell me when all my privilege makes me clueless?"

Damn her. Every time I think I might be able to get past this girl, move on to someone who will actually tell me how she feels, she does this. Shows the tender under all that tough and reminds me why not one day has gone by in eight years when she hasn't at least crossed my mind.

"I can do that," I promise quietly.

"Good, I—"

"There you are. I was looking for you guys." Rhyson strides down the hall toward us. "You both bailed on the meeting. What gives?"

"Sorry. You're right," Bristol says, eyes cool again when she looks at me. "I have too much to do to be standing around. Gotta go. Grip, I'll email you about the Target spot. Should be later this week."

I just nod and watch as she walks away.

"What's wrong with her?" Rhyson asks.

"What's wrong is your timing is shit," I snap.

I love Rhys, but this is one time I want to strangle him.

"What's crawled up your ass?" Rhyson frowns and starts walking. "Can you tell me while we walk? I don't want to be late for Kai's appointment."

"Sure." I match my long stride to his. "I wish you'd checked with me before you played that song."

"Everyone loved it." He jabs the down button for the elevator several times.

"Not everyone." I give him a wry smile. "You do know that doesn't make the elevator come any faster, right?"

"Maybe we should take the st—"

The ding of the elevator doors opening shoots down that suggestion.

"Who didn't like it?" he asks as we board.

"Bristol didn't."

"What?" He frowns over eyes just like his twin sister's. "Why would Bris not like it?"

Do I really want to do this? All these years I haven't talked about this with Rhyson. After the drama with my almost-ex-girl-friend/close-call baby mama, Bristol wanted to put that week behind us, including not telling Rhyson about it. It was kind of awkward anyway, so at first, I was cool with that. Now it just seems stupid that he doesn't know after all these years.

"Bristol doesn't like the song because it's about her." I run my hand over the coolness of my scalp, half-expecting to encounter locs hanging down to my shoulder. "The song, it's about us."

We've reached the building's underground parking garage. As soon as he steps off the elevator, he stops abruptly.

"What the hell are you talking about?" Genuine confusion clouds his expression. "When did you ever kiss Bristol at the top of a Ferris wheel? Is that like a metaphor?"

"No. Dude, I literally kissed your sister at the top of the Ferris wheel."

Rhyson looks torn between losing his lunch and punching me in the face. This might actually make the awkwardness worth it.

"When was this?" he demands. "You and Bristol? Is this recent?"

"No, when she was here for spring break. Remember we went to that carnival?" I sigh. "Don't worry. It hasn't happened again. Unless you count last night."

"Last night?" Rhyson's mouth falls open a little, even as he starts moving in the direction of the Porsche Cayenne in his parking spot. "What the hell? Tell me."

I may be enjoying this too much. Rhyson always has his shit together, so seeing him thrown for a loop is rare and wondrous. To be the cause of it, even better.

"I left my bag here yesterday, and she brought it by my place last night." I pat the hood and deliberately turn to leave, not actually expecting to get very far. "Well, I know you're in a hurry so—"

"Marlon." Rhyson leans against the SUV with his arms folded and a frown on his face. "Cut the crap. Talk."

"We kissed." I lean beside him against his car and shrug. "That's it. That's all."

"That's all?" He lifts a skeptical brow.

"For now." I grin as salaciously as I dare considering Bristol is his sister. "There's always tomorrow."

"Let that shit go." Rhyson blows out an exasperated breath. "I don't want this affecting your working relationship at such a crucial time. Your album's about to drop, and Bristol's hand is in every aspect of it. If you pursue this, it could get awkward. We can't afford awkward right now."

His phone rings with his own song "Lost", Kai's ring tone. "Damn." He glances at the screen. "That's Kai. Probably wondering where I am. She'll feel better if I'm in motion."

"Then by all means get in motion." I step back when he starts the car and pulls out of the space, driver side window still down.

"Don't forget what I said about Bristol, okay?" He gives me one last worried look.

"What? You mean to go for it?" I ask, hoping to see some hackles rise. "Got it."

"Not go for it. Did you not hear a word I . . ." He studies my face and must see the humor there. "Screw you. You know I'm right. Leave it alone."

Leave it alone.

That's what my mom used to say when I'd pick at my scabs. She warned me it would only take longer to heal, but it was a compulsion, a fascination. It's the same way with Bristol. I've been pulling this scab off over and over for years.

If I have to leave her alone for this to get better, maybe I don't want it to heal.

CHAPTER 6

"YOU'VE DONE A great job with everything, Bristol."

The praise comes from Will, Qwest's manager, as we check the set list for tonight.

"Thanks," I murmur without looking away from the document detailing the songs and cues for the performance Qwest and Grip will give soon. "Are your rooms okay?"

"That would be an understatement." His dark eyes laugh at me when I finally look up. "The Presidential Suite at The Park-LA is a little over the top, wouldn't you say?"

"The Presidential Suite?" I frown, mentally scrolling through the email I sent Sarah about accommodations for Qwest's team. "I'm glad you like it. I just don't remember reserving it for you."

"Yeah. It's a three-bedroom suite." It's his turn to frown. "Is there a problem?"

"No. Probably just a mix-up. No problem." I catch Sarah's eye across the room and flick my chin so she knows I need her before looking back to Will. "Is Qwest settled okay?"

"Um, yeah." Will's face broadcasts his reluctance. "She really wants to hang with Grip tonight instead of doing that interview, though. Any update from the reporter?"

Translation. She really wants to sleep with Grip before she goes back to New York. That's her business and his, not mine, I remind myself and draw a deep breath to support the words I need to say.

"I'm trying. I've left Meryl a message and am just waiting to hear back."

"Waiting?" Will glances at the platinum watch on his wrist. "She needs to let us know soon."

"Believe it or not," I say sharply, despite the control I thought I was exercising. "My job description as Grip's manager does not include arranging booty calls. So yes, waiting to hear back. And if Qwest needs to hear that from me, it's a message I'm more than happy to deliver personally."

Will holds up both hands, his teeth flashing white against his goatee and dark skin.

"Whoa, whoa, whoa." He takes my hand and squeezes. "You handle Meryl. I'll take care of the booty call."

"Sounds good to me."

"You must admit," he says, his eyes persuading me to smile. "It is an awful lot of booty for one person to manage."

I laugh before I catch myself. Qwest's ass is the stuff of legends.

Jaws drop over it. My laugh withers in my throat when I think of Grip spending the night holding on to that ass.

"I'm just trying to keep my artist happy," Will says. "So don't flip."

"Flip?" I find a polite smile from somewhere. "You'll know when I flip, Will. I'm far from flipping. I'll have an answer for you before the show is over."

"Grip's lucky to have you." There's sincerity in his eyes, which is something we don't find much of in this business.

"Qwest is lucky to have you, too."

Because God knows she and I would kill each other.

Will knows hip-hop, but he knows business even better. Armed only with his MBA and hustle, he started a small management firm just a few years ago. Qwest was his first act, but he's parlayed that into several others, and recently merged with Sound Management, one of the largest firms in the business.

"Congratulations, by the way, on the deal with Sound," I add.

"Thanks." Will's smile is instant and tinged with pride. "Ezra Cohen asked me to tell you hello. I didn't realize you knew him, though I shouldn't be surprised."

"I interned with Sound in New York and worked some at their office here in LA when I first moved. Ezra's been a mentor of sorts to me over the years."

"I guess with parents like yours, making those connections is easy, huh?"

I stiffen at his words, resenting any assumption that my parents' success managing classical musicians fast tracked me.

"He actually wasn't familiar with my parents at all. He's mainstream. They move in classical circles." I clip each word. "I applied for the internship like anyone else and busted my ass once I got it."

"I'm sorry." Will's dark eyes search mine, and he grimaces. "Look, real talk. I'm the only minority at the Sound Management partner table, and most of them think I'm Ezra's answer to affirmative action."

The memory of fetching coffee for some of those assholes during my internship makes me grin.

"And a lot of folks at Penn State thought of me as some kind of token. Like I was taking the spot of someone who actually deserved it," Will continues. "I guess what I'm trying to say, and not very well, is that I know what it's like when people assume you got where you are using something other than hard work. Didn't mean to imply that."

"No problem." I relax my face until my smile becomes genuine. "Sorry I got defensive."

"Then we're both sorry." Will returns my smile, straightens his tie, and nods to Sarah as she walks up. "I need to check on something for Qwest. See you in a little bit."

Once he's gone, I gesture for Sarah to join me at a nearby table to go over a few details before the doors open.

"You're feeling better today?" I ask.

"So much better." Sarah grins, looking more like the perky girl I'm used to seeing. "I went to bed as soon as I got home and woke up a new woman. Thanks for taking the bag to Grip."

"No problem." I ruthlessly suppress the images and sensations that assault me when I remember being on that rooftop with Grip, and focus on the task at hand. "Did you, by chance, upgrade Qwest to the Presidential Suite at the Park?"

I sip my water. As badly as I need a drink, I've been trying to cut back. I'm known for holding my liquor, but that doesn't mean I should. If I'm not careful, I'll end up drinking vodka for breakfast like my mother.

"No." Sarah frowns and pulls out her phone, scrolling through emails. "The reservation is for a luxury suite, not the Presidential."

She whistles and lays her phone on the table. "Somebody messed up. Costly mistake."

"Hmmmm. Maybe." I have my suspicions about other scenarios, but don't voice them. I just open a few emails that might need my attention. "Did we hear back from Meryl about Grip's date with Qwest?"

Sarah clears her throat in a way that catches my attention. I glance up from my phone and wait.

"I haven't heard back yet," Sarah says. "But does Grip know about this um . . . date?"

"I think Qwest wants it to be a surprise of sorts." I keep my face impassive.

"She's wasting her time," Sarah singsongs the words, a small smile on her matte pink lips. "Grip only has eyes for one woman."

Sarah is more observant than I gave her credit for. I stand and smooth my hair.

"I don't think all the girls Grip sleeps with really care where his eyes are," I say, keeping my tone neutral. "There are other parts of his anatomy they're much more interested in."

"If that one woman he has eyes for would give him a sign, I'm sure he'd keep his anatomy where it should be."

"Well his anatomy has to be onstage in about an hour," I tell her. "So, I'm going to make sure it is."

Did I say I liked being friendly with Sarah? Retract that statement. I don't need her that close or seeing that much. She better be glad she's so efficient.

And that I like her so much.

I prepare a mug of lemon tea in the kitchen for Grip. He's been performing so much his voice must be tired. I'm walking down the hall to the dressing room, and the door is ajar. My brother's voice reaches me through the small open space.

"Call me whipped if you want." Laughter threads Rhyson's deep voice. "You're just jealous, Marlon."

Softer, feminine laughter joins Rhyson's.

"Rhys, don't tease him," my sister-in-law Kai chides.

"He knows it's true," Rhyson insists. "You want the wife and kid now that I made it look so good, right? I see it in your eyes. You're ready to settle down. You're tired of sowing all those wild oats."

"I haven't been sowing anything." Grip's voice when it comes has a little gravel in it. "I always wrap it up."

I clench my fist at my stomach. I know he sleeps with women. If I hadn't known, he made it abundantly clear last night.

"I don't mean literally sow," Rhyson says. "You already had one baby daddy close call."

"Not funny," Grip answers. "Too soon."

"How can it be too soon?" Rhyson demands with a laugh. "Tessa was eight years ago."

"Considering what she tried to pull on me," Grip answers. "It will always be too soon."

Tessa.

Tessa was my close call, too. I may have fallen hard and fast for Grip that week, but I've been getting back up ever since. My hands and knees may be scraped, but I'm otherwise in tact, if not a little tougher and smarter. Tougher and smarter should be the natural evolution of a woman. It's the only way we'll survive as the "weaker" sex in this world.

Weaker, my ass.

"Just admit you want this," Rhyson says with a laugh.

I carefully peer through the crack to see Rhyson's very pregnant wife sitting on his lap. He brushes Kai's long, dark hair away from her neck to drop a kiss there. I can't believe Gep, Rhyson's most trusted security guard, isn't out here keeping watch. Then I notice a shiny shoe only a few feet from Rhyson's. Figures. Gep is inside with them.

"You two do make it look good." The smile in Grip's voice stills my heart for a beat. "But it looks good on you because you found the right girl. A lifetime with the wrong girl is a sentence."

"Then find the right girl," Rhyson says. "And do not say it's Bristol."

A needle pulls through my heart at my brother's words. Grip and I aren't right for each other, but to hear someone else say it, to hear my own brother say it, hurts.

"Don't start." Now Grip's voice is tight. No sign of a smile.

"Yeah, Rhyson," Kai chimes in. "I believe Bristol will come around."

You're wrong, honey.

"I already told you who Bristol will marry," Rhyson says. This I gotta hear. My brother is notoriously obtuse about me.

"She'll marry some guy in a suit with a stick up his ass and who has our mother's approval."

Okay. Maybe not completely off base.

"Don't say that about your sister," Kai says.

"It isn't a criticism," Rhyson replies, his tone ringing with truth. "Just a prediction. Bristol wants more control than what she would have with a guy like you, Marlon."

"We'll see, huh?" Grip answers softly. "You might be right."

"I still have my money on Grip and Bristol." Kai's voice is light but a little defiant.

"Don't lose our money, Pep," Rhyson says. "Ow! Why'd you hit me?"

"Because you're being a jerk," she says, laughing a little. "And I'll kiss it better."

They would turn my stomach if I wasn't getting a niece out of this in the next month or so.

"Uh . . . I'm still here," Grip says. "Don't start making out. Remember Gep's innocent, virgin eyes."

Gep's gruff hack of a laugh joins the others. I'm positive the ex-CIA operative hasn't been innocent or a virgin in decades.

"In all seriousness," Rhyson continues. "Qwest likes you a lot."

"What gave you that idea?' Grip asks. "The way she practically dry humps me onstage every time we perform? Maybe I'll wear a condom for our set tonight."

I find myself smiling listening to them laugh. "She's a sweet girl," Kai defends.

Kai actually pointed Qwest my way when the rapper asked about meeting Grip. They've developed some kind of odd friendship. Odd because Qwest may be sweet in her own way, but she's a diva. She and I would still rip each other's hair out. Kai doesn't have a drop of diva in her body.

"She's very sweet," Grip agrees. "I've been surprised by how sweet she is. And smart. And gorgeous. And funny. She's actually kind of amazing."

That needle makes another pass through the fibers of my heart as I listen to Grip's glowing words for Qwest. Why wouldn't he think those things?

"And let's not forget that asssss!" Grip laughs.

Seriously. The girl's ass has its own hashtag. I'm pretty sure it's insured. Rhyson and Gep join in the laughter, but Kai refuses.

"Does it always come down to that?" Kai sounds only slightly outraged. She has room to talk since she has "assets" in that area herself.

"No," Grip answers. "I like legs and breasts, too."

"Both of which Qwest had the last time I checked," Rhyson says.

"Oh, you checked, did you?" Kai asks.

"Not like that," Rhyson rushes to say. "I mean, not at all like that. It's just her—"

"Dude, just stop," Grip laughs. "That's a no-win grave you're digging for yourself. I may not be married, but even I know that."

"Rhyson, to misquote *Mean Girls*," Kai says. "Stop trying to make Qwest happen."

My brother and Kai are film geeks and could talk in nothing but movie quotes for days. How I ever thought they weren't perfect for each other, I'll never know.

"Maybe it isn't Qwest." Some of the laughter fades from Rhyson's words. "I'm just saying I know how important family is to you. I don't want you wasting any more time than you have to pining for my sister when she hasn't budged all these years. How long are you gonna wait?"

I glance through the crack again and see Rhyson holding Kai even tighter, his chin on her shoulder and her temple leaned against his head. With Rhyson's hand splayed across her baby bump, they're the picture of marital bliss. Happiness personified. Grip's eyes reflect the same emotions roiling inside me. Maybe a little envy. Maybe a little doubt. He's probably asking himself the questions Rhyson asked of him.

What is he waiting for? Me? To change my mind? I won't. It shouldn't be me. He needs to see that, and I know what I need to do to make sure he does.

CHAPTER 7

G_{RIP}

THE LIGHT KNOCK on the dressing room door interrupts my conversation with Rhys and Kai. And Gep, if I count his non-verbals as conversation, which I pretty much have to since he barely speaks.

"Come in." I expect a stagehand to tell me it's almost time, but it's Bristol.

God, she's beautiful.

I'd like to kick everyone out, lock the door with us on this side, and fuck her against the wall. She could keep those heels on, too. I can imagine them digging into my butt while I tear that ass up.

I'm not a gentleman.

I feel like I'm channeling Uncle Jamal for a moment. Maybe Rhyson's right. Maybe she needs a guy wearing a suit accessorized with a stick up his ass. Tonight, she looks like the definition of class.

Those heels are the color of tangerines and match the cropped top showing off the golden skin of her stomach. The long sleeves cling to her arms, and the narrow white skirt hugs her hips, ass, and the infinity of her legs. The coppery streaks stand out in the dark hair parted down the middle and pulled back at her neck.

"Hey." She hands me a steaming mug of lemon-scented something or other. "For your voice."

It takes no effort to hold her eyes with mine when I accept the drink. I will her to remember our bodies pressed together on the roof under a full moon. She's wearing blush, so I can't tell if she's flushing or not under my stare, but she gives nothing else away so I can't know for sure.

"How's my niece today?'

She rubs Kai's little belly.

"She's good, Auntie Bristol," Kai says affectionately.

"What's up, brother?" Bristol musses Rhyson's hair with her knuckles.

"Nothing much. Just supporting our artist." Rhyson swats her hand away and grins at her. "Excellent job tonight, as usual."

"Thanks." Bristol checks the items on my dressing room table. She's anal about our riders, and I know she's making sure everything we requested is there.

"I talked to Danny today." Approval lights Rhyson's eyes when they rest on his sister. "He says you laid down the law and got things straightened out for their show when no one else could. He couldn't stop singing praises of your bad assery."

"It was nothing. I'll probably join them on the road for at least one stop. Maybe after *Grip* drops." Bristol leans against my dressing room mirror to face us. "Kai, if you weren't so preggers, we'd get to hear you tonight."

"Small mercies." Kai rubs her belly and allows herself a wry smile. "Or not so small. I'm sorry I can't perform our song, Grip."

My first single from the album was a collaboration with Kai. We got the video in the can, but she ended up pregnant and having some complications that kept her from performing live. The song still stayed at number one for weeks.

"Don't think twice about that." I grab her hand. "You just keep growing my niece in there."

"If she gets any bigger," Kai says, toggling a smile between Rhyson and me. "I'll pop."

"Soon," Rhyson says with a tender smile.

"Well, I love the single with Qwest." Kai's shoulders start moving to the song she must hear in her head. Not only is she a great singer but also an incredible dancer. One of Prodigy's most versatile artists, she'll start working on her debut solo album soon after the baby arrives.

"My favorite line of 'Queen'," Kai continues. "Is the no one sees your crystal crown lyric."

"Neruda," Bristol and I say in unison.

Surprise locks my eyes with hers when she makes the connection between my current single and Neruda's poem "The Queen." Maybe the book I gave her meant something to her after all. Or am I doing what Rhyson said I do? Wasting my time and reading too much into things that don't mean anything?

"The poet?" Surprise blooms on Kai's pretty face, her tilted eyes sliding between the two of us. "You're a fan, Grip?"

"Huge fan." My eyes haven't left Bristol's face since she mentioned Neruda, my favorite poet. "I didn't realize you were, Bristol."

"Lucky guess." She shrugs and straightens from the dressing room table.

"You're still coming tomorrow, right, Bristol?" Kai tucks into the crook of Rhyson's arm.

"Tomorrow?" Bristol frowns and screws up her face. "I should know this, right?"

"Lunch at our house. The whole Prodigy team is coming over." Kai laughs and rubs her baby bump. "You have just a few things going on, so I'll give you a pass on forgetting."

"Oh, yeah. I'll be there. One o'clock?" Bristol asks.

"Right," Rhyson says. "You want your favorite? Empanadas?"

Bristol and I exchange a quick look. There's no way she isn't recalling last night on the roof. I hope she still feels my hands all over her because I still taste her. I'd back her into a corner and taste her again right now if it wouldn't horrify Rhyson. He swears up and down that Bristol would destroy me if we ever get together. He doesn't realize that's a risk I'd take every day and twice on Sunday. I'm not sure he really believes I'm serious about Bristol. Hell, Bristol may not think I'm serious. Kai would probably start cheering. She's pulling for us if no one else is.

"Whatever's easiest," Bristol says. "Grip, you're on soon."

She walks to the door, class and grace and elegance twined into one girl I can never get out of my mind. "I'm going to check a few last things."

At the door, she practically bumps into someone.

"Excuse me," Bristol says. "Oh, Qwest, hi. How are you?"

Qwest steps fully into the room, the energy that explodes when she performs on stage, latent and waiting for her to pop the top.

"I'm good." Qwest gives Bristol's toned body a head-to-toe inspection. "Damn, you look good, girl. You got a man I haven't heard about?"

Bristol's husky laugh drifts back into the room and caresses my ears.

"You never know," she says, injecting some mystery into her voice.

Tension grips my neck and shoulders. Even though I know she isn't dating anyone, our exchange last night about fucking other people has been haunting me ever since. I try not to think of her with other guys. Hell, I sleep with other girls, but if she even hinted we had a chance, that would be over before she could even ask. She knows that, right?

"How's the Park?" Bristol asks. "Your suite is okay?"

"That suite is the bomb!" Qwest's dark eyes glimmer with pleasure between the fake lashes she wears for stage. "Maybe the nicest I've ever stayed in."

"Good," Bristol says. "I've got a friend there who went the extra mile for me."

"You mean Parker, Bris?" Rhyson asks, a slight frown on his face. She looks over her shoulder to her brother. They aren't your typical twins, but every once in a while I suspect they're telepathically communicating things the rest of us are missing.

"Yeah, Parker," she confirms. "I need to go."

She's gone before Rhyson can ask the questions I see lining up in his eyes. I hadn't thought of Charles Parker since our artist showcase in Vegas. His family owns the Park Hotels all over the world, and when we held our showcase at the Park-Vegas, he was wrapped around Bristol like a damn vine. I haven't seen or heard any sign of him since, so he hadn't entered my mind. Now, I wonder if she has been seeing him and I was just that oblivious. If she hid it from me. Or worse, maybe she wasn't hiding it from me at all. Maybe I didn't occur to her and she was just living her life like she told me.

"Is Bristol dating Charles Parker?" Qwest asks Rhyson.

"Not that I know of." Rhyson shifts Kai so he can stand. "I wouldn't be surprised if he hooked her up, though. Our families have been close all our lives. Our mothers are best friends. Roomed together at Wellesley."

How did I not know this? I'll be following up with Rhyson later. But first . . . I need to deal with Qwest. Rhyson, Kai, and Gep tell us they'll see us out there, and all drift out of the room, presumably to give us some time alone.

"Hi," Qwest says as close to shy as she can get.

There's nothing shy or subtle about Qwest. Skin flawless and the color of nutmeg. Her trademark braids, which are usually pulled into a knot, flow down to her tiny waist. Her body is a series of highlights and exaggerations. The curve from her waist to her ass is positively hyperbolic. I used to wonder if that ass was real. Remembering how she invited me to touch it and find out for myself the first time we met crooks my lips into a grin. This girl makes me laugh. She's talented and beautiful. Smart as a whip. I should feel so much more for her than friendship. And maybe I would if it weren't for Bristol.

But there is Bristol.

"Hi, yourself," I answer. "You ready for this?"

"Ready to get it over with." She walks over until she stands directly in front of me. "So we can have a good time later."

"A good time?" I shrug. "Sure. We could get a crew and go hit Greystone."

"A club?" She shakes her head and reaches up and over my shoulders, pressing her body into me. "No, I had something much more private in mind for us."

She is tight and warm and curvy against me, and if she keeps doing this, my dick will get hard. But that's it.

"Okay." I rest my hands lightly at her hips to move her so I can step away. I grab the button up I'm wearing for the show. "More private, huh? Just remember we have that interview with the *Legit* reporter after the show."

"Didn't Bristol tell you?" Qwest's eyes heat up a few degrees. "She got it cancelled so we can hang out."

"Hang out" is a euphemism for screw me into next week. I'm sure Bristol realizes this, and yet, she cancelled a long-standing interview to accommodate the desire branded in Qwest's eyes.

"Bristol arranged it, huh?" My voice is plastered to the walls of my throat. "Well then it's settled. You just tell me where we're going."

She runs one long nail down the center of my chest, her eyes never leaving mine.

"Oh, I will."

CHAPTER 8

THE FIRST TIME I saw Grip perform, I literally almost came.

Standing in the wings, watching him charm the audience with his charisma, challenge them with his lyrics, and feed them from the palm of his hand. I've almost nodded off waiting for guys to find the spot, to get me off, and this man does it hands-free from fifty feet away in front of a crowd without even trying. It's embarrassing to be so aroused just by watching him onstage. A heat wave flushes my body. Tiny beads of sweat gather down the line of my back, across my lip, at the nape of my neck . . . from watching him. While the blood seems to slow to a languid creep through my veins, my heart hurtles in my chest. Fire-winged butterflies swarm in my belly. I'm wet.

Good God. When will this set be over?

Thank goodness it's the last song or I'd need spare panties. I must not be the only one feeling hot. When Grip brings Qwest onstage for "Queen" to close the show, her eyes rake his tall frame possessively, like he's already hers. Like she wants to jump him under the lights in front of everyone. When she sidles up to him before her verse begins and grinds her hips into his, the audience goes wild. They want this to be real. There's already rampant speculation about a romance between Grip and Qwest. Some even mistakenly assume the song honoring women from all walks of life was written for her. Tonight's sexually charged performance will only send it into overdrive.

She stuffs her mic into her tiny bra top, freeing up her hands.

Grip's denim button down shirt hangs open already, his chest and abs a map of muscles on display. Qwest slides her hands under the shirt at his shoulders and guides it down over his arms until it catches at his wrists. Squeals from the audience pierce the air. Grip laughs, his smile as bright as the stage lights overhead, and shakes the shirt free of his hands. Qwest ties his shirt around her waist before diving into her verse.

She's a powerful figure, the cocky feminism and hard flow of her lyrics juxtaposed with the soft curves of her body. She turns her back to Grip, pressing and circling that is-it-really-real ass into his groin. His hands at her tiny waist look huge and commanding, and I know exactly what every woman in this place must be fantasizing about right now.

Because I would be, except I'm no longer aroused. Seeing how perfect they look together, feeling their chemistry like a tangible thing permeating the whole room, cools me right off and leaves a painful lump in my throat.

"They're fire," Will says from beside me with a grin. "And it's burning up the charts. People want them to happen, and it's driving sales. Their chemistry is a huge part of why 'Queen' is number one."

"It would seem." I try to relax my face so I can smile back.

"And their night out will only fuel it. Thanks for getting the interview delayed. Qwest was very happy."

"Good. She can show her appreciation in Dubai. Meryl's expecting a one-on-one with her, too."

"She'll be more than happy to," Will says. "You should have seen her face when I told her about tonight. I haven't seen her like this over a guy . . . well, ever really."

"Grip has that effect."

He had that effect on me.

Had? Who are you kidding, Bristol? He still does.

And it's harder than I want to admit, seeing him have that effect on Qwest.

We both clap, adding our applause to everyone else's when the set closes.

My shoulders drop with relief. Not only because I'm no longer held captive to the burlesque show Qwest made of the performance but also because I didn't realize how much preparing for this show has stressed me out. It was televised, and every show, every shoot, every interview counts leading up to the release of Grip. In my gut, I know this album is special. I wake thinking about it, and it's the last thing on my mind when I fall into an exhausted heap each night. Unfortunately, that means Grip owns the first and last of my day. I keep a pad by my bed so when promotion ideas or things to do hit me, I can capture them right away. I don't know if I've ever felt this much anticipation and excitement for a project, for an artist. Whether it's because it's that great or whether it's because it's Grip, I don't let myself consider.

I'm at the bar ordering my well-earned, much-deserved vodka martini, when a hand presses against the small of my back, caressing the bare skin. I stiffen and look over my shoulder.

"Parker." I turn back to the bar and smile at the bartender as I accept my drink. "Well, that didn't take long. I texted you, like what? Twenty minutes ago?"

"More like fifteen." The hotel mogul I've known all my life grins and slides a steamy gaze down my body. "You have any idea how long I've been waiting for you to call?"

"Since Vegas?" I turn and prop my elbows on the bar. The action pushes my breasts forward in my cropped top, and his eyes predictably drop.

"A lot longer than that." He captures a lock of hair that's escaped from the knot at my neck, tucking it behind my ear. "And you know it."

"I just wanted to thank you for upgrading the suite." I force myself not to pull away from his hand and take a sip of my drink, closing my eyes in pure bliss. "God, I've needed this drink since I woke up this morning."

"We make the best vodka martini at the Park." He pauses, running a finger down my neck. "The Park-Vegas, I mean. Let's go."

"Now?" I take another glorious sip and cock an eyebrow at him. "Tonight?"

"Got a 'copter waiting on my helipad."

"I love that after all these years you still think your money impresses me." This time, my sip becomes a gulp that bottoms the glass out. "It's charming, really."

The bartender passes me another without my having to ask. "You, my man," I tell him, accepting my second drink gratefully.

"Are on your way to quite a tip."

When I turn back to Parker, the humor gathering in his eyes dissipates as he starts at my toes and takes me in, not stopping until he meets my eyes in the blue-green light of the club.

"I really miss fucking you, Bristol."

The glass stops halfway to my mouth, my breath catching. Not because his words turn me on. It's one thing to invite him here in hopes that Grip will see him and give Qwest a chance. It's a whole other thing to get entangled with Parker again. Our mothers have been planning our wedding since they discovered they were pregnant within days of one another. For some reason, Parker has always been onboard.

Onboard . . . obsessed. Semantics.

"Parker, we've talked about this." I set my drink down on the bar. "We tried and failed at a relationship. I think we've satisfied our parents' misplaced intentions."

"This isn't about what our parents want." Parker palms my hip and pulls me closer, dropping his head until his lips brush my ear. "It never has been for me. I've always wanted you, and having you for a few months wasn't nearly enough. Give me another shot."

Parker and I dated for a while from senior year in high school until I went to college. When I chose Columbia and he went to Stanford, I took advantage of the long distance to break things off. We had zero chemistry, but I think something in me recognized the promise of what he's become—spoiled, entitled, and a bit of a bully. I could so easily have become those things. Hell, I may have even been those things at various points in my life, but I didn't want to be that. I certainly didn't want to be with that.

"Sorry to interrupt."

I look just past Parker's shoulder to see Grip standing there. To anyone else, he might look at ease, but I know him better than most. I know his face intimately, have every line of it memorized. I know how frustration thins his full lips. How his eyes narrow at the corners when he's annoyed. How anger ticks the strong line of his jaw.

"No problem." I gesture to Parker. "Parker, this is—"

"Gripe, right?" Parker extends his hand, which Grip leaves hanging in the air, his eyes fixed on Parker's face.

"It's Grip," I correct, breathing a little easier when Grip finally shakes his hand. "Remember Grip is one of my artists, Parker. He performed at the show in Vegas."

"I need a minute, Bristol," Grip says, not acknowledging my introduction. He walks a few feet away without waiting for my response.

"Be right back," I tell Parker. Parker catches me by the elbow. "I'll have them ready the 'copter."

I pull free without answering and step over to where Grip waits. "What's up?" I ask him.

"Next time, before you pimp me out," he snaps, eyes darkening to hot chocolate. "Give me a heads-up, would you?"

"What are you talking about?"

"You didn't set me up on a date with Qwest?" His brows push up. "Did she misunderstand?"

"I didn't 'pimp you out.' I thought it would be a nice surprise." I shrug nonchalantly. "That you'd enjoy some time to relax. Sorry if I overstepped."

"She wants to fuck me." He dips his head so his eyes wrangle with mine under the moving lights. "You do realize that?"

"You're consenting adults," I say around the fist in my throat. "Whatever you decide to do is up to you."

"This guy, Bristol?" He twists his lips derisively and switches gears without a clutch. "The guy with the irretrievable stick up his ass. This is the guy you give the time of day?"

"Don't start."

I turn to walk away, but he clamps his hand around my wrist. Just that contact sends a smoke signal up my arm. Parker can whisper in my ear that he wants to fuck me, and I'm dry as a bone. One touch from Grip, and I'm gushing in my panties.

Figures. My vagina, the contrarian.

He doesn't get to say more because Qwest walks up to us, her smile wide with anticipation.

"Hey." Her eyes drop to where Grip still holds my wrist. "Everything okay?"

"Just touching base before Grip leaves." I tug my wrist free, looking up at the neutral expression shuttering Grip's face. "You've got a couple of days off before everything goes even crazier. Enjoy them."

Grip's eyes cool to iced mocha and freeze when they shift over my shoulder. I turn to see Parker standing there, a sober-faced gentleman in a suit standing just a few paces behind him. The man with Parker is one of those people who carries just enough menace not to blend into the wallpaper but with a face you'd be hard-pressed to remember.

"Bris, we need to go if we want to make that flight." Parker's hands, usually possessive when in my vicinity, settle on my hips as he positions himself at my back.

"Um, okay," I say, though I'm still not sure I'm going with him anywhere.

"Thanks again for the suite, Bristol," Qwest says. "It's incredible."

"You actually have Parker here to thank for that." I force myself to lean back into him, knowing I'll pay later for encouraging him. "He's the one who upgraded you."

"Anything for Bristol's friends," Parker says smoothly.

"You two together?" A smile lights Qwest's sharp eyes.

"On and off since high school," Parker says.

Mostly off, but no need to split hairs right now.

"No way." Qwest's mouth hangs open a little. "I had no idea."

Neither did I.

"I actually escorted Bristol to her debutante ball." Parker tucks his chin into the crook of my neck. "That's how it started."

In my eighteen-year-old mind, sex in that coat check was such an adventure. Little did I know that would be the high point. I spent the next four months trying my damnedest to shake Parker and have been shaking ever since. That tic in Grip's jaw tells me he remembers the story I told him about screwing my escort, but until now, he never knew the guy.

"You were a debutante?" Qwest laughs, looking at me through the lens of my family's wealth and pedigree. "Wow."

"In another life, and at my mother's insistence." I put a little distance between my ass and Parker's dick, because apparently, trips down memory lane arouse him.

"We better go." Grip grabs Qwest's hand and turns to leave abruptly without saying goodbye.

Qwest waves over her shoulder and stutter steps to keep up with Grip's swift, long-legged stride away from us.

I should feel good that this is working even better than I planned. Qwest is with Grip. Grip saw me with Parker. All is going according to plan, but it feels so wrong. I watch Grip and Qwest slip through a side exit, hand in hand, and wonder, too late, if maybe I've made a big mistake. Actually seeing him with another woman— someone he could really fall for—saws at my insides. He was right, up on that roof. It hurts me to see him with someone else, every time. I know I could have him, but not on my terms. Probably not forever. Probably not to myself. It's ironic. People think I'm heartless. That I don't care enough. That isn't it. This ache, this wound bleeding on the inside of me, it tells the truth of how I really feel.

And I'm sick and damn tired of feeling. I want to forget that Grip is probably falling for Qwest tonight. Probably sleeping with her tonight. I want to be numb. I want the best vodka martini money can buy, even if I do have to fly to Vegas with Parker to get it.

"Hey." I turn to Parker, determined to feel less by the end of this night. "What about that drink you promised me?"

CHAPTER 9

G_{RIP}

"YOU DON'T LIKE STAND-UP COMEDY?"

Qwest's question pulls me out of my own head, where thoughts of Bristol with that punk ass Parker have tortured me ever since we left the club. So Parker's the coat check guy. And the man her mother has wanted her to marry since the cradle.

"What?" I frown and force myself to focus. "No, I love Chappelle. I can't believe we caught a show."

Dave Chappelle has been doing surprise shows in the city, and we were lucky to catch one tonight.

"Do you not like steak?" Qwest points her fork at the medium rare meat on my plate, nearly untouched.

"Love it." I take a bite. "This is delicious."

I survey the private dining room of the restaurant still open solely to accommodate us at this late hour. We're the only customers here. Qwest's security guard stands just outside the door.

"So do you not like me?" Qwest injects humor, but her eyes beg the question.

I feel like shit. She went to a lot of trouble to make tonight fun, exactly what I would have chosen. I've been half here the whole time. The other half of me can't stop wondering where Parker took Bristol on the "flight" he mentioned. I need to make more of an effort.

"You know I like you, Qwest." I toss my linen napkin on the table. "I'm sorry I've been so . . ."

I search my tired mind for the right word. "Preoccupied?" Qwest finds it for me.

"Yeah. It's rude, and you're great. It isn't you." I lob a smile across the table before lifting my water for a sip.

"Would you like to fuck me, Grip?"

I almost spew my water. I grab the napkin to dab at the corners of my mouth.

"It's a yes or no question," she continues unfazed.

"Um, maybe it isn't." I would laugh if this wasn't so awkward. "I'm attracted to you, yeah. Of course."

"I know that." She walks over, slides between the table and me, and straddles my hips. "But what do you want to do about it?"

Her wrists link at the back of my neck. I run my hands up and down her back. She's slim and tight and supple beneath her silk dress. She'd let me take her right on this table where her guard could hear her scream when she comes.

"Is there someone else?" Voice dropped, she runs a hand over my closely cropped hair.

"Yeah." I release a breath, my voice low and husky, too. I shake my head. "No."

"That's also a yes or no question." She slips her hand into the collar of my shirt and runs a long nail over my shoulder.

"I don't know." I try to focus on the conversation even as her touches distract me. "I'm just realizing that she may not feel the same way."

"Then she's a fool." Qwest rocks her hips into me, the heat between her legs like a furnace on my dick.

I gently push her back to put some distance between us.

"Qwest, I like you." I look her right in the eyes. I learned my lesson with Tessa. I'm not that dude who leads girls on anymore. "I respect you and think you're amazing. The last thing I want to do is hurt you. I'm afraid that's what would happen. We got business together. We're friends. Maybe we shouldn't mess with that."

"Let me worry about it." She scoots forward again. "I'm going into this with my eyes wide open."

She leans into me and sucks my earlobe into her mouth. Fuck. It's been too long since I had some. My dick rises to the occasion, and she pulls back with a satisfied chuckle.

"So what do you say?" She opens her lips over my jaw, mumbling against my neck. "We doing this or what?"

"Um . . ." My underserved libido and my anger over Bristol riding off into the sunset with that punk ass urge me to say yes.

Gripe? Motherfucker, you know my name.

"You have a few days off." Qwest slides her hands over my back under my shirt, lightly raking the skin with her fingernails. "Fly back with me to New York tomorrow night and I'll screw myself into your system."

A million, no more, guys would kill to have Qwest and her ass in their lap right now. I know this. It isn't her. I'm just so tired of being with anyone who isn't Bristol. In all these years, I haven't figured out how to move past what started between us. I know it was only a week. And we were young. And I mishandled the situation with Tessa. I get all that, but it wasn't just a few kisses on spring break. It's the friendship we've built since then. It's her passion about my writing, about my work. Her commitment to her brother. Her knife-sharp sense of humor. The soft, sweet side only a handful of people get to see. It's the way she tastes. The texture of her skin. Her hair. Her laugh. The conversations I can have with her and no one else. Everyone who thinks we're not right for each other doesn't know her, doesn't know me, or doesn't know how good we are together.

I want Bristol. Not anyone else.

And that's a problem, because for the first time, I have to consider the possibility that she doesn't, not even deep down where I thought she did, want me.

CHAPTER 10

BRISTOL

THERE'S A MAN in my bed.

I barely know my name. I'm not sure who's leading the free world or what year it is, but I do know there is a man in my bed. I at least know that is unusual. I don't do sleepovers.

At least sober Bristol doesn't do sleepovers. Apparently, after one . . . or two . . . or eight vodka martinis, drunk Bristol does sleepovers.

The guy is naked. I do know that. Man parts poke between my butt cheeks.

My naked butt cheeks.

Dammit, I'm naked. He's naked. In my bed. At my house. The likelihood that we didn't have sex diminishes with every detail I absorb through my pickled senses. My thong and bra, a man's pants, suit jacket and shirt leave a sinful trail across the hardwood floor of my bedroom. To the left, a man's expensive watch rests on my mirrored nightstand. Under the duvet cover, which I'll probably burn later, a muscled forearm reaches across my hip, and a hand flattens against my stomach. He pushes my hair aside and trails kisses down my neck.

"Morning, Bris."

I clench my eyes closed and silently curse, dread lining my stomach. Or maybe that's nausea. There's a bass drum banging in my head, and I could vomit on my Egyptian cotton sheets any minute now. I struggle to bring the room into focus as the details swim in front of me. This is the worst scenario. I could have had meaningless sex with a stranger, but nooooo. Instead, I had meaningless sex with the man who has been obsessed with the idea of marrying me since we were ten years old. Meaningless sex that will mean something to him.

Oh, this will end marvelously.

"Parker?" I ask tentatively.

"I hope so." His husky laugh blows the hair at my neck. "Last night was amazing, Bristol. Even better than before."

"Before" set a low bar from what I recall. The orgasm I had in that coat check was the only time Parker got me off. And I think the threat of getting caught probably helped a lot then. After that, I touched myself more than he did every time we had sex. A girl's gotta DIY when he isn't getting it done. The story of my sex life.

I bet Grip would get it done.

Since when did my vagina start talking back to me? Maybe I'm still drunk. I hope so. God, please let this be a drunken hallucination. Parker's fingers wandering between my legs confirms it's happening.

"Um, Parker." I turn over, pulling the sheets over my naked breasts. "Last night is kind of hazy. I'm not sure how we . . . did we . . . you know."

"Fuck?"

Blond hair falls into his blue eyes brimming with laughter. He looks good in the morning. I remember that now, but it doesn't make up for how overbearing he is the other twenty-three hours of the day.

"Uh, yeah." My cheeks fire up. I'm blushing? Apparently, even I have some shame. Remembering who was inside you last night must be one of my standards. "

Yes, we fucked." He leans over to kiss my neck. "We took the jet back from Vegas."

"I thought we took a helicopter?"

How drunk was I?

"We took a helicopter there and the Park Hotel jet back." He kisses my shoulder. "We kissed in the car."

Jesus, Mary, and Joseph. This is worse than I thought.

"And then we came here and made love." His hand explores under the sheet, gripping my thigh and pulling my knee over his hip. "You still give the best head, Bris."

Oh. Dear. God.

Do I still have disposable toothbrushes? No way I'm using my electric. I assumed my tongue felt furry and sticky from too much alcohol. Apparently Parker's dick was down my throat last night. I don't typically swallow, but I also don't typically sleep with Parker. I want to purge the contents of my stomach just in case. I want to purge the contents of last night. To make it go away, flush it down the toilet like it never happened. All signs indicate it did happen, though. And from Parker's growing erection, he thinks it will happen again. Not when I have all my faculties.

I roll out of the bed, and it feels like my head keeps rolling. Dizziness assaults me, and I stumble back to the mattress. I look over my shoulder to find Parker watching me intently.

"You okay, Bris?"

Do I look fucking okay?

I nod as much as my pounding head will allow, grabbing the sheet and wrapping it toga style to cover my nakedness.

"Parker, I hate to rush you off," I lie. "But I have an appointment this morning."

He looks at me like I've disenfranchised him somehow. Like it's his inalienable right to screw me before breakfast.

"Re-schedule or—"

"No, sorry. This is can't-miss."

I shuffle to the bathroom, making sure the sheet covers the vital parts even though he's seen and sampled them all. When I look back, he's propped against my tufted headboard like he has all the time in the world, sheet down to his waist, hands folded behind his head.

"You should probably get going." I lean into the arched doorway of the bathroom. "I'm going to shower and then I'll be leaving, so . . ."

"You kicking me out?" His smirk works my last remaining nerve.

"Yes, Parker. I'm kicking you out. Men don't normally sleep at my house, and if I hadn't been plastered out of my mind, you wouldn't be here this morning."

The smirk dies, collapsing into a flat line.

"You're not implying that I took advantage of you somehow, are you?"

"Imply?" I shake my head. "I'm saying I'm disappointed you had sex with me knowing I was drunk and maybe not fully . . . aware."

I've known Parker literally my whole life. As slimy as he can be, I don't want to think he would drug me, but was I that drunk? To remember nothing? Everything after we arrived in Vegas is a blank sheet of paper, and as hard as I try, I can't sketch any details. I wanted a good martini. That's all. I know I had no intention of sleeping with Parker. Even drunk I can't imagine allowing this, wanting this. I've come as close as I can to an accusation without actually making it, but based on Parker's heavy scowl, it's close enough.

"Bristol, you were completely willing, and we did use protection, if that's your next question."

It was, but I still see a visit to my doctor in the very near future.

"I don't doubt that." Even sighing makes my head spin a little. "But we haven't had sex in over a decade, and you think the night I'm drunk is the night to get reacquainted?"

He climbs out of my bed, less modest than I was, not bothering to cover up. He's in good shape, but his dick is as underwhelming as I remember. I avert my eyes, embarrassed for him. Embarrassed for myself. No wonder it doesn't feel like I had sex last night.

"I know you're having a rough morning," Parker says as he steps into his pants. "So I'll excuse that. When can I see you again?"

"I think we should slow this down." I run fingers through the tangled hair hanging past my shoulders. "I didn't, um . . . anticipate any of this. I'm not in the market for a relationship right now."

"This is happening, Bristol." He buttons up his shirt, his eyes never leaving my face. "It's always been obvious that we're perfect for each other. Last night only solidified it."

"Forgive me for not agreeing since I don't remember much about last night." I turn into the bathroom. "We'll talk more later. Could you lock up on your way out?"

I don't wait for his response before closing the bathroom door and slumping against it, barely able to meet my own eyes in the mirror. Shame, frustration, disappointment swirl in my belly, joining the nausea. I feel violated, and as much as I want to put all the blame on Parker, there's really no one to blame but myself. I blink at the disheveled, puffy-eyed girl in the mirror who has tears filling her eyes.

"Bristol," I say to her. "What the fuck?"

After a few more moments of self-castigation, I start my shower. I wonder what time it is, but I left my phone in the bedroom. At least I presume that's where I left it. Hopefully, it isn't lost somewhere between here and Vegas. I have this appointment downtown, then errands, and then the Prodigy lunch at Rhyson's.

God, facing Grip after sleeping with Parker. Not that I haven't slept with other guys before, but the other night on the roof, our conversation in the hall yesterday, the confrontation in the club last night—we haven't talked this openly about what's between us in years, and now everything feels right at the surface.

An hour later, YSL Roadie bag on my shoulder and feeling only slightly more like myself, I walk into Chelle's, the high-end jewelry store I stumbled across downtown. Black skinny jeans ripped at the knee, black cashmere T-shirt, a knee-length camel-colored cardigan duster and nude ankle strap sandals. Hopefully no one will notice that I'm woefully in need of a pedicure. My head remains under attack, so I couldn't endure the blow dryer. My still-damp hair is scooped up into a topknot that I hope looks somewhat intentional. I wait until the last possible second to remove my sunglasses. My intolerance for sunlight is near-vampiric.

"Bristol, morning, love." Chelle, the owner of the exclusive, but lesser-known, shop air kisses my cheek.

"Morning." I clear my throat of the alcohol-induced Barry White effect. "How are you?"

"Not as good as you, I would imagine." Chelle pairs a knowing grin with her Stella McCartney jumpsuit. "You sneaky thing."

"Huh?" I slide the sunglasses farther up into my hair. "We have an appointment, right? My necklace came in?"

"Boy did it, you lucky girl." Chelle gives my arm a light slap and starts toward the back. "Come on. I've got it ready for you."

Either the lingering effects of my inebriation have dulled my senses, or Chelle has been imbibing, too, because she's acting strangely. I sit down at the small display table and wait. I special ordered this necklace a while ago and was giddy to get the message that it had come in. It's twenty- four carat gold with a diamond-encrusted vertical bar, which hangs just above my cleavage. The inscription on the bar is my favorite part.

"It's beautiful, Chelle." I bend over the table to examine it more closely and reach for the wallet in my bag. "Looks good. Let's settle up. I'm late for lunch at my brother's."

"Already paid in full." Chelle's smirk and teasing eyes mystify me.

"What do you mean it's—"

"She means it's my gift to you. I've already taken care of it." Parker stands in the door leading to the back room where Chelle keeps inventory. "I couldn't resist."

White-hot rage lights me up like a signal flare. I squeeze my eyes shut in a futile attempt to douse my temper.

"You didn't tell me you were dating Charles Parker," Chelle whispers in my ear. "You lucky thing."

I can't muster a smile, and my voice comes out so softly I barely hear it myself.

"Chelle, would you excuse us for a moment?"

"I get it," Chelle says. "You want to reward him in private. Just spill all the deets later."

"Oh, I'm going to reward him, all right." My eyes pin Parker where he stands, still wearing last night's clothes.

"Now don't be mad," he says. "You left your phone in the bedroom, and I saw the alert to pick up the necklace. I just thought it would be something I could do for you."

He lifts the necklace from its velvet box and goes behind me to clip it on. I step away and whirl around to face him.

"Don't you dare." Anger shakes my voice. "Who do you think you are? And what the hell do you think you're doing paying for jewelry I ordered for myself?"

His face registers what I'm saying slowly, the smile fading into confusion. "We had a great time last night, and I wanted to—"

"Thank me?" Brows lifted high, hands on hips, I cut in. "Is that what this is?"

"Well, not exactly. I just—"

"The other women you sleep with may require these little fuck tokens the next day as expression of your appreciation. I, however, do not."

"You're being unreasonable."

"I'm being independent. I'm being the woman who earned the money to buy this outrageously expensive necklace, chose it for myself, and has been looking forward to swiping my own damn card to pay for it."

"Bristol, I—"

"No, you will listen." My words butcher whatever he was about to say. "The bed you woke up in this morning? I paid for that. The house you locked up on your way out? I paid for that. The car I drove here in? All me."

I step as close as I dare and glare up at him.

"I will not be kept." My words whiz through the air like arrows. "That may be the road your mother chose, but it isn't the one mine did. Mine taught me not to rely on any man for anything, and I'm damn well not starting with you."

He blinks at me for a full ten seconds before he sighs, his tight expression relaxing into a smile.

"All that fight and pride." He grabs my upper arms and looks down at me intently. "You'll be my queen. With you at my side, we'll rule the world. Can't you see that?"

After last night's fiasco of lost memories, I can barely rule myself. He thinks I want to rule the world with him? Some replica of his committee-chairing, debutante-sponsoring, Vicodin-popping mother? She's my mother's best friend, and actually very sweet, but hell will freeze over before I become her.

"I need to pay for my necklace and go." I pull out of his hands and turn back to the showroom.

"I've already paid for it." His voice hardens. When I look back, so have his eyes. They're blue crystals in his handsome face.

"Then we'll get you a nice little refund."

I call Chelle back in and instruct her to refund Mr. Parker's card and to charge mine.

"I'll need the card you paid with." Chelle gives Parker a confused look but accepts his card. She probably thinks I'm crazy. On the surface, Parker is one of the most eligible bachelors in the country, hell, maybe in the world. Why wouldn't I want him and his gifts?

He and I stand in awkward silence while Chelle processes the transactions.

"I didn't mean any harm." He steps closer until his stale morning breath wafts over my lips. "I want to see you again. Soon."

"I don't know, Parker."

I step back and away. This is already out of control. I wanted to just wave Parker around a little so Grip would take that step toward Qwest. Somehow, I ended up sleeping with the guy I've avoided for the last decade. I grew up surrounded by people like the man Parker has grown into. Not just overbearing, but willful. Spoiled. Entitled. Combined with unlimited resources and unchecked power, that's dangerous.

"I fly to India tonight for business." He presses his hand to my back as we exit Chelle's. "Can we talk when I get back? About where we go from here?"

I'm so tired. I'm running late, and I don't feel like fighting with Parker in the street in front of half of Los Angeles.

"Okay, we'll talk when you get back," I concede. "But I'm not making any promises."

He steps closer until I'm pressed into the driver side door of the Audi convertible I treated myself to last year. Before I can object, he leans down to press a hard kiss against my lips. The contact is quick, but I still resent it.

"Fine," he says when he pulls back. "I'll make all the promises."

That doesn't reassure me. With men like Parker, there's a fine line between a promise and a threat. I hope I haven't set myself up for either.

CHAPTER 11

G~RIP~

I HAVEN'T SEEN the Prodigy team this relaxed in weeks. We're all chilling here at Rhyson's place. It's the quiet before a very big storm. Grip not only is my solo debut but also it's Prodigy's first release. It's a big deal for us all. We needed this small block of time to blow off steam. It's been so intense, and it will only intensify the closer we get to release day.

Max and Sarah are talking near the pool table. Neither of them knows how to actually play, so they just hold the cues and lean on the table, trying to look cool. Rhyson's playing Grand Theft Auto with Simon, one of the sound engineers. Several of the team members went swimming out back. The whole gang is here. Almost.

I check my watch again. I've been at Rhyson's for thirty minutes and still no sign of Bristol.

"She called to say she'd be late," Kai whispers, taking the spot beside me on the brown leather couch.

"Am I that obvious?"

Until I told Rhyson, no one else really knew about the week we shared. It was ours and no one's business, but after seeing her with Parker last night, I feel like the butt of an eight-year joke. Like everyone knows how I feel, and I was a fool for holding out hope. For still holding out hope. I'm not prepared to give up yet. I wonder some- times what will convince me to give up on the possibility of us.

"It isn't that you're obvious," Kai says. "I just know how you feel."

"Our plan isn't working." I offer her half a smile.

Kai actually suggested I let Bristol manage me to get closer to her. That if we were around each other all the time, she'd have to acknowledge her feelings, my feelings, whatever. Bristol had been trying to manage me for years, but I didn't want to just be her job. Apparently, she's now not only my manager, but also my pimp. It still burns me up that she handed me over to Qwest like some prize at the fair.

"You mean Project Proximity?" Kai grins and reaches for one of the brownies Sarita, their housekeeper, made.

"Yeah." I shrug with phony carelessness. "Maybe Rhyson's right. Maybe she wants a guy like Parker, and I should just give up."

"Rhyson isn't right. Not this time," Kai mumbles around her brownie. "He's biased. He's so close to you both, he doesn't want things to go south and become awkward. Not just personally. He's thinking about the business, too, I'm sure."

Kai laughs, the husky sound drawing Rhyson's attention. He grins over at us . . . mostly at Kai, before returning his attention to the game.

"And he's afraid Bristol would destroy you." Kai's eyes meet mine in a careful stare. Maybe she's afraid of that, too.

"I know." I grin because I ain't scared. Not even a little bit. "Most brothers would be protective of their sisters, but I get it. Bristol's a handful."

I slant her a sneaky grin and hold my hands up for her inspection.

"But I got big hands."

"Oh, God." Kai shakes her head and chuckles. "Rhyson is protective of Bristol in his own way, but he thinks she's too much like their mother."

"She's not."

Kai pauses chewing to hold my eyes with hers.

"Bristol is like her mother, Grip. I think she's aware of that, and you should be, too. It isn't all bad." She shrugs. "I'm like my father in a lot of ways, and we know his history."

Kai's father, a pastor, left her and her mother in Glory Falls, the small Georgia town where she grew up. Ran off with the church secretary and never looked back.

"Just because she's like her mother, doesn't mean she *is* her mother," Kai continues. "Rhyson got away from that house, from his parents. Bristol wasn't so lucky."

"Are you saying Rhys doesn't trust her?" I frown, because I know he does now. They've gotten past that.

"Of course not. I think Rhyson is self-aware and recognizes how much he's like his parents, and how easily that can go badly if he isn't careful." Kai offers a tentative smile. "Maybe he's just afraid Bristol won't be careful with you."

"I'm willing to take that risk."

"Apparently, she's not." Kai leans over and squeezes my hand. "Yet."

"Why couldn't it be easy for us the way it was for you and Rhyson?" I wait for the incredulous look Kai gives me. Their journey was anything but easy.

"It's funny you mention us, though." Kai rests her hand on her belly. "Bristol reminds me a lot of myself."

"Really?" If there were ever opposites, it would be Kai and Bristol. "You'll have to elaborate."

"I believe Bristol has feelings for you," Kai says. "I've told you that before, but something holds her back. That's how I was. I knew I had feelings for Rhyson, but I let all my hang-ups keep me from doing anything about it. I didn't trust him or myself."

"You think Bristol doesn't trust herself?" I smack my lips derisively.

"Not just herself." Kai's eyes fill with sympathy. "I don't think she trusts you either, but I believe she will."

That's the very hope I've been clinging to for years, but now I'm not as sure. I can't believe I thought Kai was just another thirsty chick when Rhyson first started bringing her around. She's the opposite of that, and of all the amazing things my best friend has had in his life, she's the best. She's the only one who sees what Bristol and I could be together.

"It's about time you showed up," Max says from the pool table across the room.

Kai and I follow the direction of Max's smile. Bristol makes her way slowly down the steps to the rec room, still wearing sunglasses. The grim set of her mouth and faint lines bracketing her lips speak of a rough night. I wonder how rough it got with Charles Parker.

"Sorry I'm late." Her voice a tired rasp, she pushes the sunglasses up into the hair screwed into a knot on her head.

"I hate you, Bris," Sarah says, looking over Bristol's narrow, ripped-knee jeans and long cardigan. "You look great even hungover. You are hungover, aren't you?"

"Very much so." Bristol tips her head back and closes her eyes. "Gah. Sid Vicious is playing in my brain."

"Isn't he dead?" Max squints his eyes and frowns.

"Max, I can't with you today." When Bristol opens her eyes, she looks right at me for a few seconds before looking away to Rhyson. "Hey, brother."

"Bris, what's up?" Rhyson glances away from the screen briefly. "I didn't even know you could be hungover. You hold liquor like a bottle. I've never seen anything short of a tranquilizer lay you low."

"Apparently," Bristol says, settling onto the couch across from Kai and me, "they tranquilize vodka martinis now."

"Where'd you have these vodka martinis?" I ask, addressing my first words to her since our confrontation at the bar last night.

She becomes preoccupied with the handle on her bag for a few seconds before lifting her eyes to mine. They're slightly pink and puffy, more pewter than bright silver today.

"Um, Vegas actually."

"Vegas? Last night?" Sarah plops onto the couch beside Bristol, jarring them both.

"For the love of God, it's a couch, not a trampoline." Bristol winces and raises a shaky hand to her forehead. "Yeah. Just with a friend."

"Woman of mystery." Max squeezes between Sarah and Bristol. "Give us all the details."

"No." She scoots over, her flat voice and flat eyes opaquing her thoughts from them, from me.

"Did you take anything, Bris?" Kai asks sweetly.

"You know," Bristol says, mouth tipped to the left, "I didn't. I was rushing and didn't even think to."

"Come on. We'll get you something." Kai presses her hand into the couch for leverage, and Bristol stands to help pull her the rest of the way.

"Whoa. Careful there, little mama." Bristol smiles for the first time since she arrived. She's already got a soft spot for her niece. "Let me help you."

Rhyson's eyes leave the screen and fix on his petite wife with her hand pressed to the small of her back. He and Bristol exchange a quick grin. He's still watching Kai as she and Bristol climb the steps and leave the room.

"Dude!" Simon laughs triumphantly, pointing to his winning score onscreen. "That's what happens when you take your eyes off the prize."

"Oh, my eyes were on the prize." Rhyson tosses the controller to the floor. "I'm out. Food? Sarita left raw meat. I think I can manage to get it to and from the grill without the fire department intervening."

"Maybe I should handle the grill." I follow him out onto the patio adjacent to the rec room. "Remember the last time you tried to grill?"

"Nothing was lost or destroyed," Rhyson says.

"Unless you count Grady's eyebrows."

"God, he looked ridiculous for months." Rhyson's laugh booms over the memory of the uncle he lived with here in LA when he emancipated. "Too much lighter fluid. That was the problem."

"No, you not knowing what the hell you were doing was the problem."

Max and Sarah join us, stretching out on two lounge chairs and scrolling on their phones.

"Daaaaaaaaamn." Max sits up on the lounge chair and flips his legs around to face Sarah. "Did you see Spotted?"

"No, what . . ." She checks her phone, eyes stretching. "Oh my God. Is this true?"

"Photographic evidence." Max's delighted laugh lights up his face. "Well, at least now we know who Bristol was with and what she was doing."

My head snaps around when he mentions Bristol's name. So does Rhyson's. He beats me to the punch.

"What are you talking about?" He walks over to Max's lounge chair. "What about Bristol?"

Max and Sarah pick up on the fact that neither Rhyson nor I find the prospect of Bristol on Spotted, one of the most viral gossip sites, as amusing as they do.

"Gimme your phone, Sarah." I stretch my open palm to her, waiting until she reluctantly hands it over.

Well, shit.

Spotted has a pictorial chronicling Bristol's date last night. Bristol and Charles Parker climbing into a helicopter. The two of them drinking in an intimate nook, the Vegas strip lit up behind them. Parker deplaning at a private hangar and getting into his Viper. Him pulling out of her driveway this morning. And then him kissing her in front of a jewelry store not even an hour ago.

Really? A Viper? You can't tell me this guy doesn't have a small dick. He's overcompensating for something. Has to be. But my girl . . . or I thought she would be my girl one day . . . is sitting on his fucking lap in Vegas drinking vodka martinis. And it looks like he spent the night. Every detail is a poisonous dart piercing my skin, toxic to my system. Jealousy, rage, resentment crawl through my blood.

"Charles Parker?" Max looks impressed. "One of the biggest fish you can catch. Go big or go home, Bristol."

"What are you talking about?" Bristol asks, standing with Kai at the patio door. "Go big? Go home? What?"

"You dark horse." Max crosses over to her, his grin and eyes eager. "Your secret's out."

Her eyes fly to mine, and we have a wordless conversation. My eyes ask questions that hers tell me I don't want to know the answers to.

"What secret?" She frowns her confusion at Max.

"You're all over Spotted," Max drawls. "You and Charles Parker. How dare you keep all that juiciness from us."

"What?" Panic widens Bristol's eyes. "What the hell?"

"It's all here for the world to see." He hands her his phone. "Someone took the time to document your night out."

Bristol's expression darkens while she reads the Spotted post. By the time she hands Max his phone, she's smoothed her face into a blank, shiny surface.

"Wow." She takes the spot Max occupied on the lounge chair. "Must be a really slow news cycle if that's all they have to talk about. No news there."

"Are you kidding?" Sarah leans forward, her face alight with salacious speculation. "You're dating one of the most eligible bachelors, like in the world, Bris. How could you keep that from us?"

"Bristol's business is just that." Rhyson flips steaks over the open flame. "She works hard and deserves some privacy when she finally takes some time to play. So leave her alone."

His words come casually, but we all know he means it. He knows his sister as well as I do. She may be playing it cool, but this is not the kind of spotlight Bristol enjoys. She's uncomfortable, and he doesn't like it. They exchange a look, and I suspect there will be a follow-up conversation.

Meanwhile, I may as well be that steak Rhyson's flipping on the grill.

Raw. Tossed. Seared. Hot.

I'm hot as hell. Riled like a horse with a bur under the saddle. If I don't get out of here, I'll explode all over this sunny day. And then there will be no secrets left. There won't be a person on our team who doesn't know how bad I have it for Bristol. Or how little she cares. And how sick to my soul I am of all this shit.

"I'm gonna head out," I tell Rhyson at the grill.

"Marlon, no." He stops flipping meat and gives me a searching look. He knows what this is about. "Dude, stay. Food's almost done. We can—"

"I actually have a flight to catch." I lean over and do the man pound-thump to his chest.

"Flight where?" His eyes move over my shoulder, I presume to his sister, before settling back on me.

"I got a few days off. I'm going to New York."

"But—"

I turn away from him and address everyone else.

"Yo. I'm gonna bounce, guys." I fist pound Max and Simon. Give Sarah a quick hug. "Got a plane to catch. I'll be back next week."

I head over to Kai, ignoring Bristol as she gets up from the lounge chair even though I feel her eyes on me. I feel her eyes on me all the time, but maybe I imagined it was more than it really is. After seeing those pictures of her with Parker, knowing he wants to marry her, knowing that she'll probably do it and be miserable for the rest of her life just like her mother, I'm sick of trying to crack her code. I'm done deciphering how what she actually wants differs from what she says she wants. She says she wants Parker? I'll take her at her word.

"Take care of my niece while I'm gone." I leave a quick kiss on Kai's cheek.

"Don't go." She grabs my wrist to stop me from pulling away, her dark eyes worried. "Grip, I'm sure that—"

"I'm not sure." I cut off whatever assurances she would offer.

"Not anymore."

Brushing past Bristol standing there as still as a statue, I head back into the house, through the rec room, and up the stairs. I'm in the foyer at the front door when the clack of heeled footsteps catches up to me.

"Grip." Bristol's voice at my back stops me with my hand on the door. "When were you going to tell me you were leaving town?"

I turn to face her but don't take my hand off the door handle. If I keep it in my hand, maybe I won't lose sight of the reasons I need to go.

"Bristol, I'm leaving town." I turn back to the door. "Bye."

"Grip, wait. Talk to me."

Her touch on my arm stops me. Scalds me. I hate wanting her like this. Constantly. Futilely. I lean against the door, indicting her with a narrowed glance. She wants to talk? Let's talk.

"You fucked him, didn't you?"

Her long lashes flutter in a rapid blink before lowering over her eyes. I've caught her off guard. She steps back, her hand falling away. A deep breath fills her chest and whooshes past her lips. She looks at me, biting her lip, but doesn't answer.

"Tell me." My words are chipped with stone. "Did you fuck Parker last night?"

She looks up at me, a spark of defiance lifting her chin like it's none of my business.

"Yes."

Such a softly spoken word, but it slices me down the middle like I'm a cadaver. A humorless stretch of my lips is all I can manage.

"You must have laughed at me."

"I didn't." She closes her eyes, shakes her head. "I never did." "On the roof the other night when I went on and on about how neither of us has been in a relationship in years, when you were already in one." A laugh hacks at my throat. "Can you believe I thought you were waiting for me? When all along you were waiting for him? Some medieval power couple alliance shit your parents drew up years ago."

"It isn't like that. You don't understand what—"

"Was it good?" I straighten, stepping close, invading her space. My voice, a dark rumble in my chest, boils over between us. "Did Parker figure out how to make you come? Did he fuck you again this morning at your house? In your bed? Did he find the vibrators in your nightstand? Did you show him how you like it, Bristol?"

"Stop." She tips her head back to watch me, bright eyes welling with hurt. "I hate the way you're talking to me, the way you're looking at me like you don't know me. Please stop."

I grab her hand and press it to my heart.

"Do you have any idea what we could be together? Hell, what we already are?" The hot words sear my lips. "It's rare and real and you just keep spitting on it. You just keep ignoring it. Ignoring me. And I'm so fucking over it."

She stands there in silence, eyes fixed on her hand over my heart, the muscles in her throat working as she swallows.

"You haven't asked me because obviously you don't care," I go on, my heartbeat kicking into her palm. "But I didn't sleep with Qwest last night."

When she looks at me, surprise flickers through her eyes before she veils them with her lashes again.

"You don't want to know why a guy like me would turn down top-shelf pussy?" I ask, deliberately crude.

"I don't want to know." She drops her hand from my chest and turns like she's leaving, but I grab her arm and turn her back to face me.

"I thought something happened on the roof the other night," I grit out. "I thought after all these years, it was happening. You were starting to realize we could do this. We could be an us. So, I turned Qwest down. I wanted to be able to look you in your face today and tell you that I didn't sleep with her. That I would never fuck anyone else ever again if you wanted to be with me."

The tears standing in her eyes must be for our friendship I'm going to ruin, for the hurtful words I keep making myself say. There was a time I'd fool myself that they were for something else, but that time is gone. I swallow a hot knot of hurt and pointless humiliation.

"But you don't want to be with me." I drop her arm and open the door. "So if you'll excuse me, I'm gonna get back to fucking who the hell ever I damn well please."

CHAPTER 12

B<small>RISTOL</small>

OUTWARDLY, MY MOTHER and I couldn't be more different. My cheekbones, wide mouth, dark hair—all my father. In contrast, my mother's hair is flame-bright, unrelieved red without a hint of gray, thanks to the bottle. She's like a cultivated pearl, breeding in every curve and class in every line. In the eyes, though, you find the resemblance. The silver-gray eyes I see in the mirror every morning, stare back at me from my mother's face this beautiful morning over brunch.

"I'll have eggs Benedict." Mother glances from the brunch menu for Afloat, the restaurant located on a yacht in Marina del Rey, to the server's conciliatory expression.

We've never eaten here before, and I was surprised when she suggested it. We typically eat at the home she and my father purchased when they relocated here from New York last year after his heart attack. From time to time, we'll eat in town, but never here. It's a nice change. I need the fresh air. My world has become claustrophobic since the Spotted piece outing my night with Parker. "And a

Bloody Mary," Mother adds, closing the menu and handing it to the server.

Of course. Because it wouldn't be . . . a day . . . without my mother drinking. I've only seen her actually drunk once in my life. I learned more about my father, about my mother, and about myself that day than I wanted to know. I wish I could un-learn it, but I can't.

The server clears his throat, shifting his eyes from my mother to me.

"And you, ma'am?"

"I'll have poached eggs and smoked salmon," I tell him.

"And to drink?" The young man's eyes discretely tease me, bordering on flirtatious. "Bloody Mary for you, too?"

"No, this coffee is great, and I'll add orange juice, please."

I've avoided vodka, all alcohol really, since last week's Vegas debacle. If I thought getting drunk would make me forget the look on Grip's face when he realized I slept with Parker, I'd drink myself stupid. But nothing will make me forget that. I still feel his heart pounding into my hand. His words and the hurt in his eyes have haunted me since he left.

"There was another piece about you and Parker in the *New York Post* this morning." Mother's pleased eyes meet mine across the table as the server walks away with our orders. "You looked good."

"Those same shots from Vegas?" I sip my coffee. "I looked drunk."

"No, these were new ones." She laughs lightly. "Actually old photos, old memories. Someone dug up the pictures from your debutante ball."

A groan vibrates in my chest and throat.

"Great. That's all I need. More fodder for this ridiculous narrative they're spinning. We've gone from slutty night in Vegas to epic fairy tale. I wish they'd find some other couple to obsess over."

"Well, they did feature a piece on Rhyson's friend Marlon."

I go still for a moment at the mention of Grip's name. The speculation about Parker and me has only been matched by rumors of a budding romance between Grip and Qwest.

"They can report on that all day long as far as I'm concerned." I resume sipping, hoping my face is unreadable, though my blankest expressions have never hidden much from my mother. "That's good for business. That rumor sells records."

"Hmmm, yes. That's right. You're managing Marlon now, right?"

"Right."

It didn't take long for social media to latch on to the relationship it seems Grip and Qwest are pursuing full throttle. He's been in New York for the last two days, and pictures of them exploring the city have popped up everywhere. The latest of them leaving one of Grip's favorite strip clubs, Pirouette, surfaced last night.

Of course there's already a hashtag shipping the two high-powered performers. #GripzQueen has been trending since yesterday, connecting their hip-hop love affair with "Queen," the single still sitting at number one on the charts. With Grip's album dropping so soon, it couldn't be more perfect if I'd planned it. In a way, I did plan it. Will is ecstatic, as I should be. But the pictures I've seen of them holding hands in Central Park, kissing on the Brooklyn Bridge, and leaving Qwest's Manhattan apartment building for a morning run—they all turn my stomach. I'm not sure I'll be able to eat my eggs when they come.

I feel even sicker when I think of my last conversation with Grip. I may have done irreparable damage to our friendship. At least we still have his career. We still have work. I keep comforting myself with that, though it feels hollow. I knew it might come to this, but I had no idea it would hurt this much. His crude words keep playing over and over in my head. Even if Grip and his "queen" weren't trending, I'd still be unable to get him out of my mind.

"It's nice he's found someone of his own . . ." My mother trails off as she searches for some politically correct word. "Type. You know. Another . . . entertainer."

"Yes, they make a great couple," I agree neutrally.

"And much more appropriate than the crush he's had on you all these years." Mother says it matter-of-factly, as if we've discussed this many times in the past. We have not.

"What do you mean?" I pleat my brows in a facsimile of dismay. "What crush?"

"Oh, Bristol. It's me." Mother tilts her head, her eyes sharp and brittle. "I've seen him several times over the last few years with you and Rhyson. It was patently obvious he had feelings for you."

"He doesn't," I reply softly, fixing my eyes on the boats floating around us.

"And of course that you have feelings for him, too." Mother smiles her thanks at the server who sets her Bloody Mary on the table. "But you've always hidden those feelings well, thank goodness."

I sit quietly, biding my time until the server places a glass of juice in front of me with promises to bring our food in a few moments. I save my response until he has stepped away.

"I have it under control, Mother."

There's no need to deny it. That would be useless and foolish. Even as careful as I've been, at some point, I slipped, and she saw something that told her things I've never said. Pretending she has missed the mark would be futile.

"You'd better." Mother watches my face, her bright eyes as hard as diamonds. "Because Parker would not take kindly to you tossing him over for some . . ."

"Careful," I warn, clenching my jaw.

"Musician," she says, her tone defensive. "I was going to say musician."

"Rhyson is a musician. What's wrong with musicians? And it's none of Parker's business who I have feelings for. Despite all your plotting and best efforts, I'm not marrying Parker. I don't love him."

"Even better." A bitter smile twists the thin, painted red line of her lips. "If you don't love him, Parker's mistresses shouldn't bother you."

"Parker's mistresses won't bother me because I'm not marrying him."

"Then what are you doing?" Mother narrows her eyes at the corners and her lips pinch in the center. "Parker isn't the boy you grew up with, Bristol. Do not toy with him."

"I'm not toying with him. I was very clear that I didn't want a relationship. He refuses to listen, and this media maelstrom hasn't helped. He's in India on business." I roll my eyes and take another sip of orange juice. "Very conveniently, he's been so tied up he hasn't returned my calls. Someone from his team confirmed the rumors about us. They wouldn't have done that without his consent. He's the one toying with me, manipulating me through the media. Not the other way around."

"Of course he told them to confirm." Mother takes a draw of her Bloody Mary. "Hmmm. That's good. He probably tipped them off for the pictures in the first place. Men like him leave very little to chance, and he's probably tired of waiting for you to marry him."

The thought had occurred to me. For someone to be trailing us at every stage of the evening capturing those photos seems farfetched. The photos of him leaving my house the next morning and kissing me at Chelle's definitely required a "tip" or inside track. I wouldn't put it past him.

"Be very careful, Bristol. This thing with Marlon and his new girl-friend is the best thing that could happen," Mother says. "If Parker suspects you have feelings for Marlon, that you might choose Marlon over him, he'll find a way to crush him. Do you know that?"

"Yes, Mother. I know that. It won't be a problem." I meet her eyes with a sigh. "Like I said, I have it under control."

"Oh, yes. The same way you had your brother's career under control?" Mother's eyes flash silver fire at me across the table. "And yet, instead of him playing with the Pops, as he should be, he's starting some record label thing."

"That was a misunderstanding," I flash right back at her. "You chose to believe I was moving to LA to manipulate my brother for you, to get him back under your management, when actually, I moved here to help him pursue his dream. Not yours."

We both fall silent as the server places our plates on the table.

"And that record label thing is my job," I add when the server leaves. "One I'm very good at, by the way."

"Well, I guess you made do since you had no real talent to speak of." Mother takes a bite of her eggs Benedict. "Lemonade from lemons, they say."

The words I would fire back at her die on my lips. I can shake down crooked vendors and go toe to toe with the toughest people in one of the toughest industries, but my mother . . .

She always makes me feel inadequate. As if I failed her somehow being born less talented than my twin brother. Music connected the three of them, and I could never push my way into their circle. I was left out. Disconnected. That's what surprised me with Grip. How connected we felt, and the closeness that wasn't dependent on blood or even common interest. It came from how clearly we saw and accepted each other almost right away.

It's rare and real and you just keep spitting on it.

"Did I tell you we're managing Petra now?" Mother interrupts Grip's voice reverberating in my head. There's no trace of the hateful barb she just tossed at me left on her lips. Only a smile.

"No." I look out to the harbor again. "How nice for you."

"I still think it's a shame she and Rhyson never resolved their issues," Mother says, taking a delicate sip of her liquor.

"Issues?" I snort inelegantly. "She cheated on him, Mother, with one of his classmates."

"It was high school, for God's sake." Mother sighs her exasperation. "People make mistakes when they're young. Two piano prodigies. So young and in love. God, the classical world ate up their dueling piano tour. So much potential."

I'm pretty sure Rhyson dodged a bullet with that one and has no regrets.

"Well, all is not lost." I try to keep my smile from become smug. "Rhyson has Kai now, and their first baby is on the way. I think Rhyson is fine with how things worked out."

She didn't exactly approve of Kai for Rhyson, but he hasn't considered our mother's opinion in a very long time.

"Kai's due soon." I study my mother's unreadable expression. "Have you guys talked about that in your sessions?"

My parents and brother are in family counseling, still trying to mend what was broken when Rhyson left.

"We've missed the last few sessions," Mother admits, a hint of genuine sadness in her eyes. "Not that Rhyson would talk to me about my own grandchild."

"He'll come around."

Maybe? One day?

Rhyson has made a great deal of progress with our father but remains at odds with our mother.

"Why does your father get a pass and I don't?"

That's a complicated answer that Rhyson will have to give her because I can't.

"You'll have to ask him that." I shrug. "Maybe bring it up in your next session."

"By the way, Dr. Ramirez suggested we bring you in," Mother says casually.

I nearly drop my fork. They were supposed to bring me in "soon." That was over a year ago, and I still haven't been to one session. I've been waiting so long for this, to be heard. To have my say about how all the decisions they made affected me years ago. How I'm still affected by the civil war that splintered our family.

"When?" I keep my voice free of eagerness.

"Hopefully in the next week or so. Rhyson's been busy with that record label." Mother says it with such distaste I almost laugh. "And your father and I have taken on several new clients in addition to Petra."

"Just keep me posted. I'll adjust my schedule however I need—"

A hand on my shoulder cuts the sentence short. I look up to find my mother's best friend since college standing over me, her blue eyes and blonde hair a beautiful, older echo of her son's.

"Mrs. Parker." I cover her hand on my shoulder with mine, forcing a smile to my lips. "So good to see you."

"So formal?" The gentle rebuke in her eyes coaxes my lips into a genuine smile.

"Sorry, Aunt Betsy." I kiss the cheek she offers before she takes a seat at our table.

"Betsy, hello, darling." Mother sips her third Bloody Mary. "When did you arrive in LA?"

"I left you a message that I was flying in from New York last night." She smiles at our server. "Mimosa, dear. Thank you."

They don't fool me. Like mother like son. I have a feeling Aunt Betsy and my mother have done some orchestrating of their own to make sure even with Parker in India, speculation about us remains high. I cast a quick glance around the floating restaurant, my eyes peeled for cameras and paparazzi. Not giving a hint that I sniffed them out, I scoot aside to make more room for Aunt Betsy between my mother and me.

"Nothing to eat?" I ask.

"Trying to maintain my girlish figure." Aunt Betsy winks. "Do what we have to do to keep our men, don't we?"

If by "keep" she means watch helplessly as her husband screws half of the Upper East Side, then I guess she's doing everything she can. She and my mother didn't exactly hit the lottery in the fidelity department. At least my father is discreet. I would never have known about his indiscretions had I not come home early that day.

It doesn't take long for the conversation to circle around to what she and my mother have been planning since they compared ultrasounds almost thirty years ago: my "pending" nuptials to Parker.

"We need to have you up to the house in the Hamptons, Bris." Aunt Betsy caresses the diamond at her neck. "Maybe next weekend?"

"I'm really busy right now." I smile politely instead of telling her that I will never, ever, ever, ever, ever marry her son. She'll soon see. "One of the artists I manage is about to drop his first album."

"Oh, well isn't that nice?" She sips her Mimosa.

Between Mother's Bloody Mary, Aunt Betsy's mimosas, and the pictures stacking up of Grip and his "queen", I could use a drink. I'm caving and ordering a vodka tonic. Life's too short and too tough not to.

"Bristol, over here!" someone yells from the hostess stand at the restaurant entrance.

Here we go. A camera flash makes me blink a few times. When I look back , the photographer is gone. Great. I could write the caption myself: "Bristol Gray, manager to the stars, brunches with future mother-in-law."

I pretend not to see the smug looks of satisfaction the two conspirators exchange. On second thought, forget the drink. Vodka got me into this mess. More vodka won't get me out.

CHAPTER 13

G~RIP~

EVEN THOUGH I was only here my freshman year before transferring to the School of the Arts, my old high school in Compton feels like home. As early as elementary school, Jade and I watched Greg and Chaz play football on Friday nights. Chaz was already dealing by then, already banging, but he was such a gifted athlete. Football was the last thing tethering him to school. Otherwise, he probably would have dropped out long before. Only blocks away from where Chaz died, the ink scripting his name into my arm seems to burn.

"Man, these kids are so crunk to see you today," Amir, my "security guard," says from his spot on the wall of the gymnasium beside me.

Since Amir worked airport security for years, he was a natural choice when Bristol insisted I have some kind of protection. I don't need security, but it means Amir and I get to hang all the time, and it puts him on my payroll instead of someone else's.

"Yeah. I'm pretty stoked to be here."

I slide my hands into the pockets of my jeans, studying the kids assembled. Shondra, the teacher who coordinated this assembly, told them we could do autographs after and to give me some space. I'm using this time to mentally rehearse the things I want to tell them. Things I wish someone had told Chaz. Or at least things I wish he'd listened to.

Shondra crosses the gym floor, twisting her hips like she has since the eighth grade. Only now she wears a skirt and silk blouse around those thick thighs and round hips instead of the booty shorts and oversize earrings she sported growing up. Her natural hair fans out in a curly afro around her pretty face. I watch Amir watching Shondra. He always crushed hard on her.

"When you gonna make your move?" I bump his shoulder with mine. "It's been years. Man up."

"I know you ain't talking." Amir reluctantly drags his gaze from Shondra's twisting hips to meet my eyes. "After you punked out and ran off to New York to get away from Bristol."

The teasing grin freezes on my face. The disadvantage of Amir working for me is the same as the advantage. He's around all the time. He sees a lot.

"I wasn't running away from anything." I shoot him a frown. "You telling me you wouldn't jump at the chance to spend two days and nights with Qwest? Any man would."

"Yeah, but 'any man' hasn't been stuck on Bristol forever." His face crinkles with a laugh at my expense. "You have."

"Was stuck. Past tense. I'm over it. She ain't the only girl in the world."

But she was the only girl I could think about. Even waking up with Qwest in New York, Bristol occupied my mind as soon as my eyes opened. I still feel her hand over my heart. I think it's branded there in acid.

"Please," Amir scoffs. "I was there when you met Bristol. The way you looked at her that day at the airport, I ain't ever seen you look at anybody else like that."

He pauses for emphasis, brows up in the air "Not even Qwest," he adds. "She's a great girl, but she isn't your girl."

"Neither is Bristol." My teeth clench around the words. "Haven't you heard? She's Charles Parker's girl."

"I ain't buying it."

I didn't before, but I do know. She's slept with guys in the past. I'm not an idiot. I know that, and I certainly have no room to talk. This is different. A relationship with this guy who's been chasing her for years, who her parents have always wanted her to marry. This is real, and the fact that she's with him makes me mad as hell.

"Hey, guys." Shondra finally reaches us and splits a smile between Amir and me.

I nudge him with my elbow the same way I did in eighth grade when he couldn't work up the nerve to ask her to the winter dance.

"What's up, Shon?" I bend to hug her and watch as Amir does the same.

"Thank you so much for coming, Grip." Her dark eyes shine her excitement. "It's so needed."

"Things are getting better, though, right?" I ask.

I've heard violence is down. Gang recruitment, too. I know there's still a long way to go, but progress has been made.

"Yeah, but not enough and not fast enough." Shondra's sad smile dims the shine in her eyes. "I lost a student last week, and another the week before. Both shot. Still too many funerals. And they have so much potential."

She punches my shoulder.

"Too many Crips, not enough Grips," she half-jokes.

Amir and I laugh, too, even though we feel the weight of what she's saying. I feel the responsibility of being here and doing things like this.

"You, Kendrick Lamar, guys who made it out of here, but still give back, still come back," Shondra continues. "We need you. We need more, so today means everything."

"Whatever I can do," I assure her.

"Well, there's this one student I really hope you get to talk to," she says. "He reminds me so much of you at that age. He's in my English lit class and is such a good writer. There's this writing contest I want him to enter that could lead to big things, but his friends called it 'gay.'"

I wince. We may struggle with a lot of things in the hood, but we have homophobia down. That, we're great at.

"So, of course," Shondra says, rolling her eyes, "now he won't touch it with a ten-foot pole. And both his brothers are Piru."

Amir and I exchange a look, knowing what that means. When your family is Piru, a Blood alliance gang, it probably won't be long before you are, too.

"They call him Bop," Shondra says. "What's his real name?" I ask.

"His name is Dudley," she replies with mischievous eyes.

"Dudley?" Amir laughs. "That ain't even gangsta. Your mama call you Floyd. Imma call you Floyd."

The three of us laugh at his *Coming to America* reference, and it feels good to be home. As hard as I've worked to get out, to survive it, being back here today feels right. Even though I can't ever think about *Coming to America* without thinking about Chaz's last day on earth, it feels right to be here.

Shondra's eyes shift just beyond me and light up with a smile. "Ms. James!" She reaches behind me to hug the petite woman with neat dreadlocks pulled away from her unlined face. "So good to see you. Now, it's a party."

"The whole neighborhood is buzzing about some superstar coming," Ms. James says. "I had to come see for myself."

"Ma." I reach down and pull my mother close, her small frame and fierce spirit burrowing into my side. "I didn't know you were coming."

"And I didn't know *you* were coming." Her eyes, golden brown like mine, hold a light rebuke. "I wanted to hear what you have to say about life and stuff, Mr. Superstar."

"I'm pretty sure most of it will be things you told me in the first place."

"We'll see." She studies my head, a frown on her face. "You cut out your locs. What else don't I know? I had to hear through the grapevine you were in New York with your new girlfriend."

Amir catches a laugh in his fist, and Shondra stretches her eyes with humor.

"Uh oh. Busted." Shondra chuckles and drops a kiss on my mother's cheek. "Good to see you, Ms. James. I need to go find the principal. Be right back."

"Shondra, don't be a stranger, girl," Ma says. "I can't remember the last time you came over for Sunday dinner. You ain't that grown."

"No, ma'am, I'm not." Shondra laughs and turns to leave, speaking over her shoulder. "I'll be taking you up on that. Nobody beats your greens, but don't tell my mama I said that."

"Um, is the b-bathroom still down the hall, Shon?" Amir stutters, looking all nervous.

"Yeah. Of course." Shondra looks back at him like he's crazy. "I'm going that way. You want to follow me?"

Amir grins at me over his shoulder as they walk away.

"Pussy," I mouth at him silently, laughing when he scowls and turns to follow Shondra's hips through the exit doors.

"I'm glad Amir is with you." My mom takes Amir's spot on the wall beside me. "You need somebody who's known you since jump to hold you down, to keep your head on straight the bigger you get."

"Ma, my head stays on straight. Don't worry."

"I do worry." She dips the arch of her brows into a frown. "Especially when you don't tell me things. Why'd I have to hear about you and Qwest on the news?"

"It's not . . ." I sigh, frustrated with how out of control things have gotten in such a short time. "The media's made it bigger than it is. We had a few dates. I spent two days in New York. That's all."

Any hopes I had of keeping things low-key and taking it slow with Qwest went out the window as soon as social media figured out I was staying in her apartment. In just a few days, our fans have made this into some epic love story.

"Well, maybe it should be big." A hopeful grin lights up her still-youthful face. "I need grandbabies. And Qwest seems like the perfect candidate."

"She's a great girl." I keep my tone neutral. "But I don't want you putting too much weight on this."

"It feels like a big deal because you haven't been with a girl in so long." She gives me a wry grin. "I mean like on dates and a relationship. I know you still been smashing."

I groan and close my eyes at her bluntness. She had me when she was just eighteen, and though there was never any doubt which of us was the parent, her youth often made us feel like friends, a unique closeness I usually love. Unless she's talking about me "smashing" chicks.

"Ma, please." My eyes beg her to stop because once she gets started, there's no telling how she'll embarrass me.

"Boy, what? I bought your first pack of Trojans." She smacks her lips, exasperated. "I'm the one who took you to the clinic that time you had that burning—"

"All right, Ma," I cut her off before someone comes and hears her over-sharing. "I got it."

"I thought I was #GripzQueen." She laughs at the face I make. "Seriously, when do I get to meet her?"

"She'll be here for the album release party in a few . . ."

My words trail off when two women walk through the gym doors, drawing the attention of the students waiting in the bleachers. For one thing, the girls are white. We pretty much only see black and brown here. Secondly, the girls are attractive. At least the taller one is. She's damn beautiful.

I assume that's the *Legit* reporter who's shadowing me for the next few weeks entering the gym with Bristol. I barely notice her, but I absorb every detail of Bristol's appearance, starting at her feet in ankle boots, rolling up her long legs in black leather leggings, over the denim shirt with sleeves rolled to the elbow. Hair hanging loose around her shoulders. Even angry with her, I can't ignore the elemental pull between us, like our bodies are in lock step as soon as she walks into a room. It's almost gravitational, and I need to figure out how to shut it down.

"Which one of those girls are you looking at like that?"

My mother's question snatches my attention from the gym entrance.

"Huh?" I make my face confused. "What do you mean?"

"Boy, don't play a player." She inclines her head toward the door. "You lost your train of thought mid-sentence, and looking at one of those girls like breakfast, lunch and dinner. Now which one is it?"

"I don't—"

"Marlon." Her lips compress. "I'm not asking you again."

Like I told Bristol. My mother has extra senses.

"The tall one with the dark hair." I roll my shoulders away from the wall, bend my knee to prop a foot against the wall. "Bristol."

She squints in Bristol's direction.

"She's pretty." Disappointment shadows her face. "White, but pretty."

"Don't start, Ma. And don't worry because she doesn't want to be with me."

"Why not?" Indignation straightens her back and rolls her neck. "She thinks she too good for you or something?"

"You're the one who only wants me dating Black girls, so why you tripping?"

"I never said only Black girls." She pats my shoulder. "I'd settle for Latina. Brown's a color, too, you know."

"Wow. Good to know I have options, but like I said, she isn't interested."

"Hmmmm." She considers Bristol, who's almost reached us. "I think I just saw her on the cover of some magazine in the checkout line."

"Yeah. She's dating—"

"That Parker boy!" Ma's eyes go wide when they meet mine. "His family's rich as hell, baby. So is hers. She's Rhyson's sister, right?"

"Yeah." I straighten from the wall as Bristol and the reporter draw closer. "Can we talk about this later?"

"One more question."

"Ma." Irritation huffs a breath from my chest.

"What?"

"So are you using Qwest to get over her?"

"Not exactly."

"I raised you better than that." Ma points a slim finger in my face. "Don't you play with that girl's feelings. You be honest with her."

"I have been honest with Qwest, Ma." I try not to feel like an asshole. "We were on the same page before Black Twitter blew up with #GripzQueen and #BlackLove hashtags and all that shit. In just a few days it's like . . . more. It feels like more than what she and I talked about it being."

"Shhh." Ma plasters a smile on her face. "Bristol's coming."

I turn my head to find Bristol's eyes flitting between my mother and me, questioning and wondering.

"Hey," she says when they stand in front of us. "Welcome home."

We stare at each other for a few electric seconds, caught in the memory of the last time we saw each other. Of the last hurtful words I hurled at her. The crude things I said. I feel bad for that, but I'm also still so damn frustrated with her. And yes, hurt. Hurt that she chose that Parker asshole over me when I know what we could have, what we could be.

The silence swells, Bristol slides her eyes away from my stare, uncomfortable waiting for me to respond.

"Uh, yeah. Thanks. Good to be back." I shift my attention to the reporter. "Hey. I'm Grip."

"Sorry. I should introduce you." Bristol grimaces and then smiles. "Grip, this is Meryl Smith. She'll be shadowing us . . . you . . . the next couple of weeks for the *Legit* story."

"Such a pleasure to meet you." Meryl pumps my hand enthusiastically. "I'm a huge fan. I've loved your music since that first underground mixtape."

I study Meryl with her pale skin, mousy brown hair, owlish glasses, and marvel again at the globalization of hip-hop. My music reaches the kids sitting in this gym, living in the hood, and somehow finds suburban girls like this one, who probably listened while studying for her finals at Ivy League colleges. I wouldn't have it any other way.

"Thanks." I smile at Meryl and squeeze her hand. "I'm looking forward to it."

Before we go further, Shondra and Amir return.

"Bristol, hey, girl." Amir pulls her into his side, his smile affectionate. Like he said, he was there the day I met her. She's known him as long as she's known me. "Been missing you."

"I've been around." She gives him a squeeze and leans her head on his shoulder. "You're the one who ran off to New York."

"Not me." Amir tilts his head in my direction. "Just following the boss."

My gaze wrestles with Bristol's until I break the awkward, heated moment.

"Bristol, this is Shondra," I say. "She teaches here and coordinated everything. Shon, this is Bristol, my manager."

I turn to find my mother has Bristol under her microscope. This should be fun.

"Bristol, this," I say, pulling my mother close, "is my mom."

"Your mother?" Bristol's eyes widen and swing to my mother. "But you look so young."

"You know what they say." Ma shrugs. "Black don't crack."

"They actually say that?" Bristol asks.

Shondra and Amir laugh right away. If you get Bristol, you like her. Amir's always liked her. Shondra must get her, too. Even irritated with her, I have to smile a little. Ma isn't prepared to laugh, but her lips twitch.

"I mean," Bristol rolls her eyes at herself, "I've heard so much about you."

"Have you now?" Ma looks Bristol up and down. "You're Rhyson's sister, huh?"

"Um, yes." Bristol nods, an uncertain smile on her lips at my mother's thorough vertical inspection. "We're twins actually."

"Hmmmm," Ma says. "I see the resemblance."

"Yes, well, it's great to finally meet you." Bristol glances at me briefly before turning back to Shondra, pouring all her charm into a smile. "Meryl needs to sit down with Grip once he's done, just for a few minutes. I was thinking there might be a place here on campus where they could do the interview?"

"Sure," Shondra says. "We can find a spot, easy."

"And we'll just need to get some releases signed." Bristol reaches into her bag and extracts a few forms. "In case we use pictures of any students or places here on campus. Could we scope a few possibilities?"

"We might be in *Legit* magazine?" Shondra's eyes light up. "That's great. We have a few minutes before Grip starts. Let's go."

She, Shondra, and Meryl turn to walk off.

"Amir," I say quickly. "Go with them."

"It's okay, Grip." Bristol looks over her shoulder with a small smile. "We'll be fine."

"Bristol, you're not home." I check my frustration, conscious of how closely the others watch me, especially my mom. "Things could pop off here without warning. Amir will know what to do if anything goes down."

"She'll be fine, Grip," Shondra reassures me.

"I know she will because Amir's going." I tip my head toward him . "You got it?"

"Yeah, I got it," he says.

"Amir," Bristol says pointedly, leveling annoyed eyes on me. "That isn't necessary. Really."

"Well, Amir works for me, and I told him to go with you."

A muscle tics in Bristol's jaw, but she turns without another word and starts walking swiftly toward the exit. Shondra, Meryl, and Amir trade uncertain looks before they take off to catch up.

"Oh, I see you have your emotions well in check," Ma says sarcastically, watching Bristol leave through the gym door. "No one would ever guess how you feel about that girl."

"Ma, please." Chin dropped to chest, I run a hand over my head. "Not today."

"You need to get over her." Ma shakes her head. "Just try with Qwest for me, okay?"

"It doesn't work like that." I shove my hands into the side pockets of my leather jacket. "I wish it did. I thought it could."

"Now, when did you say I get to meet Qwest?" She skips over what I've said. "You got . . . distracted before."

"She'll be here for the release party in a few weeks."

"I'll meet her then." She reaches one hand up to cup my face. "I know you don't understand, but I get sick and tired of our successful Black men ending up with women who don't look like us."

"Ma, I hear you, but you know I've dated all over and that's never been how I chose who I was with." I place my hand over hers against my face, wishing I could transmit my perspective to her through the touch connecting us. "That's not everyone and it's not me."

She drops her hands and lifts one brow. "You think I made all those sacrifices so you could be a cliché? Some Black man who thinks a white woman is the ultimate symbol of success? Like a nice car or a big house, but with blonde hair?"

"She isn't blonde, and you know me better than that. You raised me better than that." I'm losing the grasp on my patience the longer I have to defend my feelings for Bristol, since they won't be doing me any good anyway. "I didn't fall for her because she's white. I fell for her because she's . . . Bristol."

"You *think* it isn't a factor, but it is." Mama places her hand over her heart like I'm breaking it. "I was afraid of this. I wanted you to go to that fancy school, but I always knew this could happen, that it could influence you. And here we are."

"I've dated Asian girls, Hispanic girls, black girls, white girls. Why is this such a big deal to you?"

"But marrying is a different story."

"Who said anything about marrying? And it's a little late in the century to still be hating white people."

"Tell them that," she replies with fire. "And I don't hate all white people. Just like I don't like all Black people. All God's children, red and yellow, black and white get on your mama's nerves. Not hating them does not mean marrying them."

"Nobody's talking about marrying anyone," I reiterate. "She won't even date me, much less marry me. You have nothing to worry about."

If anyone should worry, it's me. Because after two days in New York in Qwest's bed, my feelings for Bristol are just as strong. My anger and my frustration lie on top of them in a thick pile, but I've come nowhere near snuffing them out.

Not for the first time I wonder if anything ever will.

CHAPTER 14

I'M NOT SURE how much more my ovaries can endure today.

As if Grip looking the way he does isn't enough, seeing him inspire these kids from his old high school is like a stick of C4 planted in my ovaries.

Boom.

It seems I'm not the only one. Meryl "the huge fan" reporter hasn't taken her eyes off him since we got here. So much for professional objectivity. She practically threw her panties at him.

Okay. I'm being ridiculous. I know it. I'm taking my frustration out on poor Meryl because the person who really deserves it can't take it. Not Grip for going to New York and sleeping with Qwest. Not Qwest for inviting him and being exactly the kind of girl he should be with. No, the person who deserves my scorn is me, but I think watching Grip fall for Qwest on every social media platform is punishment enough. So, Meryl it is.

"I know it feels like there's no way out sometimes," Grip tells the assembled students from his spot on the gymnasium floor. "I grew up just a few streets over, so I know what happens in Bompton."

Grip told me once that here when a word starts with the letter "C", you often substitute a "B" because this is Bloods, not Crips, territory. The possibility that wearing blue or saying "couch" instead of "bouch" could get you killed? I can't imagine human life being treated so cavalierly.

"Half the boys I knew when I was your age didn't make it past twenty." Grip drops his eyes to the wax-shiny basketball court before looking back to the students. "And too many others are locked up. I'm not gonna sugar coat it. The odds are stacked against us."

He steps closer, and the passion in his eyes and in his voice reverberates, reaching as high as the rafters. Reaching each student listening intently. Reaching me.

"You have to make your own way out. You're responsible for your future." He runs his eyes methodically up and down the rows of students. "You can't wait for somebody else to give you anything. My mom taught me that."

The warm smile Grip and his mother share telegraphs a closeness I envy. She's exactly as I'd imagined she'd be. Proud. Confident. Fiercely protective.

"She was the one who encouraged me to apply for a scholarship at the School of the Arts," Grip says. "Even though it meant leaving this school where all my friends were and taking a bus across town everyday alone. Even though it meant going to a new school that felt like a foreign country, where I felt like an alien. If I hadn't done that, you might not be hearing my music now. You probably wouldn't even know my name."

"He's amazing," Meryl whispers, her eyes fixed on Grip's expressive face. "I can't wait to write this story."

"Good," I whisper back with a forced smile.

My phone buzzes in my lap, and I look down at the screen. Parker.

I would ignore this call, but I've been leaving him messages for the last three days. He has to know I suspect he leaked that information to the media. I need to set him straight, and there's no telling when he'll stop avoiding me and call again.

"I need to take this," I tell Meryl quietly. "Be right back."

I bend at the waist and tiptoe, hoping I haven't drawn much attention to myself, though Grip couldn't miss me stepping out.

"Parker," I say as soon as I'm in the hall. "Why did it take you so long to return my calls?"

"Bristol, I miss you, too." His deep voice is part humor, part caution.

"Your people confirmed to the media that we're dating." I lean against the brick wall and plow my fingers through my hair. "They wouldn't have done that without your express permission."

"I've been in India. You know that. It's just a misunderstanding. A miscommunication."

"One I am fully capable of correcting if you don't do it." I pause for emphasis. "Soon."

"Is it really so far from the truth?" he asks. "Come on, Bristol. We did spend the night together just days ago."

"You know damn well I was too drunk to even know my name that night, much less choose to sleep with you. Now, everyone thinks we're practically engaged."

"I'll handle it."

"You better, or I will."

Something sinister uncurls and hisses in the silence on the other end.

"That wouldn't be wise, Bristol," Parker says quietly.

"You don't scare me." I push myself away from the wall, standing perfectly straight as if he were right in front of me to see. "I hope you know that."

"I don't want to scare you." He infuses his words with artificial warmth. "I want to love you."

"Love?" A bitter laugh leaves an aftertaste on my lips. "The way my father loves my mother? The way your father loves yours? No, thank you. If I ever do marry, it won't be to a man who needs other women like they do. A man who humiliates me with his infidelities."

"I'm sure you can persuade me not to stray," he says, sounding pleased that it matters to me. "I had no idea you were so possessive."

"I'm not possessive of you, and any man I have to persuade not to stray is welcome to do so. If I have to convince him I'm worth his fidelity, then he isn't the one for me."

"I love your spirit, Bristol." He sounds a little like he's . . . panting? "It turns me on."

"All right." I wish he were here to see my eyes rolling. He's like a hound dog after a rabbit. A swift rabbit he won't get ahold of again. "On that note, I'm gonna go."

"But, baby—"

"I'm working," I say, cutting into whatever bullshit he planned to say. "And don't call me baby."

I hang up before he has the chance to protest further and quietly ease back through the gym doors so I don't disturb Grip's talk.

Only he isn't talking. He's at one end of the court, poised to shoot the basketball. He's no longer wearing his black leather jacket and Kelly green hoodie, but just a plain white T-shirt and black jeans. One of the students, as tall as Grip and with an athletic build, guards him with a hand in his face.

"What's going on?" I ask Meryl. "What'd I miss?"

"It was great." Meryl's eyes glimmer with her eagerness. "One of the kids challenged Grip when he talked about the value of an education. He said Grip didn't go to college, but he's still, and I quote, 'stacking dollars'. Then Grip said everyone doesn't have to go to college, but an education is something that cannot be taken away."

"Wow. Sounds intense." I watch the two guys run back up to our end of the court. "How did they end up playing basketball?"

"Then Grip said he's enrolled in online courses now." Meryl gives me a curious look. "Did you know that?"

"Uh, no." I shake my head, watching the student make a difficult shot. "I had no idea."

He never told me. Why would he not tell me something that huge?

"So then Grip calls him out about some writing contest he apparently won't enter," Meryl says. "Before I knew it, Grip said he'd play him for it, one on one. If Grip wins, the student—I think they called him Bop—has to enter the contest."

"And if Grip loses?"

"If Grip loses, Bop wins his shoes."

"His shoes?"

Grip has a massive tennis shoe collection, and the classic Jordans in his closet are his prized possessions. I recognize the pair he's wearing now as especially expensive and rare.

"We haven't even sat down for the interview yet," Meryl says gleefully. "And I've already gotten a lot."

I notice Grip's leather jacket and hoodie on the floor. I pick them up so they won't get stepped on or dirty. As soon as they're within sniffing distance, his clean, masculine scent surrounds me. I hold the material to my chest and surreptitiously inhale, closing my eyes to absorb this small part of him. The items still have the warmth of his body, and holding them, even for a few seconds, warms my chilled places.

When I open my eyes, I encounter Ms. James' golden brown gaze locked on me. Even fully dressed with Grip's jacket and hoodie hugged to my chest, I feel naked under her stare. She sees everything. I clear discomfort from my throat and turn back to the court.

Grip takes one final shot, which apparently puts the game away, and the students go crazy, emptying the bleachers and rushing the basket- ball court. Even Amir, Shondra, Ms. James, and Meryl join the exuberant knot of students surrounding Grip on the court. I hang back, observing. He's laughing, at ease, at home, the basketball pressed to his hip.

I've never been in this position with him. On the outside, out of favor. It's awkward, and it hurts. Maybe I could mitigate this by telling him that Parker and I aren't dating. Parker should be telling everyone soon enough himself anyway. But do I have the right? Grip finally seems to be moving on and giving someone a real shot. I'm still not going to be with him, so what would telling him accomplish? I should give them a chance, him and Qwest.

I skirt the edges of the crowd, waiting while he signs autographs, all the while encouraging Bop to keep writing, to enter the contest. I've never seen this side of him. Listening to the songs he writes about his childhood and his old neighborhood, I suspected it, but seeing it firsthand is an entirely different thing. An entirely better thing.

Meryl steps out of the crowd until she's standing with me.

"I'm glad you invited me." Her broad grin pushes the glasses up on her cheeks. "This is a great add for the piece."

"Speaking of which," I say. "Grip has a session soon, making some last-minute adjustments for the album. We better get him into the courtyard for your interview before it gets too late."

I make my way through the crowd until I'm standing right behind Grip, waiting for him to finish the last few autographs.

"You enjoy managing my son?" Ms. James asks at my shoulder.

I turn my head, startled to find her so close, those eyes, so like Grip's, trained on my face.

"Yes, very much." I clutch his leather jacket and hoodie a little closer. "I manage several artists, but Grip definitely has a special place. He's like family, being so close to Rhyson."

"So he's like a brother to you?" Ms. James asks.

"Something like that." I lick the lie away from my lips, turning to offer her a smile. "We've known each other a long time."

I see a good stopping point, and know I have to dive in and get him out before he starts with another group.

"Excuse me, Ms. James." I smile politely and press my way to Grip's side.

"Hey." I touch his elbow, drawing a sharp glance from him. The smile on his face, the light in his eyes dies when he realizes it's me. That look drags a serrated knife over an open nerve.

"Sorry to interrupt," I say softly. "But we need to get into your interview with Meryl. I think you have a session this afternoon, right?"

For a moment, it seems he may not even acknowledge my question, but then he nods and turns back to the crowd.

"Gotta go, guys." He raises his voice to be heard by all who are around. "I'll stay longer next time."

"Sorry to break things up." I look up at him, searching the rigid lines of his face for any softening. He flicks a glance my way with a barely discernible nod.

"Oh, here's your stuff." I extend the jacket and hoodie to him.

"Thanks," he mutters, slipping the hoodie over the plain white T-shirt he played basketball in.

"Sure." I look over at Shondra to give myself something to do while things feel so weird. "Hey, can we head to the courtyard for the interview now?"

"Of course," Shondra responds. "Follow me."

Meryl gets a call on our way to the courtyard. While she's on the phone and Shondra is a few paces ahead of us, I search for something to break this awkward silence between Grip and me.

"I didn't know you were taking online courses."

"And I didn't realize it had anything to do with managing me." He looks straight ahead. "So, why would I tell you?"

He quickens his steps to catch up to Shondra, to get away from me. I notice his shoulders relax, the handsome profile lit with a smile as they talk about old times in these halls.

It's like a slap across my face, his indifference. Or was it rejection? It all feels the same now. In giving him his chance with Qwest, I wasn't prepared for what I would be giving up. Whatever existed between us, even the friendship I've grown to treasure over the years, will never be the same.

CHAPTER 15

HE'S GOING TO be number one. He's going to be number one. He's going to be number one.

That thought buzzes around my head as I obsessively check the numbers on *Grip*. It's Prodigy's first release. It's the thing I've poured everything into for months. With two number one singles already under its belt, topping the album charts would be a crowning achievement. It's critically and commercially beyond anything we could have hoped for. Reviews are glowing. Sales are shockingly good. By the time Meryl's story goes to press, Grip will be in another stratosphere.

I rarely cry, but tears stand in my eyes because no one deserves this more than he does. He's worked hard for years and is one of the most talented artists on the scene. So happy tears, but tears nonetheless.

"Knock, knock." Rhyson raps his knuckles against my open office door and pokes his head in. "Got a second?"

"Sure." I sniff and sneak a thumb under my eyes, hoping runny mascara doesn't give away too much. "Come on in, brother dearest."

"Did you see the numbers?" The eagerness on Rhyson's handsome face matches the unassailable joy leaping in me since I saw the first batch of sales figures.

"What numbers?" I blank my face, but probably can't suppress the happiness in my eyes.

"What numbers, my ass." Rhyson huffs his disbelief, collapsing into the leather chair across from my desk. "I bet you've been checking every five minutes."

Try every two.

"*Grip* is outpacing sales of my last album," Rhyson says. "You're telling me you don't already know that?"

"It's pretty freaking awesome, right?" I burst out, unable to hold it back any longer.

"Yeah, it is." His smile softens with what looks like affection . . . for me. "We did it, Bris."

"Grip did it," I reply immediately.

"Of course, he did, but this is Prodigy's first release. This is our baby, and we did good, kid."

It means everything to hear Rhyson talk about the label as ours and the work as our shared project. This feeling, this accomplishment, the possibility of it, is what compelled me to focus my college degree on business and entertainment. It spurred me to move here for Rhyson's solo career, even when he wasn't sure he wanted one after all the drama with our parents. Hell, he wasn't even sure he wanted me in his life.

"It's pretty incredible." I push the words past the pesky lump in my throat.

"So where's the man of the hour?" A grin curves Rhyson's lips.

"He's your best friend." I shuffle some papers on my desk, avoiding Rhyson's eyes. "You don't know?"

"Are you kidding me?" He barks a laugh out. "You know where all your artists are at all times."

"True." I twist my lips into a wry grin at how OCD I can be. "He's got a full day. He started off super early this morning with a call into The Breakfast Club in New York, and he's everywhere. Several in-store appearances. He's even on Seacrest, in studio."

Rhyson gives a low whistle, sitting back to cross an ankle over his knee.

"Wow." He studies my face. "So why are you here and not with our biggest star?"

"Sarah's got it." I stand and take a small stack of papers to the shredder I keep in the corner. "We do have other artists, and I've been giving so much to Grip, there's lots to catch up on. Kilimanjaro is still out on the road. Luke is finishing his album. There's a few movie scripts coming in for Kai, after the baby of course."

"No nudity." Rhyson frowns. "Like at all. Preferably no love scenes. We need final approval on the script. Aren't there any great, meaty nun roles out there? Remember Audrey Hepburn in *A Nun's Story*? She received an Oscar nomination for that."

I chuckle because my brother is notoriously possessive over his little wife. The nun stuff sounds ridiculous, but he isn't even kidding. I look back, and his face is completely serious. Poor Kai.

"Uh, got it. Nuns. I'll see what I can do." I sit again, hoping he's lost his previous line of questioning.

"So, about Marlon."

Damn, he's persistent.

"I promise you Sarah's got it. She's more than capable."

"I'm sure she's capable. You wouldn't keep her if she weren't. We're not known for tolerating incompetence. Guess we got that from our parents."

Among other things.

I leave that on the shelf because Rhyson and I have never gotten far discussing our parents. Come to think of it, there are a lot of things we don't get far discussing outside of our business dealings.

"Besides Marlon, you've worked harder on this than anyone, Bris." Rhyson leans forward. "You should be with him today, and you know it. So why are you here?"

"Drop it. Geesh." I open my laptop and pull up my checklist for Grip's listening party and release celebration. "Everything's covered."

The only sound in the office is my fingers flying over the keys. I glance up to find his cool eyes on my face. I pause my typing and lean back in my seat to cross my legs.

"What?" I lift a brow.

"Can I ask you something?"

"You just did." My lips move a degree in a smile.

"What's up with you and Marlon?" There's no trace of a smile on his face, and his eyes hold only questions, no humor.

"Rhyson, leave it." I sigh and lean toward my desk, back to my typing.

"I wasn't going to bring this up because I didn't think it would be a problem." Rhyson frowns and runs a hand over the back of his neck, uncharacteristic discomfort on his face. "But Marlon told me about . . . you know."

I stop typing to give him my full attention. "Not yet, I don't know. He told you what?"

"He told me about you guys hooking up when you were here on spring break that time." Rhyson pushes the words out like they burn his tongue.

"Oh, did he?" Irritation blisters beneath my skin. "I should go check the restroom. Maybe he wrote 'for a good time call Bristol' on the stalls, too."

"Bris, it's been a long time. He probably wouldn't have told me now if it hadn't been for the song. I had no idea 'Top of the World' was about you."

"It doesn't matter." I fix my eyes on the screen. "Water under the bridge. Water that never went anywhere anyway."

"That's what I thought, but things have been weird lately," Rhyson says. "And it's none of my business."

"Right." I don't look away from the sales report in one of my open browsers. "It's not."

"Until it affects my business," Rhyson finishes, his tone stiff. "If things weren't tense between the two of you, you'd be with Marlon today. We can't have whatever is going on with you personally affecting business."

"So what?" My eyes jerk to his face. "Are you here to write me up? Put a warning in my file? Give me a demerit? Whatever you came here to do, do it, say it so I can get back to work."

"There's no need to get defensive."

"There is when you tell me you think I'm not doing my job because of some shit with Grip."

I open yet another browser. Anything to avoid the curiosity in my brother's eyes.

"Do you have feelings for him, Bristol?" Rhyson asks softly.

In all these years, he's never asked me. Not once has Rhyson ever asked if I returned Grip's feelings. He's always assumed that when I brushed aside Grip's advances, his flirtations, there was nothing to it on my end. Any hope I have that I'll get out of this conversation without telling him something fades when he doesn't drop it.

"Bris, look at me," my brother demands.

I finally abandon my laptop, meeting his eyes. "Do you have feelings for Marlon?"

I still can't make myself admit it aloud. Even though he isn't in the room, it's like as soon as I say the words, they'll land on my sleeve for Grip to read. But my silence says it all. I've never had to deny my feelings to Rhyson, and I find it harder than when I lie to Grip.

"What the hell?" Rhyson leans back in his seat, resting his head on the back of the chair and staring up at the ceiling. "All these years and you never ... why?"

"It doesn't matter what I feel."

He sits back up, spearing me with the frustration in his eyes. "How can you say that?"

"Because I'm not doing a damn thing about it. That's why."

"But if you . . ." He pauses, obviously taking great care with the next word that comes out of his mouth, as he should. "Care about Marlon, and he's made no secret of how he feels about you, then why not?"

"Weren't you the main one afraid I would destroy him?" I pinch my brows together. "Seems you'd be the last person encouraging a relationship between poor, vulnerable Grip and your sister the man-eater."

"What?"

"Oh, please, Rhyson." I steady my voice for the next words. "Just a few weeks ago, I overheard you warning him away from me. Telling him that he should pursue Qwest instead. So, don't act as if Grip and me would be some match made in heaven. You know we wouldn't be good together."

Rhyson is quiet for a few moments, studying the clasped hands in his lap.

"I admit there are risks involved." Rhyson looks up at me from beneath his dark brows. "I have been concerned that you might hurt him."

"It never once occurred to you that he might hurt me?" A bitter laugh darkens the air around me. "That maybe he had already hurt me and I wasn't willing to risk my heart being broken?"

"You mean the stuff with Tessa? It wasn't his baby, Bris."

"It could have been." I shake my head and twirl my chair away from him to face the view through my window. "That wasn't even the point. He lied to me. He never once mentioned he was in a relationship that whole week we were . . ."

Together. To even think of us as "together" pains me.

"Whatever we were doing that week," I finish lamely. "If he would cheat on Tessa, he'd cheat on me."

Rhyson comes to stand in front of me, propping himself against the windowsill.

"You think Marlon would cheat on you?" Rhyson looks at me disbelievingly. "He was a kid!"

"He hasn't exactly been chaste since."

"Neither have you," Rhyson tosses back. "You can't hold anyone he's been with against him when you weren't together, Bris. That's ridiculous."

"You say that so easily because you'd never cheat on Kai."

"Of course I would never cheat on Kai." He looks offended that I even brought it up. "I couldn't."

"Well you're the exception to the rule. Most men have no trouble cheating." A laugh sours in my mouth. "Our father certainly doesn't."

"What did you say?" Rhyson peers at my face like he's never seen me before. "Dad cheats on Mom?"

"Oh, God, Rhyson." I lean back in my seat, part horrified, part relieved that he knows. "Yes. Dad cheats."

"When?"

"When not?" I meet the confusion in his eyes. "Almost since the beginning."

"I mean, I figured they didn't have what you would call a typical marriage." A frown settles on Rhyson's face. "But I hadn't thought about . . ."

He shrugs, his expression clearing.

"She probably cheats, too," he says. "It isn't like they have some grand passion."

"She loves him," I say softly. "She's never cheated on him." "How do you know all of this and I don't?"

"Because I've been there, Rhyson." Pent up emotion pushes my voice out louder than I intend. "You left and never looked back. I'm the one who stayed. I saw what happened."

"What did you see?" His eyes never leave my face. Maybe he's really seeing me for the first time since we were kids.

I hear my father screwing that girl as if I'm standing down in the foyer again.

"I heard him." I draw a deep breath, releasing it on a shaky exhale. "I went home after spring break but didn't tell them I was coming. As soon as I walked in the house, I heard them upstairs. Someone having sex. Like loud, so I knew they didn't think anyone else was in the house."

I lean forward, propping my elbows on my knees and scooping my hair away from my face before going on.

"There was this part of me that was happy." I shake my head, remembering the goofy grin I wore thinking I'd caught my parents making love. "I never thought they loved each other. I knew they were. . . partners, but I didn't think of them as having sex. Of enjoying each other."

"Yeah, neither did I." Rhyson clears his throat. "And then what happened?"

"Then Mom walked through the front door." I meet Rhyson's horrified eyes. "Yeah. She walked in and heard him fucking someone upstairs. And I was standing right there, thinking the whole time it was her."

I pop up, on my feet and pace around my office, because even the memory agitates me.

"She wasn't shocked." A staccato laugh chokes me. "Devastated, but not shocked. She was used to it. She accepted it."

"Why doesn't she just leave him?" Rhyson asks. "If it hurts so badly, why not just leave? Is it the business?"

"No, that's what I thought." I walk over to join him at the window, setting one hip on the windowsill and leaning my shoulder against the pane. "She brushed it off like it meant nothing, but later that night, I found her drunk and crying. Just . . . this pathetic person, nothing like our mother at all."

I bite my lip, as if I can physically hold back the last of a dirty secret, but it's about to spill out of me.

"She loves him. She doesn't leave because she can't. She loves him desperately."

I tip my head back, preferring the ceiling to the perplexed look on my brother's face.

"She has vodka for breakfast to get through the day," I say. "Did you know that? Bloody Marys if she's in public, but at home, she just drinks vodka first thing in the morning."

"Are you saying our mother is an alcoholic?" Disbelief, horror, smudge the clear gray of Rhyson's eyes. "How could I not know all of this?"

"Like I said, you weren't around." A wry grin tilts my mouth. "And you were already running from us. As if you needed more reason to stay away. I didn't want to tell you now that you're finally trying with our parents. I didn't think any of this would endear us to you."

"I don't know what to say." Rhyson pushes his fingers through his unruly hair. "What to think. It's like there was this whole world going on that I knew nothing about. Our parents. The cheating. Mom's drinking."

He gives me a direct look that probes for anything else I might be hiding.

"You and Grip. What does all of this have to do with the two of you?"

I lean my temple against the cool glass and don't respond. I don't want to talk about this with him. We go years without talking about anything but music and business and shit that doesn't matter, and he wants to go excavating my brain while our first release rockets up the charts.

"Grip isn't our father." Rhyson turns my chin with his finger until I have to meet his eyes. "And you're definitely not our mother."

"Aren't I?" I shake my head, lowering my eyes to hide anything else from him. "You don't believe that. You know how alike we are."

"Not in the ways that count," Rhyson says. "I'll be the first to admit that I didn't trust you when you first came back into my life. I thought she could manipulate you. You know that."

"So did she. That's why she didn't completely lose her mind when I left New York to come here. She thought she could get to you through me."

Rhyson's jaw becomes granite.

"I know that." He looks at me, his eyes losing some of their stoniness. "But she couldn't. She didn't. You're not her."

"She's a foolish woman who feels too much for a man who doesn't feel enough for her, and she can't make herself walk away." A hollow laugh grates in my throat. "And I'd be just like her."

"No, you wouldn't. You're not."

"I am," I fire back, holding his eyes by sheer will. "You have me pegged so wrong, Rhyson. You always have."

"What? I . . ." He dips his head to get a better look at my face. "What do you mean?"

"You think I'm this hard ass who doesn't care."

My voice wobbles, dammit. I swallow as much of the years-old weakness as I can before continuing.

"That isn't me." The words barely make it out, singed by the hot tears in my throat. "I'm the girl who cares too much. When you and our parents walked away from each other, who fought for our family? Who actually cared that we weren't a family?"

"Well—"

"Me, Rhyson." I dig my finger into my chest, pressing my point. "And when we didn't see each other, literally for years, who took the first step? Reached out? Called? Came here to see you?"

"Bristol, I—"

"That's right. Me." I can't hold back the tears that leak over my cheeks. "Who was the idiot who hadn't had a real conversation with you in years, but chose her college major based on your dreams? Bet the whole farm that you'd let me back into your life if I could help your career?"

"You did," he says softly.

"Don't you see? Can none of you see how much I care?" A sob breaks into my words. "How damn starved I am? For anything from you, from Mom, Dad."

"From Grip?"

His question slices into the quiet like a knife through butter.

Softly. Smoothly, but it still cuts.

"It didn't even take a week with him," I whisper, sniffing and letting the tears roll over my chin, down my neck, and into my collar unchecked. "I knew I was in trouble after three days."

A chuckle at my own expense vibrates in my chest.

"Maybe less. Two days." I shrug. "We talked about everything that first night. There was nothing off limits. We were so different, but I'd never felt so . . . connected to anyone."

"I guess I was working on that project, huh?" Guilt floods Rhyson's eyes.

"That was the excuse you gave, yeah." I give him a knowing look. "We both know you were avoiding me. You had no idea if I was legit. You didn't know what to make of me after all those years apart. You always thought, and rightly so, that I was too much like Mother."

"I'm sorry."

"No it's true. I am." I smile, reminiscing about that week. "But Grip didn't know that. He just got to know . . . me. For me. He was smart. So smart. And such a good writer. Sensitive. He wrote poetry, for God's sake. What grown man who looks like him writes poetry? That's just not fair."

Rhyson and I share a smile, tinged with sadness.

"And he was so comfortable with himself," I say. "So confident, and it didn't come from having money or fame or anything else. Just confident in himself. It came from somewhere I couldn't even relate to, but it was completely authentic and magnetic."

"And?" Rhyson prompts when I stop myself.

"And I didn't stop it." I blow out a breath laden with my own incredulity. "For once, I decided I was going to free-fall. I was going to kiss at the top of a Ferris wheel, swim naked in the ocean—"

"Naked in the ocean?" Rhyson does a double take. "I wasn't gone that much. I missed all that?"

"We didn't let anyone know. It was just . . . us. I knew Grip was falling for me, and I knew for sure I was falling for him, and it felt so good. Just to let it go. To just fall felt good."

"If you and Grip were together, he'd be faithful."

"You think so. He thinks so." I laugh harshly. "But I'm not so sure. What makes me so special?"

"What makes you so special?" Rhyson leans over and gently pushes the hair out of my eyes. "How much time do you have, little sister?"

"We're twins, idiot," I hiccup through the last of my tears. "Once and for all, I'm not your little sister."

"Well, I came out first."

He pulls me into a hug. My throat swells with heat, emotion closing the passageway and making it hard to swallow, to breathe. I've longed to talk like this with my brother for years. And no matter how much business we did, it never became this personal. This vulnerable. I fight it back. I pull away.

"I'm sure at some point Mother thought she was special, too, but I flew back to New York and caught our father fucking one of his clients upstairs while our mother listened in the foyer," I say in a rush. "She didn't feel special that night when I was mopping her up off the floor, drunk and miserable. She feels things so deeply she has to make you think she feels nothing to protect herself."

"And that's what you're doing?" Rhyson's question comes softly but harshly. "Denying to Marlon that you feel anything when you feel everything? Is that why you're dating Parker?"

"God, you really don't know me if you think I'm actually dating Parker," I say, my response flat.

"You're not dating Parker?" A baffled frown settles between Rhyson's brows. "I knew it! What the hell, Bris?"

"If I won't be with Grip, he should be with someone like Qwest." I swallow the hurt even linking their names in the same sentence does to me. "And he wouldn't even try as long as he thought I was . . . possible. So, I let him, along with the entire known world, think that I was dating Parker when the media reported it."

"But he . . . didn't he . . ." Discomfort tightens Rhyson's words. "Him leaving your house that morning, that was—"

"Oh, no. I slept with him. That happened." I shrug. "I guess. He says I did."

A loaded silence stretches between us as Rhyson processes that information.

"You don't remember?"

"I was taking a page out of Mother's playbook, numbing with vodka so I didn't feel." My heart twists like a knife in my chest as Grip's cutting words before he left for New York come back to haunt me. "That kind of backfired."

"Wait. Let me get this straight." Anger bunches the muscle along Rhyson's jaw. "Did Parker take advantage of you? Like sleep with you while you were—"

"I can't, Rhyson," I say so softly I'm not sure he heard me. "He says I was willing. I just don't remember much."

"He says you were . . ." Rhyson narrows the rage in his eyes to slits. "That motherfucker."

"That motherfucker," I agree with a little laugh, even though it isn't funny at all to wake up and have no memory of having sex with someone. "I mean, I've let that go. You need to let it go, too. It won't accomplish anything."

"You say you aren't dating Parker," Rhyson finally says after he's composed himself some. "Does Parker know that?"

"Kind of." I laugh at the expression on Rhyson's face. "I've tried to tell him. He insists that I'm going to marry him one day and we're going to rule the world."

"Asshole," Rhyson mutters. "Exactly."

"You should be careful of him, Bristol. All that power and money make him dangerous."

"No, thinking he's God's gift is what makes him dangerous, but I've got it under control."

"What does that mean?"

"Meaning it was convenient for me to let him play this little fantasy out in public so Grip would finally move on." I toy with a loose string on the sleeve of my blouse and bite my bottom lip. "Thinking I'm with Parker moved him on to Qwest, but I've told Parker. He hasn't accepted it fully yet, but he'll tell the media the truth soon."

"If you really think Grip is over you that fast, then you don't know him."

For a moment, hope flares inside me. Hope that maybe I didn't completely burn the bridge between Grip and me. But it's a bridge I'll never cross anyway, so what's the use?

"He has the right to know the truth." Rhyson's worried eyes hold mine. "To know how you feel."

"The right?" I scoff. "They're my feelings, and I choose not to act on them, so what good does it do for him to know?"

"So what? You just watch him fall harder for Qwest? Give him to someone else?" Rhyson's voice is so full of disappointment and disapproval I almost flinch. "You're braver than that, Bristol. You're the most fearless person I know. And you let the threat of something keep you from what you really want?"

"You don't understand what—"

"I do," Rhyson cuts in. "It's the same kind of bullshit that kept Kai from being with me. Allowing her past and the mistakes her parents made to dictate her future. Imagine if she'd just given up? Not taken a chance on me? She had every reason not to."

He takes both my hands in his, squeezing as he looks at me, through me.

"We wouldn't be married. She wouldn't be pregnant." A bleakness enters his eyes. "The prospect of spending the rest of my life without her would destroy me. Why would you choose that?"

"You think I'm fearless?" The words get hung up on the tears flooding my throat. "I'm not. I'm scared shitless, Rhyson. I care so much about the people I love. I'd do anything for them. If I let myself. . . have Grip, there would be no boundaries. Do you understand what I'm saying? What if I end up like our mother? A strong woman whose man is her Achilles' heel? A drunken fool who takes whatever scraps he leaves and shares him to have whatever he'll give her?"

"You would never allow—"

"Neither would she, but she does." I shake my head. "I've seen it. How weak she is for him. She kept it from us for years because she's ashamed."

"All I know is the very thought of Kai with anyone else drives me insane," Rhyson says. "And we may not be typical twins, but I do know we're alike in that way. Actually having to watch her be with someone else, to see her fall for someone else and know that I allowed that to happen? I would be miserable, and so would you."

Images of Grip holding Qwest's hand and of them out in New York laughing and kissing twist around my mind, squeezing like a boa constrictor. My imagination fills in the dark gaps of what they're like in bed together. Of how she runs her hands over his broad chest, over the whipcord muscles of his arms and legs. How she strokes him, takes him in her mouth, takes him in her body. Of her satisfying him in a way I never will. She knows him now in a way I don't. They've passed secrets between their bodies.

The unrelenting flow of images floods my mind, torturing me. Rhyson thinks I would be miserable?

Oh, God, I already am.

CHAPTER 16

G~RIP~

POETRY HAS LONG ~BEEN~ a habit and a comfort for me. Ever since I was a kid, I would recite my favorite poems when I was afraid, nervous, excited.

Sad.

The words pull me into a rhythm. Something set and predictable, yet brimming with the potential to break wild and free.

In my favorite poem "Poetry", Neruda said he wheeled with the stars and that his heart broke loose on the wind. It seems particularly appropriate tonight because I do feel as if, with my debut album sitting in the number one spot, I'm tumbling through some galaxy I never thought to explore. A dark sky pelted with stars, with promises masquerading as constellations.

I quoted that poem to Bristol at the top of the Ferris wheel all those years ago when we got stuck. She was frightened, but our kiss chased her fears away. She flipped my heart upside down, upending everything I thought I wanted in a girl. That Ferris wheel was maybe a hundred feet off the ground, but with Bristol's lips so soft, first hesitant then urgent, her fingers twisted around mine like she was just as desperate to hold onto me as I was to hold onto her—I was on top of the world. I didn't have two pennies to rub together or a pot to piss in, but I was happy.

So fucking happy.

And tonight, I am at the top of the world, more successful than that pauper on the Ferris wheel could have imagined. I can see Bristol on the other side of the club where we're holding my release celebration, but she may as well be in another hemisphere there's so much distance between us. I'm a fool because given the choice, I'd take the Ferris wheel with her any day over tonight. That kiss, not this celebration, feels like the best night of my life.

"You do know you have the number one album in the country, right?" Qwest walks toward the edge of the stage where I'm seated. We just finished sound check for tonight's performance. "You got nothing to look sad about, baby."

"I'm not sad." I curve my lips into something close to a smile to prove it. "Just taking a quick breather. It's a lot to take in."

"How about you take me in." She stands between my legs hanging over the lip of the stage. One hand touches my chest through my shirt and moves down while her lips wander over my jaw and down my neck. Her hand searches between my legs. I'm limp as a noodle. It's embarrassing to have a woman hot enough to melt butter practically molesting you, and your dick doesn't care.

"Sorry to interrupt."

Bristol's voice snaps my head up, our eyes catching in the dim light of the club over Qwest's shoulder. She's scraped her hair back tonight so she's all high cheekbones and matte red lips. I permit myself a glance over the naked shoulders in her strapless black pantsuit. The tight silk coaxes her breasts higher until they spill a little over the cups. A scarlet sash cords her waist, and her bright red heels scream "fuck me." But it's Bristol, so they could whisper it, and I'd still hear.

My dick presses against my jeans, poking into Qwest's hand and putting that knowing grin on her face. She assumes my sudden hard-on is for her, not my manager. I'm a fraud. This thing with Qwest has gone too far, and I'm going to have to do what I never wanted. I'm going to have to hurt her.

"Could we talk for a minute?" Bristol's eyes drop to Qwest's hand on my dick before popping back up and staring just past my shoulder. "I just need to go over a few things for tonight."

We've hardly spoken this week. All the hard work we both poured into this release over so many months, and when the project is colossally successful, we can barely look at each other.

"Sure," I mutter, not bothering to check if she's finally managed to look at me. "Pull up a seat."

"I need to go find Will anyway." Qwest kisses my cheek and steps away. "See you backstage."

She and Bristol exchange polite smiles on her way to climb the stage steps and disappear in the wings.

Bristol shifts from one foot to the other, touches the silky bare skin at her throat, bites her lip, moves her iPad from the crook of one elbow to the other. I sit in silence, waiting for her to settle and tell me what this is about. Finally, she sets her hip against the edge of the stage beside me.

"I know it's been a crazy week." She clears her throat, long lashes lowered and eyes fixed to the floor. "How are you?"

"Good." I keep my tone brusque. "What'd you need?"

She hesitates, probably still unused to the indifference I've displayed since our confrontation at Rhyson's house. Since the Spotted post.

"So for tonight," she says, glancing at her iPad. "We have you slated to do three songs."

"Yeah, we just rehearsed them."

"About that." Bristol sets her iPad on the stage. "I know you're doing 'Queen' with Qwest, obviously."

"Yeah, and 'Bruise'."

"For the third song," Bristol says, tracing the edges of her iPad without looking up. "The Target executive was wondering if you'd perform a song from their Exclusive deluxe version."

I already know where this is going, but I stay quiet, waiting for her to gather the audacity to ask me to do that song.

"They want 'Top of the World'," she says softly, hazarding a glance up at my face.

"I'm not doing that song." I give an adamant shake of my head. "Not tonight."

"Of course tonight." Bristol huffs an exasperated breath. "It's the perfect fit obviously. Your album is at the top of the charts. The song is called 'Top—"

"Do I look like I need you to break it down for me, Bristol?" The only thing moving on my face is one brow lifting. I'm barely breathing. "I understand why they want it. I'm just not doing it."

"We have a track for it. The band—"

"My not doing that song has nothing to do with having a live band or a track, and you know it." I hold her eyes captive with mine. "You didn't even want the song on the album in the first place."

"I know, but it's so good," she admits grudgingly. "It's their favorite of the ones we added. They want people to hear it and know they can only get it there."

"Too bad."

"How long are you going to do this?" Bristol asks.

"Do what?" I fold my arms across my chest, a physical barrier over the heart she jerked around like a kite for years.

"You know what."

"No, I wouldn't have asked if I knew what."

This feels good. This is my first real opportunity to growl and snarl at her since the album dropped. She's been so deliberately ghost, and I resent it. That she made this dumb decision with that dickhead and drove this wedge between us when I want to share all of this success with her. But I can't stand to look at her for more than two minutes without working myself into a rage.

"You're letting this thing with Parker color your decision making."

She dared to actually bring it up. To actually say his damn name to me.

"This 'thing with Parker', as you call it, is not the point." I slip razor blades between each word. "I'm not doing that damn song, and you and those executives can kiss my black ass."

"Wow." Irritation narrows her eyes to slits. "That's real professional."

"Professional?" I drop a laugh loaded with sarcasm. "And was it professional for you to go MIA the week of my debut release and send your junior flunky to handle me?"

It's strangely satisfying to see her cheeks flush the color of not-quite-ripe raspberries. I know I'm not being fair. Sarah did a great job, and not once did I have reason to complain. But I can't complain to Bristol about the thing I want to—the fact that she chose that entitled prick over me—so I'll complain about things that don't really matter.

She's right. Real professional, and I don't give a damn. "Hey, what's going on?" Rhyson asks from a few feet away.

Bristol and I glare at each other while we wait for him to reach us. How it got this bad, I'm not sure. I'm only sure that I'm making it worse. Every time I'm near her I want to pour accelerant all over my anger so it burns us both to ash.

"What are you fighting about?" Rhyson looks between us, his frown deepening the longer he studies our faces.

"I was telling Grip that the Target executives want him to do 'Top of the World'." Bristol sighs like I'm a thorn in her side. "But he won't."

"Bristol, could you give us a minute?" Rhyson asks.

"What?" Her expression climbs from irritated to outraged. "This is my job, Rhyson. I don't need you to—"

"If this is your job, then I am your boss." Rhyson's tone and face brook no argument. "And I said give me a minute with my artist."

"With your art . . ." Bristol folds her lips in to stem her words and draws a calming breath that doesn't seem to be working since she's still glaring at me. "Have at it, boss man."

She stalks off, her precipitously high heels clack clacking her indignation with every step she takes across the floor.

"You know you need to do this song, right?" Rhyson hops up beside me.

"No, I'm not . . ."

Reason swallows the rest of my sentence. Of course I know I need to do the song. But the last thing I want to do is get up in front of all these happy faces and sing about the first time I kissed Bristol or how she turns me inside out like a sweater running through the spin cycle.

"I'll do it." I run my hands over my face, exhaustion from the demands of the week landing on me like a brick house. "Whatever."

"This is exactly what I warned you about." Rhyson points a finger at me.

"I know you better get your finger out of my face." Involuntarily, my lips lift at one corner, and so do his. He laughs first, a small sound that loosens some of the tension bunching at my neck and shoulders. "I don't think this is going to work, Rhys," I say quietly after the short-lived laugh.

"What won't work?"

"Bristol, us working together." I tip my head back to look at the lights overhead with their multi-colored gels. "I don't want her to manage me anymore."

"Dammit, Marlon." Rhyson leans back, arms straight, heels of his hands pressed to the stage and supporting him. "You and Bristol work incredibly well together. Look at what you've accomplished."

"I know. I just . . . I can't do it. I don't want to do it." I look at him frankly. "I'll just keep antagonizing her until everything blows up, and we'll ruin even the chance to be friends some day."

"Is that what you want?" Rhyson asks. "To be her friend?"

"You know what I want." I tap out the bass line to "Top of the World" on my leg. "Wanted. But I'm finally accepting that won't happen. I only agreed to her managing me in the first place to be closer to her. Kai and I thought it would help my chances."

"Kai was involved in this shit storm?" He shakes his head. "That's what she gets for playing matchmaker."

"Her heart was in the right place." A bitter breath gushes past my lips. "Mine wasn't, I guess. You were right all those times you said I should give up on Bristol and let it go."

"Yeah, well. What do I know?" Rhyson shrugs carelessly, but

when he meets my eyes, he seems more careful than a few moments before. "I mean, what if I was wrong about Bristol? I've been wrong before. Like that one time in high school I was wrong."

"We both know you've been wrong a lot more than that." My smile starts but melts before it's fully formed. "But about this you were right."

"But, maybe if—"

"What are you saying?" I bunch my eyebrows into a scowl. "It's settled. I'm not working with her anymore."

I lace my fingers together behind my neck and heave a defeated breath.

"Dude." I meet his eyes with complete honesty. "I just can't."

Rhyson searches my face for a few seconds before nodding and sliding off the stage.

"So when?" he asks.

"After Dubai." I glance at my watch to see how late it is and hop off the stage, too. "I need to get ready."

"What do you want me to tell her?"

"Nothing." I bite the inside of my jaw, enjoying the slight pain. "I'll tell her myself."

"You sure?"

"If we're ever going to be friends again, then yeah. I need to talk to her about it. Right now, I can't be her anything. Not with things the way they are. Once I'm over her and have really moved on . . ."

I leave the thought half-done and shrug, heading back to get ready for the show because I have no idea what that will feel like.

CHAPTER 17

G_{RIP}

HIGH SCHOOL. SENIOR year. School of the Arts theatre. Empty except for Rhyson and me. We'd snuck up to the catwalk and, legs kicking over the sides, dreamed out loud. Compared to the success he'd had early in life as a concert pianist, Rhyson's dreams to write and produce music for other artists seemed modest. Mine, which were to be a voice to our generation, hear my music on the radio, and reach fans all over the world, seemed loftier than the catwalk we sat on that day.

Now Rhyson's onstage introducing me, applauding with everyone else in the packed club as I join him. I can't help but wonder if he ever thinks about the dreams we spoke into existence that day, the ones we worked into existence over the last decade.

"Here's the man with the number one album on the charts," Rhyson says, his smile wide and familiar. "How's it feel, man?"

"Surreal," I say into the mic. "I can't even believe it." "Well, believe it," he says. "You deserve it."

And I don't have to wonder if he thinks about that day, about those dreams. It's sketched on his face. The pride in his eyes and the excitement that practically vibrates off him. It isn't just my album. It's his label, something we're building together.

"Anything to say before you perform for us?"

"Just thanks to everyone for all the support." I look out over the crowd, straining to pick faces out of the clumps of people. I shield my eyes with one hand from the glare of the lights. "My mom's here somewhere."

"Over here, baby!" she screams from the left corner, making everyone laugh.

"You believed in me against every odd, Ma." I struggle to keep a smile in place, swallowing the emotion thickening in my throat. "There's no telling where I'd be if it weren't for you and every sacrifice you made so I could be here today."

"I love you," she yells back.

"Love you, too, Ma." I scan the room, packed but not so big it doesn't feel intimate. "Max and Sarah, all the engineering guys. Everyone who worked on the project, Prodigy's first, you guys are amazing. Thank you for all your hard work. Let's keep doing it."

Whoops and cheers come from the corner of the room where I know a good portion of the Prodigy team are gathered.

I could leave it there, move right into the three-song set and get this over with, but I can't. Even when we're barely speaking, when I can hardly look at her without getting pissed off, I can't ignore that so much of this night and of my debut album's success, I owe to Bristol. I don't have to scan the room or search the crowd. She's the compass in every room. I always seem to know exactly where she is. Where she always is when I perform. Backstage left.

"And Bristol."

I swing my head around to that spot where she usually watches from backstage. She's standing there, all business and sex in her suit, with her phone and those lips and those breasts and those heels that would dig into my ass with a sweet sting. Hearing her name catches her off guard, and she doesn't have time to pull that mask in place or blink away that vulnerability from her eyes. She's waiting, unsure of what I'll say considering how things stand.

"You take everything to another level," I say softly into the mic, unable to look away from the promise of storm in her cloud-gray eyes. "You're the hardest working, most committed person I know. Your passion for my work has been evident since the day we met. Tonight wouldn't be tonight without you."

"Thank you," she mouths, blinking rapidly and biting her lip.

There's no one in the room but her right now. We may as well be alone at the top of that Ferris wheel, lips seeking and hungry, trading breaths and heartbeats. The cheers, all eyes in the club on me, none of it registers. There's a web that traps us together, silky and fine, tensile and fragile. A sticky mess I've never wanted to escape until now.

Maybe it's time to let go . . .

I turn my attention back to the crowd before it gets awkward and make my smile as natural as possible. I have to shake this off. Truly this is the moment I've been waiting for and working for, and I'm not going to let my obstinate, misplaced feelings for Bristol ruin it.

"Where's Qwest?" I boom into the mic.

The room explodes with wolf whistles and catcalls and suggestive remarks as Qwest swaggers onstage, one hand wrapped around a mic, the other hand wrapped around her hip. Oversized safety pins tenuously hold scraps of material together on her tight, curvy body. Very little is left to the imagination, and I bet every man in here is imagining.

Except Rhyson, of course. He's backstage cuddled up with his wife, I'm sure.

The first hard beat of "Queen" drops, and it's like opening the gate on a charging bull. As my first verse starts, Qwest circles me in a sensual stalk that elevates the sexual tension so high the whole audience is probably lightheaded. When I reach the chorus, she bends over in front of me and starts twerking. I can barely get the words out I'm laughing so hard, and the audience is eating it like dessert. Camera phones flash all over capturing this. It'll be on YouTube,

Instagram, Twitter, and anywhere else they can find to upload it before the night is through.

When our song is over, Qwest wears my outer shirt as usual tied around her waist. At least tonight I'm wearing a T-shirt under it. I don't want to perform this next song with chest and abs out. "Bruise" means too much. I don't want to set it up, explain it, excuse it, defend it, or make either side of the black and blue debate feel better or worse.

"This song is called 'Bruise,'" I say simply and quietly once Qwest has left the stage. "It's my next single, and I hope the lyrics speak for themselves. I hope they speak up for the kids in my neighborhood who get pulled over for nothing or whose dignity is dinged and chipped from the time they understand what those flashing blue lights mean. I hope my words rise up on behalf of my cousin Greg and other cops who put themselves in the line of fire every day, running toward the dangers the rest of us flee. I hope this song is a dirge for lives lost on both sides of a debate that has divided us, when we should unite. I hope this song is common ground."

The last chorus is more spoken word than rap, with the music and the beat falling away. A capella. When the final word leaves my mouth, disappearing into thin air, it lands in the total silence I've come to expect when people hear the song for the first time. A silence loaded with contemplation. The sound of walls dropping and assumptions combusting. Ignorance running from the room. The trickle of applause swells to the loudest it's been all night in here, and now, my smile is real. That dream I sketched in the air with Rhyson, suspended above a theatre, to be a voice for my generation, that just happened.

I check stage right where I saw Rhyson last. He wears the same look he did the first time he heard "Bruise", like his eyes open wider every time. He grins and tosses his chin up. Amir stands just behind him, and I'm struck by the two friends who have been mainstays in my life. They come from completely different paths and are completely different types of men, but they are both exactly what I need them to be.

Seguing from "Bruise" into the last song I'd ever want to perform tonight is tough. I'd usually talk a little about the story behind the song, but "Top of the World" is no one's business but mine and Bristol's. Or I'd share what it was like to write it, but it wrote itself on a night when I couldn't sleep. I'd fucked some random chick, whose name I'm ashamed I can't even remember. The smell of her perfume clung to my sheets, hung on my body. She lay curled up beside me, sweaty, naked, and sated. Disgust and frustration and loneliness and longing waged a blood war in my veins while I wondered what Bristol was doing at that very moment. If she was in bed with some other guy, thinking of me. Or if she was in bed with some other guy, and I wasn't on her mind at all. And, yeah, I hated her. For a sliver of a second, I hated her for throwing up road blocks and smoke screens and barriers every time I got close enough to see she felt the same way. And there was just enough hate and too much passion to hold in. So, I'd rolled out of bed, lit a joint, and these words puffed from my lungs and fell from the burnt tips of my fingers.

I can't say any of that, so I just signal the drummer to drop the beat. And my tongue is a stiletto that breaks the seal of my lips. It cuts the lining of my jaw, every word slitting my throat. I'm bleeding out over the infectious sample of Prince's "I Wanna Be Your Lover," in a room full of people, and none of them know.

I exit the stage with the sound of their applause battering my ears. I hope the executives are happy with the pound of flesh I just carved out of myself for them. I hope Bristol's happy, too, hearing my feelings spread out and tied down on an altar like a still-breathing sacrifice for slaughter. I brush past her in the wings, deliberately not looking at her face. It's the first time I've performed the song live, and I hate it as much as I did the night I wrote it. And I love it just as much, too.

With the hard part—the performance—behind me, I'm determined not to waste another moment brooding over the woman who wants someone else, or at the very least, doesn't want me. We're popping bottles and celebrating in earnest. Only my mother would look right at home in VIP and with her very own bottle of Ace of Spades.

"Baby, I'm so proud of you." She takes a delicate sip straight from her bottle. "When Marlon was growing up, I always said my baby won't have any strikes. That was all I wanted. My dream for him was just staying out of jail and not having a bunch of nappy headed kids running wild all over the neighborhood."

"Ma, in your stories, why my imaginary kids always gotta have nappy heads?" I tease her with a grin, drawing from the bottle of Cristal on the table beside me.

"Because your imaginary baby's mama has no idea what to do with their hair." She cackles and passes a fresh bottle to Amir. "Then Grandma has to come in with bows and brushes to save the day."

Everyone cracks up. Kai and Qwest sit on either side of my mom, and her hilarious commentary keeps them in stitches. Luke, our friend since high school and a certified pop star in his own right, has been in the studio non-stop recording his next album, so he looks like a convict on furlough. He signed to Prodigy shortly after Kai. Bristol manages them both.

"Luke, where's Jimmi?" I ask. "I miss her crazy ass."

"She's in London." Luke's blue eyes are slightly glazed, maybe from smoking a little something. "She'll be back in a couple of weeks. Hates she missed it."

"She texted me, but I haven't had a chance to open it," I tell him. "She's actually back next week," Bristol pipes up from the corner of the velvet sectional taking up the entire wall of the VIP section.

Jimmi is the only non-Prodigy artist Bristol manages. They met on that fateful spring break trip, too, years ago and have been close ever since. If there's trouble to be gotten into, they'll get into it together. Jim's one of the few people who can corrupt Bristol into outrageous behavior.

Like walking naked into the ocean at midnight.

I didn't ask for the image of Bristol's long, slim body nearly naked plunging into the Pacific between waves and moonlight, but it floats to me unbidden. I wonder if she ever thinks about that night. About that string of nights when she pulled me into her unexpected depths where I've been drowning ever since.

"Well, if it isn't The One!" a slightly accented voice yells from a few feet away.

Hector, the owner of my favorite strip club in New York, Pirouette, crosses the space with sure, swift strides. His real name is Martin, but "Hector" suits his image of the first-generation Cuban- American who pulled himself up by the proverbial bootstraps. He launched his first high-end strip club in Miami, and New York soon followed. "Hector" has become infamous. His own mama probably doesn't call him Martin anymore.

"This is amazing, Grip." Hector squeezes into a small space between Amir and me, gaining a deep frown from my friend/body-guard/babysitter. "Feels like just yesterday you were in the strip club spinning for my grand opening in New York."

"That didn't even feel like work." I laugh because it's been a long time since I deejayed, and I miss it. "I haven't done it in forever."

"Come do it again!" Hector pushes an impatient hand through the dark hair that keeps flopping into his eyes. "You know we're opening a Pirouette here in LA in two weeks."

"For real?" I take another swill of my drink. "You doing big things."

"Be bigger if I had Mr. Number One spinning on opening night." Hector's already-impassioned expression brightens even more if that's possible. "And you and Qwest could perform 'Queen.'"

His VIP visit feels less spontaneous and more calculated with every idea he unpacks. I glance over at Qwest, but she's so deep in conversation with my mom, she didn't hear Hector's proposition.

Great.

Now I'll never convince Ma that Qwest and I aren't planning weddings and baby showers.

"We'll have to check Qwest's schedule." I take another look around our group. "I don't see her manager Will right now, but I can put you in touch."

"I hear Qwest's people drive a hard bargain," Hector says.

"Not as hard as Grip's people do," Bristol inserts, scooting down so she can hear the conversation.

"Well, hello there, mami." Hector's eyes touch every inch of Bristol from her bare shoulders to the heels stretching her already-long legs out even farther. "I don't believe I've had the pleasure."

"Hector, this is my manager Bristol," I say, my tone void of any warmth. I know Hector. I may not get to have Bristol, but there's no way I'm letting a sleaze bag like Hector anywhere near her.

"Nice to meet you." Bristol extends her hand, giving me an "is this guy for real" look when he lingers over her hand with a kiss. "When does your club open?"

"In two weeks." Hector drops his glance to Bristol's chest. She pretends not to notice but slides a few inches away from him and discreetly wipes her hand against the side of her pants.

"We'll be just getting back from Dubai." Bristol frowns and squints one eye. "But we may be able to make it work. I'll talk with Will to check Qwest's schedule."

"Did I hear my name?" Qwest excuses herself from the conversation with my mom and Kai, heading over to our corner where she plops on my knee. On reflex my hands go to her hips, steadying her. Bristol's eyes linger on my hands touching Qwest, but I refuse to read into it like I've done in the past. I refuse to think it bothers her.

"I have a few things I need to check." Bristol stands, smoothing a few wrinkles from her pants. "I'll reach out. Grip has your info, right?"

"He does, but I don't have yours." Hector's glance slides from her breasts and over her hips and legs before crawling back up to her face.

"Like I said, I'll reach out," she says wryly before turning to walk away.

Hector leans back to watch her go.

"Damn, Grip," he mutters, eyes still glued to Bristol crossing the room. "Your manager is fine as fuck. She like a little color in her life?"

He rubs his chin and waggles his eyebrows. "Like the color brown?"

"Not happening." The words come out like pellets, and irritation tightens my hands on Qwest's hips. She turns her head to study my face, which I know must look like a tundra.

Hector eyes Qwest in my lap.

"Seems to me you got your hands full, bruh." He laughs. "If you ain't hitting that, somebody needs to."

"She's got a man." Qwest leans back on my chest so her head snuggles into my neck. "She's dating Charles Parker. Right, Grip?"

Hector's face lights up with a cocky grin. "I got something for her I bet he ain't giving her."

"The hell you do," I snap. "Don't even think about it, Hector. Keep your greasy hands and beady eyes to yourself."

For a few seconds, our tight circle goes quiet. I feel Qwest studying me closely. The rein I've had on myself all night, all week, is slipping. I want to get out of here and take this face off. Take these reins off and just . . . rage in my loft playing something angry like Public Enemy at full blast. As much as I want to ignore it, forget about it, I'm still mad as hell that Bristol isn't mine. And pretending I don't care is wearing my ass out.

"She's Rhyson's sister and my friend." I harden my eyes when they meet Hector's. "And if you want me performing at your opening, take her off your hit list."

"You got it." Hector's hands go up defensively. "I wouldn't be a red-blooded male if I didn't try. You say she's off limits, she's off limits."

I jerk my head in a nod and gulp down a mouthful of Cristal and irritation.

"You okay, baby?" Qwest leans back and turns her head so she can whisper in my ear, her back pressed to my chest, her ass pressed into my crotch.

"Yeah. I'm good. Just tired." I roll my neck against the tension vising it. "It's been a long week."

I rub her arm, regret nipping at my insides because I don't think I can let this thing go on with Qwest much longer. It's gone deeper than it was supposed to. She's gone deeper than she was supposed to, and the longer I put this off, the worse it will be.

"I've got something to make you smile." She sits up, clapping as Will comes into our section. "You made it!"

"Yes, barely." Will hands her a black velvet box. "Traffic was a beast because of some accident."

"Thank you." Qwest takes the box and then turns to me. "A little gift to celebrate the number one spot."

"Oh, wow." A surprised breath escapes my lips. "I didn't expect anything. You didn't have to do this."

"I wanted to, and don't say wow till you've seen it." Qwest puts the box in my hands, eyes lit with anticipation. "Go ahead. Open it."

It's gotten quiet, and everyone's conversations have died out as they watch and wait for me to open the box. When I pop open the lid, I'm nearly blinded by the bling.

"Shit." My jaw drops. A diamond and platinum watch glints against the black velvet bed. "What the . . . Qwest, you really didn't have to do this."

"Well, I noticed you wearing this thing." She gestures to the nondescript black watch I always wear. "And I knew I needed to light that wrist up."

I bite back an objection when she undoes my old watch, which is made of nothing but cheap rubber and vivid memories. That day at the carnival, I won Bristol a whistle and she won me this no-name watch. We joked that they were the worst carnival prizes we'd ever seen, but I can count on one hand the times I've taken that watch off since that carnival. And now this mammoth, glittering hip-hop cliché is strapped to my wrist, and I already can't wait to get home so I can shove it to the back of a drawer.

"I don't know what to say." I turn my arm back and forth, the overhead lights bouncing off the watch and making me squint. "It's . .
. I've never had anything like it."

"Lemme see," my mother says. She comes over, grabbing my arm and admiring the watch. "Ooooh, Erica. So nice."

"Erica?" My eyes flick between my mother and Qwest.

"She told me to call her by her real name," Ma crows. "Ain't that sweet?"

"That's great." I look around on the floor and the couch, unreasonable panic ripping through me. "Where's my watch?"

"What do you mean?" Qwest frowns, looking down at my wrist. "You're wearing—"

"No, the other one." I move her off my lap and bend to search the darkened floor. "The black one. It was just here. Where . . ."

It doesn't take the strange looks from Qwest and Ma to know I sound like an idiot. I've barely glanced at the expensive new watch, but I'm on the verge of losing my shit because I can't find some cheap watch no one would even want.

But I want it.

"Do you see it?" I ask my mother. "Check down by your feet." "Baby, I don't see it," Ma says with a laugh. "But I doubt you'll miss it."

I don't answer as I continue to scan the floor and couch around me.

"Got it!" Amir says from the floor on his hands and knees. "I guess it fell."

He hands it back to me, and my heart slows. I almost had a stroke when I thought I'd lost the thing. Losing Bristol has left me in even more of a panic, only it isn't evident on the surface. It's like pins under my skin. Needles under my scalp.

Of all things, my stomach growls loudly. I frown and realize I'm starving.

"Do they have actual food here?" I ask no one and everyone. "Or is it all libation?"

"See he always had a way with words," Ma brags, touching Qwest's hand. "You know he started with poetry. Won a poetry contest in the sixth grade and has been writing ever since."

"Ma, don't," I groan. I know she's going to embarrass me. That's a given. It's just a matter of how much.

"I actually think I have a picture here." She digs around in her purse and pulls out a falling-apart wallet. "Here we go."

"I wanna see!" Qwest laughs and settles down beside my mother. "So do I." Kai shoots me a wicked grin. She knows I hate this stuff. "Are there any naked baby pictures in there?"

"Food?" I repeat. "Is there any?"

"Why don't we go back to the house?" Ma doesn't look up from the stack of pictures ranging from toddlerhood to adolescence she must carry in her purse. "I could make chicken and waffles."

"I vote for that," Amir says, smacking his lips. "I haven't had chicken and waffles in a long time."

"Boy, you came by the house last week and had chicken and waffles," Ma says.

"I know." Amir rubs his stomach. "A week is a long time in waffle years."

"Did that actually just come out of your mouth?" I raise both brows. "For real, bruh? Waffle years?"

He doubles up, flipping me off with both middle fingers.

"Okay." I stand up. "I'm gonna go grab my stuff from the dressing room before we head out."

Amir stands with me, but I wave him back to his seat.

"Please don't try to 'guard' me," I say. "I hate it when you do that."

"It is my job."

"Well, right now you're getting paid to sit your ass back down and leave me alone for a few minutes."

"Give a man a little money." Amir grumbles, grins, and takes his seat. "And he gets all new on you."

I'm still smiling about that when I enter the dressing room to collect my bag and the clothes I wore to the venue. I almost run right over Bristol leaving as I enter.

"Sorry." I grab her to keep her standing upright. I intend to let her go, but my palms linger on the warm, silky skin of her shoulders.

"No problem." She steps back, looking up the few inches to my face, her eyes guarded. "I was just, um, leaving. Straightening up and then leaving."

I notice her hands behind her back, and the shifty look on her face.

"What you got there?" I reach behind her, but she steps back, deeper into the room and out of my reach.

"Nothing." She shakes her head, a self-conscious smile tugging at the fullness of her lips. "It's just ... nothing."

"If it's nothing, why are you hiding it?"

I slide my hands down her arms until I encounter her death grip on the handles of the bag. I don't bother actually reaching for the bag, but give myself a few seconds with her pressed against my chest. She swipes her tongue over her bottom lip. I'm riveted by the motion of her tongue and how her breasts lift against my chest as her breath shallows. Her lashes flutter closed, and her sigh lands heavily in the quiet dressing room. She steps out of my hold and offers the bag to me, breaking the moment fusing our bodies together.

"For me?" I glance from the brightly wrapped box in the bag to find her gnawing on her lip, a tiny frown sketched above her eyes.

"Just a little something for, you know." She gestures vaguely in the air. "Congrats or whatever."

"Oh, you shouldn't have," I murmur, setting the bag on a side table so I can open the box.

She starts toward the door. "Well, I'll just—"

"Hold up." I gently shackle her wrist, pulling her up short and stopping her from leaving. Our eyes collide over her shoulder. "Don't you want to stay while I open it?"

"Obviously not." She tugs on her wrist uselessly. "Grip, come on. Let me go."

"I've been trying to," I say softly. "It's harder than you think."

She stops struggling, going still in front of me and pulling a breath in through her nose, huffing it past those cherry red lips. A fiery chord bridges the distance between our bodies, and I want to pull her close enough to burn me, to hurt me, to destroy me. Sometimes I don't think I care as long as she's close. I just want to feel her, even if it burns me alive.

But she pulls away.

"Like I said, it isn't much." She shrugs, clasping her hands in front of her while I rip the paper away. "Just something I kind of picked up on a whim."

When I open the box and see what's inside, I'm like a kid at

Christmas. The limited edition silver Jordans with the black sole and laces are like polka dot unicorns for a collector.

"You say you got these on a whim, huh?" I take them out and resist the temptation to remove my boots and put them on right now.

"Yeah." She shrugs, but I don't miss the anxiousness in her eyes or the way she twists her hands. "Just thought you might like them. I know they're not—"

Her words fall off a cliff when I hook an arm around her neck and pull her against me. I drop the shoes and bring my other hand to her waist.

"That's some whim." My voice dips to a husky whisper that disturbs wisps of hair escaping by her ear. "Considering there's only maybe ten pairs of these ever made."

"Really?" The word comes out high and breathy, and the controlled line of her mouth melts and softens. "I had no idea."

I drop my head until my forehead presses against hers.

"Thank you, Bris." I sneak a kiss into the hair pulled back at her temple. "I meant what I said tonight. I know how much you've done for this project. How much you've done for me."

She only answers with a nod, but her lashes fall to cover her eyes, and her hand holds me at my hip as if she might fall if she lets go. I'd love for us to fall together.

But we can't. Or she won't. Whatever it is, I refuse to let this feel like something it's not. Or something she won't allow it to be because I'll go to my grave believing Bristol cares about me. That doesn't do me any good when she chooses to be with someone else. And at least for now, so am I.

"I better get going." I pull back, but somehow, my hand finds her neck, and my thumb caresses the warm skin over her hammering pulse. Somehow, her hand is still at my waist. "My mom's making chicken and waffles."

"Sounds good." She looks at me, and though we both keep asserting that we need to go, we can't seem to separate.

"You wanna come?" I know she won't, but the question is out before I can stop myself.

"Um, I doubt your mother would appreciate that." Bristol looks at the ground, a wry grin teasing one corner of her mouth. "She and Qwest seem to be getting along well, which is great. I'm glad. I'm happy for them . . . for you."

She nods, like she's convincing herself as much as she's convincing me.

"I'm . . . yeah. Okay." She raises her glance from the floor. "Maybe I'll come another time. I've never had chicken and waffles together."

The smiles we trade carry traces of sadness. I don't know what we will become. I'm not looking forward to telling her she won't be my manager anymore. Obviously, any hope that we'll be lovers is fading fast. And I can't stand by and watch her with that asshole, so even friendship feels like torture. Whatever we will be, for a few minutes, we're . . . us. All I've ever wanted was for Bristol and me to be an us. I don't know what that looks like anymore, but I'll fight to keep her in my life.

Later.

But not while I can still taste her wild kisses in the fun house from years ago, where even distorted in mirrors, our bodies looked right together. So letting go of the us I always thought we would be . . . it's too soon for that.

"I better get going," I say. "They're waiting for me."

My hand falls from her neck, and the fluorescent lights glint off the watch on my wrist. Bristol's eyes follow my arm down to my side.

"Nice watch," she says, her eyes set on the gaudy thing that feels like an albatross tied around my wrist.

"Yeah." I lift it for my own inspection.

Her lips concede a smile before leveling out.

"Grip, Ms. Mittie said come on!" Amir's voice reaches us just before the door opens and he appears, flicking a surprised glance between Bristol and me. "Oh, sorry. I didn't know you were in here, Bristol."

"It's okay." She smooths her hair. "I was just going. I assume you're in for chicken and waffles?"

"Best believe it." He grins a little uneasily, still not sure what he walked in on. "You coming?"

"No, I need to go," she says, glancing at her watch.

"Parker waiting for you?" I ask grimly. The thought of him at her house, in her bed, or her in some penthouse with him, erases the goodwill of the last few moments.

"No." She looks back over her shoulder, one brow lifted at the return of my censure. "He's still in India."

She makes her way to the door, stopping to give Amir a hug. He's one of those few she loves. They couldn't be more different, but they get each other. In the beginning, I was their common denominator, but they've formed their own friendship over the years.

"Your passport is current, right?" She pulls out of the hug and pats the side of his face affectionately. "You ready for Dubai?"

"More than ready." Amir rubs his hands together. "I hear they got some of the most beautiful scenery in the world."

"I have a feeling you're not talking about the landscape." She laughs and heads for the door. "Sarah will get you all the details."

"Hey, Bris," I say.

She turns to me, the ease she shared with Amir evaporating as she waits for me to finish. "Speaking of Sarah, why don't you let her reach out to Hector?"

"Sarah?" She frowns, but nods. "Okay. Why?"

I could tell her that soon Sarah will be handling all of my day-to-day. Or I could tell Bristol that Hector has a thing for her, and I don't like guys who have a thing for her.

"Why not?" I counter, since we don't already have enough to argue about.

"Because it's my job." She rests a fist on either hip. "Because I'm usually the first point of contact, and—"

"How did Rhyson put it earlier?" I touch my chin and glance up at the ceiling like I'm trying to remember. "Oh, yeah. If this is your job then I'm your boss, and because I said so."

That goes over about as well as it did when Rhyson said it, but the irritation clouding her expression when she leaves is better than what we were feeling before Amir came in. A bristly Bristol is safer than the vulnerable one who makes me want to kiss her and make her scream my name.

"So?" I grab my box of one-of-ten kind Jordans and head for the door, checking to see if Amir is following. "Chicken and waffles?"

CHAPTER 18

B<small>RISTOL</small>

ARE YOU THERE, God? It's Bristol.

Please make it stop.

For the love of all that's holy, if Qwest kisses him one more time, I'm breaking out my Dramamine. And the woman has a perfectly good, overstuffed leather seat. Must she perch on Grip's knee the whole time? The poor man's leg must be asleep by now. I mean, sure she's small, but still . . . all that ass . . .

Whoever said traveling by private jet was "flying in style" was never trapped in close quarters with the hip-hop lovebirds, also known as Grip and Qwest, for sixteen hours.

They look great together. Perfect together. I get why their fans still have #GripzQueen trending and want more of them as a couple. It's great. He's moved on. He looks happy. She's happy. Hell, even his mother is happy. In a small way, I helped orchestrate this. The least I can do is watch my handiwork unfold.

Only I can't.

I pull my sleep mask over my eyes and lie back. I'll just drift off into the darkness, take advantage of the quiet.

"Excuse me, Bristol." A low whisper comes from beside me. So much for quiet.

I lift one corner of the mask to peer at Meryl in the seat beside me.

"Sorry." She nudges her glasses up the bridge of her nose with an index finger. "I had a few questions."

Of course you do.

"Yes?" I draw on my dwindling reservoir of patience to respond with some civility. The girl has been our freaking shadow, and I'm regretting bringing her with us to Dubai, but I don't see where we had much choice. The price you pay for publicity.

"When do I get my sit-down with Grip and Qwest together?"

"It will be the middle of the night when we arrive in Dubai," I reply. "So we'll go to sleep, acclimate our bodies some. I thought you guys could do the interview over brunch tomorrow?"

"Oh, that works." Meryl jots something down in the notebook I've never seen her without. "And the desert shoot with Grip? Can that still happen?"

"Yes. I just need to confirm details with my liaison there. I think it can happen tomorrow afternoon, if your photographer will be ready?"

"Yeah, should be fine." Meryl looks down the aisle to where the photographer she brought along snores faintly. "I think he wants to keep it simple."

"Simple we can do." I lower the sleep mask and cross my fingers that she'll leave me alone.

"I've never flown on a private jet," she says. "Hmmm." I refuse to encourage her.

"I guess you have, huh? I mean, you're dating Charles Parker, so of course you've been on a private jet. We saw the pictures."

"Hmmm."

My monosyllable won't give this little newshound anything she doesn't already have. Parker said he would "take care of" the media's impression that we're dating. He needs to deal with it soon.

I've never been sure I believed in God.

My family wasn't religious in the least. In a clan of prodigies and pianists, a concert hall was our cathedral. But here in a vast desert of Dubai, I'm positive that only the deft hand of a higher power could have crafted beauty like this. Not the rolling landscape of sand and sun, but the right angle of jaw lightly dusted with shadow, the bold slant of cheekbones, the heavy sweep of brow and lashes, the lavish spread of soft lips and white teeth.

"Grip, could you turn a little to your left for me?" the photographer asks from behind his rapidly clicking camera. "That's it, and just prop your foot up?"

Grip bends his knee, setting his foot against the quad bike he's leaning on. Wide rips in his dark wash jeans flash the sculpture of muscles in his thighs. The slashes in his Straight Outta Compton T-shirt give glimpses of the bronzed skin wrapped around his ridged torso. Even in the hour we've been out here on the glorious Red Dune, the sun has bronzed him, heated the rich, caramel-colored skin to a deeper hue. "We almost done?" Grip asks for maybe the tenth time. "It's hot as hell out here."

"Sorry." Meryl scrunches her expression into an apology. "Paul, how close are we to getting what we need?"

"Just a little bit longer," Paul says distractedly, still snapping photos. "I want to get a few more before the light changes."

"If by light you mean that sun beating down on my head for the last hour," Grip says, a grin tipping one side of his mouth. "I'm ready for it to change."

"Sorry." I say. "Almost there."

His eyes flick to me briefly, sliding over my arms and shoulders in the tank top I've tucked into my black jeans. He hasn't looked at me, has barely spoken to me since we landed in Dubai. As much as I've pushed him away, avoided him, I miss looking into his eyes and seeing the things we don't say to each other, but feel, even though I've never voiced those feelings to him, and probably never will. One day

I'll look into his eyes and they'll be void of whatever he felt for me before. It'll be gone because I killed it. Maybe it's already dead.

"And we're done." Paul lowers his camera and squints up into the bright sun overhead. "Just in time."

Grip relaxes against the ATV, running big hands over his head. His hair has grown just a little since he cut out the locs. Still not long enough to pull.

Right. Must stop thinking of someone else's man in terms of pulling his hair when he comes inside me since . . . he never will.

"Any chance I could take this thing out?" Grip asks the guide who brought us out here, patting the huge ATV.

"To-to ride, yes?" the man asks in his stilted English, his expression uncertain.

"Yeah." Grip's smile is all persuasion. "Come on. I'll sign a waiver or whatever anyone else would do."

"Alone?" the guide asks with a frown.

"I was gonna take her with me." I'm knock-me-over-with-a-feather shocked when Grip tips his head at me. Since he's barely acknowledged me in days. "You down to ride, Bristol?"

Maybe it's the desert heat suddenly beading sweat on my neck, sand in my throat so I can't breathe easily. Maybe I didn't eat enough at lunch, and I'm lightheaded. More likely, it's Grip's gorgeous eyes waiting on me, resting on me when he's barely looked at me in what feels like forever.

"Um, well . . . I guess so." I search his face for some clue in this puzzle.

"Good." He nods and turns to the guide. "There's a set path, right?"

"Yes, but . . ." The poor little man still isn't sure, but sighs and relents. His supervisor probably told him to give the rich Americans whatever they want. Being guests of the prince probably doesn't hurt our case. "I'll get papers."

"And you'll take them back?" Grip points to Meryl and Paul. "Yes, of course."

I glance at Meryl because I feel her glancing at me.

"So I guess I'll see you guys back at the hotel," I direct my comment to Meryl and her curious eyes. "The party is at eight o'clock."

"I'm not sure how to dress for a royal Sweet Sixteen Party," Meryl says, splitting her attention between me and Grip, who's signing paperwork.

"I'd skip it if I could. I'm so ready to go home tomorrow."

"I guess I'll have everything I need for the story," Meryl says. "I think it's going to be awesome, especially with Grip hitting number one, and this gorgeous setting for the cover."

"Yep." I listen to Meryl with half an ear as Grip walks over. "Thanks for everything, Meryl."

Grip's slow smile makes a little bit of color bloom on her cheeks. I, unlike him, am not oblivious to her crush. "I can't wait to see how it turns out. See you at the party tonight."

Without waiting for her response he returns to the guide who has the helmets for him.

"Come on, Bris," he yells, swinging his leg over the ATV.

"See you tonight," I tell Meryl hastily as I go to join him.

The guide gives us some quick instructions. Grip nods, but it's obvious he's only half-listening. He and Rhyson love these things. The prospect of riding one on the Red Dunes has him excited and impatient to get on with it.

I climb on the back, not sure about this. Not sure why he asked or why I'm going. I slip my arms around his warm, hard body. My fingers brush against ladders of muscle peekabooing through the rips in his shirt. I jerk my fingers back, unprepared for the jolt the intimate touch sends through me.

"Hold on," Grip says, his voice a little muffled by the helmet. "Or fall off. Those are your options."

Riding wrapped around that hot, hard body, my thighs bracketing the power of his? The center of my body fitted to the curve of his ass? And the primal growl of this desert beast carrying us over the sand, vibrating beneath me for the duration of the ride? As horny as I am, I'll come before the ride is over. Not a good look.

Using the electric boyfriend in my suitcase would be less mortifying.

"Another option would be not to ride at all." I scoot back and lift my leg to get off.

"Too late."

Before I can get any further, Grip revs the engine and takes off.

I'm forced to hold onto him tightly or get dragged by one leg. "Motherfucker," I mutter through my helmet.

"What was that?" Grip shouts over the engine.

"I said you could have warned me," I scream back.

I've seen Rhyson and Grip ride at the beach, but this is so far beyond that. The dunes climb so high and drop so low, making my stomach loop with each crest and valley. No matter how much I try to put some distance between our bodies, the motion of the vehicle, the speed of our ride pulls me inexorably into him. My breasts flatten against the wide, solid expanse of his back and shoulders. His muscles shift and flex beneath my arms with every rise, fall, twist and turn. Involuntarily, my limbs stiffen as I fight the pull toward his body, not just gravitational, but the sensual tug he always exercises on my senses.

"Relax, Bristol," Grip shouts over his shoulder. "Or you'll take us both down."

I give in, allowing the force and speed to collide our bodies. My legs mold to him, my nipples pebble at his back. I know I'm wet, and him securing my arm tighter around his waist with a rough hand doesn't help. To distract myself, I take in the scenery rushing past us. We soar over this mountain of scarlet sand, so high if I reached up to touch the azure sky, my palms might come away blue. The sun, high and saffron, splashes violet and pink through the clouds, a child playing with watercolors. Vivid color saturates the landscape, like a fresco stretched and painted, left out to dry in the sun.

We stop at the pinnacle of a dune, and just sit there for a few moments, the quad an idling beast beneath us. Grip kills the engine, swinging one leg over to get off. I carefully follow suit.

I steal a glance at Grip, who has walked a few feet away and surveys the same vibrant vista that captivated me during our ride, the helmet hanging from his hand. I take a few steps until I'm right in front of him, ready to ask what we're doing out here and why he brought me if he has nothing to say. The guide gave him a black bandana to wear over his nose and mouth, protection from the sand flying from our wheels. With just his dark eyes and the slashing, inky brows visible above the bandana, he looks part outlaw, part Bedouin prince. He stows the helmet and pulls the bandana beneath his chin, revealing the rest of his face, the lips finely chiseled and full, the strong, square chin. He squints against the sun, his bold profile sketched into the horizon behind him, and my heart performs a perfect ten somersault.

It's so quiet, the air rides a fine line between peace and desolation. It's like we're in a vacuum, void of time. Like we're the last two people on a deserted planet, and everything except him and me and what's between us dissipates. Every thought escapes me, except one.

"I miss you," I whisper.

His head jerks around, his eyes meeting mine, going so narrow his long lashes tangle at the edges.

"You don't get to say that to me, Bristol."

I know why he says it, but it still feels like rejection.

"Grip, I just mean . . . your friendship. With things the way they've been, I miss us as friends."

"My friendship?" He cocks his head, a humorless laugh escaping him and echoing over the dunes. "We're not friends. Not right now."

"We are," I insist. "I need that."

"You need." Grip wads the bandana up in one hand and clenches the back of his neck with the other. "I've let you have that, let you do that, for too long. Ignore what I need. Fuck what I want. I've settled for whatever I could get from you for years."

I want him to stop, but anything I could say to stop him stalls on my lips, so he just keeps going.

"Even this setup, you managing me, was an attempt to be closer to you," he says, anger powering his words. "And what do you do? Go off and start dating that asshole. Choosing him when I've been patient. When I've been here."

The explanation I should have given him weeks ago fills my mouth, collects on my tongue. I know if I tell him the truth about Parker, it could mess things up with Qwest. And I want to. Even though it may mean the end of them, I want to. I'd rather have the back and forth of him wanting and me resisting than not having him at all. It isn't fair, but sometimes we do things that aren't fair to protect ourselves. To survive.

"I've let you make all the rules, but I'm changing them. I have to," Grip says before I can decide what I should say. "I was going to wait, but now's as good a time as any. You won't be managing me anymore."

And just like that, the words I would say are sawdust in my mouth.

"Wha-what?" I never stammer. I have this one part of him, of his life I've allowed myself, and he's taking even that away, and it makes me stutter. "What do you mean?"

"Sarah's going to handle my day-to-day—"

"Sarah?" My strident voice punctures the surrounding quiet. "Sarah isn't a manager. She's my assistant."

"I know." Grip nods, his expression pinched. "Like I was saying, she'll just handle the day-to-day stuff till I find a good fit for my manager."

"I'm a good fit!" Stupid tears dampen my eyes, and emotion watermarks my throat as the hurt rises inside me. "You have the number one album in the country. I'm not saying that's because of me, but—"

"Of course I know you're a huge part of that." He frowns and tosses the bandana back and forth between his hands. "This isn't about that."

"I did a good job." My voice falls to a dismayed whisper.

"I don't want to be your job." He blows his frustration out in an extended sigh. "I never wanted that. I wanted . . . more, and know that we're both with other people and it's obvious what I wanted can't happen . . ."

"What?" I demand, crossing my arms under my breasts, steeling my heart. "Then what?"

"I thought if I couldn't have a relationship with you, I didn't want anything."

His words crash land in the pit of my stomach. I grasp desperately at my composure, determined he's got as much of me as he'll get. My dignity at least is mine.

"But I was wrong, Bris."

His anger fading, his voice almost gentle, he reaches for my hand and dips his head to catch my eyes. I resent how my insides start melting.

"I do want us to at least be friends," he continues. "Right now I don't like who we are. Sniping at each other. The arguing and antagonism. It isn't us. I think we just need to go our separate ways and let things even out, so down the road, we can be friends again."

"So you just ruin a great partnership?" I shake my head and snatch my hand away, refusing to believe this is his solution. "When we talk to Rhyson about this—"

"He already knows."

"He knows?" Betrayal chokes my words. "You talked to him about this already? You decided this without talking to me first?"

"It isn't a decision we're making together," Grip says. "I decide who manages me, and it just can't be you right now."

I'm done with this shit. I shove my helmet back on and take my spot on the back of the ATV, waiting for him to get on.

"Bristol, let's talk about this."

"Oh, now you want to talk?" I snap. "After you've gone to my brother and gotten me fired?"

"Fired?" He frowns. "Come on. It isn't like that. You have plenty of other artists you're managing."

He doesn't get it. Of course I have plenty to do. Between Kilimanjaro, Luke, Kai, Rhyson, and Jimmi, I could have two more assistants and still need help with everything I do for all of them. But if Grip and I aren't lovers, and we're not working together, and we can't even be friends, then we're nothing. I haven't been "nothing" to Grip since the day we met.

"Take me back to the hotel," I say woodenly. "Bris."

I pour my anger into the look I level on him. "Right. Now."

He probes my eyes, and I make sure all he sees is anger. I stuff the hurt, bury the pain, keeping an impenetrable shield over my face, over my heart. He finally climbs onto the quad and starts the engine.

As we ride back, I resist the forces, physical and otherwise, that would slot our bodies together. He doesn't encourage me to hold him any tighter. He doesn't urge me to relax, to hold on, now that he's letting go. Maybe he senses that anything he said would bounce off me like a coin from a sheet drawn taut. I just want to get through this ride and back to the States. The glamour that shrouded these ruby-tinged dunes on our ride here lifts, leaving stark reality. What I thought was peace is actually the loneliness of an arid land. The Bedouin prince doesn't want me anymore, and all that's left is this dry, barren desert.

It's nothing but dust and sand.

CHAPTER 19

HELL HATH WINGS.

This airplane is pretty much airborne hell. If I'd thought the flight to Dubai was torture, the flight home would give Dante new inspiration.

"Grip, what's wrong, baby?" Qwest asks . . . you guessed it . . . sitting on his lap.

"Nothing." He sits with his hands on the armrest while she snuggles into the nook of his arm and shoulder. "I'm good."

"You sure?" She squeezes his shoulder. "You're so tight."

"Just a long few weeks." His head drops back against the seat. "I'll be glad to get home."

"I know how to loosen you up." She inches closer and whispers in his ear, a husky laugh invading the space where Will and I sit across from them. Grip's eyes open to clash with mine. Despite my best efforts, I can't look away. I can't help but remember what he said to me that night on the roof. That I can't keep my eyes off him. It's true, but it shouldn't be an issue any more since he won't have me around. I deliberately look away and down to the phone in my lap.

"Great idea," Grip says.

They stand and walk to the back where there is a bed. I don't look up even at the sound of the lock turning. I guess it's the Mile High Club for them. My jaw clenches. My lips tighten, but otherwise I show no sign that it bothers me.

"What's wrong with you?" Will asks from beside me.

Okay. Maybe I'm not hiding it as well as I thought.

I convinced Meryl that Will and I needed to discuss a few things, so she should probably sit with the photographer. Looks like I won't fare much better with Will.

"Oh, nothing." I roll my neck and stretch in the wide legged jeans I chose to wear for the flight. "Just tired, I guess. You must admit it's been a lot lately."

"Yeah, Grip's on top."

"Qwest, too," I murmur, rubbing the denim covering my legs. "'Queen' is still number one."

"She'll want Grip for her next album. You know that. We'll need to coordinate."

A gust of air imitating a laugh rushes past my lips. "Oh, there's no doubt she'll want him."

Will turns in his seat to stare at my profile. I ignore him, taking my laptop from the bag by my seat and answering a few emails.

"What's up with you and Grip, Bristol?"

My fingers pause over the keys for just a second before I resume typing. "What do you mean?"

Will's fingers cover mine over the keyboard.

"Stop." He waits for me to look at him. "I know there's something going on. If it affects my artist, I need you to level with me. Are you guys . . ."

I fill in the blanks. He has picked up on something obviously. I'm glad I can look him straight in the eyes and tell the truth. Though, I can look people straight in the eyes and lie just as easily.

"Grip and I have been friends for a long time, Will, but it isn't like that."

"You sure?" Will asks. "Sometimes I think I pick up a vibe between you guys."

"Like I said, we've been together a long time." I shrug, slamming my laptop closed. I don't feel like faking work right now. "Friends for a long time. That's all."

"Okay, good." Will laughs his relief and leans back in his seat. "'Cause I'm pretty sure Qwest's in love with that guy."

His words spear me right through the middle. I could see that for myself, of course. She's completely into Grip. And he really likes her, but I know he doesn't love her. I don't want anyone to get hurt. If Grip stops trying with her, breaks things off, she'll be hurt. If he keeps trying and really falls for her, I'll keep hurting. In neither scenario am I brave enough to do anything about it, to stop this train I'm at least partially responsible for setting on its course.

Sixteen hours just fly by when I don't have to stare at Grip and Qwest the whole time. They never came back out. I guess they put that bed to good use. The thought of him inside her, of her wrapped around him takes my breath with a sharp pain. I grab my bag and head toward the exit. As soon as I step onto the tarmac, I spot a black SUV with a vaguely familiar figure standing to the side. The man who accompanied Parker that night in Vegas. I think Clairmont was his name. I already know who will step out of the vehicle before Parker appears.

"You're a lucky girl." Meryl comes to stand beside me. "We can't all have billionaire boyfriends to come home to."

"Lucky me." I give her my fakest smile ever.

Will joins us, accessorizing his roguish grin with a wolf whistle. "No wonder you looked at me like I was crazy when I asked about you and Grip," Will says. "I almost forgot you have one of the richest men in the world on a string."

Right about now I'd love to choke Parker with said string.

"I'll touch base about the Pirouette gig in the morning," I say, not acknowledging his comment. I scrounge up a smile slightly more sincere than the one I offered Meryl. "I'll see you there tomorrow night. Get some rest."

I start toward the SUV like I had expected it to be there waiting. Halfway to the SUV, Parker covers the ground between us swiftly, stepping into my path.

"It's been too long," Parker says. Equal portions of ownership and lust mix in the eyes studying me. He takes my bag and snakes an arm around my waist, pulling me into him. His erection pokes my stomach, and I draw a shallow breath.

"Someone's happy to see you," he whispers through my hair, into my ear.

I can't take it. I didn't want to cause a scene, especially with Grip and Qwest deplaning behind me, but I instinctively pull out of his body lock.

"What are you doing here, Parker?" I leave my irritation close to the surface where he can see it. "How did you know I was landing today?"

"I have my sources," Parker says with a smile. "I have my ways."

He wraps possessive fingers around my elbow, and I jerk out of his hold again.

"Don't." I chop the word up and serve it cold. "You said you would fix this. To spare you the public embarrassment, I've left it to you. You've done nothing to address the rumors and then show up here like my long-lost lover. Who the hell do you think you are?"

"Who do I think I am?" His voice is a brick in a kid leather glove, a buttery soft blow. "You know who I am, Bristol, and I'm here to remind you who you belong to since you seem to think this is a negotiation. It's not. I've waited. I've been patient. That's over."

"Belong?" I keep my voice low and trap my outrage between Parker and me. I can practically feel Grip's eyes on us, and this could get ugly quick. "Parker, you're right. This isn't a negotiation because I'm giving you nothing, and I want nothing except for you to leave me the hell alone."

He grabs me again, and I jerk my arm, but this time Parker doesn't let go.

"Bristol." Grip's deep voice rumbles from behind me, and I go still, my eyes snagging with Parker's. The less contact he has with Grip the better.

I turn to face Grip, still clamped to Parker's side.

"Hey." I curve my mouth into a smile that I hope fools him. "What's up?"

His eyes move from Parker's iron hold on me to my face. The concern, the question in his eyes, doesn't bode well for things remaining drama-free.

"Everything okay?" he asks. "You need a ride home?"

"She has a ride home," Parker answers before I can. "It's Grip, right?"

Grip's icy eyes freezer burn Parker's face.

"Bristol can speak for herself." Grip's answer comes dangerously soft.

"Of course she can." Parker leaves a soft kiss at my temple. "Tell the man, Bristol."

The muscle knotting along Grip's jaw tells me I need to diffuse this. Even as angry as I am with him, I can't have him caught in Parker's crosshairs. He's mad with me, and I'm mad with him, but we're both still trying to protect each other.

"I'm fine, Grip." I loosen the hold Parker has on me so I can loop my elbow through his. "I'd forgotten Parker was picking me up."

"You sure?" He makes the mistake of touching my hand, and I feel Parker stiffen beside me. He's inspecting Grip with new, alert eyes.

"I am." I pull my hand away and pat his shoulder. "Your girlfriend is waiting. It's sweet of you to check, but I don't want to keep you away from Qwest."

He glances over his shoulder to find Qwest walking up with Will in tow, her eyes inquiring about the tableau playing out on the tarmac.

"Okay." He still doesn't seem sure, looking at Charles Parker like he might be Charles Manson. "We'll touch base about Pirouette tomorrow then?"

"I'll have Sarah call you." I inject a little venom into the statement, a small jab that he'll feel, but no one else will notice. "May as well start as we mean to go, right?"

He sighs and turns to join Qwest and Will without saying another word.

I keep my silence until we reach the SUV. I stop in front of Clairmont who stands guard at the door.

"Take me home right now." My voice and glare are low-level radioactive.

I don't wait for Clairmont's response before climbing through the open rear door and waiting for the reckoning that's long overdue between Parker and me. As soon as the door closes, I turn on him.

"Let's get something absolutely straight," I bite out. "You and I are not in a relationship. We aren't dating. We aren't getting married. I had to be so far under the influence of hard liquor I didn't even know I was in the world to fuck you again after a decade, and I guarantee that was the last time you get anywhere near this pussy."

Maybe I went too far, too hard. I've seen Parker's eyes cold, but they've always held a warm center for me. There aren't even trace amounts of heat in the subzero look he directs my way.

"Careful, Bristol." He covers my hand with his, a gesture intended to smother. "You don't want to make me angry."

"Why?" I elevate my brows to the appropriate level of disdain. "Would I not like you when you're angry? Who are you? The Incredible Hulk? And like I've told you before, you don't scare me."

"Maybe I should. Love and hate and fear and respect are all bedfellows."

"That sounds like one messed up orgy, if you ask me."

"Huh." His casual shrug comes at odds with the whipcord tension of his shoulders. "Maybe you and I will try the real thing once we're married, and you can tell me how you like it."

"I'm not a doll in the window." I shove his hand away from me and press my body into the leather seat as far from his as I can. "You don't just decide you want me and expect me to fall in line. How many ways can I tell you it isn't happening?"

"Is there someone else?" The question falls from his tongue so smoothly, but I know there's a dagger tucked into the silk of his words.

"If there were someone else, it wouldn't be any of your business."

"You know, through the years, I've given you space to sow your oats, so to speak, but I need to settle down. You've been groomed for me, Bristol, since we were kids. I'm ready for this to happen."

"You're crazy, and I don't want to see you again, Parker."

"And I want to see you for the rest of my life." He crooks stiff lips into a one-cornered smile. "Is that what they call an impasse?"

"No, an impasse is when there is no apparent solution." I channel all my frustration into my words. "I have a solution. Leave me alone. It's something stupid our parents dreamt up. Let it go."

Through the tinted window I see that we're already in my drive-way. My cottage is my refuge. I need to get inside, lick my wounds from the disagreement with Grip, and shower Parker's touch away from my body.

"This is over," I tell him. "Don't call me again. Our families will, of course, remain close, but we don't have to. I don't want to."

"You don't decide how this ends, Bristol." A fiery tongue of rage licks through the cold eyes. "I do."

I nod to Clairmont, who opens the door and holds my luggage. I take the bag from him, not wanting him or Parker anywhere near my front door.

"Either you address the rumors in the press," I tell Parker, who watches me stonily from the back seat. "Or I'll do it. That's the only end you can control."

I don't look back as I make my way up the cottage drive, but I know he's still there and he's still watching. He won't let this go.

My cottage, though empty and completely quiet, welcomes me home like a friend. This place is all mine, from the decorations I personally chose to the plants I potted myself. Of all the things I've accomplished, my home is one of the things that makes me most proud.

I drag the luggage back to my bedroom and collapse onto the bed I didn't get the chance to make before I left for Dubai. The last few hours land on me like bricks. I don't even bother stripping away my clothes, but crawl in just as I am, under the fluffy duvet. I toe my boots off under the covers, leaving the shoes in the bed with me.

I have no idea how Parker will retaliate. That nefarious brain of his is hatching a plan to either trap me or to make me suffer for defying him. Not wanting him, not grasping the privilege of his desire is, in his mind, my gravest infraction. If he had an inkling of my feelings for Grip, that would add insult so egregious to an injury so deep, I have no idea how he would retaliate. But I know it would be swift and unreasonable.

On top of that, the full implications of Grip firing me unravel the last of my fraying composure. I'll have no place in his life. He wants us to "go our separate ways."

Separate?

When I've felt more connected to him than to anyone else? Even when I was spitting mad over Tessa, I felt his guilt and his regret. I felt how it tore him up that I left and gave no sign we would ever make good on the promise of the week we shared. Wanting him, pushing him away, watching him with other women, knowing I could stop it but too afraid to try. What I want more than anything, I deny myself. I deny him.

I sit up in bed, longing for all I have left of that week we shared. I open the drawer housing all my vibrators and sex toys, reaching to the very back until I touch a key. I carefully unlock the bottom drawer and pull out the worn leather volume of poetry a boy gave a girl years ago, a guarantee of his affections. The page corners are dog-eared, and the margins are filled with notes written in a brusque, masculine hand. I trace the bold strokes of Grip's handwriting, the audacious hope in his g's and p's, the impatience of the I's he took no time to dot and his hastily half-crossed t's.

I flip the page to a poem so familiar I could almost recite it backward, Neruda's "Sonnett LXXXI." In one of my favorite lines, the poet tells his love that already she is his, and implores her to rest with her dream inside his dream. That he alone is her dream. The note of possession, the inextricably linked futures, speak to me, especially with Parker's possessive claims still ringing in my ears. I would never belong to him, but how would it feel to love someone so deeply you relinquish yourself that way? To embrace the responsibility of them belonging to you. And to know whatever the future holds, you face it together. Whatever you accomplish, you celebrate together. When there is pain, you endure it together. I'm not sure I'll ever know.

Grip's scrawled note written to the side in black Sharpie cuts my heart.

BRISTOL, never forget our ocean. Remember our last night together. Your dream was inside my dream. Please believe that I would never hurt you. Give me a chance to explain. I need that second chance.

I CAN'T READ ANYMORE. Not that I need to. I've read each poem, each note countless times since he mailed this book to me. By then I understood the curse I carried in my blood. Loving too deeply, too fiercely, too wholly. A love like that for the wrong man would ruin you.

I'm about to replace the book of poems when something silver in the drawer caches my eye. It's a cheap whistle, tarnished by age. I pull it out by the discolored string from which it dangles. I don't have to blow it to hear its piercing shrill. It's as sharp and clear in my head as the smell of funnel cake and the cool night air on my face at the top of a Ferris wheel.

I fall back into my bed, placing the whistle and the book of poems on the pillow beside me. They're like artifacts from another age that was marked with the promise of love. Marred with the agony of loss. It wasn't eons ago. It wasn't a light year away. It was eight years, and now the man who scrawled in these margins and presented this whistle to me like a piece of his heart, is cutting me out completely. This is all I have left of that night, of those days. Of the man who begged me to never forget.

CHAPTER 20

G_{RIP}

MY BODY HAS no idea which damn time zone it's in. I couldn't sleep last night, but it wasn't the jet lag. I kept thinking about the interaction with Bristol on the tarmac. Something's off with Charles Parker. When Bristol jerked away from him, I knew it. I think I've known, but that one moment confirmed the suspicion I hadn't allowed to fully form until yesterday. I tried to dismiss it as a lover's quarrel, but I still found myself standing in front of them on the tarmac, prepared to punch Parker if he grabbed her like that again, even with that meathead security guard standing there.

I check my playlist one last time. Typically when celebrities deejay, there's little pressure to be any good. They don't have to actually know what they're doing. All they have to do is pick great songs and press play. But I used to live by the spin. Deejaying in between the songs I would write for other artists kept a roof over my head and ramen noodles in the pantry.

"We ready?" Hector asks from the floor.

I save the playlist I have loaded on the laptop set up for tonight before hopping down off the stage to join him.

"Yep, let's get it."

"You laced tonight, bruh." Hector points to my feet. "I heard your shoe game was beast. Which ones are those?"

"The Space Jam Blackouts." I grin and bow at the waist. "I broke out the classics for your grand opening."

"I feel honored." He laughs and looks around the stage. "Where's Qwest? She here?"

"Yeah, she's already in our dressing room and we've sound checked."

I look around the mostly empty club for anyone from my team. Sarah is at a table, her curious eyes glued to the scantily clad strippers onstage rehearsing their routines.

"Hey, let me introduce you to Sarah from the label." I start across the room with Hector falling into step beside me. "If you need anything tonight, she'll be your contact."

"Not Bristol?" Mischief sparks in Hector's eyes. "Does Qwest know you're sprung for your manager?"

"Shut up, man." I shoot him an annoyed glance that just makes him chuckle.

I'm more annoyed that he brought up my dilemma with Qwest than I am that he peeped my feelings for Bristol. I'm getting through this performance, and then I'm ending things with Qwest tonight. I have to. The flight home was a disaster. I didn't want to have sex with her, so I didn't, which definitely raised her suspicions. We shared a room in Dubai, but nothing happened. I told her I was tired and that my body was off because of the trip. Lame excuses. My dick would be ready in an outer space time zone if the need arose. It's not that she isn't beautiful. She's fine as hell.

It's that she isn't Bristol.

And as much as I wanted to try with someone hoping to get over Bristol, it isn't working. And it isn't fair. Not to Qwest. Hell, not to me. This isn't about convincing Bristol to be with me. I'm done with that shit, too. If she wants me, wants to dump Parker, she knows where to find me. That doesn't mean my feelings have changed for her. Bringing Qwest into this only made a bigger mess. One I have to clean up tonight.

"Sarah, hey," I say when we reach her table.

"Hey." She hugs me and smiles politely at Hector. "Is this Mr. Abrentes?"

I already gave her a heads-up that she would be the contact for anything Hector needs. I'll let Rhyson and Bristol determine when she finds out she'll be handling a lot of things for me until I find a new manager.

I give her and Hector a moment to talk through a few details before asking her the question that's been on my mind since I arrived.

"Sarah, have you heard from Bristol?" I ask. "Seen her?"

She's always at venues well ahead of her artists, and I've been here for more than an hour with no sign of her.

"She told me she'd be here by the time the show starts," Sarah says.

"Why so late?" The frown feels heavy on my face, so I can only imagine what it looks like. "She's usually here hours ahead."

"Oh." Sarah bites her lip and blinks a few times too many, betraying her nerves. "She said this would be a good training opportunity for me. Is that not okay?"

"No, no, it's fine." I squeeze her hand and reassure her with an easy smile. "I was just curious."

I ignore Hector's knowing grin. He's got my number now. But that's okay. Hector may be a dog, but he knows not to shit where his friends eat, to be crass about it. And even though Bristol and I aren't together, in his mind, that's where I eat. Nasty code, but it works.

I notice Sarah keeps looking back to all the nipples and ass onstage. I'm betting this is her first time in a strip club.

"Don't get any ideas, Sarah," I tease her. "Prodigy pays you well.

Don't be working that pole tonight."

She gasps her shock but laughs when she realizes I'm playing with her.

"I think I . . . no, that wouldn't . . ." Her cheeks burn pink. "I mean, I won't."

I'm halfway through spinning the first set when I spot Bristol at one of the bars. Damn, she looks good. The dress shouldn't look good. It has no shape. It just hangs off one shoulder, but every time she moves, it molds to the curves and lines of her body beneath the blue silk. The hem doesn't even hit mid-thigh, and her long, toned legs go on forever, the high heels emphasizing the cut of her calves. My mind goes blank of every image except those legs wrapped around me as I pound into her. I don't need this hard-on within fucking distance of Bristol.

The blonde beside her makes me set aside my reservations about going over. If it weren't for her, me and my hard dick would run in the opposite direction.

"If it isn't my favorite rock star," I say from behind Jimmi. She turns, squealing and hurling herself into my arms.

"I won't tell Rhyson I'm your fave if you don't." She lets out that rich, husky laugh that hints at her top-charting singing voice. "How the hell are you, Grip? I mean, besides having the number one album!"

"I definitely can't complain." I press a kiss into her soft blonde hair, which is flying all over the place. "Missed you, girl."

"I'm sorry I didn't make it to the release celebration." A grimace crosses Jimmi's pretty face. "I think I was in London that night. Great show, but I would rather have been here."

She links her arm through mine, and we lean against the bar. I don't speak to Bristol, who's sitting on a barstool with her legs crossed, and she doesn't speak to me. Jimmi bounces a glance between the two of us but doesn't comment on how tight the air is around us. Jimmi knows the score. She knows I've always had it bad for Bristol.

"Can you even believe this?" Jimmi's blue eyes soften, losing some of their usual cynicism. "When we were at the School of the Arts painting backdrops for musicals and dreaming of making it big, we had no idea. You, me, Rhyson, Luke. It's crazy."

"Right." I shake my head. "I still wake up some mornings thinking I'm supposed to be sweeping studio floors and rent's past due."

"Same here!" Jimmi's laugh mixes with the heavy beat of the Future song playing in the club. "I still have my name badge from Mick's."

"I would have starved those first few years without all the free food you hooked me up with from that place."

"Like your mom would ever let you starve." Jimmi turns to Bristol, who has been considering the stage intently ever since I walked over. "That's where we first met, Bris."

"Huh?" Bristol turns slightly glazed eyes to Jimmi. "Sorry, what?"

"Bris, what planet are you on tonight?" Jimmi bumps Bristol's shoulder with hers. "Grip and I were just talking about the good old days. Remember how we met at Mick's that first day you came for spring break? Grip brought you to lunch."

"You had on a bikini top and heels and cut-offs." Bristol scrunches her nose, her throaty laugh rich with affection. "You were such a skank."

"Yeah, well you were an uptight asshole prude." Jimmi leans into Bristol, her grin wide. "Who thought she was better than everyone else."

"I totally was." Bristol's mouth opens in a silent laugh. "I totally did."

"And Grip kept looking at you like he'd discovered chocolate." Jimmi bends at the waist, laughter shaking her shoulders.

The humor drains from Bristol's face. The club is so dark I almost miss the anger, the residue of hurt in Bristol's eyes from our argument.

"No, he didn't," Bristol murmurs into her vodka martini.

Yeah, I actually did.

Jimmi grabs Bristol's drink and gulps down most of it.

"Hmmm. That's good. I shoulda been drinking that." She licks her lips and wiggles the nearly empty glass before handing it back to Bristol. "Be a doll and get me one."

Bristol leans back, catches the bartender's eye, points to her glass, and then holds up two fingers.

"I was looking for you earlier, Bris," I say.

"Why?" Over the rim of her martini glass she spears me like the toothpick through the olive in her drink.

"You're just usually early, and I didn't see you."

"Didn't Sarah take care of you?" She cocks one brow. "I thought that's what you wanted."

"Bristol, yeah, but we need to talk about—"

"I could totally do that, Jim," Bristol cuts over my comment, gesturing with her glass toward the strippers onstage.

"Do what?" I demand, deciding not to pursue the Sarah conversation right now.

"Yeah, do what?" Jimmi asks.

"That upside-down move she's doing and make my ass clap," Bristol says, taking a sip of the new drink the bartender just gave her.

"Me, too." Jimmi sips on hers. "It isn't as hard as it looks. The one girl in the red . . . what was her name, Bristol?"

"Champagne," Bristol says. "I'm pretty sure she said her name was Champagne. It was something . . . festive."

"I think you're right." Jimmi tilts her head, her eyes never leaving Champagne as she hangs upside down on the pole, legs straight in the air. "Though they are rather athletic and well-trained, you must admit. I think one day stripping will be an Olympic sport."

"If strippers were men," Bristol says with an inordinate amount of conviction. "It already would be."

"There are male strippers," I remind her.

Bristol's withering glance makes me want to guard my testicles. "Don't you have a performance to get ready for?" She looks past my shoulder. "Where's your girlfriend? I almost didn't recognize you without her in your lap."

"Is she clingy?" Jimmi whisper-shouts as if I'm not standing right there listening. "I hate clingy girls."

"Clingy like ivy." Bristol stares into her drink, her mouth sullen. "Like a particularly aggressive strain of rabid ivy."

"Don't talk about her that way," I say. "She doesn't deserve that, Bristol, and you of all people should know that."

"Oh, me of all people?" Bristol leans across Jimmi until her nose almost touches mine. "Why me of all people?"

"You know why," I grit out.

"Why?" Jimmi interjects, round eyes ping ponging between Bristol and me.

"I didn't make you fuck her," Bristol snaps. "No one twisted your dick to sleep with her or any of the hundreds of other girls you've been with over the years."

"Hundreds?" I shake my head. "Not hundreds, but at least none of them had a stick up their ass."

"Oh, I bet there was a stick up somebody's ass at some point along the way." Bristol signals for another drink. "Maybe even yours."

"Musicians do like to experiment," Jimmi agrees. "Believe me. I know."

"Nothing has ever been up my ass," I say harshly. "And, Bristol, I think you should slow down on the drinks."

"You're not my father." She laughs bitterly. "Or maybe you are. You probably are. Yeah, you're my father."

"What the hell does that even mean?" I demand.

I don't get to the bottom of her glare because Sarah comes over to get me.

"Hey, you ready?" she asks. "Qwest is already backstage. You guys go on soon."

"Ooooh! I get to see you and Qwest perform live." Jimmi claps her hands. "I've heard you're fire together onstage."

"Oh, three-alarm fire," Bristol says sarcastically. "We had to add a hose to Qwest's rider."

"You're becoming a bitch, Bris," I snap.

"I'm factory order bitch." She toasts with her martini. "I came like this. Maybe you just never noticed."

"Grip, we gotta go," Sarah reminds me, but her worried eyes rest on Bristol.

"Stay out of trouble, Jimmi." I hook an elbow around her neck and whisper. "Watch Bristol. She's drinking too much."

"But drunk Bristol is so much fun," Jimmi whispers back.

"What are you guys whispering about?" Bristol asks, her eyes narrowed on Jimmi and me.

"You," I say without missing a beat. "Now I have to go do my job."

"How nice for you to still have a job," Bristol says, her words slurring more than they did four martinis ago. "Some of us got fired."

"Okay, Jimmi." I grab her by the shoulders to look her in the eyes. "I'm counting on you to keep her safe."

"You snot it." Jimmi cackles and sloppily covers her mouth. "I mean, you got it."

"Are you drunk, Jim?" I note her glassy eyes and flushed cheeks. She's a very functional drunk. You never realize she's drunk until she starts breaking shit and hooking up with strangers in port-a-potties. I've had whole conversations with her and not realized she was lit. I think I just had one.

"Just a little." Jimmi holds up her thumb and index finger, the smallest sliver of space separating them. "Lil' shit. I mean, lil' bit."

I search the club for Amir. I usually hate having him with me as "security", but I need him now. When I spot him talking with a very limber stripper, I know he'll hate me for breaking that up, but I wave him over.

"What's up?" He glances back over his shoulder at the girl now giving some dude a lap dance.

"Keep an eye on Bristol and Jimmi." I tip my head in their direction. "You know how they get when they drink together. It's never good."

"Got it." Amir assesses the two girls who are slumped against each other laughing over nothing.

"Break a leg, Grip," Bristol says, sober enough to be snide. "No, really. I hope you break your leg while Qwest is humping it."

I can't do this with her right now. With one more death stare, which she returns in triplicate, I head back to join Qwest in the dressing room. She's already in her skimpy costume, fake lashes on, braids spilling down to her waist. Her eyes light up as soon as I enter the room. I can't help but wonder if that's how I look when I see Bristol. If maybe sometimes, just maybe, she's ever looked that way when she saw me.

"Where've you been?" Qwest slips her arms around my waist. "My friend Jimmi is here, so we were just catching up." I set my hands at her hips, putting a little space between us. "Look, Qwest, can we talk after the performance? There's just some stuff I need to get off my chest."

"I was hoping you'd say that." She smiles up at me impishly. "I think we're on the same page."

By the mischief and lust in her eyes, I doubt that very seriously.

I'm grateful we're only doing one song. We power through "Queen," which is as energized and sexy as usual. Qwest actually steps up her game and is borderline indecent being that we're in a strip club. When in Rome.

When we come offstage and head back to the dressing room, I can tell the performance turned her on. She locks the door and presses me into a wall before we've said one word. Her tongue is so far down my throat it would take a Saint Bernard to retrieve it. I'm horny and it does feel good, but I can't do this again. I can't do this to her any more.

"Qwest," I say against her lips. "We need to talk."

Her mouth slows over mine until the kisses are just pecks on my lips and across my cheeks.

"I know." She nods, looking down at the floor. "I figured after what happened . . . or rather didn't happen . . . on the plane."

"Yeah, that's what I want to talk about."

"You don't have to. Hectic schedule. Crazy week." She gives me a sly look. "I even wondered if you might be bored."

"No, it isn't boredom. It's—"

A knock at the door interrupts.

"Who could that be?" Qwest asks in mock innocence before opening the door.

Champagne stands in the hall, her shy grin at odds with the cupless bra displaying her pierced nipples.

"Hey, Qwest." She wiggles her fingers, and her words are directed to Qwest, but her eyes are on me.

"Come on in." Qwest steps back, looking at me like I should be thanking her. "Voila."

"Sorry?" I run a hand over the back of my neck. "What is this?"

"It's your surprise." Qwest locks the door, stalking over to me and dragging Champagne with her. She leans up, kissing my neck, and nods to Champagne to get to work on the other side. Champagne's overachieving ass reaches straight for my dick, running her hand up and down my stiffening erection. I've had my share of threesomes, but having sex with Qwest hasn't solved anything. Having sex with Qwest and some random stripper certainly won't. I know how to fix this, and as much as it may hurt Qwest, I'm fixing this tonight.

"Whoa." I step out of their clutches. "What the hell? This isn't happening. Qwest, we need to talk."

"Not happening?" Champagne pushes out her bottom lip. "You promised I'd get to fuck Grip."

"Well, Grip didn't promise that you'd get to fuck Grip." I walk swiftly to the door, wrenching it open and gesturing to the hall. "Bye, Champagne."

"But will I still get—"

"See my boy Will out front." Qwest sighs, watching me as if I were a house pet who just bit her. "He'll pay you."

Once Champagne leaves, there's just Qwest and me, and all the things I need to say that may hurt her.

"I'm sorry." She walks over and loops her arms at the back of my neck. "I just thought when you couldn't get it up on the plane—"

"Hey. Don't be telling people I couldn't get it up." A sharp laugh slices the corners of my mouth. "That's how rumors get started."

"Sorry." Her smile makes a brief appearance before disappearing again. "What's going on?"

"Let's sit down." I lead her over to the plush couch in the center of the room, never letting go of her hands. "Qwest, you're an amazing girl. You're smart, funny, talented. Total package."

"If there's one thing I know," Qwest says, her full lips twisting wryly. "It's big butts, and I hear a huge *but* coming."

"But." I pause meaningfully and squeeze her hand. "This isn't gonna work between us."

"Why?" The dismay and hurt on her face drives a knife into my heart, making me feel like an even bigger jerk. "Things have been good, haven't they?"

"Yeah, but it's going so . . . fast." I shrug and look at her apologetically. "Once the media got ahold of us, it just went so damn fast. And before I knew it, we were being hashtagged and shipped and made into something other than what we said we would be. Bigger than what we said we would be."

I look at her frankly.

"I was honest from the beginning that I wasn't sure we should do this."

"But we're so good together." Tears stand in her brown eyes. "I thought we were . . . that maybe things had changed."

She bows her head, swiping at a tear.

"Things changed for me, Grip," she whispers. "I love you."

Even though my mom warned me, even sensing it myself, to actually hear her confirm it makes me feel worse.

"I told you not to do that, Qwest. You know I don't feel that way."

"You also know the heart doesn't always do what we tell it to." She lifts her head, eyes wide. "That's what this is about. It's that other bitch?"

Anger sparks life in her dulled eyes. "Grip, if you cheated on me—"

"No, I wouldn't do that to you."

Even if Bristol had turned to me, I would have broken things off with Qwest first.

I hope I would have.

"Did she finally decide she wants you?" Qwest asks, the flare of anger yielding to the hurt again. "That's why you're breaking up with me?"

"No, she still won't be with me."

The words are barely out of my mouth before Qwest is on the floor between my knees, her hands pressing my legs apart.

"Then let me have what she's missing." She pulls my zipper down, slipping her hand inside, her fingers going by memory to cup and stroke my balls.

"Qwest," I groan, pushing at her shoulders. "No. Stop."

"But you want it." She looks pointedly at my growing erection. "I know you do."

"No." I shake my head and zip my jeans. "That doesn't mean anything."

"But if she still doesn't want to be with you then—"

"But I still want to be with her." I lean my elbows on my knees and wipe a hand across my face. "Only her. Feeling this way, it isn't fair to be with somebody else. Not fair to you, and not fair to me."

"She doesn't deserve you," she whispers, leaning her head on my knee, tears now freely streaking down her face.

"But she has me." A sad smile rests on my lips as I swipe a thumb over her tears. "Whether she deserves me, whether she wants me, I'm hers, and I want her. I've tried to stop, but I can't. While that's the way it is, I can't be with you. I won't do that to you anymore. I won't do that to anybody. You deserve better."

A heavy knock at the door interrupts. "Who is it?" I shout, frowning.

"It's me, Grip." Amir's voice comes muffled but urgent through the door.

I cross the room to let him in, and Amir's eyes drift over my shoulder to Qwest still on her knees wearing her barely decent costume. "Sorry, man." Amir's wide eyes zip back to mine. "But that, uh, project you had me watching is a little out of control."

"What project . . ." My eyes snap to his. Bristol. "What's up?"

"Um . . ." Amir glances at Qwest. I look back to see her standing, eyes watchful and antennae up.

"Hey." I walk back to her, gently cupping her face and kissing her forehead. "I need to check on something. You'll be okay getting back to your hotel? Should I send Will back here?"

"Yeah, send him." She folds her hands over mine at the curve of her neck. "I guess I'll go back to New York. Nothing's keeping me here now."

"We still have some shows scheduled," I say carefully. "Will you be okay for them?"

"If you know anything about me, Grip, it's that I don't let nothing mess with my money." A choked laugh escapes her lips. "Not even my stupid heart."

"Your heart isn't stupid. It's a good heart, and some guy's going to be really lucky to have it."

She nods, fresh tears springing to her eyes and streaking through the heavy stage makeup on her cheeks.

"Be safe." I drop another kiss on her forehead and walk out into the hall where Amir waits.

"What's going on?" I ask once the door is closed. In the light of the hall, I notice some slight puffiness around Amir's eye. "What happened to you?"

"Bristol happened to me." He touches around his eye. "That's what I was trying to tell you. She's turnt up out there. I tried to check her, and she hit me in the face. Jimmi jumped on my damn back. You know that lil' white girl scratched me? You think I'll have to get a tetanus shot?"

"What the hell, Amir?" I push past him and barrel down the hall. "I told you to watch her. You know how Bristol and Jimmi are when they get together."

"Uh, I was watching her until she and Jimmi climbed up onstage with the strippers and started talking about making their asses clap."

I keep moving forward but glare daggers over my shoulder at him.

"If she's out here naked your ass is mine."

She isn't naked, but pretty close. She and Jimmi are on one of Pirouette's three stages along with a few professionals who are "coaching" them. Bristol's blue dress lies in a crumpled mound of silk at her feet, leaving her in a nude-colored strapless bra and matching thong. She's a hair from naked, and all the guys clustered around the base of the stage are salivating for that last hair to fall out. Jimmi isn't much better, also in bra and panties.

By the time Amir and I make it to them, one of the guys with a hundred dollar bill clutched in his fist has his other hand wrapped around Bristol's leg. Fury erases caution and discretion. I grab him by the shoulder and shove him to the side.

"Get your damn hands off her." The guttural growl of my voice barely registers above Lil Wayne's "Lollipop" blasting through the system.

"Nigga, who you think—"

The anger melts away from his face, morphing into a wide grin. "Grip!" He reaches to dap me up. "You did it tonight, dawg. And that song 'Bruise' you got out is deep. You telling our story, bruh."

"Uh, thanks."

With a curt nod, I reach up and grab Bristol's hand. I can only hope Amir has made more progress with Jimmi.

"Bristol, get your ass off that stage," I yell up at her.

She tugs at her hand, glazed eyes squinting down at me.

"No." Her other hand goes to the front closure of her bra. "I'm trying to get this thing off. It won't . . ."

She looks so confused by the uncooperative clasp, pouting and frowning down at her fingers that don't seem to want to work properly.

"I can do it," she yells at me. "Just give me a sec."

"Fuck this." I scramble onstage, pull the chambray shirt over my head, not bothering to unbutton it. "Bris, put this on. We're getting out of here."

"I'm not going anywhere with you," she slurs, pointing a loopy accusatory finger at me. "You fired me. Asshole."

I pull the shirt over her head, shoving her arms through the sleeves. I bend at the knees and haul her over my shoulder, ignoring her pounding on my back. Fortunately, a few "amateurs" were onstage trying their hand at stripping, so most people weren't paying as much attention and were focused on the main stages. Hopefully, I was able to stay under the radar as much as possible and none of this will land in tomorrow's news cycle.

I make my way through the crowd back toward the dressing room, Bristol still bouncing against my back. Farther down the hall, Amir has Jimmi propped up against the wall. Like me, he had to sacrifice his shirt, and we face each other, both wearing wife beaters and jeans.

"Does Jimmi not have security with her?" I ask.

"She said no, but she isn't exactly reliable right now." A tiny beaded clutch looks incongruous in Amir's beefy hands. "I found a valet ticket in her purse, so looks like she drove."

"You take her home, and I'll get Bristol to her place." "You sure? I don't know if I should leave you."

The skepticism on his face is like a straw breaking the camel's back of this night.

"I grew up same place as you, Amir." I hitch up my wife beater to show him the 9mm tucked into my waistband. No way I'd be in a club like this without it. "I'm strapped, same as you. You may be on the payroll to shadow me, but don't forget who you're dealing with. Now, you get Jimmi home. I'm pretty sure I can make it to Bristol's house without getting jacked."

He nods and starts herding Jimmi toward the private exit. By the looks of Jimmi's face, he'll be lucky if she doesn't vomit on his bright white Nikes before it's all said and done. With Bristol still slung over my shoulder like a sack of potatoes, upside down with as much liquor as she's consumed, I'm surprised she hasn't vomited down my back already. She's gone quiet and still. She may have passed out.

I carefully bend and flip her back, sliding her down my body until she's pressed to my chest, my arms folded at the small of her back to keep her upright. Her hands go to my shoulders, and she slumps against me.

"Bris," I say softly, saving the anger urging me to lambast her ass for later when she'll remember it. "Let's get out of here, okay?"

"No." She shakes her head, the burnished hair tangling around her shoulders and over her eyes. "It's fun. Don't . . . don't wanna go."

"Bristol," I say firmly, glaring down at her. "We're leaving right now."

"It's fun," she whispers, her face crumpling and tears rolling over her smooth cheeks. "I'm having so much fun. Can't you see I'm having fun?"

Still in my arms, she drops her head into the curve of my neck and shoulder. Her tears rain over me, dampening my skin, and her heaving sobs jackhammer my heart. I rub her back in soothing strokes.

Dammit, I can't take Bristol's tears, not even the drunk ones. "Hey, it's okay." I try to pull her back so I can see her face, but she presses closer.

"Don't." Her broken whisper is muffled into my neck. "Don't push me away again, Grip."

"I wouldn't." I palm the back of her head, rubbing the soft, wild hair. "I didn't."

"You did." Her tears come faster, her erratic breaths hiccupping her words. "You don't-don't want me-want me-around. You f-fired me."

"Bristol, you know—"

"You just want her." She trembles against me, folding her arms between her chest and mine. "You just want Qwest."

I know she probably won't remember this tomorrow, but as much as it cuts me open to see her like this, it's this raw, vulnerable version of Bristol that will tell me the truth. And I'm not noble enough not to take advantage of it to finally hear her confession.

"Does it hurt you when I'm with her?" I peer down at Bristol's face in the muted hallway light, hunting down the truth in her eyes.

"So much," she whispers, fat tears squeezing from under her clenched-closed-tight eyelids and leaving trails of mascara. "It hurts so much."

"Why does it hurt so much, Bris? Do you . . ." I swallow around the emotion clogging my throat at the sight of her tears, unsure if I really want to hear her say this knowing that tomorrow she'll probably just deny it. "Do you have feelings for me? Do you care about me, Bristol?"

With eyes the silver of moonlight, illuminative, so clear and unprotected, not fogged by her fears, insecurities, or questions, she tells me.

"So much." Another tear skids over the silk of one high cheekbone. "I care so much."

Something breaks free in my chest. Knowing I'm not crazy loosens a vise from around me. Knowing I haven't imagined that the connection we had all those years ago never went away.

"Bris, then why do you—"

My question never makes it out. With green tingeing her tear-streaked face, Bristol doubles over, clutching her stomach and puking all over my Blackout Jordans.

CHAPTER 21

BRISTOL

I HAVE TO stop doing this.

Not that drinking myself into a coma is a regular occurrence, but when the pain and pressure are too much, I find myself reaching for the same bottled oblivion my mother favors. And there's no doubt I've been drinking. Demons are line dancing in my skull. My furry tongue clings to the roof of my mouth. The morning chill creeps under my duvet, and I pull the chambray shirt I'm wearing closer around me. I tug the collar up to my nose, inhaling the clean, masculine scent. It's familiar. It smells like . . .

"Grip," I say into the quiet of my bedroom. "What?"

I literally jump and screech, flipping onto my back to find Grip staring at me unsmilingly, wearing a white tank undershirt. I have no idea how I came to be wearing his shirt from last night, or how he came to be sitting in my bed, broad shoulders overpowering my tufted headboard.

"You scared me half to death." I clutch his shirt over my pounding heart and touch my bare legs. My dress is nowhere to be seen, and under Grip's shirt I'm wearing only a strapless bra and a thong. I have to wonder if I did anything regrettable last night.

"Did we . . . um . . ." I lick my dry lips, not sure how to ask this question. The same one I had to ask Parker just a few weeks ago. Shame curdles in my belly that I'm repeating this destructive cycle. "Did we have sex?"

Grip cocks one dark brow, his lips not even twitching. "Do you feel like you could walk straight?"

I nod and move my legs experimentally to check for partial paralysis. "Um, yeah."

"Then there's your answer." He shrugs. "We couldn't have had sex."

"Very funny." I drag myself up to sit beside him against the headboard.

"Not being funny. Just stating fact."

His eyes remain sober. There was a time when he would have made this easier for me, allayed some of my discomfort with a joke. But there's no levity in his expression.

"Did you roofie me or something?" I try to lighten the heavy atmosphere since he won't.

"You roofied your damn self with that bottle of vodka you poured down your throat." If anything my attempt at a joke makes things worse. A scowl forms on his face. "What the hell were you thinking?"

"I wasn't thinking." I shield my eyes from the light intruding through my wide windows, curtains undrawn. "I was drunk, in case you didn't notice."

"Yeah, what the hell were you thinking getting drunk?" He shakes his head as he lifts a knee under the duvet and props his arm on it. "In a strip club. Do you have any idea how vulnerable you were in a place like that drunk off your ass?"

"I don't need a lecture." I swing my legs over my side of the bed, pausing for my head to spin. "What I need is . . ."

The words trail off when I see the water and aspirin on my bedside table.

"Thanks," I mumble around the two pills before gulping down

water. I lift a hand to touch what feels like involuntary pageant hair. "My hair situation seems dire."

I try to run my fingers through the nest tangled around my head, but they stall at one knot after another.

"Yeah, your hair looks like shit. Your lipstick is smeared all around your mouth, and you have mascara running down your face like some emotionally unstable clown. You look like a circus refugee. Also, you reek."

I swing him an affronted look over my shoulder.

"Why are you being so mean to me?"

"Because I'm pissed, Bristol." He flings the covers back and stands, facing me with my unmade bed between us.

Even at this time of morning and under these circumstances, he looks highly fuckable in his jeans and undershirt, with a shadow coating the chiseled jawline. There isn't enough alcohol in my system to wash the horny away. I need to have actual sex with an actual person and actually remember it. Being this close to the sexiest man I know isn't helping.

"If I hadn't been there," Grip continues, blissfully unaware that I'm mentally dry humping him. "It could have been much worse."

Worse than what? I try to reconstruct the events from last night. I remember still being angry at Grip for firing me. I remember drinking lots of vodka with Jimmi. We asked that nice stripper Champagne to show us how to make our asses clap. And then . . .

"Oh, God," I gasp. "Did I take my bra off? Like in front of people? Did I make it rain?"

He sucks his teeth, exasperation in every chiseled line of his handsome face.

"You were damn close," Grip snaps. "If I hadn't pulled you off the stage, you and Jimmi both would have been butt naked in there."

"Where's Jimmi?" I ask, my voice constrained by embarrassment.

"Amir took her home." Grip walks to the bench at the foot of my bed to grab his backpack. "You owe him an apology, by the way. You hit him in the eye."

"What?" I slap my forehead and close my eyes, mortified. "Oh my God, no."

"Oh my God, yes, and you owe me an apology." He gestures to his shirt covering my almost-naked body. "I want that dry cleaned, by the way."

"Yes, sir. Right away, sir." I load the words with a double helping of sarcasm and stumble toward the bathroom. "If you'll excuse me, I need to figure out what died in my mouth."

I'm practically brushing my teeth with eyes closed to avoid the road kill of my reflection in the mirror.

"You just keep getting better and better, don't you, Bristol?" I mutter around my electric toothbrush. I splash my face, but don't even bother with my hair and the rest of my bodily disaster. I'll shower once Grip's gone. I walk back into my bedroom to find Grip on his knees, ass up, looking under my bed.

And what an ass it is.

He glances over his shoulder from the floor, one brow lifted when he sees my head bent at just the right angle to peruse his butt.

"Um, can I help you?" he asks.

"Oh . . . no." Embarrassment at getting caught checking him out fires up my cheeks. "Were you looking for something?"

"My shoes." He stands and glances around the room. "Did I mention that you threw up on a pair of thousand dollar vintage Jordans?"

"I'm sorry." I walk around to the side of the bed, joining the search for his shoes. I spot the worn leather book of Neruda poems and the tarnished whistle on the floor. My heart, my thoughts, my whole body goes still.

"Have you been going through my things again?" I snatch the book and the whistle up and cram them into the bottom drawer, which is usually locked. "How dare you?"

"How dare I?" Incredulity widens his eyes. "I didn't have to go through anything. That was on your pillow when I brought you in here. I just moved it out of the way so I could fall asleep."

Maybe he didn't recognize it. I know it's a feeble hope, but it's the only one I have. He quickly disabuses me of any possibility that he doesn't remember those items. Doesn't recognize their significance.

"I'm surprised you kept them." Grip hitches his bag onto his shoulder and steadily watches me.

"Well you kept the watch," I say defensively before I realize this only pulls me deeper into a conversation I'm too addled to have.

Grip's lips thin, and his jaw clenches.

"I kept the watch because that night at the carnival was one of the best nights of my life, Bristol. That night with you meant a lot to me." Grip crosses his arms over the muscled width of his chest. "But you already knew that. So, why did you keep a worthless whistle from that night? Why is the book of poems I mailed to you beside your bed?"

Anxiety prickles my scalp and heats my skin. I'm exposed, and my habit is to hide.

"No reason. I wouldn't throw that away," I mumble. "That would just be rude."

"Not only did you not throw it away," Grip says, walking to stand in front of me. "You highlighted. You folded down pages. You circled. You starred."

"You did go through my things." I glare feebly up at him. "I knew it."

He tips his head toward the drawer where I stowed the book and whistle.

"You've obviously handled that book, read it over and over. I'm asking you why, Bris." His voice drops and his eyes soften. "I've told you what that watch and what that night meant to me. Can you tell me what that night meant to you? What it still means to you?"

My defenses slam over my heart like a gate. He's much too close. Much too dangerous to someone like me who would not know how to stop loving him when he hurts me. When he cheats on me, lies to me. And he would. How could he not? I refuse to be my mother.

"It was a long time ago." I caress the buttons of his chambray shirt I'm wearing, fixing my eyes on my trembling fingers. "Don't read too much into a drawer full of old memories."

When I glance up at him, his face has cemented into a mask. His eyes are like iced coffee.

"Forget it." He turns abruptly and leaves the room, tossing the last words over his shoulder. "Never mind."

His proximity was causing my anxiety, but seeing him walk away only increases it. I sense that if he leaves this house, if he walks out that door, that's it. I'll lose him forever. He's already fired me, so we won't have work. We can't be in the same room for five minutes without fighting anymore, so we can't be friends. And I've made sure we'll never be lovers.

And why the hell not?

It's a rebel cry from my heart. That stupid thing pounding with angry fists against my ribs, demanding attention. Demanding him. Commanding me to find a way to make him stay. I'm not sure what I could say at this point as he crosses my living room with swift strides that take him closer and closer to the front door, but I have to say something, even if it's the wrong thing.

"I guess Qwest is waiting for you, huh?"

Yep, the wrong thing.

He's at the front door but turns to face me, irritation and disappointment on his face.

"It wasn't cool, Bristol, you talking about Qwest that way last night with Jimmi. She's been nothing but nice to you."

He's right, but him defending her only agitates me more.

"Well, it's the truth." I assume my face is resting bitch, but I can't fix it. "She is clingy. The girl doesn't know how to sit unless she's on your lap."

He stiffens, eyes hard and lips set in a flat line when he crosses his arms over his chest. "You sound jealous."

"Of her?" I bark out a disdainful laugh. "I don't think so."

"At least Qwest doesn't have to be high or drunk to tell me how she feels."

That low blow lands just above the belt in the vicinity of my heart.

"Fuck you, Grip."

"I already know you wanna fuck me." He raises both brows and tilts his head to the other side. "I'm wondering if you'll ever tell me how you feel about me."

He drops his bag to the floor and settles against the door, as if he has all the time in the world to wait.

"Or are you such a scared little girl you can't?"

"Scared little girl?" Indignation starts at my feet and works its way up to my head. "I'm not . . ."

I can't even finish the sentence. The truth smacks me across the face, and Rhyson's words ring as clearly in my head as if he's standing beside me.

You're braver than that, Bristol. You're the most fearless person I know. And you let the threat of something keep you from having what you really want?

Am I? Brave? Fearless? In most things, yes. But with this, with Grip, there's too much at stake. Too much to lose. If I give him a little, I'll give him everything.

Grip's waiting for me to finish, to respond, but whatever I was going to say flies right out of my head. While I'm standing here, trying to figure out how to hide from him, he's hiding nothing from me. There's so much raw longing in his dark eyes. There's so much emotion on his face it punches right through my heart. I've taken years to build a fortress against this man. I've learned to resist him. And he has over and over, time and again, put his heart on the line. Worn it on his sleeve. Persisted when I turned him away.

He's been brave. He just kept coming after me like a tank, even when I refused. Even when my brother told him he shouldn't. Even when I steered him in the direction of someone else. He even let me manage him for the chance to be closer to me. While I've drawn my armor tightly around myself, Grip stood naked in the heat of battle, stripped all of his armor away and made himself vulnerable. In my fear of becoming my mother, I think I'm becoming my father instead. The one who takes and takes, risking nothing. Always defining the relationship and expecting Grip to take whatever terms I offer. To take whatever's left. It's so selfish and so weak and so unfair, I feel sick, not because of the alcohol, but sick of myself. Sick of living in fear.

He wants to know how I feel? As if seeing that book of poetry didn't tell him. As if finding that worthless whistle didn't show him. As if I haven't already told him in a million silent ways. He already knows, but he wants to hear me say it.

I want him.

For the first time, watching him poised to leave my front door, poised to walk out of my life, my want feels stronger than my fear. The threat of Grip breaking me weighs less than the possibility of never having him. Before I know it, I'm swallowing my pride. I'm eating my words and mustering the courage to tell him everything and praying it isn't too late. I'm walking to stand in front of him.

"You want to know how I feel?" I can barely push the words past the tumbleweed in my throat.

He doesn't nod. Doesn't speak, but I know him too well not to recognize something flicker in his eyes. Hope? That I'll finally be brave enough to be honest?

"I want you so much it scares me," I say in a rush before my fear stops me. "The way I feel about you terrifies me."

I train my eyes on his Jordans because I can't look at him.

"I'm afraid you'll cheat on me, take advantage of me, and that I won't know how to stop wanting you. I'm afraid I'll settle for less than I deserve because I'd take whatever you'd give me."

He's completely silent, but his chest in front of me rises and falls with deeply drawn breaths.

"You want me?" he finally asks, voice husky, making no move to touch me.

I nod, sliding my glance to the side, looking for an escape route, though I already know there's nowhere left to hide.

"You want to be with me?" he presses.

I hazard a glance up, not sure how to take his impassive expression.

"I know you're with Qwest, and this is awful timing, but I—" "I broke things off with Qwest last night," he cuts in softly. My eyes zip up to meet his head on.

"You did?" His words kindle a small, fiery hope to life inside me. "Why?"

He tilts his head, a smile tipping one side of his mouth.

"You know why, Bristol." A small frown bends his eyebrows to meet. "It wasn't fair letting her think there was a chance when I couldn't get over you."

The blood slams against my wrists and at my temples in a frantic rhythm. My breaths grow shallow, fear and excitement and possibility mingling in my veins. He tilts my chin up until I'm forced to meet his eyes again.

"I won't be getting over you," he says softly. "And I would never cheat on you. As long as it's taken me to get you, you think I would jeopardize that with some piece of ass that doesn't mean anything to me?"

His words, his reassurances, loosen some of what's been tight inside me since I walked in on my father.

"You don't have me yet," I whisper, managing a tiny teasing smile.

He takes me by the hips, pulling me into his big body against the door, dipping his head until he hovers over my lips.

"Keep telling yourself that, Bris."

Anticipation crackles between us as I wait for him to take me, to claim me. Because there's no way I can stop him now. Despite any fear that may still linger, I don't want to stop him, but he's made every move for years. It's time for me to move first.

I tip up on my toes and press my lips to his, tentative as if it's our first kiss. I'm careful, as if he might turn me away, but he doesn't. With a groan, he spreads one hand over the small of my back and slides the other up into my wild hair. He angles my head just the way he wants and commandeers the kiss, nothing tentative or uncertain about him pulling my lips between his. Nothing careful about the way he plunges into me, his mouth slanting over mine, his tongue sweeping against mine. On repeat. Over and over. Avid. Desperate. Hungry.

He slumps against the door and takes me with him, searching

hands venturing under the chambray shirt to cup the bare cheeks of my ass. With one foot he kicks my legs apart until he's between my thighs. I gasp at the stiff erection pressing into my panties. Involuntarily, my hips roll into him. We groan into each other's mouths at the heat, the hardness, the wetness of us touching. Of us together.

"Bristol." He trails his mouth down my neck to the spot that's basically a blank check to my body. "I want to hear the whole sordid story of why you've put me through all this shit all these years. I really do."

I nod, hastily loosening the buttons of the chambray shirt and sliding my arms out until I'm only wearing the strapless bra and the thong.

"Damn, baby," he whispers, dipping his head to nudge the sheer material of my bra down, baring my breast. He takes my nipple into his mouth, drawing on me so hard it's almost painful, but I'm glad he doesn't stop when I whimper.

"Grip." I clutch his head to my breast and grind myself into him over and over, a hurricane building inside me. "Please."

"Please what?" He paints my areola with his tongue. "What do you want?"

"You know." I'm almost in tears it feels so good and I want it so bad. "You know, Grip."

Without asking for more, his fingers slip into the sides of my panties, rolling them over my hips and down my legs. His eyes eat up my nudity. I feel exposed, and realize that my head may not be pounding as badly and I managed to brush my teeth, but the rest of me still looks and smells like last night. I'm a wreck from head to naked toe.

"Grip, wait." I pull back, reaching down to grab the shirt from the floor and sliding my arms in.

"You're going in the wrong direction, Bris." Grip shucks his shoes off again and rips the tank over his head, revealing his sculpted chest. "Clothes should be coming off."

"I . . . well, um . . ." My breath stutters when the jeans slide down his powerful thighs. Through his briefs, I see what he's working with, and it's more than I've ever had.

Shit.

My poor pussy may not be ready for this. I feel like I should have been in training to fuck him, the way I would for a marathon. Surely, all that dick isn't something you just wake up one morning and take.

He hooks an arm around my waist and drags me against him, his erection announcing his intentions. He teases my lips apart and sucks on my tongue until my knees turn to rubber. For a second, my brain is gooey with desire, and I can't think past the throbbing heat between my legs. I pull back to speak before I lose the ability.

"Remember I reek?" My lips lift at the corners with the relief of not having to hide from him anymore. "And our first time will not be with me looking and smelling like drunken debauchery."

His eyes are so open and tender on my face, and he laughs with me, dropping his lips to my ear.

"Okay, Bristol." His warm breath in my ear makes me shudder. "We'll do it your way. First I wash you."

He steps back, sweeping a smoldering look over my nearly naked body, his desire stroking me like a physical hand.

"Then I fuck you."

CHAPTER 22

G_{RIP}

I'VE HAD SOME pretty wild dreams about Bristol Gray. But in my wildest dreams, I couldn't imagine that, not the nakedness of her body, but the nakedness of her soul, would be the thing that tempted me the most. Her eyes, so open and vulnerable—I couldn't have known that would be what was most precious to me. I feel like the guy who ran around for years screaming that the world was round when everyone insisted it was flat. I knew I wasn't crazy, that Bristol cared about me. I knew there was something undeniable between us. The greatest validation lies in those silvery eyes, completely unshielded for the first time in years.

"I guess I'll shower," she says once we're in her bathroom, reaching into the spacious, tile-walled unit to turn on the water.

"That's a great idea."

I peel back the flaps of my chambray shirt, which she has folded over her chest instead of buttoned. Her bra is right where I left it, tugged under her breasts so her nipples are exposed. We left the thong at her front door. I push the shoulders back, watching the sleeves skid down her arms. The shirt puddles around her feet. I take my time surveying the finely boned ankles, the infinite legs, tanned and toned. I devote a moment to appreciate the smooth triangle of flesh at the juncture of her thighs. I'm planning to gorge myself on that pussy. When I force my eyes over the curve of her hips and the dip of her waist, the tight tips of her breasts, it's her cheeks that make me smile.

"Are you blushing, Bristol?"

She's so bold, so brazen. I would never expect a little nudity to embarrass her.

"Shut it. Don't make fun of me." Her nervous laugh floats away on the steam from the shower. "I'm just . . . self-conscious."

"Maybe it's because I have on too many clothes."

I tug my briefs down, freeing my rampant erection. Her eyes drop to my dick and go wide. Under her stare, I get harder, my balls feel heavier as the seconds tick by. I've been with a lot of girls, but never has anyone made me feel like this without even touching me. I'm so ready, Bristol could breathe on me and I'd probably come all over her. I need to get this under control because from what I've inferred, the men in her life, in her bed, have not impressed her. I don't want to think about them too much because it makes me slightly insane. If she can put up with all the women I've been with, the least I can do is pay her the same courtesy.

But that doesn't mean I have to like it.

"If you're wondering," she says softly, lifting her eyes to my face. "You don't have to worry about Parker. There's nothing...we're not together."

I can get details on that later. It actually hadn't even occurred to me to ask.

"I wouldn't care if Parker was in the next room." I take her hand and place it on my bare chest, dipping my head to whisper in her ear. "I'd make sure he heard you scream."

She scans my face for any signs of distress, curiosity—I don't know what she's looking for, and I don't care.

"Parker and I aren't together," she says again.

"I know you're not, because you're with me."

"But what I'm saying is that we . . ." she lowers her lashes over cheeks still marked with faint mascara tracks. "We aren't—"

"Bris." I press a finger over her lips. "The last thing I want to talk about is the last asshole in your bed. He's rearview, just like Qwest and anyone else I've ever been with."

She nods, and her eyes lock with mine as she kisses my finger. I trace around her lips, tugging them open, touching her tongue, her teeth, the lining of her jaw. It's painful how badly I want this warm, wet mouth around my cock. I take her hand and lead her into the shower, gently setting her against the tiles to kiss her. Her arms climb over my shoulders and clench behind my neck. She's pressing against me, her breasts straining against my chest. She's wet and slippery, and I could lift her legs around me and take her right now, but I have no plans to rush.

Instead, I turn her to face the wall, reach for her shampoo, and slowly work the lather into her tangled hair. Her head falls back, and she sighs as my fingers massage her scalp. I pull the showerhead off the wall, rinsing out the shampoo and repeating the process with her conditioner. Still with my front to her back, I soap up my hands and run them over her firm thighs, tight waist, under her arms, and over the slender bones of her shoulders. I squeeze her breasts, rubbing my thumbs over the distended nipples until she cries out. Languidly, my hand journeys between her breasts and over her hipbone to palm her, my middle finger sliding into her slit and over the bud of flesh tucked inside.

"Grip."

My name on her lips when she's on the verge of coming hums through my blood. Knowing it's me doing this to her. Hoping that no other man ever has the privilege of touching her this way again, it's almost more than I can stand. I trap her clit between two fingers, rubbing up and down between the lips. My other hand roams over her ass, and I slip a finger between the firm cheeks. She stiffens, unsure of what I'm about to do. I sip at the water flowing in rivulets over her satiny skin. My teeth nip at the curve of her neck, at the elegant slope of her shoulder.

I match the rhythm I set in her pussy with the rhythm between her cheeks, caressing that puckered hole with each stroke, gathering her wetness and then slowly inserting my finger.

"Oh, God." Her face crumples as she pushes against my finger, urging me deeper in. "You have to . . . I'm going to . . ."

Her words twine with the steam, hotter than the steam. She slaps one hand against the wall, her head tipping back on a silent scream. Her knees buckle, and I catch her under her arms, seating her on the small bench tucked into the corner of the shower. Her head lolls back, eyes heavy-lidded, mouth slack, breasts heaving. She looks undone, but I'm far from done with her. I go down on my knees between her thighs.

"Spread your legs for me, Bris."

It's part plea, part command. Either way, she complies, her long legs yawning open for me. I swallow deeply at the sight of the thick, slick lips, pink and wet. Her clit is swollen from her orgasm. I have to resist the temptation to take it in my mouth and suck until she comes again.

"Hold your lips open." I can barely get the words out. My teeth slam together and my jaw clenches painfully as she obeys, opening herself with her fingers, her hungry eyes watching and waiting.

I set the showerhead to massage and let the warm water flow between her legs. She jerks, her eyes going wide and her mouth gaping on a sharp cry.

"That's it, baby." I roll the showerhead up and down and over her, watching her eyes squeeze closed and her face collapse when she loses the fight to maintain control. I twist the setting to vibrate and press it into her. Leaning forward, I capture one piqued nipple between my lips, rolling my tongue over it, drawing it deeply into my mouth.

"Grip, oh God. Please."

Her fingers tremble holding the lips open. Her head thrashes against the tiles. All the while her hips gyrate into the spray desperately, her rhythm uneven and broken with her desire. I need to taste that desperation. I drop the showerhead to the floor, not bothering to turn it off before I bend at the waist and pull her clit into my mouth.

"Bristol," I groan against the plump flesh. "You taste . . . Fuck."

I shove her fingers aside, spreading her as wide as she'll go, nipping at the lips with my teeth, slipping my tongue inside.

"Ahhhh." One of her hands clutches my shoulder, the other grabs my head, pressing me deeper into her rocking hips, deeper into her sweetness. Her taste intoxicates me. I hook her legs over my shoulders and devour her, my head bobbing furiously between her thighs. I want my mouth right here waiting to receive her when she comes. I take her nipple, rolling it between my fingers while I continue licking and sucking and supplicating at her altar.

She comes, shattering against the wall, shoulders shaking with dry sobs, her thighs trembling on my shoulders. I drink from her like a fountain. I'm thirsty, zealous. She claws the skin off my back, but I don't care. I want her wild, and the pain of her unleashed passion is worth it. I want her unhinged. I want her to feel what I've felt every day since we met. I've dreamed of having her a million times, and when she jerks and weeps and writhes under my hands, my name coming to life and then dying on her lips, I finally do.

CHAPTER 23

OBVIOUSLY I'M DEAD.

I can't feel my body and a dark angel hovers over me, so this must be heaven. The fluffy white duvet covering my bed is a cloud at my back.

"Bristol, baby." Grip's gruff voice reattaches me to the present, to the memory of what just happened.

Me, the queen of DIY orgasms, just came twice in the shower without a dick or a vibrator, or even at my own hand. Unless you count the massaging showerhead as vibrating. I try to speak, but my throat is scratched out from the hoarse screams Grip took from me.

"Yeah?" I finally croak.

"Before we do this," Grip says, a tightness around his eyes and his mouth. "I need you to believe I would never step out on you. I—"

"Grip." It's my turn to hush him, resting my finger against his lips. "You don't have to explain. We weren't together."

Anything else he would say stifles in his throat when I stroke him with a tight-fisted, steady rhythm.

"You were saying?" I whisper, lowering my head to suck on his nipple.

"Bristol, I'm not going to last long." His head drops. "Please don't take that as a sign of how it will always be, but watching you come in the shower has me halfway there already."

A shaky laugh breaks up his words.

"I've waited so long for this." The laugh dies, giving life to a tenderness in his eyes that pries my heart open another inch. "I've waited for you."

He pushes my damp, tangled hair back from my face, his touch rough and reverent.

"I've thought about this moment almost every day since we met. Not just the sex." His smile is so beautiful it literally hurts to look at it knowing it's for me. "I mean, yeah, of course, the sex. But the first day I met you, I wondered what kind of man it would take to win you. I wondered if I could be a man like that."

I slowly shift, nudging his shoulder until he's on his back and I'm looking down at him. I kiss a hard pectoral muscle and dip my head to lick between the ridges of his abs, his sharply indrawn breath making me smile against his skin.

"And what kind of man are you?"

His expression sobers, his eyes a mesmerizing night I lose myself in.

"The kind who would do anything to keep you." He brushes a thumb across my cheekbone. "Be sure because I won't let you go after."

I bite my lip to keep the tears at bay. He has no idea what it means to hear him say that. For the girl who had to beg for scraps of affection, for attention from the people she's loved the most, hearing him say that sets my fears free. All my life I've been the chaser. Chasing my parents' approval. Chasing my brother's love and friendship. I went to extremes to make them notice me, to make them love me.

I was right to be cautious. This heart of mine that has no borders, no bottom, no ceiling, would be crushed by the wrong man.

I could easily end up a shell bent to his will and settling for leftovers and reheated affection, but Grip is not the wrong man. He may be the only man I can trust with a heart like mine.

And I finally do.

"I'm sure." I rest my chin on his flat, hard stomach, reaching up to trace the bold bones of his face, the soft lips and thick, curling lashes. "Are you sure? I'm not like other girls, Grip. You have no idea."

He props up on one elbow to probe my eyes, palming my head and running his thumb over my brows and across my cheeks.

"Tell me what I'm in for," he says softly, his eyes serious, really asking.

"I'm going to be unreasonably possessive." I scatter kisses across his stomach, and the muscles clench beneath my lips. "I won't hesitate to destroy any bitch who tries to take you away from me."

"Okay." His breath hitches. "What else?"

I sit up, settling my legs on either side of his magnificent naked body, the narrow waist widening to the sleek muscles of his chest, the heavier muscles of his shoulders and ink-splattered arms. I admire the contrast of my thighs against his skin so deeply bronzed.

"I will hurt anyone who tries to hurt you." I laugh self-consciously. "If you hadn't figured it out, I'm kind of protective of the people I care about."

"I had noticed that, yeah." Grip caresses my hip, his fingers splaying possessively over me. "Anything else I should know?"

I lean forward until our flesh is flush, positioning myself over him, poised to inaugurate our bodies.

"Yes." I lean to reach my nightstand, grabbing a condom and barely fitting it over the thick, swollen head. "I like to be on top."

I slide slowly onto him, unprepared for the stretch. Not only am I tight, but Grip is wide and long. I breathe through the initial pinch, determined to take all of him, even if my body has to accommodate him inch by slow inch.

"You okay?" His concerned eyes scan my face. I offer a wobbly grin, biting my lip.

"Why is your dick so big?"

He chuckles, sitting up to kiss along my jaw and piercing his fingers into the hair at the base of my neck.

"You'll get used to it. It's the one stereotype about black guys that I'm glad is true, at least in my case. I can't speak for the rest of the brothers."

Our laughs meet between us, and I rest my temple against his.

"Besides," he groans when I roll my hips to sheath him completely. "You were made for me."

Our breaths catch, our chests press together, our bodies interlock. He caresses my back and then spreads his hands across my butt in ownership. Gently at first, he takes control of the pace. I pant with his every thrust up and into me, tightening my thighs around him. A blistering hunger burns away all discomfort as my body molds to his, as if we were carved to fit, as if I truly was fashioned to take him. I swoop to kiss the chiseled line of his jaw, and he turns his head, highjacking the kiss. Our mouths battle, each of us going deeper into the other with every parry of our tongues. The taste of him obliterates everything else. I can't see. I can't hear. I'm consumed, blindly grabbing his hard body anywhere I can—his biceps, his back, his thigh. There's so much of him and not enough time.

My frantic touches seem to shred his control. With a growl, he flips us, reversing our positions so I'm on my back, the bed cushioning my fall. He drags my leg over his hip and opens me up, grinding back in, his cadence merciless, all gentleness gone. He stares down at me, and it's hypnotic, our eyes locked as intensely, as intimately as our bodies. I hook my ankles at his back and meet every thrust, enslaved to the pace he sets. He's dictating my heartbeat, governing my pulse, holding my next breath cupped in his hands. I'm at his mercy, and it doesn't frighten me. With our bodies meshed, our hearts sharing beats, there's no room for fear. He lifts me up to pull my breast into his mouth, every tug of his lips, every delicate bite, lures me deeper under his spell.

"God, Bris." He groans against my swollen nipples, his breath a glorious burn on the sensitive skin. "I can't get enough of this. Baby, of you."

I don't want him to ever get enough, because I already know my desire for him is a bottomless well. He reaches between us to rub that cluster of nerves that combusts me in his arms. I cling to him as I explode, particles of myself floating in the air around us and settling onto the sweat-dampened sheets.

Guttural, groaning, he stiffens and floods me. My waters rise, and like a river bursting free of its banks, I overflow.

CHAPTER 24

G~RIP~

"SO YOU CAUGHT your dad banging one of his clients," I say to Bristol over the large steaming pizza recently delivered to her door. "And that made you mistrust me?"

"It isn't that simple." She picks off a mushroom that landed on her half of the pizza. "Halving never works. The crap you don't like always ends up creeping to your side."

"One mushroom does not constitute creeping." I pop the discarded mushroom into my mouth. "Don't get distracted. You were explaining why you kept me and that tight, sweet pussy apart for so long."

The slice she's holding pauses on its way to her mouth. Her eyes smile back at me, though she censors the rest of her expression.

"Just because we're sleeping together doesn't mean you can objectify me."

"How is that objectifying you?" I laugh before taking a bite of my pizza. "I said it was sweet and tight. That's high praise."

"You're ridiculous."

She rolls her eyes but laughs and stretches on the living room floor, her back against the couch. She looks completely relaxed, wild hair tucked into the neck of her Columbia University hoodie, legs bare in her boy short underwear.

"And you're stalling." I tweak her big toe. "You were telling me about your dad."

Any humor drains from her face. She tugs one string of the hoodie, folding her legs under her.

"I was already wrestling with my feelings for you." She puts the pizza down, dusting her hands of crumbs. "I knew I felt too much too fast."

"It wasn't too fast."

"It was a week, Grip." Bristol reaches for the bottle of red wine, giving me a wry look. "I'm not saying it wasn't real. Just that it was fast. Throw the drama with Tessa into the mix, and I was already regretting letting my guard down."

Hearing Tessa's name replays that scene at Grady's house before Bristol flew back to New York. Tessa screaming at me about being her baby's father. Bristol witnessing it all with wide, devastated eyes.

"I didn't handle that well." I capture her hand, tracing the love line in her palm. "I should have officially broken things off with her before letting it go as far as it did between you and me."

"I didn't know what to think." She runs her thumb along my finger. "I felt so connected to you, but Jimmi and Rhyson had painted you as this player."

"And I was a little bit." I shrug, my smile rueful. "I was young and feeling myself. Just because I wasn't a cheat doesn't mean I wasn't a player."

"I know." She pours a glass of red, offering it to me, before pouring one for herself. "I was this close to writing you off anyway after Tessa, but when my mom and I walked in on my dad with that girl . . ."

She tips her head back, the wine untouched.

"That wasn't it, though." She grimaces. "It was seeing my mother after we caught him. She just . . . let it go. She put up a good front, but later I found her drunk and weeping because she loved him and couldn't make herself walk away. It was pathetic what she was willing to take from him. All those years Rhyson and I assumed she didn't love him, and the whole time she loved him too much."

For the first time since she said she wanted me, her eyes become guarded again.

"And I realized that I'm like that." She releases a disparaging puff of air. "That's what I did with my parents, with Rhyson. I took whatever they had to give, scraps, and even when they hurt me, like a broken spigot, I couldn't turn it off."

"You group Rhyson with your parents?" I hate hearing that because he would hate to hear it.

"Not him as much as how I responded to what I processed as rejection." She sips her wine, cynicism coloring her laugh. "And yet after years of silence, I still wagered my future on him, on the possibility that he would take me into his life."

I'm silent, giving her space to express this her own way while my pizza goes uneaten, growing cold.

"It's like I only have a few spots in my heart, but the people who have one, I'd do anything for. I'd accept anything from them because they mean so much to me. It's needy and weak and I hate it about myself."

Emotion blurs her eyes with tears.

"I knew you were one of those people, Grip. That you had one of those spots, and when I saw how giving that kind of power to the wrong man has destroyed my mother, I just couldn't risk it with you."

Hearing her refer to me as "the wrong man" hurts, but I understand her caution. I just hate it took this long for her to trust me. Or for me to prove myself to her.

"I guess it didn't help that I've been smashing everything that moves since you came back to LA." I tear a slice of pizza into crusty confetti.

"And guys in your line of work aren't known for staying faithful."

"I ain't gonna lie. You know I've had my fair share of . . ."

Ass.

"Fair share of girls," I amend. "But I promise you I always let one go before I grabbed another."

"You're not helping your case," she says wryly.

She's probably right. I should move on. "What changed your mind?" I ask.

She shrugs, picking pepperoni from her side of the pizza and chewing it slowly.

"I think seeing you with Qwest was a big part of it." Her lashes shield her eyes from me. "And Rhys calling me a coward."

"He knew about this?" I'm stunned for a moment. He wouldn't have let me suffer for years this way.

"Only a few days ago. He confronted me about it when things started falling apart between you and me. When I wasn't with you for the release, he kept digging until he figured out what I felt."

That's my boy! I owe him something overpriced or inebriating.

"I still have reservations." She draws her legs up to her chest, resting her chin on her knees. "We've only been together once, and I already feel like it would be impossible to walk away."

Her admission is a huge step, one I relish, but I think she's looking at this all wrong.

"Bristol, having the capacity to love that way, as fiercely as you do, is not in and of itself a weakness."

She doesn't reply, but that curiosity that first drew me to her sparks behind her eyes.

"My mom has it." I chuckle and shift to lie on my side, propped up on my elbow. "I think every strength has a dark side, can be a weakness. She's learned to manage hers."

I think of how hard it will be for Ma to accept my relationship with Bristol because of her desire to see me with a Black woman. Or Latina. She did say brown was a color.

"Well, she's learned to manage most of her weaknesses." I shake my head. "There wasn't anything she wouldn't do for me. She always said sacrifice is the essence of love. It was the same for her sisters and her brothers, but I saw her draw lines, set limits as she got older and

KENNEDY RYAN

more mature. She didn't take shit from anybody, especially if it affected me."

I lift up to lay a soft kiss on her lips, and she opens up, tangling her tongue with mine for a few seconds before I pull back.

"And you won't take shit, either, not even from me." I cup one side of her face. "Not that you have to worry."

I rest my forehead against hers.

"Bris, you have to know how crazy I am about you."

The lingering uncertainty in her eyes tells me, as much as I've chased her, showing all my cards for years, she doesn't really know. She doesn't know it's her and no one else. And who can blame her with my dick waving like the state flag for the last few years?

"The thing you think is your greatest weakness," I assure her. "Is your greatest strength. That capacity to love, everyone doesn't have it. That grit to fight for the people who mean the most to you, it's priceless."

"You think so?" she asks softly, not looking away from my face.

"I know so, and I feel honored that I have one of those spots in your heart." I lay a palm against her neck. "I promise I won't abuse it. You can trust me."

She closes the space separating us, taking my chin between her lips, meandering over my jaw and finally touching my mouth with hers.

"You know what I want?" Her question lands on my lips in a husky breath.

"Yeah. Me, too."

I sit up, reaching for her, my dick solid as a rock, but I come up with thin air. She's on her feet and walking toward the kitchen.

"Ice cream." Over her shoulder her eyes tease and torture, but I know she needed to change the conversation. So, I let her.

The sweatshirt hits the top of her thighs, and the occasional glimpse of her ass in the white boy short underwear isn't helping my erection. I follow her to the kitchen like she knew I would. When I swing open the kitchen door, she's bent over, her upper body buried in the freezer, the sweatshirt hiked up to show off the firm lines of her thighs and curves of her butt.

"I know I have ice cream in here somewhere." She shifts frozen meat and vegetables until she finds what she's looking for. "Aha!"

She turns to face me, bumping the freezer door closed with a hip.

"Found it." She shakes a quart of Ben & Jerry's Cookie Dough ice cream. "This is my fave, not that I can afford it."

I inspect the lean grace of her body, punctuated by subtle curves. There's so much more to Bristol than her body, but it's a really great place to start.

She hops up onto the kitchen island, swinging her legs and banging bare feet against the base.

"Want some?" She proffers a large spoon loaded with ice cream to me.

I definitely want some. I stalk over to her, insinuating myself between her knees and leaning forward, my mouth open and waiting. I can tell the moment she realizes it isn't ice cream I really want. Her eyes go smoky and her pink tongue swipes over the fullness of her lips. She takes the large spoonful into her mouth instead. I lean into her, my palms pressed into the island surface and my arms bracketing her slim body. She brushes our noses together once, twice before opening my lips in a frozen kiss that shivers through my whole body. Her icy tongue plumbs the recesses of my mouth, brushing the back of my throat in chilly strokes. She cups my chin and holds me still to control the tempo of our tongues twisting together. When we finally pull away, harsh, frosted breaths gust the air between our lips.

She slides off the counter and maneuvers me slowly until my back is against the island. Without ever looking away, she scoops another spoonful of ice cream into her mouth and drops to her knees. She holds the ice cream in her mouth while she deftly unzips the jeans hanging low on my hips, already unbuttoned at the waist. The pants drop and collect around my ankles.

Please let this be happening.

She touches my hips under the briefs, coaxing the underwear down my legs, too. With no preliminary, she stretches her mouth to take my dick between her lips, rolling her cold tongue around the throbbing head.

"Oh, dammit, dammit, dammit, Bris." I clench my fingers in her wild hair.

The wintry mix of her tongue taking me in rough strokes and the smooth sides of her throat clamping around my dick push me to the edge. Brows knit, eyes press closed, her blissful groan vibrates around me. She clutches my ass with one hand and takes my balls, heavy and tight, into her other hand, caressing them.

"I'm gonna come," I rasp in case she doesn't swallow. A lot of girls don't. Groupies tend to swallow because they want to leave an impression. They'll do whatever they think you want to get another night with you. I only want Bristol to do what she wants to do. She doesn't have to perform. I'm hers already, and I want her to enjoy everything we do as much as I do.

Because I'm enjoying the fuck out of this blow job.

Never pulling back, she reaches up and finds the quart of ice cream again. She pauses only to load her mouth with another scoopful of the frigid creaminess before she possesses me again, her head bobbing at a deliberate pace between my legs. It's apparent to me that Bristol will, like she does all things, finish what she starts, but I'll have to watch her swallow me down to the last drop some other time. I want to be inside her again. Now.

With gentle fingers, I tug on her chin until her mouth drops open. She looks up at me from her spot on the floor. I reach down under her arms and raise her off her knees.

"Rain check." I hoist her onto the kitchen island and yank the underwear down her legs. I lay her back flat and lift the heels of her feet to the marble surface, leaving her knees up and her legs wide open.

"Hold on, baby." I push into her, and we groan when the cold from the ice cream melts into her wet heat. I pound into her so hard she has to latch onto the counter to keep from sliding away. I break rhythm to check her face for pain or discomfort.

"Don't you fucking stop," she moans, her neck exposed, back

arching, pushing her breasts up under the thick cotton of her sweat-shirt. I shove the material over her torso, scrunching it at her shoulders and below her neck so I can watch her breasts bounce with every thrust. I bend to take one in my mouth.

"Take it," she pants. "Baby, take it."

The exquisite slide of flesh against flesh is like nothing I've ever felt, and I realize I'm in her with no rubber.

"Bris, I'm in raw." I grit the words out because I want to stay right where I am, flesh on flesh. "I need to pull out."

"No, you don't." She pants, her nails digging into my ass. "I'm clean, and I'm covered. You?"

"Yeah," I answer unhesitatingly. "I'm clean. So we can . . ."

She nods frantically, shifting her hips forward on the counter to change the angle, to deepen penetration. She wants deeper?

I pull her legs straight up on my chest until her feet rest at my shoulders, leaving me nothing but ass and pussy. I slam into her at a bruising pace, hoping I'm not hurting her, but unable to imagine stopping. It's a primal mating—a feral rutting, and I'm the wild beast reduced to a clump of nerves and instincts.

"Grip." Her hands climb her chest to touch her breasts, twisting her own nipples. Watching that, there's no way I'm not coming, but her next words do the impossible. They stop me.

"I love you." Tears slip from the corners of her closed eyes. "Oh, God, I love you so much."

My breaths are choppy, my heart seizing in my chest. "What'd you say?"

Her eyes pop open, briefly touching on my face before fixing to the ceiling.

"Um . . ."

I pull her up so her legs fall alongside my hips, our bodies still joined at the center, but her chest pressed into mine.

"Did you mean it?" I demand, cupping her butt.

"Grip, I—"

"Don't play games with me." Desperation sharpens my voice. I need to know she means it. She lifts her lashes, and fear saturates her beautiful eyes. Linking her fingers behind my head, her thumbs caressing my neck, she nods.

Not good enough.

"Say it again." I resume pumping in short and shallow thrusts that will stoke the fire, but won't satisfy.

"I'm scared to death." Her words come on choppy breaths. Without breaking rhythm, I bend to her ear.

"You have nothing to be afraid of." I press her hand to my chest, over my heart. "This is yours. No one else's."

I dip my head, slowing to nothing, but keeping her eyes.

"I'm yours. No one else's." I scatter kisses over her cheeks. "Even when we fight, I feel you. Your anger, your frustration. I feel your pleasure like it's mine. Your emotions like they're mine."

I peer into the flushed beauty of her face. Her sweatshirt is still pushed up so her breasts press into my naked chest. I give her a moment to recognize the syncopation of our heartbeats.

"Don't you feel how connected we are?" I ask. "If I break your heart, I break mine."

A sweet smile spreads over her lips and she nods.

"I love you." She laughs, shaking her head. "Eight years in the making, but I love you."

"I love you, too," I whisper into her hair. "You're everything to me, Bristol. You gotta know that."

Her tears come even as our bodies resume a ferocious pace. We splinter into a thousand pieces in her kitchen, becoming more together than we were apart. More than we were alone. With whispered promises and words of love, we exchange hearts.

CHAPTER 25

B<small>RISTOL</small>

BRIGHT SUN BEAMS through Grip's windows, letting me know we've slept later than I usually do even for a Sunday. We spent the night at the loft, and as I shake off a veil of dreams, lines from Neruda's "Night on the Island" filter through my consciousness. The poem follows a long night between lovers. Though I've read those lines more times than I can count, they were always beautiful hypotheticals. I never expected to sleep through the night with Grip or to wake with the possessive weight of his arm around me, welcome and beloved. I never expected any of what has transpired over the last two days.

And I almost gave him away.

I would have forfeited the perfect weight of his body over mine. Would never have felt the sweet heat of him wrapped around me, or the bold sweep of his hands over my nakedness under our covers in the morning. These are the things that cost nothing but are precious. And I almost never had them.

"What are you thinking about?"

Grip's whispered question mists the sensitive skin of my neck, and I scoot back to snuggle under the covers and against his hard, naked body.

"'Night on the Island.'"

"Fitting." He opens his mouth over the curve of my shoulder in a kiss. "Because you were definitely wild and sweet last night.'"

"You weren't so bad yourself." I turn over to run my thumb over his full lips. "Neruda was so romantic. I'm glad you introduced me to him."

"Dude had serious game." Grip laughs. "No one writes about love and sex and passion like Neruda."

He grins down at me, a hint of mischief in his eyes. "The original Chocolate Charm."

We both laugh at that. I haven't heard it in so long. It's our own inside joke, from the first day we met, but Grip really could charm lint from your pockets.

"I believe you promised to make me come with words alone." My husky laugh puckers the smooth quiet of the room. "Will you be using his words or your own? Or was that an empty threat?"

"You'll just have to wait and see," he teases me.

He pauses before going on with a more solemn tone.

"When I saw the book and the whistle on your bed, I didn't know what to think. Even though I knew the connection between us was undeniable, the last few weeks had me questioning everything I believed was possible for us."

"I'm sorry." I swallow my uncertainty and force myself to tell him things I've kept for years. "When it first came in the mail, I wanted to burn that book. I was furious with you over Tessa. I didn't want it to mean anything to me."

Despite his hand caressing my hip, I sense a stillness in him behind me, an alertness that tells me he's listening with every part of him.

"But even after I told myself I would put that week behind me, put you behind me," I continue. "I found myself reading it at night."

"Yeah?" He pushes my hair aside and traces the downy line of my nape with a finger. "Why?"

I shrug, reaching for the ease we shared yesterday at my house. In my shower. In my bed. Sex has always been much easier than intimacy, but with Grip they're inextricable. One giving rise to the other. One and the same. Sex with other men never meant much to me, but taking Grip inside my body shook me, rearranged me. Sharing the thoughts I've kept private for so long, I feel just as naked as I did in the shower when he commanded me to open myself for him. I feel more exposed.

"I kept going back to the book, reading your notes in the margins and searching between the lines for what it could tell me about you," I say. "When I moved to LA after college, the memories and emotions from that week all came back, and I had to freeze you out or I knew I'd give in to the pressure you put on me."

"You acted like we'd never been anything to each other," he says softly. "And despite my part in screwing things up, it pissed me off."

"Oh, so was that hate fucking you did with all those other women?"

I turn onto my back to look into his eyes, the lighthearted note in my voice forced. There's more than a granule of truth in most jokes, and this one is no exception. It's levity with talons, and I take the chance to dig in, even if it isn't entirely fair.

There's regret, but no apology in his eyes. "Nope. Just plain old fucking fucking."

He props up on one elbow and splays his hand possessively over my stomach.

"At first, I told myself I would win you back. I would remind you of how it had been between us, but you wouldn't budge. After a year or so, I promised myself I wouldn't give up on you, but I also assumed we'd circle back to each other when the time was right. In the meantime . . ."

"I get it." I rub the soft heather-colored comforter pulled around us. "It wasn't cheating, but it still felt like a betrayal."

I hastily glance up at him, spreading my fingers over the hand resting on me.

"I know that isn't fair, but it's how I felt."

"You felt that way because even though we weren't together," he says, caressing my collarbone. "We were supposed to be. Inside you knew us being apart wasn't right. Me with them wasn't right, and you with anybody other than me sure as hell wasn't right."

His chuckle loosens some of my tightly wound places. He settles his eyes, still slightly sleep-glazed and growing more solemn, on me.

"I don't want to rehash everything." He cups the side of my face. "We've wasted too much time. I want us moving forward from now on."

"Starting today." He drops a quick kiss on my lips. "I've got a surprise."

"A surprise?" I trail fingers over the carved strength of his shoulders and down the hard biceps.

He shifts until he's over me, notching his hips between my thighs. With both of us naked, we're one deep breath away from penetration. His lips wander down my neck and to my breast. He takes his time with each nipple. The suction of his mouth, thorough and voracious, stirs desire low in my belly.

"We are not having sex." I moan, wetness pooling between my legs and my hips circling beneath him, seeking friction. "I can barely walk."

He releases my breast with a pop, his smile triumphant. "What'd I tell you?"

"Like your other head isn't big enough, you had to go and have a big dick." Our laughter shakes us under the covers.

"If you're not giving up that ass," he says, the smile lingering. "Get dressed so we can go. I don't want to be late."

"Go where? Late for what?"

"Pretty sure I said surprise, and last time I checked, you don't know about those before they happen."

The thought of leaving the loft freaks me out a little for more reasons than one, but I'll start with one.

"Grip, as far as the world is concerned," I say carefully. "Qwest is still #GripzQueen. I don't want to embarrass her, or for people to assume we've done something wrong."

"We know we didn't cheat." Grip's frown and the hard set of his lips indicate this is as important to him as it is to me.

"I know, but I pushed you guys together, and I feel bad that she's gotten hurt in this process."

"So do I." Regret shades his eyes. "She cried when I broke it off. She thinks she's in love with me, and I feel like an asshole."

"So do I. And she *is* in love with you. It's obvious." I trace a thumb over the thick brows and chiseled bone structure that have fascinated me since the first time I saw them. "I know how much it hurts to love you and think someone else has you."

"You were jealous?" He echoes my caress, his thumb tracing my features, his eyes searching mine, his fingers working through my hair spread on the pillow.

I nod, biting my lip.

"And scared that you would fall for her. I know that sounds stupid since I pushed you together, but the reality of you wanting someone else . . ."

My words die around the painful lump in my throat. "Bris, I've never wanted anyone the way I want you."

He kisses me deeply, long strokes of his tongue inciting the same insatiable desire we've indulged in over the last day and a half. When he finally releases my mouth, we face each other on the pillow, foreheads pressed together, exchanging short, heavy breaths.

"We'll be careful," he concedes. "But I want you to do this with me today."

"But, Grip—"

"As far as the world's concerned, you're my manager, and it won't be unusual for us to be seen together."

"True." I still hesitate.

"Should we coordinate a statement with Will? Formally notify the press that Qwest and I aren't together anymore?"

"That feels . . . I don't know. Slimy. Like we're shoving her out the door."

"So we what?" A frown knits above the frustration gathering in his eyes. "Just wait for someone to ask me or her if we're together and then deny it? That's too passive. I'm not waiting for that."

He presses my hands over my head, his rough palms scaling the sensitive skin inside my arms and wrists. He dips his head to hover over my lips.

"I'm ready to be with you."

He pulls my bottom lip between his, nipping the softness and then trailing kisses down my neck. He pauses when the intercom system buzzes. Someone wants in. They must know the code to have gotten all the way up the elevator.

"Probably Amir," Grip mumbles, rolling out of bed, treating me to the glorious sight of a taut bronzed ass, the flare of muscled thighs, and the tempting breadth of smooth back and shoulders. Two columns of abdominal muscle stack above his navel and the fine trail of hair leads down to his long, semi-erect south pole. He slips on a pair of gray sleep pants flung over a bench at the foot of the bed.

"Shame to cover that." I drag myself up, resting my shoulders against the headboard. "I was really enjoying the view."

He looks at me from under a dark line of brows, his sculpted lips tilting at one corner.

"I thought you didn't wanna fuck." He leans one hand on the bed for support and palms my throat with the other, gently tilting my chin. "Them's fucking words."

"I am a little sore." I release the sheet tucked under my arms, the rush of cool air when it falls piquing my nipples. "But who needs to walk?"

The heat in his eyes scorches my bare shoulders and breasts. He pulls one knee onto the bed and captures my nipple between his lips, his tongue like fire licking around me. His thumb teases the other nipple tight.

"Grip." His name rushes from my mouth. My head falls back, and my fingers find his neck, pressing his teeth and lips harder into my flesh. "Please."

"Shit," Grip mutters against the underside of my breast. He pulls me down flat to the bed, rips the sheet back and pushes my legs open, his eyes locked on my center.

He presses my knees up and drops to his elbows, his long legs stretched behind him on the bed. I'm writhing at the first long swipe of his tongue. He's lapping at me. There's a fire hidden in my slit, and every nip of his teeth and tug of his lips fans a desire in me so strong it clenches my belly. To want him this badly and not have him buried inside me hurts. Even knowing Amir could be on his way in, I clutch Grip's head. I roll my hips into him, a hungry undulation. Amir could walk in right now and I'm not sure I could stop. In an instant, in a matter of a few touches and kisses, I'm starved for Grip like the first time, like I've never had him before.

The buzzer comes again, insistent and extended.

"Grip, you know I got a key." Amir's irritated voice comes through the speakers. "Got me standing out here waiting on your ass. I'm coming in."

The front door beeps when it opens, and the sound of Amir's heavy footsteps climb the stairs ahead of him.

"Dammit." Grip pulls the sheet over me and bounds off the bed, crossing swiftly to the open door of his bedroom.

"Grip, you taking a shit or what?" Amir reaches the door just as Grip does, his wide eyes connecting with mine over Grip's shoulder. "Oh, hell. I'm sorry, bruh."

My cheeks burn. I tug the sheet tighter over my breasts and lift my chin, refusing to hide. From the rest of the world, yes. From one of Grip's most trusted friends who has seen all the bumps in our road, no.

"Out." Grip shoves Amir's shoulder, pushing him back onto the landing overlooking the open floor below. He gives me a quick glance over his shoulder, his mouth set. "Sorry 'bout that."

The door closes behind them, and my embarrassment whooshes

out of me on a lengthened breath. The door pops open, and Grip sticks his head back in.

"Shower and get dressed. If we leave soon, we won't be late." Chagrin twists his lips and pushes his brows up. "And I'm sorry again about..."

He points a thumb out the door.

"It's okay." I muster a weak smile. "How should I dress? Where are we going?"

"Remember? Surprise." A devilish grin widens on his face. "Just be beautiful."

I slip on a silk robe against the slight morning chill. When I walk into Grip's massive closet, his prized shoe collection takes up an entire wall. My eyes immediately go to the gap he left for me to hang the things he suggested I bring and leave at his place. This is happening fast. I mean, I know it's been coming for years, but still.

"What are you doing, Bristol?" I ask myself, dropping to the bench planted in the middle of the closet, toying with the belt of my robe. "Are you sure about this?"

Amir showed up, the first contact we've had with the outside world in two days, and all my insecurities and doubts followed him through the front door. Are things really so different than they were before I told Grip how I feel? He's still a star with an all-access pussy pass. Still the kind of man who, even if he weren't famous, would attract women effortlessly. I'm still the girl who can't draw lines around her heart where he's concerned.

"Hey." Grip props a shoulder at the arched entrance of the closet. "You're supposed to be in the shower by now. I was hoping to ambush you all wet and naked."

"Um, I was just wondering what Amir said?" I wrinkle my brows. "What did he think?"

"I'm pretty sure his exact words were, 'Took you long enough, pussy.'"

His teasing grin melts when I don't manage a smile back, too disoriented now that the sex haze has cleared. He walks deeper into the closet and sits beside me, taking my hand. He kisses the inside of my wrist and clasps an arm around my shoulder.

"What's wrong?"

"I don't know." I shrug and press into the warm strength of his chest. The longer I'm tucked into his arms, the faster my fears drain away. "I guess seeing Amir just reminded me that there's a world out there that will be hard for us to navigate."

"Just out there?" He lays his lips against my temple. "What about the world in here? In your head?"

I glance up at him and hate seeing the guard going up in his eyes.

"I told you I'm not letting you go again, Bristol." The strain in his voice tightens his lips. "You don't get to have second thoughts. You can't—"

I grab his neck and slant my lips over his, invading the warm silkiness of his mouth, aggressively thrusting and seeking. Passionate. Certain. I've allowed these fears to rule me for years, to delay this for years. I'm not giving into them again. I won't ruin this. Grip said my capacity to love can be a strength. I'll let him show me how.

He hums against my lips, a greedy sound as his hands brand my back through the silk robe. He digs into my hips, molds my thighs and arms, possession in every touch. He pulls out of the kiss, cupping my chin and forcing my eyes to his.

"You can't take this away from me. Not again." His jaw clenches. "You start having doubts about me, about us, we talk about it. It's one thing to have to negotiate the Qwest situation or the pressures that come with this industry. Those aren't the things that kept us apart. I can fight all of that. I can't fight you."

"I know," I whisper. "I was having doubts for a minute."

"Was?" He's watchful and waiting. "Not anymore?"

"Not anymore." I lean in for another kiss, and his hand presses at the back of my head when I would pull away, maintaining the sweet contact. Ravishing my lips until they throb in time with the rhythm of our kiss.

"Don't doubt me, Bris."

A fist closes around my heart at the plea on his lips, in his eyes.

"I won't." I cup the side of his face and give him one last kiss. "I promise."

"Good." The tight line of his mouth eases. "Now we really will be late if we don't get cracking."

"I'm not gonna ask again." I stand and walk over to the bag of clothes I brought.

"Good, 'cause I still ain't telling you nothing." He laughs, but there's no mistaking the quiet satisfaction in his eyes as he watches me hang the few items I packed in his closet.

I've finished my shower and am wiping steam from the mirror when he comes into the bathroom, still wearing the sleep pants hanging low on his hips. I'm tempted to tug on the drawstring holding them up so I can see all his bare magnificence again, but his frown quells all my playful instincts.

"Now what?" I scrub cleanser onto my face, leaving untouched circles around my eyes.

"You said you and Parker are done, right?" His question and his tone ring abruptly in the bathroom.

My fingertips go still on my cheeks, and my eyes meet his in the mirror. Before I can answer, he reaches into his pocket and pulls out a phone. My phone.

"You left this downstairs." He places it on the bathroom counter. "Why's he blowing you up?"

"Is he?" I carefully re-tuck the towel under my arm, at least making sure it is secure since this conversation could quickly become less than safe. "I don't know."

I splash water onto my face, wishing I could wash away all those messages and the last few weeks with Parker altogether.

"Like four missed calls, text messages, voicemails." He rests a hip against the counter, waiting, expecting an explanation from me.

"Were you snooping, Grip?" My smile in the mirror as I dry my face is strained.

"I heard it ringing downstairs when you were in the shower." Grip crosses his arms over the width of his chest, biceps flexed with the motion. "Does he understand that it's over? Why all the calls?"

I dot moisturizer on my face and shrug.

"I'd have to listen to the messages to know what he wants for sure."

He picks up the phone and extends it to me, one brow cocked. "No time like the present."

My short laugh sounds uneasy even to me. I grab the phone, but set it back on the counter.

"Later. Aren't you the one who said I need to get ready?"

I run a brush through my hair and don't look at him even though his scrutiny in the mirror never wavers.

"I said I didn't want to re-hash everything," Grip says. "But just tell me what happened with Parker."

Shit.

"Um, what do you want to know?" I drop the question but walk away before he has time to respond, heading into the closet and flicking through my limited wardrobe options. "You really should tell me what to wear for this surprise of yours. Is this okay?"

I hold a romper to my chest, taking his "I don't give a damn" expression as a no and discarding it to search the rack for something else.

"Okay, maybe this one?" I hold up a cotton candy pink belted tunic dress with a high-low hem for his inspection. He still doesn't respond with anything other than the exasperation on his face. "Yeah, I like this one, too."

He snatches the dress from my hand and tosses it onto the padded bench in the center of the closet.

"Stop avoiding my question." Impatience disrupts the rugged beauty of his face. "What happened with Parker?"

"I thought we were short on time." I turn my back to dig in my carryall, searching for ankle boots. "I know I had a pair of—"

He pulls me around by my shoulders to face him. His hands glide down my still-damp arms to link his fingers with mine, the warmth of his bare chest emanating to my chilled skin.

"Tell me. Now."

I sigh and slump my shoulders before starting.

"I used Parker to push you to Qwest." I chew the corner of my mouth for a second. "We weren't ever actually in a relationship."

I roll my eyes and gesture vaguely.

"I mean, we dated a few months, yeah, back in high school."

"And fucked in the coat check." Grip's words emerge controlled, but a savage objection flares in his eyes, a warning that beneath the placid surface, a beast bides its time.

"Yeah." I rake my fingers through my hair. "But it didn't take me long to figure out it wasn't gonna work. I broke things off when I started at Columbia and he went off to Stanford. He's been trying to wiggle back in ever since."

"So you fucked Parker, after all these years, just so I would try with Qwest? You went that far to manipulate me?"

The scariest part of what he says is what he doesn't say. The things that, even though not voiced, take flight behind his eyes. Disappointment. Anger. Disgust.

"Not exactly. I—"

"Then what exactly?" he slices over me.

"Give me a chance to explain."

"That's what this is. The chance to have your say." He narrows his eyes. "I just hate everything you're saying."

I sit on the bench and press my knees together under the thick towel, trying to keep my back and my facts straight.

"That night on the roof you said neither of us had been in a serious relationship, and that seemed to make you think there was a chance when I really didn't think there should be. Then before the show, I overheard you talking with Rhys and Kai in your dressing room."

"You eavesdropped on us?" It comes as a quiet demand.

"Not on purpose, but I could tell that you wanted . . . more. That you wanted to be with someone the way Rhyson is with Kai, and you were held up with me."

I lean forward, resting my elbows on my knees.

"When Parker upgraded Qwest's room at his hotel that night, it was perfect timing." I dip my head until a fall of hair hides my face from him. "So I invited Parker to the club. I wanted you to see us together and thought it might give you a little push in the right direction."

The silence swells with all the emotions he's suppressing, but they bubble up to the surface anyway, tightening the air in the closet until it feels like a tomb.

"I can tell you're frustrated with me," I say softly. "You don't have to hide that. I can take it."

"You wasted more time." He walks over to the few of my items hanging in the space he allotted for me, back turned to me. He lifts the sleeve of a dress and lets it fall. "And we involved Qwest. She got hurt because of us. And Parker?"

He aims a hard look at me over his shoulder.

"You fucked him to advance this dumb ass plan of yours?"

"No." I squeeze my eyes shut, but that doesn't keep me from seeing myself clearly. "I had no intention of sleeping with Parker. I was so drunk I didn't even know what had happened when I woke up with him in my bed the next morning. He had to tell me we had slept together."

"Don't tell me that." He squeezes his eyes shut, a growl rumbling in his chest. He links his hands behind his head, pacing back and forth in front of the bench. "If you were anywhere near as drunk that night as you were at Pirouette, I can't believe you had sex with someone in that state. Do you have any idea how irresponsible that is? He could have done anything to you. You're supposed to be the rational one. The level-headed one, and you pull this shit."

I surge to my feet, reaching for anger. Anything to distract me from the shame and regret weaving together like a chain-link fence around my self-respect.

"I never claimed to be perfect and you aren't my keeper. I don't need a lecture, Grip. I'm just trying to tell you what happened."

"And I'm telling you it's fucked up!" Grip's voice reverberates in the confines of the closet. "All of it. You pulling in Parker to get me to sleep with Qwest."

"I didn't force you to sleep with her."

"You getting drunk," he continues as if I didn't correct him, "and riding off into the night with that asshole."

"Riding off into the night?" I scoff. "Glad we're not resorting to the dramatic."

"Sleeping with him when you weren't even lucid enough to remember." He pauses, giving me space to object, but I don't have an objection. He can't be anymore disappointed in me than I am in myself for that. My anger deflates as quickly as it rose, and so does his. He steps close and brushes a knuckle over my cheek before cupping my face.

"Bris, what's up with all the drinking lately?" His voice is a balm over the self-inflicted wounds of my own actions. "I mean, we've always joked that you can outdrink us all, that nobody holds their liquor like you, but it was never like this. Should I be worried?"

A heavy laugh tumbles out of my mouth. I lean into his warm palm and close my eyes against the concern on his face.

"I'm not an alcoholic if that's what you're asking." I step even closer to him, so close I can drop my head to his chest and mumble my words into the smooth skin. "Lately I just needed to be . . . numb."

"Why?" When I don't respond for a few seconds, he lifts my chin and searches my face. "Numb to what?"

I pull away to show him the truth in my eyes.

"You and Qwest. That night I sent you off on a date with her, I was miserable. And I knew I did it to myself. Not just involving Parker or arranging the date with Qwest, but letting my fears rule me. Denying myself the one thing I really wanted."

"And what was that?" His eyes rest intently on my face. He already knows the answer, but I know he needs to hear me say it. After all I've put him through, he deserves to hear it. "What do you want?"

"You," I whisper.

There's no gloating, no smugness in his expression.

"You've got me." He presses his forehead to mine, angling my chin to kiss me with quick tenderness. "I just hate how we got here."

"So do I."

I place my hands flat to his chest, hesitating before going on. "If it's any consolation, Parker and I were never actually dating. I'm pretty sure he leaked everything that night to Spotted. He thought the media storm and all the coverage would somehow pressure me into giving in and making it real."

"Giving in?" The muscle tenses beneath my palms. "What does he want?"

"He wants what he's always wanted." I shrug, frank when I meet his eyes. "He wants me. Ever since we were kids he said he would marry me. Our mothers started it, and he just latched on. He sees himself as the king of his family's empire, and me as his . . ."

I stop short of the word so closely associated with Grip and Qwest.

"Queen?" The word trips, loaded with irony, off Grip's tongue.

"He's crazy." I dig my fingers into my hair. "I keep telling him I won't marry him, but he won't take no for an answer."

"Why did you let it go on for weeks?"

"He was in India almost the entire time, and the media had, for the most part, lost interest." I force myself to tell him the truth; though, I know it will only anger him. "I knew you gave Qwest a chance because you thought Parker and I were serious. I'd just started pressing him to tell the media the truth."

"When I think about you basically unconscious, of Parker taking advantage of you like that . . ."

He holds my hand, his gentle grip tightening around my fingers. He lifts his lashes to reveal the leashed violence in his eyes, and he doesn't have to finish the sentence. It's written there what he wants to do to Parker.

"Then don't think about it." I stretch up to kiss him, deliberately stroking my tongue deeply into his mouth, an exclusive, intimate exchange I don't want to have with anyone else. "Think about us. Think about what we feel, what we've said to each other. Think about today."

"Today he's still calling you." A bunched muscle interrupts the smooth, lightly scruffed line of his jaw. "You told him it isn't happening, but he's still calling and texting."

"I know. I'll—"

"I want it to stop."

I blink a few times, waiting for the ferocity to clear from his eyes, but it only intensifies the longer I stay silent.

"Okayyyyy. I'll check the messages, and I'll handle it."

"If you don't handle him, I will," he warns.

Oh, the fuck no. That's the last thing I need. "That isn't a good idea. He's . . ."

I focus on our bare feet just inches apart, our toes pointing to each other.

"He's a very powerful man, Grip, and I don't want you hurt."

There's an ominous quiet before the storm I should have known my comment would stir.

"You think I'm scared of that son of a bitch?" A dark cloud breaks on his face, his voice a boom of thunder. "You think you have to protect me from him? Is that what you're saying?"

"You don't know him. He—"

"You get one shot." He clips the words, anger still brimming in his eyes. "Listen to the messages. Deal with him or I will."

"You don't boss me around." My words land heavily between us. I hate to say it, but I have to say it. I have no plans to be anyone other than who I am. "Let's be clear about that."

The bands stretching tightly over his expression loosen just a little bit. His eyes crinkle at the corners, and he drops a kiss at the corner of my mouth.

"That's my girl."

A confused laugh pops from my mouth. I assert myself, expecting resistance, and it only draws him closer.

"I have no desire to boss you around, Bristol. I love that you're a boss. It's sexy as hell."

"Well, thank you for—"

He cups my pussy under the towel tucked around me, his eyes heated, holding me hostage.

"This is the only part of you I want to boss around." His middle finger strokes along one side of my clit and then the other.

"There won't be any doubt who's the boss right here between these legs."

The lazy motion of his finger snatches the breath from me. I'm wet and anaerobic, unable to even pant while he tends to my clit, brushing a rough finger pad along the slickened nub. One thick finger breaches me and retreats. Breaches me and retreats, a rough repetition that soaks his hand and makes my thighs tremble. Holy hell, I may not want to be bossed around, but Grip is Commander-In-Clit. He can get it anytime he wants.

The unapologetic possession in his eyes as he watches me unraveling, my knees weakening so badly I have to hang on to his shoulders, tells me he knows it. I can't even care. If he does this to me when no other man has been able to, he gets to be smug about it. He's earned that shit.

The orgasm propels harsh breaths from my mouth. I come hard and with a crash, landing limply against his chest. The pleasure so overwhelms me that tears christen the corners of my eyes.

"That's right. That's my girl." He licks at the tears as if they're an offering, like they're his due. He palms the small of my back, and the possessive weight of his hand alone has my most hidden, private muscles clenching again. He holds complete sway over my body.

"You're right, Bristol," he whispers into my hair, humor rich in his voice. "You're the boss."

CHAPTER 26

GRIP

GROWING UP, DRIVING a Range Rover like this one—overloaded, latest model, and just over two hundred thousand dollars—seemed about as likely as scoring a ride in Cinderella's pumpkin. But here I am.

Or rather here we are.

"This car's gorgeous." Bristol caresses the stitch pattern perforated leather seats. "I didn't even know you were in the market for one. You've never cared much about cars before."

"True." I merge onto the 5, shrug, and shoot her a quick grin. "I'm good with my Harley and my six four."

"And what's so great about the six four?" Bristol laughs when I look at her like this should be self-evident.

"They don't make 'em like the '64 Impala anymore," I say. "That's when American cars were the bomb. It takes more than money to appreciate them. You gotta maintain and know your way around that beautiful body. She won't purr for just any dude."

"Why am I not surprised this became a thinly veiled conversation about sex?" Bristol laughs, opening the bag in her lap and finishing her makeup since I rushed her out of the loft.

"What can I say?" I grin. "Amir rolled through to drop it off."

"It's yours?"

"I'm test driving it."

"Hmmm." She flips down the visor mirror and applies lipstick. "I'd never picture you with this car, I guess."

"Maybe I'm full of surprises."

She'll soon see that for herself. I know she's gonna kill me for what I'm doing today, but she loves me. They say love covers a multitude of sins. We'll see. In the words of that great comedic philosopher Kevin Hart, "We gon' learn today!"

"And what is this surprise?" Bristol follows up predictably.

I only give her a shrug and grin in response. If she weren't distracted, she'd probably pay closer attention to the route we're taking.

"You'll have to wait and see."

She rolls her eyes and takes off her seatbelt to reach her purse on the floor, putting the makeup bag away.

The loud "whoop" from behind freezes my blood, and for a second, my heart isn't sure it's safe to beat. The flashing blue lights in the rearview mirror confirm what my body has already warned me of. Growing up in Compton, guys like me have an almost Pavlovian response to cops. Instead of salivating, we auto-perspire and run through the mantra our mothers drilled in our heads before we could even drive.

Keep your hands where they can see them. Never make sudden movements.

Have license and registration already out so you don't have to reach into any pockets or compartments. Always answer with respect. And most important.

Do whatever it takes to make it home.

"Put your seatbelt back on." I slap my license on the dashboard. "Now, babe."

I feel her eyes boring into me, but I'm too focused on getting through these next few minutes to address her questions. It feels like the gun I stowed in the glove compartment, the one I carry for my own safety, just turned its barrel on me, adding a complication to a situation I always hate finding myself in.

I resent the sheen of sweat covering my skin. Adrenaline pours through my system, spiking my blood, crashing my heart behind my ribs. No matter how much I remind myself that I've done nothing wrong, that I have the number one album in the country, and that I could afford to buy this car several times over and not even dent my bank account, I can't undo years of conditioning that tell me I have reason to fear. To be cautious. Even before that summer day with Jade on the playground, I had an uneasy relationship with law enforcement. We all did in my neighborhood. After that, it only worsened. After that, it was never the same. Since Greg joined LAPD, I've met many good cops, and things have changed a lot in my neighborhood, but it's still a deeply rotten system. When the cop taps the window, that's something I can't forget.

"Is there a problem, officer?" I ask through the half-open window.

His assessing eyes flick past me and over my shoulder, roaming over Bristol. I don't have to look at her to know what he sees. I've memorized her. The burnished hair is wild and loose around her shoulders. Her lips, pink and soft. Her dress reaches mid-thigh, but sitting, the hem rises even higher. His glance, though impersonal, lingers on her long, toned legs. The longer his eyes rest on her, the less I feel like dealing with this shit. I'm relieved when he looks back to my face.

"There's been suspicious activity in the area, so we're doing some routine stops." He steps back. "License and registration, please."

Suspicious activity my ass. I am the suspicious activity. My driving a two-hundred-thousand dollar Rover in this neighborhood is grounds enough. My driving this car here with a white woman in the passenger seat? An imperfect shit storm.

"Any weapons in the vehicle?" he asks.

Here we go.

"A 9mm in the middle console." My eyes don't stray from his. "I have a permit for it."

"I'd like to inspect the firearm and conduct a search," the officer says. "Could you step out of the vehicle?"

I could refuse, but the last thing I need is for him to feel like I'm being "uncooperative" and that he needs to call for back up. I pass the license and my permit through the open window.

"What's this about?" Bristol leans over to demand of the police officer. "He isn't getting out until you tell us what this is about."

"Bris," I say. "I've got this."

"But he hasn't even really told us why we—"

"Be quiet." The words come out sharp and short. The hurt in her eyes twists my heart around, softening the shell that started forming as soon I saw that blue light. "Please. Just let me handle it."

She sits back, rebellion in the tight line of her mouth. She studies her nails as if she couldn't care less what happens next, but I know her better than that.

I open the door and step out.

"Sorry about that, officer, she just—"

"I'm putting these cuffs on as a precaution," he cuts in. "Just while I search the vehicle."

Cuffs? Shit.

He turns me roughly, rocking my chest into the car, pulling my arms behind my back, and clamping the cuffs on my wrists.

Bristol isn't pretending to be fascinated by her nails anymore. I feel her eyes latched onto me. I asked her to be quiet, but her shock and dismay at how quickly the situation has changed create a choking silence. He pats down my shoulders and arms, at my waist, inside my thighs and all the way down to my ankles. Rage boils up from a long-stirring cauldron in my belly, but I hear my mother's voice.

Do whatever it takes to make it home, Marlon.

When he's done, I turn and stand toe to toe with him for a few seconds, towering over him, dwarfing him. I have every advantage except the one the badge affords him

"The car isn't mine yet," I say calmly, ignoring the chafe of the cuffs. "I'm test driving it."

"All right." He tilts his head toward the curb. "Why don't you test drive that curb while I check the vehicle?"

A battle cry shreds the inside of my throat, desperate to escape. But it isn't time for fighting. I have to maintain control in what could, with one wrong word or move, become a volatile situation. I can't afford to lose control.

How many times did I sit on some damn curb, my boys and me? Pulled off basketball courts, out of cars, laid on our stomachs, stretched in the middle of streets like animals? Humiliation and rage linking us like some urban chain gang. If I think about it too long, I'll do something stupid. I just want this over so we can be on our way. I keep telling myself that, but the longer this goes on, the harder it is to remember.

"Ma'am, you can join him on the curb while I conduct the search," the officer offers.

Bristol scrambles out of the car, walking swiftly to sit on the curb beside me, the pink dress falling back to show another inch of her tanned thighs.

"Pull your damn dress down," I say around the gravel in my mouth.

She glances from the expanse of legs back to my face. She drops her knees and tugs at the hem of her short dress.

"We didn't do anything wrong," she says.

"This isn't about we, Bris." I look at her meaningfully, keeping my voice low even as bitterness rises in me. "This is about me. Driving that car in this neighborhood with you in the passenger seat."

"You think he stopped you because I was in the car?"

"Remember you asked me to let you know when your privilege makes you clueless?" I ask. "Well, that just happened."

Contrition pinches her brows together, and she lowers her eyes to the road before going on.

"I'm sorry." She shakes her head and then searches my eyes for answers. "I want to . . . I'm trying to understand. Can you just tell me why you have that gun in the car? I hate guns."

"I carry it all the time. You just never knew, I guess."

"Why? You have Amir."

"Yeah?" I ostensibly look around the surprisingly calm street. It's a Sunday afternoon, and I would expect at least a few kids popping wheelies. "And where's Amir now?"

"If you need him to—"

"That's my point. I don't need him to. I can protect myself."

"Hey." She presses a gentle kiss on my mouth, her soft lips opening briefly under mine. She rests her cool, soft palm against my face, and I lean into her, needing the contact. "I'm sorry if I was insensitive. I know this makes you think about what happened with Jade, but it isn't the same thing."

Ancient guilt cuts off my air for a moment, gagging me. I was a kid, just like Jade was. And he was a cop. I don't know what I could have done, but it kills me all the time that I did nothing.

"I know that." But the helplessness feels familiar. It feels the same. "But I'm never gonna be caught in a position where I can't take care of someone I care about again."

"I'm done," the officer says, walking toward us. "Well, almost. I've searched you. I've searched the car." His eyes light on Bristol.

"Ma'am, would you stand against the car for me?"

"No." My voice is an abrasion in the pleasant Sunday afternoon quiet. I'm cuffed, but I lean my torso in front of Bristol's chest so she can't stand. "She's clean."

The officer's brows lift at my challenge.

"I'll be the judge of that." He nods to Bristol. "Ma'am, may I search you?"

"I said she's clean." I swallow the helpless frustration bubbling in my throat, scorching the lining of my stomach. "Don't touch her."

Those are the words I said in my mirror for weeks after that officer crossed the line with Jade.

Don't touch her.

Words I never said to him that summer day when I was a kid.

Bristol glances from me to the officer, concern knitting her eyebrows. She understands my fear, as irrational as it may seem. She tries her best not to flash the officer when she stands from the curb. I surge to my feet and step between them, ready to beat him if I have to, literally with my hands tied behind my back.

My fists clenched behind me belie the calm forced into my voice and onto my face.

"I've cooperated fully with you, though you still haven't even given me a reason for the stop," I say. "You and I both know you don't need to search her. And you won't."

Am I imagining the touch of satisfaction in the look he gives me? That I may have the expensive whip and the beautiful girlfriend he could never pull in a million years, but today he gets to feel like the bigger man? In this neighborhood, just a block away from that playground where Jade lost a measure of her innocence, it's hard for me to tell where my preconceived notions end and reality begins. Is it as hard for him to look at me and not see what he expects instead of who I really am?

That moment of clarity doesn't change our circumstances. That he wants to search Bristol, and whether I'm right or wrong, he isn't touching her if I can help it. I need to calm down. I know the rules, I hear the mantra.

Do whatever it takes to make it home. Always answer with respect.

But there is no respect, not for me from him. Not for him from me. There is an unspoken feud pitting us against one another, and every cell in my body rebels against following the rules.

I try the old trick from my childhood, reaching for poetry—for Neruda, Poe, Cummings, anyone whose eloquence will calm the clamor of my heart and ease the riot in my chest. But all I find is the revolt of NWA's "Fuck Tha Police," chanting that a young nigga got it bad because he's brown. The lyrics gather in my brain like an unruly mob. Every word uproarious and disorderly. They swell in my head and crack my skull like a Billy club. My wrists strain against the cuffs, and the outrage of a million men who've sat on curbs and lay in the streets on their bellies strikes a match in my heart.

If I'm not careful, it could burn me to the ground.

The officer and I face off, an unbridgeable distance between us, when another cop car pulls up. Relief flashes over the officer's face to see one of his own arriving at the scene just in time. My anxiety doubles seeing another set of blue lights. Another cop to compound my trouble. But when the car door opens, it isn't just one of the officer's own. It's one of mine.

My cousin Greg gets out of the car like a guardian angel, and my shoulders sag. I didn't realize how painfully tight I held my muscles until he stepped out with his badge and all the tension drained from me.

"We got a problem, Dunne?" Greg triangulates a look between the officer, me, and Bristol.

"Routine stop, sarge," Dunne says. "I was just about to search the other passenger, but was getting resistance from the driver."

"That right?" His mouth kicks up at one corner. "You causing trouble, cuz?"

"Cuz?" Officer Dunne looks from me to Greg and back again. "You know this one?"

"So do you." Greg laughs and shakes his head. "You told me you liked his song when I was playing it in the locker room this morning."

"What song?" He searches my face and then looks at my license he's still holding. "Marlon James. You're—"

"Grip," my cousin finishes for him. "Get the cuffs off, Dunne."

Officer Dunne reaches for my wrists.

I jerk back, trapping his eyes with mine, silently showing him my resentment

"Don't," I tell him with deadly calm, my brown eyes locked onto the cop's blue. "You've touched me enough."

An awful quiet follows my words. I don't look away from Dunne even while Greg removes the cuffs himself.

"I'm a huge fan," Dunne says awkwardly. "I wouldn't have . . . well, I didn't recognize you with your hair different."

Like that should make any damn difference. I don't respond. I can barely breathe, suffocated by my own vulnerability. Living in my luxurious loft, driving my expensive motorcycle, performing for sold-out crowds. This lifestyle insulates me from just how vulnerable I am when it comes down to it. Just breaths away from helpless. Herded and branded like cattle, emasculated, unable to even properly shield the woman I love. Fully clothed but naked on the side of the road, stripped of all dignity. No matter how many albums I sell, no matter how much money I make, I will never forget this feeling.

Officer Dunne mumbles another apology for any inconvenience. When I keep stone facing him, he wisely gets in his car and drives away. I watch his taillights until he turns the corner and they disappear.

"Sorry about that, cuz." Greg daps me up. "We're working on it. Retraining the force and making sure we're in the community, not just policing it. It's slowly getting better. I hope.Dunne isn't a bad guy. Just still conditioned to make some assumptions."

"You mean conditioned to profile."

Greg doesn't address my comment. He knows it's true, but there's no good answer. He and I both know his colleague was wrong for that. His eyes urge me to let it go. I'm one of the few in my family who has a relationship with Greg. The others can't forgive him for Chaz. Even knowing Chaz probably would have killed others that day, even if by accident, had Greg not taken that shot. Greg joining the force always felt like a betrayal to them. Cops were in our neighborhood to harass and arrest, not protect and serve. They couldn't comprehend Greg crossing enemy lines. I understood why he wanted to change the problem from the inside. Despite the run-in with Officer Dunne, maybe because of it, I still understand, but we have a long way to go. It will take more than him on the force and some "retraining" to fix a system this broken.

"Who's this?" Greg smiles at Bristol, and she offers a stained smile in return.

"You know my boy Rhyson, of course. This is his sister, Bristol.

She's my manager." I capture and kiss her hand before she can stop me, pulling her into my side. "And my girlfriend."

Bristol's surprised eyes clash with mine. I squeeze her hand, mouthing, "He's cool," to her.

"Ohhhhh." Understanding and confusion wrestle in Greg's eyes. "I thought you and—"

"Nope. Not anymore." I convert my grimace into a smile. "Look, we're keeping this on the low for now. If you can keep your big mouth shut until we want the cat all the way out the bag."

"Got it. You can trust me." Greg's grin grows wide, pride in his eyes. "You doing it big, ain't ya? Number one album. Got that top spot."

I welcome the change of subject, chuckling, shaking my head. "Still can't believe it myself."

"And this whip." Greg whistles, running a hand over the glimmering black paint covering the Rover. "Nice."

"It's actually for Ma." I smile at Bristol's look of surprise. "I've tried to give her like four cars, and she hasn't taken any of them. I'm hoping this one will be too much for her to resist."

"Good luck with that." Greg shakes his head. "She's about as stubborn as you are."

"I prefer to think of it as determined."

"That you were. You had to be. It's in everything you write. And that new track 'Bruise' is deep." He looks at me directly. "Made me proud."

After what just happened, my own words, the lyrics to 'Bruise' that urge us to understand and empathize, mock me. Do I really think I should try to walk in Officer Dunne's shoes? I notice the impression the cuffs left on my wrists. You don't see the impression they've left inside me, not just this time, but the time before and the time before. How can I walk in his shoes? How can he walk in mine? He's never lived with this constant threat, and I've never lived without it. Living those lyrics is so much harder than singing them from the safety of a stage.

Greg looks over his shoulder at his idling car. "I need to go. I guess you're on your way to Aunt Mittie's for Sunday dinner."

He glances at his watch, unaware of the bomb he just dropped on Bristol's world.

"You know how she hates it if you're late."

"Sunday dinner?" Bristol gasps when Greg climbs into his car, her eyes storming and hands balled at her sides.

I know what's behind her anger. Fear. Fear that my mom will reject her. Keeping it one hundred, Ma probably will reject her at first, but the woman who raised me will eventually see in Bristol what I see. And maybe not today, maybe not right away, but she'll be happy for me. She'll fall in love with Bristol like I did. Even with the humiliating confrontation still smarting like a third-degree burn on my pride, I'm excited about the two women I love the most starting the process today.

"What the hell, Grip?" Bristol demands. "You can't do this. Not like this."

I'm determined to shake off the unpleasantness we just experienced. I refuse to let that shit ruin a day I thought would never come. I lean my back against the passenger side door and bring her close until we are flush, front-to-front.

"Are you okay?" I ask softly.

"No, I'm not okay. You can't just spring this on me. I—"

"Forget dinner for a sec." I push her hair back from her face. "What just went down with the cop. Are you okay?"

Her irritation fades, concern taking its place.

"Am *I* okay?" She rests her elbows against my chest, leaning into me. "You were the one in cuffs. That wasn't fair. I'm sorry if I made it harder for you."

"You being here made it harder, but only because I couldn't protect you the way I wanted to."

"Not my privilege making me clueless?" she asks weakly, her eyes only half-joking. "I'm sorry."

I don't need her apologies right now. I need her. I slide my hands down her back leaning in a few inches and hovering there until she comes the rest of the way. As soon as our lips touch, all the tension, frustration, anger, and yes, fear—I let it go. She opens for me, taking me in. The world falls away, and I'm lost in her. We kiss until I feel her lose herself in me, too. Until the tension leaves her shoulders and her hands come up to frame my face.

"You're still in trouble for springing dinner on me like this," she says against my lips.

"I did say if you ever gave me a chance," I drop one last kiss on her lips. "I'd take you home to my mama."

CHAPTER 27

B<small>RISTOL</small>

I ONLY HAVE my own vanity to blame.

If I hadn't been so concerned about my makeup, I probably would have realized where we were headed.

I would have demanded he turn the car around, or as a last resort flung myself into traffic on the 5. Now I have no recourse but to endure this. The woman will hate me. She hates the very idea of me with her son. She loves Qwest because . . . Black. She hates me because . . . white. I know that's an oversimplification. There are a lot of things Mittie James loves about Qwest that have nothing to do with the color of her skin. But I could be Mother Theresa and she wouldn't approve of me because of the color of mine, or so it feels.

At least having to deal with this distracts me from the clusterfuck of that "routine" stop. I've never seen anything like it. That officer cuffed Grip for no reason, with no provocation. It's the kind of thing I might have doubted at one time if I read on Facebook. I might assume the driver exaggerated for the sake of the story. But I saw it with my own eyes, and I'm still holding my previously held notions up against what just happened and wondering how to reconcile the two.

"It's gonna be fine." Grip's hand braves the space across the console to capture mine.

"You should have asked me or at least warned me."

"I'm sorry."

"No, you're not."

His wicked laughter fills the car until his shoulders shake and he bends over the steering wheel.

"Yes, by all means wreck us. That would be a reprieve," I mumble, looking out the window to study my surroundings.

The community teems with life. A cohort of guys riding dirt bikes pop wheelies down the street. Young girls play hopscotch, their braids bouncing as they jump the squares. A man wearing a bright red apron stares appreciatively at the Rover through the steam rising from his front yard grill. I don't see the war zone Grip has often talked about when he was growing up. But we are sometimes in the most danger when we let our guards down, when we let peace deceive us and trick us into forget- ting. Being at Grip's old high school, hearing about the funerals, the gangs, the volatility—it all tells me there is more to Compton than what this Sunday drive reveals.

A man in conversation with two others leans against an Impala, not as well kept or tricked out as Grip's, but a six four all the same. A blue handkerchief encircles one thickly muscled, ink-marked arm. Nothing's amiss in his actions, but maybe there's violence in the eyes tracking us. Something about him seems lost, desperate, dangerous. Or is that just my perception of him? Am I as bad as Officer Dunne? Fear and ignorance driving my assumptions? I'm discombobulated in this zip code, on this block, and the only things familiar to me are the opulence of this car and the man driving it.

I love him. Grip's fingers wrap around mine, and he darts concerned glances my way when he thinks I'm not looking. His beautiful words. His outrageous humor. The way he looks at me and makes me feel. Ms. James may not like me, but her son loves me. Obstinately, unwaveringly loves me. I'll hold onto that like an anchor.

"We're here."

Grip kills the engine in front of a small house in a row of houses that look almost identical, differentiated only by color and the front porch decorations. Ms. James' house is blue. A tributary of cracks run through the short span of concrete leading to the entrance. Three chairs squeeze onto the tiny porch, a vibrantly colored pillow in each one. I envision Ms. James and her friends seated there, inspecting the neighborhood and keeping watch. The wooden door stands open, leaving only the black-barred screen between me and Grip's child-hood home.

"Stay right there." Grip gets out and stands just outside. "I have to open the door for you. We have an audience."

"An audience?" I peer through the tinted windshield.

It's a sci-fi movie out there, with all the inhabitants frozen in some time warp, and apparently this expensive Range Rover is the space-ship from outer space. And when I step out, I am the alien.

"Um, I feel like everyone's staring," I side-whisper as we approach the house.

"Yeah." He gives me a cocky grin. "I'm a pretty big deal." "Oh, God." I have to laugh. "Your conceit knows no bounds."

"Well, and it isn't every day they see a car like that." He turns to me on the front porch. "Oh, and you're the only white chick for miles."

Great.

"Anything I should know?" I ask.

"Nah, Ma's easy." Grip shrugs. "Oh, just remember it's sweet potato pie, not pumpkin."

That matters?

"Okay. Got it. Sweet potato."

"And the greens, they're collards, not kale."

"I've never had collard greens. You think I'll like them?"

"If you don't," Grip says, eyes stretched for emphasis. "Pretend you do. And eat. This ain't the day to diet, baby. Ma doesn't trust people who don't eat."

"Why is every tip you're giving me about food?"

"Food's her love language. Everything you need to know about my mother is on her table."

My palms are sweaty. Why does this feel so important? I glance at Grip's strong profile, and I can't help but think of all it took for him to emerge from this neighborhood as the man he is today. The talent. The strength. The intelligence. The perseverance. The kindness.

He wouldn't be the man I love without the woman on the other side of this door, and against the odds, knowing she wants him with a woman who "looks like her," I want her to want him to be with me. I want her to like me.

"Collard greens. Sweet potato pie," I rehearse under my breath.

"Hey." Grip grasps my chin, his touch gentle and his eyes intent on my face. "Scratch all that. I fell for you. Not the edited, censored version of you. That's who I want my mom to see today. I want her to meet the real Bristol."

The tightness in my shoulders eases, and the breath I was holding whooshes over my lips.

"Thank you." I lean a few inches toward him, poised for a quick kiss.

He puts his hand between our lips, the look he gives me completely serious. "But for real, though, eat those greens."

He opens the door and pulls me in behind him by the hand. "Ma!" He steps into the immaculate and modest living room. "I'm home."

There's energy in the steps shuffling up the hallway. The closer they come, the tighter my nerves. I wiggle my fingers free of Grip's, ignoring his chastening look.

"You're late is what you are," her disembodied voice tosses up the hall. "You ain't been to church in I don't know how long, barely make it home for Sunday dinner, and when you do come you're . . ."

Mittie James' feet stop abruptly at the threshold, but her curiosity leaps into the room ahead of her and seesaws between her son and me. She's still wearing her church clothes and stockings with her bedroom slippers.

"You're late," she finishes, her eyes locked with mine. "Hello, Bristol. This is a surprise."

I want to look away, but I can't. A weak smile hangs limply between my cheeks.

"Sorry, I'm late, Ma." Grip closes the space separating them, scooping her petite frame into his broad chest. "It's okay that I brought Bristol, right?"

The caramelized eyes, so like Grip's, do a slow slide from me to her son.

"Of course. Welcome to our home, Bristol." She smiles politely and starts back the way she came. "Dinner's ready. Come on."

"You heard her." Grip smiles, takes my hand, and turns up the hall, dragging me along. "Dinner's ready."

"Hey, wait." I dig my heels in, making him stop, too. "Was it pumpkin or sweet potato?"

"Babe." He sighs and deposits a quick kiss on my nose. "Just come eat."

The small dining room feels full, even though there are only a few people at the table. I've met everyone here, but they receive my presence with varying degrees of surprise, curiosity, and animosity. Fortunately, Amir is here, and so is the sweet teacher from Grip's old high school, Shondra. I'm guessing Jade's in the animosity camp. Even with her hard, almond-shaped eyes tracking my every move, I feel a tug of sympathy for her. How could I not after what Grip just withstood? Knowing at such an early age, Jade was violated by one who was supposed to protect her. When I think of all these things, I see Grip finding it in his heart to write a song like "Bruise" as a miracle.

"Here's another plate." Ms. James rearranges the place setting by Jade to accommodate me. "Amir, grab that other chair out of the kitchen."

He jumps up to do her bidding but offers me a reassuring smile on his way. I look at the chair beside Jade, unsure if I should take it or let Grip have it and wait for the one Amir is bringing.

"We don't bite." Jade nods her head to the empty seat, her lips twisting derisively. "Sit down."

I offer her a small smile, which she doesn't bother returning. I take a deep breath, sit, and try to relax my shoulders.

"Good to see you again, Bristol," Shondra says, her smile warm and genuine.

"You, too." I'm so grateful for even that small kindness. "How have you been?"

"Good." Shondra sips from the glass of iced tea at her elbow. "Kids crazy as ever, but good. Still talking about Grip coming to see them a few weeks ago."

"It was fun." Grip leans back and drapes an arm across the back of my seat. I sit up right away, leaving plenty of space between his arm and my back.

"Well, fix your plates." Ms. James gestures to the table crowded with enough food to feed ten more people. "Nobody serving you here, Marlon. You know how to get your own."

"Yes, ma'am." His grin comes easy, and where I'm strung tight, he's as relaxed as I've ever seen him. There's a comfort, an ease, to him like I've never seen.

He's home.

He stands, stretching to scoop generous portions of everything. I'm about to do the same when he picks up the plate in front of me and replaces it with the full one.

"Here ya go," he says softly, his smile down at me intimate and affectionate.

He served me.

Oh, God. It shouldn't be a big deal, but it feels deliberate. He's expressing something. He's telling them all, without saying a word, that I'm special to him. I glance around the table, noting the smirk on Amir's lips, his eyes teasing me. The speculating surprise in Shondra's glance. The narrow-eyed resentment coming off Jade beside me like a radioactive wave. The disappointment on his mother's face before she stows it away.

"Thanks." I muster a smile for him. "You didn't have to."

"No problem." Grip metes out his own portions, sits in the extra seat, and turns his attention to the people still watching us closely. "So, catch me up. What's been going on?"

His question seems to crack the wall of tension some, and everyone eats and laughs and talks. I dig into the food. I've never tasted any vegetable like collard greens. I'm tempted to scoop up what's left with my fingers and turn up the plate to slurp the juices. Everything tastes so good, and I don't care if the greens are collard, kale, or Crayola, I want seconds.

They talk about people I don't know and things I don't quite grasp. I never watched *Martin*, so when they reminisce about a particularly funny episode, I smile and try to follow. Even without context, it's hilarious the way Jade tells it. I find myself laughing along.

"What you laughing at, Bristol?" The laughter drains from her face. "Have you ever even seen *Martin*?"

Busted.

"Um, no." I bite the inside of my jaw. "It just sounded funny the way you were telling it."

She rolls her eyes and sucks her teeth.

"Don't start, Jade." Grip's voice holds an unmistakable, quiet warning.

"What?" Jade grabs the Raiders cap off the table and shoves it on her head, leaning back in her seat. "Just didn't seem like her kind of show."

The sound of forks and knives scraping over the plates is magnified in the deep pool of silence following the exchange. It's because of me. Everyone is uncomfortable because I'm here, but I have no idea how to fix it. I'm just a girl having dinner with her boyfriend, as desperate for his mother to like me as you'd expect.

"You missed a great party, Jade," Amir finally says while serving himself another helping of everything. "Grip's release party, I mean."

"Girl, it was incredible." Ms. James beams with pride, her eyes set on her son.

"Yeah, sorry I couldn't make it." Jade doesn't sound sorry to me. "I guess you supposed to be a big deal now, huh?"

Grip bends a longsuffering look on his cousin and keeps eating without responding.

"Anybody can sell records," Jade continues. "But is it quality? I mean, is it real hip-hop?"

Grip tightens his lips, but there's otherwise no sign that what Jade says bothers him. I'm beginning to understand the dynamic between the cousins better now. Knowing about the incident with Jade and the police officer when they were kids, and Jade missing her chance to apply to the School of the Arts, I wonder if she's jealous. And maybe Grip knows it, but his guilt eats away at him, so he let's her get away with things no one else would.

"Grip's shit is legit, Jade," Amir says. "You still haven't heard the album?"

"I'm sure I heard everything he has to say before," Jade says. "No one's original anymore."

"Grip is."

It's out of my mouth before I think better of it. I really wish I'd thought better of it, because everyone, including Grip, turns a collective stare on me.

"I just meant, um . . ." I bite my lip while I collect my thoughts. "Grip's writing is excellent. His lyrics are incredible. As a matter of fact, the reviewer from *Rolling Stone* called the album innovative and revelatory. It's still the number one album in the country, and actually not just anyone can sell records in this market. In a climate where sales are down everywhere, Grip's are up. And that's because his work is stellar and resonates with a wide audience."

Grip's mouth tips at the corner, and I know he's laughing at me the way he and Rhyson always do when they say I love everything Grip writes. I do. And I probably sound like an infomercial, but it's all the truth.

"It's good, Jade." Ms. James addresses Grip's cousin, but her eyes rest on me, a little softer. "And you know I'm old school. I don't cut no slack, even for my own son. If it was weak, I'd tell you."

"And at this party I missed," Jade says. "Did you perform with Qwest, your girlfriend?"

She throws it out as a challenge, a dare to Grip to explain our situation.

"Qwest and I did perform," he says simply. "But she isn't my girlfriend anymore."

A bubble of silence swells, and Ms. James pops it with her next words.

"What do you mean?" She looks like Grip just kicked her puppy. "But she was just—"

Her eyes meet mine, and she cuts herself off, leveling her mouth into a flat line and pouring another glass of tea for herself.

"Ma, I told you not to get attached like that," Grip says softly with his eyes on his plate. "It just didn't work out."

He looks at me, taking my hand under the table and linking our fingers on his knee.

"I'm with Bristol now."

Shit. Fuckity shit.

Looking for something to do, I pour more gravy over my mashed potatoes, drowning the poor side dish. I'm so flustered my hand shakes and I spill the thick, hot liquid in my lap.

"Oh!" I scoot back from the table, fanning the scalding spot on my thighs.

"Are you okay?" Grip grabs a napkin from the table and starts mopping at my lap.

Embarrassment and discomfort constrict my throat until I can't swallow or breathe. I manage to stand under the weight of everyone's scrutiny and choke out a few words.

"Where's your bathroom?" I gesture to the spot on my dress. "I'd like to clean up a little."

Really I just want to get out of this room where it feels like I'm being bludgeoned with their stares.

"Right through there." Ms. James points down the hall, her voice flat, her eyes sad.

"Thank you," I whisper, moving in the direction she indicated.

"Can I help?" Grip follows me into the hall. "Do you need—"

"No, just go back." I don't turn around because I don't want him to see the tears in my eyes. The stupid tears of rejection. I knew she wouldn't like me. Why was I not prepared for this feeling? "Please. I'm fine."

I know he's still there. His concern wraps around me from behind. I feel his solid warmth at my back and his breath in my ear.

"Baby, it's okay," he whispers.

I take a step forward, putting distance between my back and his tenderness, which will only break me down more.

"Grip, just . . . I'm fine."

I don't wait for anything else before I step gratefully into the small bathroom. As soon as I'm behind the door, hot tears stream down my cheeks. I'm a fixer. It's what I do for a living. I fix everything for everyone, but there's nothing I can do to fix my skin. To fix the fact that everyone wants Grip with Qwest, and I can't ever be what his mother wants me to be. I know what she means to him and that he wouldn't be the man he is today without his mother's influence and guidance. That he disappoints her by loving me burns more than the gravy I spilled in my lap.

I allow myself a few moments of the lavatory pity party before wetting my napkin and wiping the dress, which is probably ruined. That's the least of my concerns, though. I splash water on my face until it looks sort of normal and steel myself to go back out there. It would be wonderful if Ms. James and Jade liked me, but they don't. I tell myself that Grip likes me, he loves me, so it doesn't matter.

I'm walking up the hall but stop when I hear my name.

"And you tried to tell me you and Bristol was just friends. Like I'm blind, dumb, and stupid," Jade says sarcastically. "You a trip, cuz."

"Oh, I'm a trip?" Irritation coarsens Grip's words. "Why?"

"You weren't satisfied with the fancy loft and the motorcycles and the cars and flying around on private jets," Jade says. "You just had to go and get you a white girl, didn't you? She's the last piece for your collection."

"Jade, lower your voice," Ms. James says softly.

"No, Jade," Grip snaps. "Shut the hell up."

"You had a queen but just had to go get you a Becky." Jade loads her voice with contempt before pulling the trigger. "Just like all them other niggas. Forgetting where they came from."

"I haven't forgotten a damn thing." Grip's words scrape against each other like iron sharpening iron, slicing into the thick air filling the house.

"Forget *who* they came from." Jade presses on like he didn't speak. "Like the sisters need another reminder that we ain't good enough. Ain't pretty enough. You sorry ass sellouts gotta stay true to form and choose them every time you get a little cash."

"My being with Bristol has nothing to do with you or anyone else," Grip says.

"Doesn't it?" Ms. James counters softly. "I'm sorry, but Jade's right. I didn't raise you to be a cliché, Marlon. Some man who thinks he needs a white woman on his arm to be successful."

"If you think that's what I'm doing," Grip replies softly, disappointment heavy in his voice. "Then you don't know the man you raised at all."

"I know you had a good woman, a beautiful Black woman who understands where you come from," Ms. James replies. "Who understands our challenges and knows how to support you."

The incident with Officer Dunne haunts me. How Grip had to guide me. Calm me. Correct me. How I had no clue about any of it. She's probably right. Qwest probably would have had Officer Dunne in his own cuffs when it was all said and done. In this moment, I feel completely inadequate.

"And last we heard, you were with Qwest," Ms. James says, her voice unapologetic. "Next thing we know you bring her in here uninvited and unannounced like some trophy we should put on the mantel. What am I supposed to think?"

"A trophy, Ma? Come on. This is me," Grip fires back. "You're right. I should have handled it differently and eased into it, but this is happening, whether you found out today or later."

"But you chose today to rub her in our faces," Jade cuts in.

"I'm not rubbing anything in your face," Grip says. "You're a part of my life. Bristol's in my life. I just want you guys to get to know each other."

"We should at least give her a chance," Shondra speaks up for the first time.

"Shondra, don't act like you don't feel the same way," Jade says. "When that basketball player got married last week, first thing you asked was did he marry a Black woman."

"Well, I like Bristol," Shondra says, not addressing the reminder of what she said before. "She's good people, and if you want to be with her, Grip, I got your back. It's fine with me."

"Well, it ain't fine with me," Jade says.

"Jade, come on now," Amir interrupts. "You don't even know Bristol."

"So what are you, Amir?" Jade challenges. "Another nigga with his nose wide open for this white chick? You know they freaks, so she might take both of you at the same time."

"Dammit, Jade!" Grip slams the table, rattling the plates and making the glassware sing a dissonant note. Anger edges his words. "You don't talk about her like that. What the hell is wrong with you? With both of you? You can't just be happy that I found someone I love? No matter if she's black, brown, white, whatever?"

"Love?" Ms. Mittie scoffs. "Once the novelty wears off, we'll see about love. For you and for her. Not to mention you'll undermine your credibility with a lot of people who saw 'Queen' as their song, our song. You'll lessen the impact you could have had in the community."

"Just because I love someone of a different race doesn't mean I'm not passionate about my own," Grip disagrees sharply. "About the causes that affect my community or the things that need to be said on our behalf."

"Well, you should ask yourself would she even give you a second look if you weren't who you are now?" Jade spews. "Would she have given you a second look if you weren't rich, famous? If you were just another nigga washing her car or changing her oil?"

Every insult, every assumption, every preconceived notion fell on me like a bag of stones. My arms are heavy with them. My neck, bowed. My back about to break. It took a lot for me to even admit I loved Grip, and I had to overcome so many fears to be with him. I'm trying to understand how his mother and Jade feel. I want to, but I can't listen to another word. I walk into the room, and for the first time, feel like myself. Feel like the girl I know Grip needs at his side.

"Bristol, hey." Grip tries to fix his face so I don't realize what I'm walking into. Tries to make this less uncomfortable for me, but it's too late. I'm well past discomfort.

"First of all," I start softly, spreading my glance between every one at the table, but ending with Ms. James. "Let me just say dinner was delicious."

Contrition darkens her eyes, but she doesn't look away.

"I'm sorry you heard all of that, Bristol," she says. "You're a guest in my home, and that isn't how I treat guests."

If Qwest had come here today, she probably would have been welcomed not like a guest, but like family. I remember the ease between her and Grip's mother at the release party. Like they had known each other for years even though they had just met. Jealousy stabs my heart. It's familiar, this stupid longing for someone's love, but I still hurt when it's withheld.

"I came here not sure if I should say sweet potato or pumpkin, kale or collards." I continue, shrugging and laughing a little. "Hell, I'm still not sure. I had no idea what to expect, but that was some of the best food I've ever had in my life."

Grip looks at me like he wants to check me for a fever or slip me a Valium.

"Also," I say, turning my glance to Jade. "You don't have to wonder if I would have given Grip a second look if he wasn't rich or famous because I fell in love with him when he was neither."

I look at Grip and don't give a damn that they can all probably tell how gone I am for him.

"He was sweeping floors and living in an apartment that quite possibly should have been condemned."

The jagged line of Grip's mouth softens just the tiniest bit, and he doesn't look away from me and I don't look away from him.

"It took me years to let Grip know how I felt, not because I didn't think he was good enough for me, or because he was Black. I can honestly say I never cared. He spoke to me in poetry and listened to my opinions and argued with me when he didn't think I was right and admitted when he was wrong." I smile, remembering my first night here in LA when we talked half the night away. "I started falling for him the day we met."

I look to his mother.

"You're right, Ms. James. I don't know how it's been for you, for your family. Our challenges may be different, but that doesn't mean I haven't known struggle. I may have grown up with plenty of money, but I know what it's like not to have."

My mother's coldness, my father's infidelities, my brother's distance all mock me, reminding me that no one in my family ever wanted me as badly as I wanted them.

I look at Grip's mother frankly, openly, a small smile pulling at my lips.

"I was so nervous coming here today," I tell her, my voice barely clearing a whisper. "I wanted you to like me. I didn't want to say or do the wrong thing to offend you, but now I understand that it isn't about anything I say or do. You're offended by who I am, by the things I can't change about myself. As I listened to you, I heard a pain that, you're right, I've never experienced. And for a moment, I said maybe they're right. Maybe Grip does need to be with someone like Qwest, but that was only for a moment."

I lift my chin, will it not to wobble, and will my words not to shake.

"Grip told me he wanted you to meet the real Bristol. Well, the real Bristol doesn't give up on the people she loves." I shrug, biting the inside of my jaw and blink rapidly, but a tear still escapes down my cheek even though I swipe at it impatiently. "I don't know how to. I can't stop loving your son. You wonder if I'll leave him. I won't, and if he leaves me he knows I'll probably chase him."

I allow myself to glance at Grip, but his familiar grin is not there. His eyes are sober, and I can't gauge his thoughts.

"And Qwest may understand where Grip is from, where he's been, better than I do. I can work on that. I *will* work on that." I look back to Ms. James. "But I know where he's going, and wherever he's going, I'm going with him. So, you and I should get used to each other because I'll be around."

I call on the impeccable manners of Miss Pierce's Finishing School.

"Thank you again for a lovely dinner, Ms. James," I say. "If you'll excuse me, I think I'll wait in the car."

I brush past Grip, who's probably going to skin me alive for talking to his mother that way. I rush down the short hall decorated with pictures of Grip from infanthood through high school, through the living room, down the cracked pavement, and to the car. When I yank the door handle, I realize my grand exit can only be so grand with the doors locked.

I'm not sure if Grip will be another five minutes or twenty, but I'm determined not to go back in there, even though I fidget when a few neighbors stare at me leaning against the passenger door. He emerges almost immediately, swift strides eating up the space between the black- barred door to the Range Rover. His face is grim as he clicks the remote to open the car. I scramble to get in and away from any prying eyes. Grip climbs behind the wheel, draws and releases a deep breath, and pulls away from the curb without looking my way once. The quiet is killing me slowly, like Chinese water torture, but with drops of silence.

"Grip, I—"

"Don't." His voice comes husky and heavy. "Not yet."

I swallow my hurt. People say they want the real you, but when you give it to them, they reject you. I should know that by now. I've encountered it all my life, but I hoped it would be different with the man I loved. And I do love Grip. He can be angry with me. He can give me the silent treatment. He can try to shut me out, but there's no way he's getting rid of me. He thinks he loves me? He hasn't met a love like mine. My love is Pandora's box. Grip snapped my hinges and pried me open. He let this love out. My love has a wild streak. Good luck trying to tame it.

I didn't pay attention on the way here, but I do recognize we're not getting on the 5. Just two minutes from his mother's, Grip pulls behind a building that seems completely abandoned.

He's quiet, eyeing his hands on the wheel. I brace myself for his anger, his displeasure. I don't know what I expect to see when he finally glances over at me, but it isn't the look on his face. A look that says he loves me. A look that says he's proud of me. He says so much with just a look, but I want the words. And after a few moments he gives them to me.

"That was amazing," he says softly. "You're amazing. There's nobody else I'd choose."

Relief and gratification burst in my chest and push out on a long breath.

"You're not . . ." I swallow the lump that's refused to leave my throat since I heard the truth of what they thought about us, about me. "You're not mad?"

"At you?" He rests his elbows on the steering wheel and drops his head into his hands. "If anything, I'm mad at myself. I was so eager for you and my mom to . . ."

He trails off, shaking his head and grabbing my hand, linking our fingers on the middle console.

"I messed up." His eyes offer an apology. "I put you and my mother in an awkward situation. I should have handled it differently."

"It's okay. Hopefully in time . . ." A fragile laugh slips from me. "Like I said, I'm not going anywhere."

Grip's tender smile reaches across the small space separating us, and he kisses my fingers meshed with his. The brush of his lips drops feathers in my belly. I pull in a breath to suppress the shivers even that soft touch sets off across my skin.

Grip's smile fades, and the air thickens between us, making it harder to breathe. He leans across the console, takes my chin between two fingers, and kisses me, softly at first. As soon as I open, inviting him into me, his mouth demands my surrender. With a needy moan, I open my heart wider, taking as much of him in as I can. The kiss becomes compulsive, something I couldn't stop if I tried. My lips, my hands, seeking and hungry. His response, possessive, ravenous.

Grip hauls me over the middle console, squeezing me between his chest and the steering wheel, fitting my thighs on either side of him, shoving my dress up around my waist to expose my lacy panties. His hand wrings in my hair, pulls my head back, holds me still.

"I love you." His eyes probe mine so long I'm sure he plucks my thoughts from my mind, the emotions from my heart. "What you did back there, what you said . . ."

He presses his lips to mine, groaning against my mouth, his tongue diving in over and over until my head is spinning. I hold onto him, my arms clamped about his neck. He digs into my hips, urging me over him in a rolling rhythm, in the groove he sets. I assume the pace, riding the hot beam of flesh and steel behind his zipper. He lifts me to capture my breast through the thin cotton. He doesn't nibble at me like a delicacy. He gobbles at my nipple, pinching with his lips, nipping with his teeth. He shoves the collar aside with his chin, suckling me, singeing me through the sheer layer of my bra for long seconds before pulling my arms out of the dress, leaving it a strip of bunched material encircling my waist. He jerks the bra straps down to cage my elbows and finally takes my naked breast into his mouth.

"Oh, God." I rise and fall over him, my thighs trembling. "I need this."

"I know." He slides a hand into my panties, rubbing my slickness between his fingers. "Please say you're ready for me."

"I am." I drop my lips to his neck, sucking the skin roughly. "Get it."

He doesn't bother removing my panties, but shoves them aside. I can't wait, fumbling with his belt and zipper. He's hot and hard in my hand as I position myself and slide down, the scrape of flimsy lace against our joined flesh only intensifying the pleasure. He's wide and thick, and there's still a sting when his body insists past my tightness, still a kiss of pain underlying the rapture as he drills all that dick to the bottom of me. Oh, but God, it's worth it.

"Shiiiiiiiit." Grip's brows scrunch, bottom lip trapped between his teeth, head dropped back against the headrest. "I wanna die this way. In here. Inside you. Just like this. Promise you'll fuck me on my deathbed."

Laughter erupts in the luxurious confines of the car, mine and his.

"Oh my God," I gasp, laughing but so close to coming I already see spots. "You're crazy."

I twist him impossibly deeper into my body, wanting to feel him where no one has ever been. Where no one's ever touched me.

"Bristol." My name bursts from his mouth as he explodes inside me, his passion warm and liquid. "God, what are you doing to me?"

Making you more mine every time.

A smug, satisfied smile rests on my lips a few moments later. He's still inside me, and I'm slumped onto his chest, the steering wheel digging into my back. I know we need to move. There's a sticky mess between my legs, and we could get caught at any moment, but I can't stop kissing him, my tongue in his mouth sustaining our intimacy like a note held at a conductor's command.

"We need to go," he whispers, his breath still labored, his palms starting at my feet folded under me and sliding up my thighs and under the panties I never took off. He fills his hands with my ass, the leisurely caress of a satisfied man, and I revel in the fact that I did that. That I satisfy him.

"Hmmmm." I snuggle deeper into him.

"Bris." His hands wander over my back and then coax my bra straps into place on my shoulders. "For real, we need to leave before we get caught. We already had one close call today, and that wouldn't exactly be the low profile we're supposed to be keeping."

"You're right. I'll move in a second." I chuckle, eyes closed and depriving my other senses so I can fully absorb the scent of him. "You were the one who couldn't even make it home."

"True." He pauses, lifting my head from his chest. "What you said at my mom's house . . ."

"I meant every word." I frame his face between my hands, my eyes latched with his. "I'm going wherever you go."

"And you think I would object?" He tilts his head, his eyes so warm as he looks at me. "You're everything I wanted before I even knew what I was getting."

I kiss him thoroughly, deeply, surrendering everything before pulling back to smile down at his contented expression.

"You wanted me, you got me." I kiss him one more time, branding him mine as surely as I'm branded his. "Be careful what you wish for."

CHAPTER 28

G<small>RIP</small>

IT SHOULD SCARE me how much I missed Bristol after just one day away from her, but it doesn't. I fully embrace my addiction to the girl. Luke and I flew out to join Kilimanjaro for the show in Chicago, their hometown. Bristol's brilliant last-minute idea of Prodigy solidarity, but even that one day without Bristol has me fiending. We've only been official a few days, and I don't sleep right without her. I'm so bent out of sorts waking up alone in an empty bed that I had Sarah change our flight to the earliest out this morning so I could get home sooner.

I need my girl.

"You don't wanna go home first?" Amir asks from the seat beside me.

The SUV picked us up at the airport, and I told the driver to go straight to the Prodigy offices.

"Nah, I'll take my stuff home later."

A knowing grin spreads across Amir's face. His eyes drop to my bouncing knee. "You got it bad, don't you?"

My knee stops bouncing long enough for me to scowl at him, but I can't hold back an answering smile. He's watched Bristol and me from day one. Knows the full story. I turn my head to watch the cars zooming by on the interstate.

"Damn right I got it bad," I mutter. "Look how long it took to get her."

"How was she after . . . well, you know?" Amir lifts his thick bushy brows. "Dinner."

"She's Bristol," I say wryly. "She's fine. Ask me how my mom is. That's a better question."

"You guys talked since Sunday?"

"Have we talked?" I pffft. "She's called me like eight times. She felt bad about the way things went down, but she still wants to talk sense into me. She thinks I'm in some kind of phase with Bristol. It's not like I haven't dated white girls before. I've dated Black girls, Asian, Latina. Everything in our species."

"Yeah, but you ain't ever brought a girl to Sunday dinner. Ms. Mittie knows you're serious about Bristol. She knows you think Bristol is the one, and she ain't okay with you marrying a white woman. She told us that when we still thought girls had cooties."

"Ma has been consistent, but Bristol is the one. She always has been. She just had to trust me to be her one."

"It's like that?" Surprise stretches Amir's face from top to bottom. "So, y'all are already talking marriage?"

"Hell, no." I laugh at the thought. "Do you have any idea how long it'll take to convince Bristol to actually marry me?"

"It was obvious on Sunday she's into you. I mean, I wanted to salute after the speech she gave."

I saluted her, all right. My dick was at attention under the table the whole time she was talking and was not "at ease" until I had her bunched up against that steering wheel with every inch I got fucking the hell out of her.

"I've made studying Bristol Gray my life's work." I lean back in the comfort of the SUV's leather seat. "Marriage will scare her to death.

She's seen too many bad ones. The worst up close. It'll take some time, but I think I've proven I'm a patient man."

"And what about Qwest?" Amir's frown comes quick and heavy. "You heard from her?"

"Nah." It pains me to think of how Qwest got caught in the drama between Bristol and me. "I ended things almost a week ago, and we agreed we wouldn't talk for a while."

"So does she know about Bristol? Does she know you're already with someone else?"

"I never gave her a name, but I told her there was someone I wanted to be with who didn't want to be with me." I shake my head. "Then Bristol and I got together the next day. We're keeping things quiet until it's public that Qwest and I called it quits."

"Yeah, if it comes out about you and Bristol while folks still think you're with Qwest . . ." The look he gives me has "oh shit" written all over it.

Qwest in the role of woman scorned, even if I didn't technically cheat, would not be a good look. For any of us.

"Yeah, we need to get ahead of it," I say. "I'll bring it back up with Bris."

"Does Rhyson even know yet?"

"No." My cocky grin comes fast. "Serves him right, too. Bristol told him how she felt about me weeks ago and he never let on. Asshole."

"You think he'll be happy for you?"

"Yeah, but Rhys can't figure out if he should protect me from Bristol, or Bristol from me. He knows for sure he wants to protect the business in case anything goes wrong between us. He doesn't have to worry about that. Bristol and I are solid now. Ain't no going back."

"Is she back to managing you?"

"Yeah, no reason not to now." I shrug and turn my mouth down at the corners. "She's so damn good at it."

"And that dude she was, um, dating?" Amir asks the sentence like he's tiptoeing over a minefield and Parker is a trip wire.

"They weren't dating."

I trap the truth behind my teeth. I can't even tell Amir that Parker slept with Bristol while she was basically unconscious. I can't get it out of my mind, the way he grabbed her on the tarmac. All the messages he's left, even though she's told him it's not happening. The extra senses my mama says we have tell me this dude's nature is fundamentally crooked. He won't hesitate to play dirty to get what he wants, and he wants Bristol. I may have grown up in the hood, but I've been straight as an arrow all my life. For this man, I won't hesitate to get a little bent if it means protecting her.

"Hey, you still got them contacts with Corpse's boys?" I ask.

Amir looks at me like I'm smoking crack and just offered him the pipe. Our moms steered us clear of the Crips, but Amir's cousin Corpse crossed over to the dark blue side. With a "b" name like Brandon, he changed his name when he joined, and became Corpse when it was clear he had a talent for assassination.

"I ask you about Charles Parker—one of the richest dudes in the world, by the way—and then you ask me about Corpse? Uh-uh. Nah, bruh."

"I'm not putting a hit on Parker." I run my tongue over my teeth, squeezing my hands into fists on my knees. "But he isn't taking Bristol from me. And I'll be damned if he's gonna hurt her. I just want options."

"Corpse ain't an option. Ever." Amir glances at the raised glass partition insulating our voices from the driver's ears. "And I'm gonna forget we had this conversation."

"I don't want you to forget." I level a hard, narrow look at him, everything in me pulled tight. "He's your cousin. Just reach out to him."

"I don't fuck with Corpse, and you know it."

"I got pulled over for no damn reason Sunday before we got to Ma's, Amir." My voice carries the bitterness of that memory. "Bristol was right there while some no-nut cop threw me against the car and cuffed me. He had me hemmed up, sitting on a curb. He could have hurt her. He could have touched her, and I wouldn't have been able to do a damn thing about it. Do you know how that made me feel?"

It's quiet in the car while Amir studies me with grave eyes. He's been beside me on that street before. The two of us in a line of our friends, bellies scraping asphalt, plastic cuffs cutting off circulation, dogs sniffing around us like hounds scenting prey. All while cops searched the car for drugs. And me, a music student making straight A's.

"The power we have, the control we think we have, it's an illusion. We can lose it in an instant." Cynicism roughens my voice. "Now, I'm a lucky man with more blessings and opportunities than most people, no matter what color they are, but in the end, it comes down to this skin I'm in. And I know all cops aren't bad, but it's the damn system. I can't even call it broken because it's functioning exactly how it was designed to - profiling us, prosecuting us for shit other people get away with, scot free."

We pull up to the imposing glass building housing Prodigy, but I'm not getting out until I know Amir understands how serious I am about this.

"You know how it is, Amir. There's a whole system stacked against me, and this motherfucker who's out to get my girl has every advantage. I just want options. Ya feel me?"

I sit with a stony face while Amir weighs what I just told him.

"I'll call Corpse," he finally says softly.

"Good." I open the car door.

"But," Amir reaches over and grabs my arm, "I'm talking to him, not you. We can't have any of this shit anywhere near you if things . . . if anything ever happens."

I stare at the face I've seen evolve from acned adolescence to the grown ass man still trying to protect me.

"It won't come to that," I assure him. "These are just precautions, but yeah, you can deal with him. Unless I need to."

Amir drops my arm, sucks his teeth and shakes his head. "Fool."

"You the fool." I chuckle. "And don't think I didn't see you tryin' to holla at Shondra Sunday."

He groans, but a smile illuminates his face. "We're going out this Friday."

"No way." I lean into the open door, arms braced against the car. "You finally grew some balls and asked her out."

If his skin wasn't so brown, I bet his cheeks would be red. Chagrin and embarrassment sit together awkwardly on his face. "She actually asked me out."

"She . . . so wait. You been crushing on this girl half your life, working up the nerve to ask her out, and she . . ." I press my fist to my lips to stifle the laugh. "So what you're saying is Shondra's balls are bigger than yours."

"Hey, some might say the same about you and Bristol," he says defensively.

"Oh, no, homey. Bristol loves these big balls. Trust." I propel myself away from the car with a deep laugh and yell, "Deeze nuts!"

CHAPTER 29

B<small>RISTOL</small>

"BRISTOL, GIVE ME <small>YOUR PHONE</small>."

Sarah is posted against my office door when she makes the odd request. She came in, closed the door behind her, and demanded my phone.

"What?" I return my attention to my laptop with a laugh. "My phone? Why?"

When she doesn't answer, I look back up. She's still standing there, back pressed to the door as if she's keeping something at bay. Her eyes are round. Her lips are tight. Her hands wring around one another at her waist. She catches sight of the phone on my desk at the same time as I do. We both dive for it. Somehow from across the room, that little ninny manages to snatch the phone that was only two inches from me.

"Give me my phone." I hold out my hand. "Right now."

"Bristol, let me just paint a picture for you first." Sarah tucks my phone behind her back.

"Let me paint a picture of you in the unemployment line if you don't give me my phone."

"Are there actual lines anymore, though?" Sarah stalls. "I mean, it's all computerized now, right?"

"You'll know for sure tomorrow unless you give me my phone." I sigh, exasperated. "How bad can it be, whatever it is?"

Her silence and the eyes shifting from me to the floor tell me it's bad. The worst things I can imagine immediately leap to mind.

"It's Grip? Rhyson? Kai? The baby?" Sarah's unchanging expression gives me no assurances. "Just tell me."

Sarah blows out an extended breath and starts tapping keys on my phone. When she finds what she's looking for, she turns the screen around for me to see.

"Let's start here," she says.

I take the phone, my eyes still trained on her face. At first, I'm not sure what I'm seeing. It's surveillance footage from the "routine" stop on Sunday with Officer Dunne.

"What is this?" I search Sarah's face for an answer. "This happened Sunday when Grip was stopped by a cop."

"Yeah, someone got ahold of the surveillance footage and posted it." Sarah bites her bottom lip. "There's a lot of talk about the irony of Grip being stopped DWB when 'Bruise' is just coming out. But there's a lot more . . . discussion about you and Grip. Keep watching."

I look again, and then I see it. I get out of the car and join Grip on the curb. I remember this moment when his forehead presses to mine and we whisper to one another, the intimacy between us obvious. Our lips touch and our eyes hold onto each other.

Oh, God, please no.

Our lips touch and linger. We kiss.

I slowly lift my eyes to meet Sarah's. Hers are wide and questioning. "It's just a . . . an itty bitty kiss, right?" False hope lilts my voice.

"Well, yeah," Sarah agrees and bites her lip. "But there is that other part."

"Other part?"

I look back to the phone. There's another clip after Officer Dunne leaves. A different feed, different angle. Maybe from a nearby pole. Who knows. We're chatting with Greg, and Grip kisses my hand and presses it to his chest. He pulls me into his side. I lean into him. There's nothing platonic about any of it. We look like we're in love, but it's nothing too incriminating until Greg leaves. The footage shows the long kiss we shared against the Rover. If there was any doubt we're more than friends, this kiss eliminates it.

The first few comments, like Sarah said, focus on the stop itself. But slowly, comments about me, about Qwest start trickling in. The comments become accusations about the white bitch with Grip. Dozens of commenters post about Grip cheating on Qwest. About him caught "creeping." With every comment, the vitriol, the outrage on her behalf increases. The hashtags stack up.

#GripzQueen. #BlackLove. #CheatingAss. #SellOut.

The room tilts. The floor beneath my feet becomes Jell-O. I stumble to my desk, perching on the edge.

"How long has this been up?" I ask between hyperventilating breaths.

"Um, maybe fifteen minutes," Sarah answers cautiously. "It's getting a lot of traffic, though."

"I can see that."

I scroll and scroll and scroll, but still haven't reached the end of the comments. Every once in a while, one commenter will mention the stop itself and how this is exactly what "Bruise" talks about, but it's drowned in the sea of speculation about Grip and me.

"What's a thot?" I look up from the phone, eyebrows bunched. "They keep calling me a thot."

"Um . . ." Hesitation is all over Sarah's face and in her answer. "That Ho Over There."

My mouth drops open. I was a damn debutante in the most exclusive circles of Upper Manhattan, and I'm a thot?

"Qwest." I look at Sarah with horrified eyes. "Oh, God. What must she be thinking?"

"Yeah, that's kind of its own thing, so to speak," Sarah says carefully. "I think that's why some of the comments are so vicious."

"Oh, my God." I pull up Qwest's Twitter account.

@YesItzQwest "When he get on, he'll leave your ass for a white girl." Kanye ain't never lied. Bruhs, don't forget the sisters who put u on. #QueenWithNoKing

The humiliation, the hurt, and dismay I experienced at Ms. James' dinner table Sunday has magnified, globalized. It isn't one, two, three women side-eyeing me because I'm with Grip. It's an entire socialsphere. I don't want to be pitted against them. Grip and I aren't what these comments suggest we are. I'm not some trophy to him. And he didn't choose me because I'm a symbol of unattainable success. I want to chase down every comment, recall every retweet, share and like. To tell them he quotes poetry to me. I know his favorite foods. I know he'd rather have Classic Jordans than a gaudy watch. We talk about real things, and even when I don't understand everything, he's patient with me because he loves me. I know him. I knew him first. I had him first. I loved him first. He's mine.

I want them all to know.

Sarah and I both jump when the office door swings open. Rhyson's hair stands all over his head like he's been plowing his fingers through it.

"Bris, have you seen—"

"Yeah." I collapse into the chair behind my desk. "Sarah just showed me."

"How are we dealing with the calls?" He sits on the edge of the desk, eyeing me with a mixture of caution and sympathy.

"Calls?" I split attention between my brother and my assistant. "Already?"

"I hadn't gotten to that quite yet." Sarah winces. "The front desk is flooded. Press, bloggers, news outlets asking for comments on the incident and the . . . status of you and Grip."

"It's all a misunderstanding," I tell them.

In synch, both of them stretch their eyebrows as high as they'll go. I get it. There's no mistaking that Grip and I are more than friends in that footage.

"By misunderstanding, I mean that Grip had ended things with Qwest by the time that footage was taken."

"But they performed at Pirouette together Friday night, and were by all accounts, still together at that point, right?" Rhyson asks.

"They broke up right after the show." I look at them helplessly. "We didn't want to hurt her. We wanted to give her some time to process everything and release a statement later. We were being careful."

"You call this careful?" Rhyson's sigh is powered by frustration. "How do we handle it? Where's Grip?"

"Oh his way back from Chicago," Sarah says. "He caught an earlier flight."

That's welcome news to me. Maybe my heart will stop hurting once he walks through that door.

"He needs to address this," Rhyson says. "'Queen' is such a huge part of his brand now, and like it or not, Black women took that as theirs. As an affirmation, and him cheating on Qwest with you—"

"He did not cheat on her." My voice cracks like a whip. "Are you not hearing me? He broke it off with her before we started . . . seeing each other."

"I get it. I know your history," Rhyson sighs. "But from the outside it looks like he cheated."

"Qwest certainly seems to think so," Sarah offers, her voice weak.

"This is just one tweet. There's a series of them and Instagram posts. And there are a few FaceTime Live posts from fans calling Grip a sellout and expressing their disappointment."

"This will start affecting sales, Bris." Rhyson shakes his head.

"Sales?" A humorless laugh comes out with my gasp. "You're thinking about sales?"

"Okay. Let's just start with you knowing me well enough to assume you and Grip are the most important parts of this for me, okay?" Rhyson's brow pleats and his mouth flatlines. "Now that we have that established, of course not just sales, but it is our job to protect the interests of the people who've invested in this label. The people who make their living from this label. They rise and fall with us, and right now we have one album out. Grip's. So yeah. I have to think about sales."

"I know, I just . . ." I've lost my bearings. There are so many important things competing in my head. I want to strategize about sales. I want to figure out how to correct this PR fiasco. I want to figure out who the hell did this to us. I want to protect Grip. He's worked too hard and for too long for this to derail his success.

"Yes. You're right, of course." I press my head into the supple leather of my seat. "Let me think about this for a second."

But any strategizing I would do goes right out of my head when Grip walks into my office. The worry in his eyes wrenches my heart. I'm jeopardizing his success. He has to be questioning whether or not this is worth the trouble. Whether I'm worth the trouble.

"Grip, I've been calling you, dude," Rhyson says.

"I literally just turned my phone back on after the flight from Chicago." Grip answers Rhyson, but his eyes never stray from me. "Could you guys give me a minute with Bristol?"

"We need to talk about how we'll handle this," Rhyson says, but his voice has lost some of its heat. "We need a plan because this has gone the worst kind of viral."

"Yeah, I know." Grip sits on the couch against the far wall in my office, stretching his legs out in front of him like we're not standing naked in a shit storm. "But I need to talk to my girl first."

Sarah immediately heads for the door, but turns just before leaving.

"His girl!" A sudden bright smile illuminates her face. "I know things look bad right now, but I just want to say yay. Like it's about time and yay for you guys!"

She scampers into the outer office, and if I wasn't feeling like the whole world is pointing out the stubborn cellulite on the backs of my thighs, I'd muster a smile.

"I'm not trying to be the hard ass," Rhyson says. "I hate having to think like this, but we do need to deal with it. It goes without saying that I'm happy for you guys."

"You could still say it." Grip's comment comes softly, but with a mild rebuke. "Your sister needs to know you support her and that she's more important to you than how this affects my sales."

Grip's so right. I hadn't realized how fragile I was feeling or how anxious I am about Rhyson's response.

"Bristol." Rhyson searches my eyes, his softening at whatever he sees there. "You're more important to me than all of this. I'm sorry if it didn't feel like it when I came tearing in here. You know how intense we are. You, me, Mom, Dad."

"It's okay." I push the hair behind my ears. "I get it."

"It isn't okay." He leans down to take my hand. "I've screwed things up with you more than once. I lumped you in with our parents and didn't stay in touch. I've been an awful brother most of the time, but I love you, Bris."

He flicks his head toward Grip without looking away from my face. "I'm happy for you, but I'm really just glad this guy can stop moaning like a little bitch about how much he's into you. It's so fucking awkward."

The three of us laugh, and the tension eases some.

Rhyson pulls me to my feet and into a tight hug. He kisses my hair and dips to catch my eyes.

"We all know you're a badass and don't need to hear this kind of thing," he says, even though I do. "But I love you, and you're so far beyond the best sister a guy could have it isn't even funny. The investors, this place, so many things that have happened for me wouldn't exist if it weren't for you. I want you to know I realize that."

Tears sting my eyes. Hearing him voice the things I've needed to hear, to know for years, moves me deeply, even in the midst of this craziness.

"I'll give you guys a few minutes," Rhyson says. "When you're ready, come to my office and we'll hammer out a plan to deal with all this."

Rhyson looks at Grip for a long moment, one brow lifted.

"And you," Rhyson says to Grip, his voice serious, but his eyes laughing. "Try to keep your hands to yourself."

"I'll see what I can do. Lock the door on your way out," Grip replies. "Or you might see more than you want to see."

"Oh, I've already seen more than I wanted to see. Believe me."

Grip tosses up both middle fingers, and Rhyson's laugh taunts us as he leaves the room. It's quiet in here, incredibly quiet as we stare at one another. What's felt so special, so intimate, so *ours* is being maligned and memed. Hashtagged and reposted and ridiculed. In here it's just us, but it feels like everything and everyone beyond that door is against us.

"Come here." Grip extends his arms, concern evident in his eyes. I drag my feet to get to him, not because I don't want him, but because I feel awful. As soon as I'm within grabbing distance, his hands encircle my waist, and he pulls me to his lap.

"Hey." He nuzzles his nose into my neck, behind my ear. "It's okay."

"I'm so sorry." I turn into him, tucking my head in the warm sleek curve of his neck and shoulder.

"This is on me." He shakes his head, a self-directed frustration on his face. "You didn't want to go to my mom's. You said be careful. I should have listened."

"I guess we won't know who leaked it, huh?"

"Does it really matter? It could have been anyone with access to those tapes. Who knows."

"It feels like the worst thing that could have happened," I whisper.

"No." Grip leaves a kiss in my hair. "The worst thing would be if you decided not to be with me. If you regretted us. That's my worst-case scenario. Not sales or any of that other shit."

"But you've worked so hard. I just hate being the reason it's diminished in any way."

"Listen to me." His hand splays across my hip and he brings me so close I feel his heart thumping into my ribcage. "Remember the release party? We were celebrating the album going number one?"

"Of course I remember." I cup his face and lay my head against his chin. "I was so proud of you. We all were."

"Yeah, well I was miserable."

I pull back to peer into his face.

"I mean, yeah. I was happy, excited for the album, but you know what my mind kept going back to?"

"What?" My voice is hushed, my heart waiting.

"Our first kiss." A smile crooks the corner of his full lips. "That night at the carnival, no one knew who I was. My bank account was sad. Not one of my dreams had come true yet, but I had you. That night I had you, and it was the best night of my life. And the night of the party, when I thought you might marry Parker, that we might not ever get back to what we started on that Ferris wheel, I could barely focus on the songs. That let me know what is the most important thing to me, and it ain't sales."

I don't know what to say. I thought I would. I'm rarely speechless, but him saying these things and hearing that I'm the most important thing in a life like his, when I haven't been anyone's most important thing ever before, something inside of me that has always been searching, settles. Something that has always been circling, lands.

"You are just making things worse for yourself," I finally whisper into his neck.

"How so?" He feathers kisses around my hairline, down my neck.

"You'll never get rid of me now."

"Good. That was the goal." He tips my face forward and kisses me lightly. "Now that we have that settled, let's go tell Rhyson how you're gonna make this all better. I know you have a plan."

Now that I've had a second. Now that the man I love has settled any lingering doubts . . .

"I might have a few ideas."

CHAPTER 30

Bristol

"YOU'LL OWE ME big time for this, Bristol." Ezra Cohen stares over his thick-rimmed glasses, the New York skyline sprawled behind him. "I'm also not entirely sure this is the best way to handle such a . . . shall we say, delicate matter."

"Will and Qwest haven't left me much choice. I need to staunch the bleeding on this, and they won't take my calls." I hesitate before giving him my most grateful smile. "Thank you so much for your help."

"If I didn't love you so much, kid, there's no way I'd even entertain a scheme like this." Ezra points a bony finger at me. "But in all my years knowing you, you're right ninety-nine percent of the time. This better not be that one percent."

He's right. This could backfire badly. If I miscalculate, I'll only make things worse. Before I have time to reconsider, Ezra's assistant opens his office door, showing in Qwest and Will. Qwest pulls up short as soon as she sees me, tilting her sunglasses down to look at me disdainfully over the cat eye frames.

Will comes in right behind her, shock flickering across his face when our eyes catch. "Bristol, what the hell are you doing here?"

"This bitch got some nerve." Qwest adjusts the Louis Vuitton bag on her shoulder. "I'm outta here."

"No, you're not." Ezra stands to his full five foot seven. His towering authority has nothing to do with his physical stature, and everything to do with the reputation he's carved out for himself and the business he's built. "You've been very publicly critical of the man who has the number one album in the country. And the two of you have the number one single in the country. That feud is bad for business, and I want it put down."

"I'm sorry to handle things this way," I interject. "But you wouldn't return Grip's calls, Qwest, and Will, you haven't returned mine."

"That's 'cause I got nothing to say to cheating sellouts or their skinny white bitches." Qwest's voice rings hard and harsh in the understated luxury of Ezra's office, but I see the hurt behind her eyes. Grip isn't an easy man to lose.

"He didn't cheat, Qwest," I say softly. "We need to clear the air."

"So he sends you to do his dirty work," Will scoffs. "This is highly unprofessional, Bristol."

"What's unprofessional is you not responding to my calls or emails for the last two days while your client went on a Twitter tour denigrating my client's character." I tilt my chin and remind him with a glance that he does not want to mess with me. "And Grip doesn't know I'm here."

He does know I'm in New York, but he thinks it's just to see Kilimanjaro on tour.

"Oh, so you go behind his back, too, not just mine," Qwest says sarcastically. "Good to know."

"I'm here to apologize," I say softly. "Not for cheating, because we didn't. We wouldn't, but for how you found out about our . . . relationship. For how things happened. Please give me a chance to explain."

For a moment, it looks like she won't yield. Her lips pull into a tight line, and her long nails dig into her palms.

"Five minutes," she finally says. "That's all you get."

I look to Ezra, who takes my cue and walks to the door. "Will, let's give the ladies a few moments alone," he says.

Irritation and indignation gather on Will's face, and he's torn between following his boss' orders, and protecting his client.

"Go on, Will. I'll be fine." Qwest looks me up and down.

Once we're alone, Qwest settles onto a couch across from the Ezra's desk and leans back, stretching her arms behind her.

"Clock is ticking," Qwest says.

"I know Grip told you from the beginning that there was someone he had feelings for," I say, sitting on the couch, crossing my legs. "He had reservations about getting involved feeling that way for someone else. He was honest about that."

"Yeah, but he also told me he didn't cheat on me."

"He didn't. He ended things with you at Pirouette Friday night, right?"

Pain breaks through the ice of Qwest's eyes for a moment before she tucks it back under and nods.

"You trying to tell me what I saw on that footage happened between Friday and Sunday?" she scoffs. "I wasn't born yesterday at ten o'clock, honey."

"We talked Saturday, the next day," I say. "About things we should have discussed years ago and decided we would try."

I look down at my hands folded in my lap and then force myself to meet her eyes again.

"I've loved Grip a long time and let stupid things keep us apart. We never meant to hurt you, and were trying to work out the best way to handle the public finding out about you and Grip since your relationship became such a huge part of everything."

"He should have told me it was you." Something beyond anger rises in the heated glance Qwest flicks my way. Resentment. "He's just like all the rest of them. He couldn't choose someone who really understands him."

"What makes you think I don't understand him?"

"He needs a sister who knows how to fight at his side and fight for him."

"So it would make it better if I was Black?"

"You have no idea what it's like seeing the best of our men always choosing you. As soon as they get a little something, make something of themselves, they need to go get a white woman to feel validated."

"That isn't Grip. That isn't what this is."

"Oh, please tell me what it is, Bristol," she says, her words soaked in sarcasm.

"I *have* experienced rejection," I say, my voice quiet.

"Rejection?" A harsh laugh erupts from her and she crosses her arms over her chest, tips her head to the side and cocks one disdainful brow. "Is this where you tell me about your *struggle*, Bristol? About all you've endured in your privileged life?"

Even the feigned amusement fades from her expression, leaving only cynicism, hurt.

"Let me tell you what rejection is. It's being told by an entire culture outright and in a million subtle ways that you're not good enough, not beautiful enough. These athletes and musicians, actors —most of 'em raised by single Black women, and when they find success, do they choose someone from their own community? No, they want someone who's nothing like the very women who sacrificed to make their success possible."

As she articulates it, I see not just her pain, but the pain behind what Jade and Ms. James said. What Shondra didn't voice to me, but felt, too. I see the truth of it and for a moment, nothing I would say feels good enough, feels right, but I have to say something.

"I hear you," I finally tell her. "And I'm sorry, but that isn't what this is. Not what *we* are. We aren't a statistic or a trend. I've had these feelings for years, and Grip wasn't successful or rich or famous when I met him. He was just . . . himself. And I loved that about him."

"I do, too." Qwest blinks at the tears accompanying her soft response.

"I'm so sorry it happened this way." Tears come to my eyes, too. I look down at the carpet to hide them. "I know you care about him."

"I do. That's why it hurt to think that he . . . well, that he cheated." Her bark of a laugh cuts into the air. "It still hurts that I lost out to a white chick. Maybe it shouldn't make a difference, but if we're being honest, it does."

I can't change or apologize for what I am anymore than she can change who she is.

"Qwest, I—"

"Your five minutes are up." Her voice wavers just the slightest bit. She sneaks a finger under one eye to catch a tear.

"Okay. Thank you for listening." I stand and grab my purse. "Grip is doing an online interview with *Legit* tonight to address all of the craziness that's been going on. I wanted to give you a heads up. Once you knew how how things actually happened, I thought you might want to . . . well, put out your own statement so your stories line up."

"You've got all the bases covered, don't you?" Qwest's eyes remain averted, her mouth pulled tight.

"That's my job."

She looks up and sees right through me.

"Only Grip's a lot more than your job, isn't he?"

She knows he is, or I wouldn't have made this risky move. There's nothing more to do here, so I head for the door.

"Bristol," Qwest says, causing me to turn at the door. "You're a very lucky woman. Any woman, Black, white whatever would be lucky to have a man like Grip."

I don't think anything I could say would be the right thing, could ease the pain I see behind her eyes, so I just nod and close the door behind me. But in my heart, despite all the crap we've waded through over the last few days, I agree.

I just might be the luckiest girl in the world.

CHAPTER 31

G_{RIP}

BRISTOL'S IDEA FOR me to address the rumors and misunderstandings directly in an online sit-down with Meryl from *Legit* helped a lot. It was short and to the point, mostly me laying out that I didn't cheat on Qwest and made sure to end one relationship before beginning another. Some will still call me a sellout, but I think most people get that it isn't about the color of our skin.

I wish my mother were one of those people. We've gone from me dodging her calls, to her ignoring mine. After the *Legit* Exclusive aired, I reached out, but she hasn't called me back. It's always been us. We've never fallen out this way, and I can't pretend it doesn't hurt. I keep telling myself I'll go to the house Sunday for dinner and we'll chop it up. Work it out over her sweet potato pie, but there's a part of me that knows it won't be that easy.

All of that aside, right now I can't pretend I'm not excited for my first night out with Bristol. Even if it is just a charity dinner, not a real date. I was scheduled to appear at this fundraiser weeks ago. After the *Legit* interview, Bristol wants me to be business as usual and show people I have nothing to hide. Of course I insisted that if we really have nothing to hide, she'll attend this event with me. It's been over a week since the footage leaked, and a few days since the interview. Surely people have moved on to something else. Something that has nothing to do with my girlfriend and me.

Who looks so damn gorgeous tonight.

I come out of the shower, towel tied at my waist, to stand behind her, settling my hands at her hips as she's putting on makeup in my bathroom.

"I've changed my mind." I kiss her neck. "This event's a waste of time. We should stay home and make love."

She smiles at me in the mirror, pausing in applying mascara.

"I could stay home and you could go."

There's hope on her face and in her voice.

"No way. I thought we had a point to make tonight." I squeeze her waist. "That we have nothing to be ashamed of or to hide."

I turn her around to get a proper look at her. She's wearing this green dress that cuts low between her breasts. The quarter-length sleeves cling to her arms, and the rest of the dress flows freely to her knees. A fragile gold chain adorns the bare strip of skin just above her cleavage.

"This is pretty." I lift the delicate gold links.

Her breath catches when my knuckles brush against the warm satiny swell of her breast. Looking into her eyes, I slip my hand into the bodice of the dress, cupping the weight of one breast, bringing the nipple taut with my thumb.

"Grip, don't start or we'll be late." Her voice is husky, her eyelids half-mast over the desire building in her eyes.

"Uh huh." I squat until I'm level with her chest, pushing the dress aside to expose one full, berry-tipped breast. I lock eyes with her when I take the nipple between my lips, sliding my hands down her waist and spreading both palms over her ass.

"Grip, stop." Her hands contradict her words, pressing my mouth deeper, urging me to scrape my teeth over the nipple. My hand wanders under her dress, skates over one silky thigh and into her panties.

"Shit." I massage her clit, plumping it between two fingers before slipping them inside of her with shallow pumps. "How am I supposed to get through this dinner knowing your panties are soaked?"

"I've got a solution for that," she says breathlessly. She reaches under her dress and slides the panties off, letting them ring around her bare feet. "No more wet panties."

I step back, gripping the knot of terry cloth at my waist, and pointing a warning finger at her.

"You know you're getting fucked so hard when we get home."

"Promises, promises." She turns back to the mirror with a smile, her cheeks and the soft skin of her throat and chest still flushed.

I'm dressed when the buzzer sounds. It's probably Amir. As much as I typically discourage him from "guarding" me, there will be a lot of people at this event tonight. For whatever reason, much of the shade seems directed at Bristol. I want him along more for her safety than for mine.

"That's Amir." I kiss her cheek on my way to the bedroom door. "I'll be down in a sec. Just finishing my hair."

"'K. We're downstairs."

Amir comes in, surveying my black dress shirt, gray slacks and short black boots hidden under my pants.

"Nice." He nods like I pass inspection.

"I try." I walk back into the loft. "Bris'll be right down. You want something to drink before we hit the road?"

"Nah." He glances up the staircase at my closed bedroom door and then back to me. "I do have an update on that thing we talked about."

"What thing?" I ask absently, strapping on my old black plastic watch. It's become a habit I can't break, and it feels good to wear it again even if it does seem cheap and out of place.

"You know," he says, voice barely audible. "The thing."

I sit down on the couch across from him and give him a puzzled look. "Why you talking in code?"

"Corpse, dude." He looks cautiously up the stairs again. "I talked to my cousin."

"Oh." I lean my elbows to my knees, now on high alert. "And?"

"I just asked him if he was still, you know, handling things for people."

"And is he?"

"Yeah." Amir looks like I'm pulling his back teeth. "But on a very limited, exclusive basis."

"I can be limited and exclusive." I pause to catch his eyes. "You know I'm not asking him to kill Parker, right?"

"Man, are you crazy?" Amir eyes the corners of the room, searching the ceiling, I presume for cameras or other devices. "You can't be saying that shit out loud."

"It's my house," I say wryly. "I think if there's anywhere we can safely talk about this, it's here. And I just want options. It would be a drastic situation. He'd have to do something pretty stupid for me to need Corpse, but I just want to know what's out there."

"Well you may have provoked him in that *Legit* interview," Amir says, mild reproach in the look he gives me.

"I just told the truth." I shrug. "When Meryl asked about Parker, I said I'm the only man Bristol's in a relationship with. End of story. It's true. What was I supposed to say?"

We shut the conversation down when the door above opens and Bristol comes out on the landing. For a moment it's just the two of us, her smile for me and me alone. Yeah, Corpse is just insurance, but I'd use him and anything else at my disposal to protect her. I glance back to Amir, wondering if he can read my mind as my girl comes down the stairs. The grim set of his mouth and the concern in his eyes tells me that he can.

CHAPTER 32

B<small>RISTOL</small>

"I<small>NTEREST HAS DIED</small> <small>DOWN, HUH</small>?"

I throw that lightly in Grip's face as we pull up to the charity dinner where there's a small mob of fans and media behind the ropes flanking the red carpet.

It isn't a ball or gala, thank God. Just your standard sit-down, five-thousand-dollar plate dinner. Grip was invited to talk briefly about the importance of giving back to the community. Meryl included parts of his talk at his high school in the *Legit* piece, along with a clip from her phone of him playing basketball with the student. Between that piece, and all the publicity "Bruise" is getting in the debate over tensions with law enforcement, Grip's being perceived as an artist with a conscience. I love it because I think it reflects who he truly is.

"It is crazy out there." Amir considers the crowd lining the red carpet leading to the hotel where the charity dinner is being held.

"It'll be fine." Grip gives Amir a pointed look. "Stay with Bristol if we get separated."

"He's here to guard you, not me." I adjust my dress before the door opens and we have to get out. I'm terribly conscious of the decision to leave my panties on the bathroom floor. I've been exposed enough without flashing my naked girl parts to the world.

"Amir, you heard me." Grip looks from me to his friend. "I'll be fine."

"Gotcha, bruh." He looks at the throng of people pressing closer to the car with cameras and microphones. "Bris, stay close."

I roll my eyes, but nod. I know it bothers Grip that a lot of the hate has died off for him, though some of the more vocal critics call him a sellout, but the lion's share of the vitriol seems to be for me. They've called me so many names, I may as well be doing business as "That White Bitch" by now.

"You ready?" Grip grabs my hand and doesn't wait for me to confirm.

We're on the red carpet sooner than I want to be. I don't answer any of the questions hurled at us, but one question makes me stiffen, and has the same effect on Grip.

"Bristol, what about Parker?" one reporter yells. "How does he feel about your new relationship?"

I hope I've adequately dealt with Parker. All of his messages were the same. I want you. You're mine. We're meant to be. You will marry me. Blah, blah, fucking blah. I left him a voicemail telling him to seek professional help and leave me alone. I haven't heard from him since, even after the police footage was leaked, but that doesn't mean anything. This man has persisted for years. We're into decades now that he's believed some day we'll get hitched and endure years of miserable matrimony just like our parents have. I'm not naïve enough to think one voicemail will kill that delusion.

"Bristol, are you with both of them?" another reporter asks.

I ignore the horrible question, but Grip turns in the direction of the reporter, glaring, his hand still holding mine, tightening around mine.

"What did you ask her?" His voice, a dark growl, has the reporter looking like a mouse caged with a snake. "Does it look like she's with him? She's with me."

"Grip, don't." I tug on his hand, pulling until he's walking with me. "Let's just go in."

The hotel entrance is a blessed end to a walk that only took a minute, but felt like forever with the glare of the spotlight. As soon as we're inside, I pull him into the nearest discreet corner. I reach up to frame his face, undeterred by the irritation stamped there.

"Hey, don't let those stupid questions get to you, okay?" I whisper. "You know I'm with you. You know what happened with Parker. That's all that counts."

"I know." He closes his eyes, turning his head to kiss the inside of my wrist. "But the Parker thing . . ."

Displeasure rattles his throat in a low rumble.

"You're mine. You're with me." He squats a little to kiss me, his lips possessive and commanding. He presses me into him, splaying his hand across my lower back. Even though we've stepped to the side, I know there have to be people watching us, but I sense he needs this, so I tamp down my self-consciousness and surrender. His kiss slows, his tongue doing a languid sweep inside like he's marking my mouth. He drops his forehead to mine.

"I know I'm overreacting." He sighs, tipping his head back and studying the chandeliers dotting the high ceilings. "I just hate that anyone would even think he has a claim on you."

"Hey, from their perspective, it was a blur." I take both of his hands in mine. "All of this—you and Qwest, me and Parker—it's all really tangled in their heads. They don't know I've been in love with you for years."

His eyes soften, like I knew they would, and he laughs, cupping my neck.

"You think you can charm your way out of that hard fuck you have coming tonight, don't you?"

"When have I ever run from a hard fuck?" My voice comes out low and sultry, my smile slow and only for him. "I'm earning it."

A hand on Grip's shoulder pulls us out of each other.

"They're going in," Amir says, eyes discreetly lowered. "Just letting you know."

"You ready for this?" Grip asks.

"You're the one who has to speak. I just look pretty and eat rubbery five-thousand dollar chicken."

Apparently I know my stuff, because that is all that is asked of me for the rest of the night. Our table is full of people much older than we are, community activists who probably couldn't give a flying fig about what's trending on Twitter. I doubt any of them know what a "thot" is either. And I'm so grateful.

Grip is extraordinary in this context. His background and child-hood mean that he is in touch with real need like many celebrities aren't. It isn't just something he shouldn't forget. His mother still lives in the house where he grew up. His cousins and aunts and family are all still in that community. He talks about how he would have gone hungry at school if there hadn't been a free lunch program, and about the years when he was younger and his mother was on welfare. He smiles when he tells us how proud she was when she no longer needed it.

I marvel again at how we found each other, at how natural it has felt with us from the beginning, considering how vastly different our lives have been. Like someone gave him the answers to a test, as if he had a Bristol cheat sheet that no one else received. I can't take my eyes off him. He thought I watched him before. Now that he's mine, now that we're together, it's even worse. He rivets me, and it doesn't scare me anymore. Maybe I do love him too much and don't have boundaries. I don't care. This love is the stuff of magic, of fantasy, but so raw and real I can touch it. I can taste it. If for some reason I fall, how many can say they soared this high?

"You were excellent," I whisper to Grip as we stand from the table to leave. Amir sat at a separate table designated for security and bodyguards, so we wait for him to make his way over to us.

"Thank you, baby." Grip leans down to my ear, his voice dark and dirty. "Knowing you are naked under that dress has been driving me crazy all night. The napkin was barely big enough to hide my hard-on."

There is some secret switch he planted in my body that responds to him instantly. Heat and wetness collect between my thighs. For a moment, I consider dragging him to the nearest bathroom stall and slaking my lust before we make it home, but a voice from behind me dumps ice all over the flame building inside me.

"Bristol," my mother says. "Good evening."

I turn to face her, braced for her censure. I may have ignored several of her calls when the footage of Grip and me leaked.

"Mother, hello. I didn't know you were here."

"Well, it's a big crowd." She glances around the ballroom. "Betsy's here, too, somewhere."

She shifts her eyes to Grip.

"That's Parker's mother, by the way." She looks at my hand linked with Grip's. "We've been best friends more than forty years."

"It's good to see you again, Mrs. Gray," Grip says politely.

He and my mother haven't been around each other much, but he knows more about my family's dark secrets, dirty laundry and skeletons than just about anyone else.

"Marlon, good speech tonight," Mother replies stiffly before looking back to me. "Maybe my messages got lost in the . . . chaos of your life, Bristol. I needed to speak with you quite urgently."

"Really?" I frown and twist my mouth to the side in concentration. "Not sure how I missed that. What did you need?"

She squeezes her eyes at the edges, shoving as much condemnation into her narrow glance as possible.

"Maybe we could speak privately," she says.

Amir walks up, his eyes moving between the three of us before finally connecting with Grip. He lifts his brows and tilts his head, a silent query. Grip just nods, but keeps his eyes on my mother.

"Mother, this is our friend Amir." I give Amir a warm smile, hoping it defrosts the atmosphere my mother is creating. They exchange brief pleasantries, but the ice remains untouched.

"We need to get going, Bris," Grip says softly. "But there was a room they had for me before I got up to speak. If your mother wants to talk before we go, we could swing that."

I search his face, tightened into impassivity, giving nothing away.

"That isn't necessary." I dip my head, trying to catch his eyes. I already know what my mother wants to talk to me about. So does he. Why does he even think I want to listen?

"It actually is, Bristol." She looks to Grip, her eyes unthawed. "Marlon, show us where."

When we reach the small room, Mother walks in ahead of us. I linger in the hall and step close to Grip. Amir takes a few steps away, out of earshot, but within helping distance.

"Why are you accommodating her?" I lean into his chest, running my hands up to his neck. I lift up on my toes to whisper in his ear. "You could be fucking me by now."

"She's your mother." He pulls back a little, setting me away from him and gently nudging me toward the room. "Give her a few minutes."

It means something to him it's never been for me, the connection to a parent. I know the distance between him and his mother bothers him. As close as they've always been, discord isn't natural, when for me that's par for the course.

"Okay," I agree. "But can we work out some signal so if I need you, you'll come rescue me from this lecture?"

"Just hurry up." He turns me toward the door and swats my bottom. "So I can keep my promise."

I'm still thinking about how good that promise kept will be when I face my mother. I don't bother closing the door, even though I know Grip and Amir are in the hall. Maybe that will deter her from saying anything too insulting.

"What the hell do you think you're doing, Bristol?" Her voice thwacks me like a wet towel as soon as I enter the room.

"I'm giving you your private moment, Mother. What's this about?"

"You know exactly what this is about." She gestures toward the hall. "Is this what you call having things under control? Being broadcast kissing that . . . man all over the world?"

"That . . . man is my boyfriend, Mother," I snap. "And if you say one disrespectful word about him, I warn you, this conversation is over."

"Bristol, Parker—"

"I told you before I don't want Parker. I don't want anything to do with him."

Her expression cracks, irritation rearing from behind the protection of the smooth mask.

"Bristol, let me speak frankly. You aren't your brother. Rhyson is a musician with a rare gift. That is not your strength."

The words I've always known she felt even when she didn't express them land heavily on my chest, suspiciously close to my heart.

"I know you're playing around with this management business," she continues. "But you need to think about your future."

"Mother, you're a businesswoman with your own money. Why would you want anything different for me? Expect anything less from me?"

"Park Corp is worth billions, Bristol. You don't ignore that.

Charles Parker is a once and a lifetime opportunity."

"Opportunity?" I shake my head disbelievingly. "Is that how you went into your marriage, Mother? How's that worked out for you?"

As much as I believe my words, I regret them. I don't want to see my mother in pain, and the hurt that pinches her face before she can hide it hurts me, too.

"Don't turn this on me, Bristol. We're talking about you. I told you not to toy with Parker."

"And I didn't. I was clear with him that we weren't going to happen."

"Well Betsy asked him about this . . . scandal you're in with . . ." She gestures out toward the hall. "Him. Parker pretended to be fine with it, but I don't believe it. I can see Marlon holds a certain appeal. You want a good lay, a man with a lot in his pants, go for it. Understand the consequences, though. Parker won't give up."

"Bristol." Grip comes to the door, that muscle bunched in his jaw that usually means he's pissed. "Baby, let's go."

"We aren't done," my mother says testily.

"Yes, you are." Grip's fists are in his pockets, tucked away with his patience. "I couldn't imagine turning my mother down if she asked for time with me. I'd have to at least hear her out. So, I encouraged Bristol to do this, but I'm not going to stand out there while you insult her."

"I'm trying to protect her," my mother says. "Parker isn't easily deterred. I just want Bristol to understand what she's giving up having this . . . affair with you."

"Affair?" Grip glowers. "I've been in love with your daughter for a long time. For years. I didn't wait this long so we could have some affair, as you call it."

"Oh, and you're serious about Bristol." My mother rolls her eyes. "Because of you, my daughter is the butt of jokes. The names she's being called. The way people are talking about her. It's beneath her."

She doesn't say it, but her eyes do.

You're beneath her.

"Mother, I have put up with your shit for a long time." My voice vibrates with the anger overtaking every inch of me. "I can take it. I have taken it. I've listened to you tell me that I'm not as talented as Rhyson. You've made me feel worthless."

"I've never—"

"Yes, you always have, but no more. I'm in love with Grip. Not only do I want to be with him, I'm proud to be with him. And anyone who doesn't like it, that goes for you and any idiots hiding behind their Instagram posts or trolling Twitter, can go to hell."

I turn to leave the room, and am at the door when Grip's words stop me.

"Mrs. Gray," he says softly. "I've heard a lot of things about you over the years, and I can't say much of it has been good."

"Excuse me?" Mother's indignation blares in the two words.

"You have an awful relationship with Rhyson, and from what I can tell, it's just as bad with Bristol. The only difference is she stayed and he left."

"You don't know anything about our family, Marlon."

"Actually, I do. Your son and I have been best friends for over fifteen years." He pauses. "And I'm going to marry your daughter one day."

I swing around, my chin dropped to my chest, shock trilling through me.

"Not today," he goes on like he didn't just topsy-turvy my world. "Not tomorrow. We'll know when the time is right. That isn't my point. My point is despite all the evidence to the contrary, I think you love your daughter very much."

"I do." Mother's bottom lip quivers before she pulls it back into the disciplined line I'm accustomed to. "I'm only trying to protect her."

"You're trying to control her," Grip counters. "You tried to control Rhyson, and you lost him. If you don't want to lose Bristol, don't make her choose between us, or you'll lose her, too."

She and Grip stare at one another for elongated seconds, reading one another. My mother reads people like a polygraph. She smells lies and eats their weaknesses. They don't make peace. I don't think I've ever seen my mother make peace with anyone, but I think they understand each other. But who knows because she walks toward me, giving me a brief look, and then sweeps into the hall and out the door.

Very rarely am I speechless, but I don't know which words are the right ones. I know Grip loves me, but I can honestly say I haven't seriously thought about marriage. That's crazy, I know. Marriage is not the end all, be all to me. Rhys and Kai are rare. Happy marriages are rare from my experience. My parents' marriage is an unnatural disaster, a lame horse that should have been put down years ago, and yet it keeps limping on.

Grip walks over to me and lifts my chin, his eyes scanning my face.

"Breathe." A small smile tilts one corner of his mouth, but serious eyes search mine.

I draw a deep breath in and exhale long and slow. He's right. I think I've been holding my breath since I heard the word "marry."

"I didn't say tonight." He cups my face. "I didn't mean to freak you out. That was the worst way to bring it up. I just . . . I'm not going anywhere. Are you?"

"No, of course not." My voice comes out from whatever rock it was hiding under. "I see nothing but you in the future. No one but you. You know that."

"Then don't freak out on me."

"I guess I . . . we just haven't talked about it, and we haven't been together long and—"

He presses a finger to my lips. "Bris, it's okay."

"I guess I just didn't know what to say."

He dips to take my lips between his, exploring me, searching me until he's satisfied with the answer my body gives. He pulls back, his eyes taking me in.

"When I do ask you, just say yes."

CHAPTER 33

G~RIP~

I'M SO HUNGRY I could eat my tires. If I didn't need them to get home to Bristol, I probably would. I pull the Harley into the underground parking garage of my loft. Bristol's Audi convertible sits in the neighboring spot. An involuntary grin works its way from the inside to land on my lips. Seeing her here at my place makes me think about the future. After last night, I've been thinking about the future a lot.

I couldn't have chosen a worst way or time to bring up marriage than during a confrontation with her mother . . . who happens to hate me.

It's beneath her.

Angela Gray's words echo back to me. Yeah, I got the message, lady. I'm some Boyz n the Hood thug rapper and your daughter will come to her senses when the novelty of how I lay down this pipe wears off.

Got it. Loud and clear.

Bristol's mother is the high priestess of veiled messages, though she wasn't hiding much last night.

Billions?

Damn. That's a lot of money Bristol's walking away from.

I look around the lobby of my loft building. It's nice. Luxurious even. Nicer than anything I ever would have imagined for myself growing up. Better than anything anyone in my family has ever owned.

But billions? Parker is worth billions.

I've been wrestling with this unfamiliar sense of inadequacy ever since last night. Unfamiliar because my mother raised me to assume I was up for any challenge, as if I could accomplish anything. That kind of confidence in a kid from my circumstances is rare, and not for the first time, I thank my mother. She'll come around. She has to. I told Mrs. Gray that Bristol would choose me. I know this because I would choose her. It wouldn't be fair, and it would cut me open and gut me, but if my mother insists on this attitude—on treating Bristol the way she did—I'll have some choices to make, too.

An odd, bitter smell hits my nose as soon as I enter the loft. An investigative sniff doesn't do much good. I still can't place that awful smell. Is it garbage or . . . what?

"Grip." Bristol bends over the rail up on the landing. Her dark hair hangs a little wild and completely free down her back. She rushes down the stairs and hurls herself into my arms. I stumble back, laughing with an armful of my girl.

God, yes. This.

Parker can have his billions and his hotels and his helicopters. This is all I want. I squeeze Bristol so tightly our hearts converse through our clothes. I lean into her, sliding my hands down to her waist and kissing her.

"Are you hungry?" she asks against my lips. She's wearing a simple black dress with short sleeves. She's barefoot and has on no makeup. I could eat her for dinner she looks so good. Or actual food and then just make love to her afterwards. I like that option even better.

"Starving." I peck her lips and squint toward the take out menus under magnets on the refrigerator. "We can order whatever you want, just make it fast."

"No need to order." Bristol pulls back, her eyes gleaming with anticipation. "I cooked."

So it wasn't the garbage.

"Um, why?" I pose the question cautiously because . . . why would she try to cook? That one good pot of chili hasn't convinced me.

"Grip." She pouts her lips so prettily that I'd eat her shoe if she pulled it out of the oven. "I wanted to make something you'd enjoy after that long photo shoot. How was it by the way?"

"It was great. I missed having you there, but Sarah did great."

"She did? Good. You were wrong for firing me. Of course, you were, but it made me realize that Sarah needs broader experiences. And if I don't recruit some help, I'll be working eighteen-hour days for the foreseeable future."

"The hell you will. Some of those hours are mine," I mumble against her neck.

"Not the neck." Her husky protest is half-hearted at best as she arches her neck to give me easier access.

"I really am starving." I laugh when she looks disappointed that I don't have her up against the wall yet. As hungry as I am, I'd probably drop her.

"Well, like I said." She pulls back, humor restored and eyes gleaming again. "I cooked."

She takes my hand and pulls me toward the dining room table. It's set beautifully with dishes I've never seen before, and lit with candles I know I didn't buy.

"What's the occasion?" I take the seat beside hers.

"Us." She leans down to kiss me. "Us is the occasion."

"I like the sound of that." I pull her into my lap, ignoring the hunger pains. She wiggles, which does not soften my dick any, until she squirms free.

"Dinner first." She's practically beaming.

"And what's for dinner?"

"Collard greens. Like the ones your mother made."

Her grin stretches across her face, and I don't have the heart to tell her how hard they are to get as good as my mom's. It's a start.

"Oh. Great." My mouth is already watering. Even knowing how other-abled Bristol is in the kitchen, I'm sure something turned out edible. "And what else?"

"Um . . ." Her face falls. "Else?"

"Yeah, you know. Like meat, potatoes, or whatever. I'm really not picky, just hungry."

"I spent a lot of time on these collard greens." She bites her lip. "I wanted to cook something I knew you liked, and they were so good at dinner that Sunday. And I think they turned out great."

"Are you telling me you only cooked greens?" My stomach howls like a coyote.

"But it's a lot of them." She grimaces and shifts from one bare foot to the other. "I guess I didn't think this through."

"Babe, it's okay." I stroke one cheekbone, tracing the few almost undetectable freckles scattered over her nose. "I can't believe you went to the trouble of making one of my favorite dishes. Let's eat."

How bad could it be? I mean, they're greens, not escargots.

Can I just say . . . damn.

At least now I know how bad they could be. I run my fork through the leathery green leaves on the pretty plates Bristol set. They also taste like I imagine leather would taste . . . but not as well seasoned. Meanwhile, my stomach is at my back. I should have eaten the Craft service on set today. I will suffer in silence because there is no way I'm telling her how bad these greens are.

"They're not great, huh?" she asks.

"They're the worst," I say before I can stop myself.

We consider each other across the table and the steaming crap pile of collard greens and laugh together. She gets up and climbs into my lap, sliding her hand into my jeans pocket to get my cell phone.

"Pizza?" She rests her forehead against my chin.

"With every meat known to man and some that haven't been FDA approved."

Once the pizza is ordered, she doesn't leave my lap, which is fine with me.

"I really wanted to make dinner special for you," she whispers into my neck, dotting kisses into the edge of my shirt and across my collarbone. "Those greens at your mom's were so good."

"It's taken her a long time to get those right. She used her mother's recipe, and her mother used her mother's recipe. They can taste really awful if not done right."

"So I discovered." She shakes against me with laughter.

"Maybe my mom can share her recipe one day," I venture softly. I know the things Bristol overheard my mom say hurt her, but she hasn't brought it up.

Bristol's laugh this time is a humorless huff of air.

"That would be an interesting development since she can't stand me."

"She'll come around, baby. She has to. She's just recalibrating her expectations. Like I'm sure your mom is doing."

Bristol shrugs one shoulder. Sending one side of the dress down her arm and leaving her shoulder bare.

"What your mother said last night about what you're giving up to be with me, to not be with Parker."

"What about it?" She doesn't know where I'm heading.

"Billions, babe." I kiss the top of her head, cupping the back and tugging my fingers through the soft strands. "It's a lot, right?"

She's silent for a few seconds before she glances up at me through her long lashes. Her fingers drift to the necklace I noticed last night. The thick gold bar hangs from the chain. It's obviously fine craftsmanship.

"You admired my necklace last night," she says. "But you didn't read the inscription."

I study her face while I lift the gold bar and turn it over.

Etched into the gold is the inscription "My heart broke loose on the wind."

For a second, the space of a heartbeat, I can't breathe. This means so much to me I literally cannot breathe.

"When did you get this?" My voice is hushed, reverent with the thought of what that night on the Ferris wheel must have meant to her, too.

"Months ago." She cups one side of my face. "We didn't even seem to be a possibility when I ordered this."

"But why . . . even then?"

Months ago, Bristol was deep freezing me, so it's hard to imagine that night was on her mind then. That I was on her mind then.

"Even if we hadn't gotten together, I was still going to wear this next to my heart because I knew I would never love anyone else that way." She shakes her head, eyes bright with conviction. "Not the way I felt that night. That night was awesome, magical, but it was just a glimpse of the man you would become. And I knew even if I couldn't have you, I'd carry this piece of you with me. This piece of your prophecy."

That poem inspired me in a way I have only ever put into words for one person. The woman sitting in my lap. The woman who has held my heart for years when I wasn't sure she even wanted it. And the whole time, this night, these moments, burned in her memory like they did mine. I'm torn between spreading her on the table and having my appetizer before the pizza arrives, or kissing her until she's limp in my arms. Before I get the chance to do either, the buzzer sounds.

"Pizza," we say together with grins.

"I'll get my wine," she says. "And your beer."

I clear my throat of the emotion still clogging it.

"Sounds good." I take one more look at her, how naturally she fits here, but she'd fit anywhere I was, and I'll fit any place she'll be. I guess we'll spend the rest of our lives chasing each other.

And getting caught every night.

I swing open the door, cash tip already in hand, but it isn't the pizza guy.

"Officers." I suppress the Pavlovian response. Obviously they're here for a reason, and I've done nothing wrong, so I'll just wait to hear them out. "What can I do for you?"

There's no answer from either of them, and they look like undertakers.

"Something wrong?" I ask.

"We um, need to search the property." One of them flashes his badge, and I note the name Officer Mars.

"Search?" I frown and glance over my shoulder into the loft. "For what exactly?"

"What's this about?" Bristol comes to stand beside me, hands already on her hips.

"We were tipped off that there may be a significant amount of cocaine in the residence connected to a recent bust over on Rosecrans."

"What?" I give an incredulous laugh. "In here? Nah, you got that twisted."

"You have search warrants?" Bristol demands. "You won't be searching anything until you show me one."

Amazingly they produce one.

"It was a huge bust connected to one of the largest operations on the West Coast," Officer Mars says. "We have to follow every lead in a case as significant as this."

"That may well be," Bristol says, eyes glowing the color of gunmetal. "But that has nothing to do with Mr. James."

"Ma'am, we have this warrant." He shifts his weight and hooks a thumb in his belt loop. "And we need to conduct a thorough search."

"This is ridiculous." I shake my head dazedly. "A tip? From who?"

"We aren't at liberty to say," Officer Mars asserts. "May we come inside?"

"No, the hell you may not," Bristol says. "I'm calling our lawyer. This is ridiculous."

"Bris, it's obviously just a misunderstanding." I lead her over to the couch and sit. "Just let them get it over with. They won't find anything."

"Sir, we're just doing our jobs," Officer Mars says softly. "It isn't personal."

"Not personal?" Bristol shouts. "What the hell do you mean it's not—"

"Babe, it's okay." I wrap my fingers around hers and pull her to wait with me on the couch. I wave a hand to the room. "Knock yourselves out for nothing. Waste our tax dollars doing this when you could be doing something real."

"I don't like this," Bristol whispers to me as they search the room systematically, finding nothing, of course. "I'm calling our lawyer."

"They're almost done. They won't find anything."

"What's this?" Officer Mars pats the back of my backpack, which I notice for the first time bulges more than usual. "I'm going to have to open this."

He pulls out a pocketknife and slits the back off the bag.

"This is outrageous." Bristol's voice stings like a scorpion. "Now you'll have to replace his bag . . ."

Her voice trails off as a huge block of cocaine in an oversize Zip Lock bag falls from the lining of my backpack.

Officer Mars swears softly, flicking a surprised glance my way. I surge to my feet and point to the bag.

"That shit isn't mine."

"It's in your bag, in your residence," the other officer says carefully. "Your ID and other items that clearly belong to you are here."

"Grip, don't say another word." Bristol has her phone to her ear. "I'm getting our lawyers on the phone right now. I knew this was some kind of setup. God."

"Tell the lawyers to meet him down at the county jail."

"Jail?" The word torpedoes from my mouth at full speed. "The hell I am. I've never been to jail a day in my life, and I'm not going now. Not for some shit that isn't even mine."

"I'm sure we'll straighten it out then," Officer Mars says, his face set in impassive lines, though I can tell it isn't what he wants to be doing. "We have to take you in, Mr. James."

It's all surreal, and none of it sinks in. Not the officer reading me rights I promised my mother I'd never have to hear. Not Bristol's urgent conversation with Prodigy's lawyer. Only the cuffs feel real, enclosing my wrists again for something I haven't done.

"No cuffs," Bristol's hard voice batters the officers. "You'll take the private exit where no one will see, and keep this off the radar as long as you can."

"Ma'am, with all due respect—"

"You left respect behind when you came into our home and found drugs that don't belong to us."

"This isn't a negotiation," Officer Mars interjects almost gently.

"Oh, you better believe it's a negotiation." Bristol folds her arms over her chest, managing to look imposing even in her casual dress and bare feet. "Here's the terms. You follow my instructions for getting him out of here and keeping this off the radar as long as possible. How well you follow my instructions determines, when I bring a wrongful arrest suit against LAPD, how deeply I drag the two of you into it."

There's no sign of the soft, pliant woman who was in my lap just minutes ago. In her place stands a coldly enraged Valkyrie who looks fully prepared to escort them to the afterlife.

"Which exit did you want us to use?" Officer Mars asks reluctantly.

While Bristol goes over the plan to get me out of the building and down to the county jail, all I can think of is my mother telling anyone who would listen that all she ever dreamt was that I'd have a clean record and never spend a day behind bars.

Sorry, Ma.

CHAPTER 34

B~RISTOL~

"THIS CAN'T BE ~HAPPENING.~" No matter how many times I've said that over the last several hours, this is happening.

Grip is behind bars, and we can't get him out on bail. With all the money and connections at our disposal, he's still stuck in county jail with no chance of getting out tonight.

"It's the weekend," Barry, the lawyer says again. "There won't be a hearing until Monday."

"You're telling me Grip has to stay in jail until Monday?" The disbelief and fury on Rhyson's face may match mine, but I doubt it. "For something we know he didn't do? Hell, even if he did it, we should be able to get him out."

"He has no criminal record whatsoever. He should be released on his own recognizance." I've said this over and over, and Barry's answer remains the same.

"They found a lot of cocaine in his possession. Enough to bump this up to a felony." Barry polishes his glasses and shakes his head. "Because they have reason to believe it's connected to a larger case, to a case they've been working and a group they've been trying to prose- cute for years, the typical strings I would pull aren't working."

Barry stands to his feet and gathers his briefcase and jacket. "Where do you think you're going? Rhyson, he isn't leaving." I grab Barry's briefcase and hold it hostage behind my back. "You're not leaving."

Rhyson and Barry stare at me, mouths hanging open. "Bristol, listen," Rhyson says. "I know you—"

"No, you don't know." My voice breaks. My heart breaks. "If you're willing to leave this place, to let Barry leave this place with Grip still behind bars, then you don't know."

"Bris, I get it." Rhyson says. "He's my best friend."

"But he's my . . ."

I drop the briefcase and turn my back on the two of them, my heart like a spinning speedometer, completely out of control and reckless. I cross one arm across my waist and chew my thumbnail. The sound of Barry leaving the room barely registers. A horrible suspicion sprouted like a weed as soon as the officers found that cocaine, and has grown into venomous certainty. It's choking every lucid thought and killing off my reason.

"Bristol, we have to go home." Rhyson turns me gently by the shoulders to face him.

"I want to see him." Tears flood my throat and emotion weakens my mouth into a trembling mess. "He didn't get to . . . to eat . . . and I need . . . I need to see him before we go."

"We can't tonight, Bris. It's . . ." he pulls his phone out of his pocket and grimaces at the screen. "It's one o'clock in the morning. Tomorrow. He's asleep anyway."

"Asleep in jail, Rhyson. We can't leave him."

"Look, we'll be back at it first thing in the morning. I am ordering you to go home, get some rest so you'll be ready to fight tomorrow. We can at least try to find some way to get him out before Monday, despite this hearing thing. But nothing more will happen tonight."

He heads for the door, looking over his shoulder at me.

"Let's go, Bris. I need to get home to Kai anyway. She's so close now, I hate leaving her alone."

Guilt pricks me as I think about my sister-in-law home alone, ready to deliver at any moment.

"You're right. Of course, go. I'll work on this tomorrow morning."

"Make no mistake about it," Rhyson says gently. "So will I. If there was more we could do tonight to get him out, you know I would do it."

I nod and walk with him into the hallway outside of the room we've occupied the last few hours, crawling up walls and shaking trees to make headway.

"Rhyson, what if I told you I think Grip being here has something to do with me?" I ask softly, finally voicing the noxious thought that has been scratching the inside of my head the last few hours.

"You mean Parker?" Rhyson slides a glance my way and nods. "It occurred to me."

I stop, grabbing his elbow to stop him, too. "So you do think this is my fault?"

"No, not your fault." Rhyson squeezes my hand. "But I wouldn't put it past Parker to be involved somehow. This was all too orchestrated. It smacks of foul play. If Parker is involved, I bet some high-ranking judge is in his pocket."

"My thoughts exactly."

"Bristol, promise me you won't contact Parker." Rhyson looks down at me sternly. "We knew he was dangerous, but now we know the lengths he'll go to. Or at least we think he'll go to. We'll work on this together tomorrow."

All the pieces start coming together in my head while I'm driving home. Once I know for sure that Parker is behind this, I'll feel better. He never does anything unless there's a gain. A measurable gain. I know what, or who he wants to gain. For the first time I feel some control. Steel enters my spine. I can fix this. I don't know what I'll have to do to fix it, and I honestly don't care as long as I can get Grip's name cleared and him out of this ridiculous situation.

I should be surprised to find the same black SUV that met me on the tarmac after Dubai in my driveway, but I'm not. Clairmont steps from the driver's side and crosses around to open the rear door for me. I don't look at or otherwise acknowledge him, but climb in, taking the seat across from Parker.

"You twisted motherfucker." I keep my voice even and calm despite the violent emotions howling inside of me. My fingers spasm with the base compulsion to claw his throat out.

"Bristol." Parker's blue eyes gleam with dark smugness. "Now is that any way to greet the man who holds the key to setting your lover free?"

"How soon can you get him out?"

"It took me very little time to break it. I can fix it just as quickly, with your cooperation, of course. And you should call your brother's lawyers off. They're wasting their time, though I must admit I am enjoying blocking them at every turn. I have the right judges so deep in my pocket they lick my ass."

"Who are you?" I lean forward, searching his face for an answer, looking for the monster hiding behind the polished mask. "What is wrong with you? Ruining an innocent man's life for what? Me? To marry me, a woman who doesn't love you?"

"Why would I care if you love me or not?" The razor edge of Parker's laugh slices through my nerves. "But a marriage offer isn't on the table anymore. How could it be now that the whole world knows you've soiled yourself with that thug?"

I watch him with no expression, waiting for his terms. It doesn't matter what they are. I'll do them to clear Grip's name. Parker may not realize it, but he has me exactly where he wants me. He can bend me, position me, do whatever the hell he wants with me. He's found my weakest point, and I'll say 'uncle' before he even asks.

"Just tell me what you want and stop playing games."

"Oh, but the games are the fun part." His lust pollutes the air. It's thick, a heavy fume filling my nostrils, gagging me. "And you know what I want, Bristol."

"Sex."

My steady eyes and matter of fact tone don't betray my insurgent heart, bawling at the thought of anyone but Grip inside of me.

"Well, of course. That's a given." Parker smiles at me like I'm a slow child. "You could have been my queen, but now you have to bow to me."

He drops the smile and nods to the spot in front of him. "I said now, Bristol. On your knees."

Teeth locked painfully and eyes hot with tears I will not give him the satisfaction of shedding, I drop to my knees and face him. He reaches out, pushing down one shoulder of my dress and then the other, until my breasts lay bare except for the gold chain dangling between them. My nipples go hard in the cool air, and I hope he'll take it for desire. A man like Parker needs to feel wanted, and my heart may have no limits where Grip's concerned, but my body does. And it refuses to want Parker.

He licks his lips, eyes brimming with greed, and cups my breast, squeezing with no mercy. I swallow a cry of pain, knowing it would only feed his appetite for my suffering.

"This body was made for me," he says huskily. His eyes lift to mine, hard as blue crystals. "Mine, and you humiliated me in front of the whole world, flaunting your sordid affair with him."

"There's nothing sordid about my relationship with Grip."

I stiffen when his hand slides down my torso, slipping past the material puddled at my hips and into my panties. His fingers play between my legs, but I remain obstinately dry. There is nothing about this, about him that excites me. I'm disgusted I ever shared my body with this man. Even as a naïve girl still in high school I should have recognized him as a monster.

"You're not as . . ." He withdraws his hand. "Ready for me as I would have hoped."

"I can get myself ready, if you like." I barb the smile before I give it to him. "It'll be like old times."

I'm not the only one holding back my true feelings. Despite the calm veneer, I see barely restrained rage in Parker's eyes. I'm just waiting for him to take it out on me.

"The whole world is laughing at me, Bristol."

"They aren't."

"To the world, you played me with that thug of yours."

I don't defend Grip. That would only make him angrier.

"I asked you to tell the press, Parker. I wasn't cheating on you, and you know it. Now let's get this over with." Urgency to free Grip, to clear his name, rides me. "Tell me what you want. I'm on my knees here. You want head? You want to fuck me in the ass? You want to invite a couple friends? I don't care, just tell me you'll clear his name and do it as soon as humanly possible."

Though I have my doubts about Parker's humanity.

"God, all that loyalty and fire. That was supposed to be mine, too." Parker runs a finger down my cheek, smiling when I flinch. "You think I'll make this simple for him? For you? No, he needs to be humiliated the way I was. Everyone has to know."

A cesspool of dread stands in my belly.

"Just tell me what I have to do, and give me the assurances I need that you'll get him out as soon possible."

"So impatient." He pushes my hair back from my face, his touch lingering at my neck with deceptive gentleness. "You and I leave for the Amalfi Coast tomorrow."

"All right." I have no idea why this is necessary, but I also can't care anymore. I just need to get Grip free.

"We'll fuck on my yacht, out on the upper deck."

My acquiescence freezes on my lips, horror seeping slowly into every fiber of my body.

"The upper deck?"

"Yes, the same reporter who leaked the Vegas pictures is standing by." His frigid smile is an icy warning. "The whole world will know that you may be with him, but you're on vacation fucking me. More importantly, he'll know."

I don't know if I can do it. For a moment, my will wavers.

"Do you think I've done my worst, Bristol?" Parker's smile is a sutured curve, a jagged row of stitches stretching over a wound. "Oh, it could get worse for him. What if there's a body somewhere connected to these drug deals of his? What if his DNA can be matched to any number of crimes? He could be put away for life, if I try just a little harder."

I think of Grip behind bars, possibly for years, life in ruins because he loved me.

"So tomorrow?" I pull my dress up over my shoulders, forcing the words past the heart trapped and bleeding in my throat. "What time?"

"I'll pick you up at two."

"I'll be ready."

I start to get up from my knees, but he grabs my elbow and turns me back to face him.

"One more thing, Bristol."

He jerks me into him, his mouth rough and cruel, and his teeth sharp on the tender swell of my bottom lip. My own blood rushes into my mouth. He flattens his hand to my chest, and my heart tattoos fear into his palm. A smile slashes his face before he snatches the chain from my neck.

"You really should have let me buy you this necklace."

CHAPTER 35

B<small>RISTOL</small>

"THE LAWYERS ARE <small>WORKING</small> on it, but we keep hitting a wall." Rhyson shakes his head, dismay darkening his gray eyes to slate. "It's the weekend, so that's part of it, but these guys can usually break through anything. Even getting this private meeting room was near impossible, and usually a good bribe can pull that off easily. Some high ups must be monitoring your case really closely."

He splits a careful glance between me and Grip, who faces us from the other side of the table, dressed in royal blue scrubs with "LA County Jail" emblazoned on the back. It's incongruous. Awful and incongruous to see my brilliant poet in this garb. This man whose record is cleaner than mine when so many things where he grew up could have left smudges on him. That was the thing his mother was most proud of, and because of me, that's gone.

Grip has been uncharacteristically quiet. Anger dulls the eyes usually lit with humor, intelligence. For me—desire, love.

"My mom's coming?" he asks, not acknowledging Rhyson's comment at all. "She knows to come here, right?"

Rhyson and I exchange a concerned look.

"Yeah, Gep made sure she knows we got this room. Did you hear me, Marlon?" Rhyson presses. "We keep running into walls, but we're working on it."

"Any idea what's behind it all?" Grip asks the question of Rhyson, but his eyes rest on me. "Why I was set up in the first place?"

With a look, Rhyson and I silently agree to tell him.

"We think it may be Parker." I clear my throat and drop my eyes to the imitation wood of the table. "So, it's probably my fault."

"Not your fault, Bristol," Rhyson says quickly. "But I do agree that Parker is the only person with motivation and power enough to throw up the kind of road blocks the lawyers keep encountering."

"They won't make any headway." I run a trembling hand through my hair.

"How would you know that, Bristol?" Grip's question, his voice so hard it hurts my ears. "You sound really certain."

"I mean, I'm guessing." I shrug one shoulder, toying with the bangles on my wrist "If it's Parker, he'll have thought of everything."

"I bet he has." Grip's eyes rest so heavily on me I feel them even though I'm still not looking at him. I tuck my swollen bottom lip in my mouth, hoping he won't notice.

"Well, we're not giving up. Gep's calling in favors with all his old fed contacts. See what we can find." Rhyson glances at his watch. "I gotta run. Luke's got a session he needs me to sit in on, but the lawyers will keep working."

He stands and crooks a grin at us.

"Besides, I assume you guys want a few minutes alone." He tips his head toward the cameras in the corner of the ceiling. "Don't give 'em too much of a show."

I glance at Grip, but there's no answering smile. No acknowledgment of Rhyson's joke. He stands, and they do that man hug thing, pounding on each other's backs.

"I'm gonna get you out of here," Rhyson says. "I'm sorry you're not out already."

"Not your fault, man." Grip fist pounds Rhyson before taking his seat, his eyes latching on to me again. "Thanks for all you're doing."

"Bye, sis." Rhyson drops a kiss on my hair. "Stay out of trouble. Let me handle this Parker shit."

I nod but focus on the hands in my lap. I'm usually an excellent liar, but the dilemma with Parker has stripped all my guard away, and I don't trust my own subterfuge to hold under their sharp eyes.

Once Rhyson leaves, I'm not sure what to do with myself or with Grip. I lay my hand on the table, in hopes that he'll reach for it, but he doesn't. He's quiet and intent, dissecting me with his stare.

"What?" I hazard a glance up to meet his eyes. "Why are you so quiet? You're angry. I understand. You wouldn't be here if it weren't for me."

He doesn't reply, but the expressive curve of his mouth is stiff as wax. He slumps in his seat and links his hands behind his head, the muscles of his arms flexing.

"Say something." I gnaw at my bottom lip. "I promise I'm going to fix this."

He reaches into his pocket and pulls out his closed fist. Slowly, his eyes never leaving my face, he opens his fist and drops a delicate gold chain on the table.

"Did you lose that, Bristol?"

My hand flies to my throat. I know the necklace isn't there. Parker took it from me last night, and now Grip has it. I can't assemble these pieces into anything that makes sense.

That son of a bitch.

"Grip, where'd you get that?"

"Oh, it came with my breakfast this morning." He slides a slip of paper across the table to me. "Along with this."

Your queen or mine?

Parker's scrawled words may as well be carved into my skin. That's how much they hurt, how badly Grip reading them hurts. I must be bleeding subcutaneously. Just under my skin, I'm hemorrhaging pride and self-respect.

"I can explain." I look from the damning note, the gilded evidence glimmering against the cheap wood. "Parker and I, we aren't—"

"I know you aren't cheating, so don't even bother explaining that," Grip says. "We're so far beyond that. What does he want? Besides for me to know he's using me to get to you?"

How much should I tell him? I have no idea.

"Don't think about lying to me." His glance peels my skin back, and any lie I would tell him crumbles under that stare.

I have to tell him everything. I wanted to do this on my own because I knew Grip and Rhyson would try to stop me. Of course, they would. It's insanity to even consider what Parker has proposed. It's demeaning and soul-destroying.

And I have every intention of doing it and whatever it takes to get Grip out of here and his name cleared.

"Parker was at my house when I got home last night."

He flattens his hands on the table. His fingers twitch, but there's no other indication that he hears. That my words might infuriate him.

"He . . . he admitted that he did this. That he has at least one high-ranking judge, probably more, in his pocket. This case isn't going anywhere unless he says so."

"Again I ask, what does he want?"

There's no curiosity behind the question. He already knows and just wants to hear me say it.

"He wants what he's always wanted." I force myself to look at him. "He wants me."

"He wants you to marry him?" Grip asks dispassionately.

"No, he says he'd never marry me now that I've 'soiled myself publicly with you.'"

"Well, at least there's that." The tight line of Grip's mouth loosens just a little. "So then what?"

"He wants to take me to the Amalfi Coast today."

All pretense that he doesn't care, that he knows everything, disappears. Urgency charges the stale air in the small visiting room.

"Today?" he demands. "What's his plan?"

"We'll have . . ." The word sits so foul, queued up and rotting on my tongue. I press my lips together against emotion and tears so I can go on. "Sex, we'll have sex on the upper deck of his yacht."

I push the words up my throat, as heavy as a boulder up a hill. "And the reporter who leaked the Vegas pictures will leak pictures of us . . . together."

"Fuck!" He bangs the table, the sound echoing like a clanging cymbal. It rattles my teeth. "You won't."

I keep my head lowered. I figure it isn't a good time to remind him he isn't the boss of me. We have so little time before I have to go, and I don't want to spend it arguing about something that, in my mind, is done. Is happening.

"Look at me, Bristol."

I clutch my conviction and raise my eyes to his.

"You are not doing this. Not for me." He does take my hand then, both of them between his, and squeezes. "We'll find another way."

"No, we won't. You don't know him."

These dull concrete walls are closing in on me, and the thought of Grip in here even another day traps my breath in my chest. Panic crushes me from the inside out.

"There isn't another way." I lift his hands to my lips, kissing his knuckles, his thumb, turning his hand and leaving a dry sob in the palm of his hand. "He's made sure of that. If there was a way, Rhyson would have found it by now."

"I won't let you do this."

"You can't stop me." I pull my hands clear of his, my resolve weakening the longer I touch him. The thought of anyone else touching me the way these hands did, with love and reverence, turns my stomach. "I told you. I warned you that I'm not like other girls."

My laugh leaves traces of poison on my lips.

"I don't have those limits." One tear at a time scalds my cheeks. "I'd do anything for you. It sounds romantic until it crosses your lines, huh? Until it goes too far."

I look at him, my smile ironic.

"Are you afraid, that like Parker, you won't want me either, after I've 'soiled' myself with him?"

"I'm afraid it would destroy something in you that I can't ever get back," he says earnestly.

I haven't admitted it even to myself, but so am I.

"If that happens," I say, dropping my eyes to my lap. "Whatever's left is yours."

"Don't, Bris." He crosses around the table, sits on the corner, and pulls me to stand between his legs, his hands running up my arms. "I'd stay before I'd let you do that."

"That's ridiculous. Oh my God. Don't even ..."

I drop my head to his shoulder, horrified he'd even entertain sacrificing his career or years of his life for something he didn't do. That he would do that to spare me this indignity.

"I would never let you do that for me," I say, my breath hiccupping in my chest.

"I won't have to, but now you know how I feel." He bends his brows over the torture in his eyes. "You think you're the only one who loves without limits?"

"That makes no sense, Grip."

"Like it made sense for me to wait around for years while you figured out you loved me." His mouth pulls into a warped smile. "But who did that? This guy."

A breathy laugh breaks through my tears.

"I love you," I whisper, stepping back and giving up the warm safety of his arms. "There's nothing ... nothing I wouldn't do for you."

The vestiges of his smile fall away. He runs his thumb over my lips, tugging at the flesh I know to be red and swollen.

"He did this?" There's brimstone in Grip's demand, fire in his glare.

"It doesn't matter." I pull away from his hand, embarrassed that Grip's seeing the results of Parker's rough kiss. It's a dim reflection of what he'll do to me later, I'm sure. "I need to go."

"The thought of him touching you ..." Grip swallows, his voice falling into a dark abyss. "Of him hurting you, kills me, Bris. That I can't protect you, it kills me."

There's blood thirst in his eyes, and I have no doubt if Parker were in this room he'd be dead. But he isn't here. He's out there wreaking havoc on our lives, and I have the means to stop him.

"I need to go."

He catches my elbow, his touch firm and gentle. In his outstretched palm he holds the gold necklace.

"Don't forget this." He proffers it to me.

"Keep it till I get you out of here." His handsome face wavers as tears fill my eyes but don't fall. "If you still want me . . . after, I'll take it back."

I glance up at the camera in the corner before leaning in to lay my lips against his, pouring everything into that brief contact. When my lips would cling to his, I force myself away and out the door without looking back. Tears blur everything ahead of me, and I slam into someone right outside the door in the hall.

"I'm sorry," I mumble to the person I almost ran down. "Oh, Ms. James, excuse me. I wasn't . . . watching."

"How is he?" She skips past my apology, looking over my shoulder to the closed door.

"He'll be better when he's out of here." I brush the useless tears away, reaffirming my commitment to this course.

"This is some bullshit." Ms. James' righteous anger shines from her dark eyes. "My boy has never done drugs, much less would be carrying enough to sell."

Her mouth pulls into an unexpected grin.

"A little dro every once in a while, yes, but slanging 'caine? No way."

"I know. We all know. It's a setup, but we're getting to the bottom of it. I promise you he'll be out soon."

"A setup?" Her question is a rapier pressed to my neck, a threat to draw blood if she doesn't get answers. "Who set my boy up?"

"My ex-boyfriend." I face her head on, knowing this will only add to the myriad other reasons she has to dislike me and want me away from her son.

"You ain't been nothing but trouble to him," she says harshly, tears liquefying the chocolate eyes. "I knew it. I knew him being with someone like you would only mean trouble."

"You were right."

"First the traffic stop and turning my son's community against him."

"I wouldn't say they turned against him," I disagree carefully. "Calling Marlon a sellout?" Her head tips, her brows lift. "Saying he disrespected Black women when he chose you over Qwest? That ain't turning against where you come from?"

Every one of her accusations is a tiny arrow that finds its mark. "I'm sorry." I force myself to meet her eyes. "Not for being with Grip, but that being with me brought this on, but I'm going to fix it."

"The damage has been done. My son's record—"

"Will be cleared."

I look at her. I feel so hard right now inside. I'm marbleizing my heart to get through this ordeal with Parker. I do that to protect myself, but I crack the shell long enough to say what I need to say more gently.

"Ms. James, I'm going to do whatever it takes to get him out, to fix this," I say. "But when he's out, I'm still going to be with him, if he wants me. All the things you love about him, I love about him. He isn't a sellout because he loves me. And I'm not just after him for whatever you think the novelty is. We love each other."

I dredge up a smile and hope she doesn't notice the tears I can't seem to clear from my eyes.

"I need to go, but he wants to see you, and our 'favor' only extends so far. He won't have much more time to visit."

Even with her looking at me as if I've committed a crime or personally put her son here, I want to ask her for a hug. For a touch that tells me I can go through with this. That as abhorrent as it will be taking Parker into my body, having him leave his filthy fingerprints on my soul, that it will be worth it. That Grip is worth it. I want that from her because she's the one who taught him that sacrifice is the essence of love. She's the only one who would love him as much as I do and would do anything for him, too. I see it in her fierce eyes, in her warrior stance.

But of course she doesn't offer a touch or a word. She doesn't know I need it, and if she knew, I'm not sure she would care.

CHAPTER 36

G_{RIP}

I'VE BEEN IN the LA County Jail all night and most of the morning, but this is the first time I've felt truly caged. I prowl the tiny visiting room like a starved beast. And I'm so hungry. I need to feel my sharp teeth tear into Charles Parker's skin. I want to eat him alive and spit out his bones for putting Bristol in this position. There has to be another way, something I'm not considering.

Like a dark shadow, Corpse looms in my brain. I wanted options for desperate situations. Am I willing to go that far? I can't even allow myself to imagine what I'll feel if Bristol goes through with this. She thinks she has no limits? I'm not sure of mine anymore. Fury blots out everything else. I clutch my head, pacing from the table to the wall, back and forth, the problem winding around my brain like a serpent. Looping, coiling, poised to strike. I bang my head against the wall, impervious to the pain. I'm just praying the blow will jolt me; show me a way out of this.

"I always said you were hard-headed."

My mother closes the door behind her. She crosses over to me quickly and wraps her arms around me, collapsing and sniffing against my chest. She's the toughest woman I know and only has one weak spot.

Me.

This is the first time we've seen each other since the fiasco of Sunday dinner. This shit situation has hurdled any awkwardness between us. She knows I need her, and any differences we have we set aside at least for now.

"Are you okay?" She explores my arms and shoulders. "Did they hurt you?"

"Ma, this ain't exactly *Letter from Birmingham Jail.*" I manage a weak chuckle. "The guards have been getting my autograph and taking selfies. They asked me to freestyle at breakfast. I'm good."

"Good?" She rears back, running disparaging eyes over LA County's standard issue blue scrubs. "This ain't good, Marlon. I never thought I would see you here. Not you."

"And I haven't done anything to be here, so I'll be out before you know it," I tell her with more confidence than makes sense.

"You know I didn't do this, right?" I dip to catch her eyes, not thinking I would even have to defend myself. Not to her. "Somebody set me up."

"I heard." Her glare is a laser cutting through any secrets I would keep from her. "I saw Bristol in the hall."

I close off my expression. I can't hear any shit she would say about the woman willing to sacrifice her dignity, her body, pieces of her soul to get me out of here. I can't even wrap my brain around the money and power at Parker's disposal. Abuses like these, he's probably been inflicting his whole life.

When I get out of here, however it happens, I'll make sure he regrets this one.

"She told me this is her fault." Ma's disapproval is palpable.

"It isn't her fault," I say impatiently.

"I know it isn't the best time to bring it up," she says, her elevated brows indicating it must be said. "But if you had stayed with Qwest, this wouldn't be happening."

"I don't love Qwest, Ma." I blow out a weary breath. "And I don't need this right now."

"You didn't give her a chance. You could have—"

"I fell in love with Bristol years ago," I break in. "In a week. Did you know that?"

I grasp her hands and press them to my heart. "She's here, Ma. In my heart. In my head. I can't get rid of her."

I shake my head, a sad smile on my lips.

"I don't want to. I want to spend the rest of my life feeling this way, like I'm only half alive when she isn't here. There's nowhere she could go I wouldn't chase her. Have you ever felt that for anybody?"

Shock rounds my mother's eyes, and her fingers tremble against my chest.

"No," she whispers, her eyes searching my face. "I don't think most people ever do."

"It's painful." A hefty sigh heaves from my chest. "It's precious, though. I won't give it up."

Pain tears my heart in half as I look at the woman who, on more than one occasion, went hungry sitting across the table making sure I ate—who literally went without so I could have.

"I won't give her up for anyone." I lean to kiss her forehead. "Not even you."

"I only wanted . . . I only want what's best for you." Her bottom lip trembles, but she traps it in her teeth, eyes to the concrete floor. "A woman who knows how to fight. Who will stand with you and understands you. Who would do anything for you."

The irony of it runs me through like a sword.

"You always said you prayed I'd find someone just like you. As fierce as you, ride or die like you, as strong as you." I shake my head, rubbing her fingers between mine. "You don't realize your prayers were answered, exceeded. Why do you think I fell for her? Bristol's just like you. Don't miss that because she doesn't look it on the outside."

"I can't make myself want her for you, Marlon." She doesn't waste tears, but her eyes are sad. "I've always had this idea of who she'd be, and a debutante from New York isn't what I was expecting. I guess we mothers always have expectations. We always assume we know exactly what to do in every situation."

"Well, most of the time, mothers do . . ."

My words open up a path in my mind I hadn't seen before.

Dammit. I'm an idiot. Why am I just now considering this?

"Ma, I need you to do something for me. Someone I need you to call right away."

CHAPTER 37

WHAT DOES ONE pack for a trip like this? Will it really matter? The whole world will end up seeing my ass on Parker's upper deck off the Amalfi Coast.

I hold the pantsuit I bought at Fashion Week last year up to my chest. I'm not sure that Alexander McQueen's fall line is fitting for what amounts to rape and ignominy.

"Needs must when the devil drives," I mutter, tossing the grandma period panties that cover my whole butt into the pile. I'm not wasting my good lingerie on Parker's sorry ass. As long as my things are on the bed and not in the overnight bag, it's easier to pretend this isn't happening. That I'm not going anywhere.

The doorbell startles me since Parker isn't due for another hour and a half. I've been relishing every minute I have before he comes to get me. I peer through the small window of my cottage door.

"Mother." I stand there staring at her. She's been to my home exactly once since I moved into the cottage last year. After our fight the other night, I wasn't expecting her to darken my door anytime soon. "Is someone dead or giving birth?"

She walks past me, not waiting for an invitation.

"Don't be vulgar, Bristol."

Mother's eyes trace over the warm simplicity of my living room. I can't imagine where she would find fault in the understated elegance, but then she never ceases to astound with her innovative ways to find fault.

"I didn't realize death or birth were vulgar. My apologies." I gesture for her to sit, but I remain standing. "What can I do for you? I thought we said all we had to say the last time we saw each other. I don't have much time to spare."

"Packing for your trip, are you?" Mother's eyes heap disdain on my head. "Speaking of vulgar."

My breath hovers in my throat, drawn but not released. How does she know? I mean, soon everyone will know, but I was clinging to my last days of dignity.

"Trip?" I choose to play dumb, but I've never been good at pretending to be anything but intelligent.

"Oh, God, Bristol." Mother sets her Celine bag on the couch beside her. "From what I understand, we don't have much time, so dispense with the games. What time will Parker arrive?"

I blink at her, disoriented like I'm an actor in the wrong play. I flounder for my line and wonder who this character is in front of me.

"Mother, what are you talking about?" I perch on the edge of the love seat across from her.

"Marlon's mother called me and told me everything, so let's figure out how to save you."

"Ms. James?" It could be no worse than Grip's mother knowing this about me. Knowing that her son's girlfriend, whom she already dislikes, will be bartering her body for all the world to see. "She knows . . . she called . . . what's going on?"

"Bristol, do keep up." Impatience wrinkles my mother's smooth brow. "Marlon asked his mother to call me about your predicament.

Wisely, I might add. How could you even consider such nonsense? I raised you better than that."

With everything else I've had to endure the last twenty-four hours, my mother's selective memory is more than I can withstand right now.

"Actually nannies were primarily responsible for my upbringing, if you'll recall, since you were managing Rhyson all over the world and couldn't be bothered to actually parent."

The temperature in the room drops so drastically, my words crystallize in the air as soon as they leave my mouth.

"Maybe I should have been more involved if you think this is acceptable behavior." Mother tsks and studies her wedding rings. "Debasing yourself this way for a man."

Laughter stirs in my belly and spills over, shaking my shoulders. I throw my head back and howl with it. I may be hysterical, but she is absolutely blind if she can say that to me with a straight face.

"The joke?" Mother asks with quiet dignity. "Please share it." "You accused me of debasing myself for a man."

My laughter does a slow leak until it's all spent, leaving me hollow and insulted. "At least I know the man I debase myself for is worth every minute of it. I'd debase myself for Grip every day if I had to. And the man you've been debasing yourself for the last thirty-odd years? Is he worth it?"

Mother's hostile eyes narrow on my face. Her hands clench into slim, beringed fists.

"You have no idea what my marriage is, what your father and I have."

"Don't you think I got an inkling when I caught him fucking a girl my age in our house? In your bed, and you did nothing but get drunk and cry about it?"

"How dare you." Mother snaps to her feet. "I came here to help you."

"Help yourself, Mother." I stand, too, needing to be on level ground with her. "Do you know how much time I wasted trying to please you? Trying to be you? Trying not to be you? You were such a contradiction, I wasn't sure if I should emulate you or eradicate you from my nature."

"Only you can't, can you?" Her eyes are solemn. "You think I wanted to fall in love with a man who cared so little for my feelings?"

Her bitter laugh echoes in the empty living room.

"It doesn't pay to love, Bristol. I had hoped you learned that lesson from me with your father. With your brother."

"Is that what happened?" I blink against tears that have nothing to do with Parker and everything to do with my mother standing in front of me telling me not to love. "You gave all your love to them and there was none left for me? They were worth the risk and I wasn't?"

"What in heaven's name are you talking about?" Mother frowns but takes her seat again by the Celine bag. "I guided you as much as you would let me."

"I didn't want to be guided, Mother. I wanted to be *loved*, but there was always a distance. You would only allow me so close."

"That was for your own good. You were already too much like me."

"It doesn't have to be a weakness, you know," I say softly. "With the right people, with the right man, love rewards hearts like ours."

"Oh, so it's strength that has you ready to fuck Charles Parker?" Mother asks, the crudity so at odds with her refined appearance. "Is that your reward?"

"No, Grip is my reward," I volley back without hesitation. "For him, I'll do whatever needs to be done."

I look down at my bare feet sunken into the plush rug covering my hardwoods.

"I love him. He loves me. You do crazy things for the ones you love sometimes. You accept things you thought you never would. You know that better than most."

Mother studies me appraisingly for a few moments before speaking.

"I do know." She twists her wedding band. "It's liberating knowing there's nothing you wouldn't do for him, to keep him. And it can also be a dark lonely trap, with love as your prison cell."

"Not for me," I say softly. "Not with Grip. It's taken me years to realize that I'm like you, but I'm not you. And Grip is nothing like my father. I almost lost him running away from this kind of love, but it's giving me the strength to do what has to be done."

"Let me tell you something about your father, Bristol." Usually I'm not even sure if my mother is breathing she's so serene, but today she draws a deep breath. "I don't talk about my marriage. Not with anyone."

This I know. I fasten my eyes to her lips like I might miss something and need to catch every word.

"I know what you saw that day." She looks down at her lap and licks her lips, the only sign of discomfort she allows. "It wasn't the first time, and I wish I could say it was the last. Do you remember when your father had his heart attack?"

I nod. We thought he would die. It was the impetus for Rhyson and my father to start repairing their relationship.

"I said I was away on a business trip," Mother says. "But I was actually leaving your father."

Mind. Blown.

And like a child the only thing I can think is I can't wait to tell Rhyson.

"Yes." She nods, a regal movement that barely disturbs her hair. "I'd had enough, and thought I could finally do it. I could leave him. I could *not* love him just enough to go."

My cottage is quiet, like even the furnishings, the walls, the bulbs hold the same bated breath as I do waiting for her next words.

"When I got the call that he'd had the heart attack." Mother pinches her lips together and blinks rapidly. "I knew I'd never leave him. It was like fate or some force didn't want me to go."

She looks at me frankly, her eyes as vulnerable as I've ever seen. As unguarded as mine when I'm alone.

"Things changed between us after that. Slowly, but they changed."

My father had a difficult recovery, but my mother stayed with him throughout.

"When he told me he was working on things with Rhyson and wanted to move out here, I jumped at the chance." Her knuckles whiten through her skin as she clutches the expensive handbag. "I thought maybe I can finally have my husband back."

She swallows. "My children."

Shock skitters over my nerves and short circuits my synapses.

Say what?

"When we started therapy sessions with Rhyson, we also started counseling for our marriage." Her laugh is truncated. "Can you imagine it? After thirty years? But we are trying."

"I had no idea, Mother."

"Why would you?" Mother's haughtiness snaps back into place. "It's private between your father and me. I didn't run to you every time he cheated, so I'm certainly not running to you now that he's trying not to."

"So you're in family therapy with Rhyson and marriage counseling with Dad, making things right with them, but didn't bother with me."

I will never figure out how not to be hurt by this woman. It's like some claw dug into my heart in vitro, and I don't know how to free myself from feeling anything for her.

"We have brunch," she says defensively.

"Brunch?" My voice pitches to the ceiling with my outrage. "You mean those regular intervals when you find new and inventive ways to criticize me over vodka and a meal? Oh, very healing, Mother."

"It's different with you, Bristol. You're . . . you're all the best parts of me," she says softly. "The tender parts, the tough parts, the smart and fighting parts. I've damaged you enough, and I don't know how to fix it between us."

"Well, manipulating me into marrying a tyrannical pervert isn't best place to start, if you're taking suggestions."

"I just . . . I don't know. I thought you could have all of that. That everyone wants all of that on some level. I didn't want you to turn it down."

"Maybe if I hadn't met Grip I would have settled for that." I shake my head, fresh tears burning my eyes as time disintegrates, and the time to go with Parker approaches. "I love him, Mother. You saw that even though I tried to hide it."

"I recognized the signs, yes," Mother says, a wry twist to her lips. "You were just like me when I met your father. I tried to hide it, too."

"Is that why you didn't want me with Grip?" I ask softly.

"Maybe in part." Mother shrugs elegant shoulders, turning clear eyes to me, or as clear as hers can be. "At any rate, he must love you to come to me after our confrontation the other night."

"He loves me very much." Just saying the words and believing them thaws some of the ice collecting around my heart.

"If you love him, then don't give yourself to Parker, and in such an undignified way." The distaste in her voice matches or exceeds the distaste on her face.

"I can't just stand by and watch . . ." My words drown in my guilt. "Grip's there because of me. His life, his career, his good name—all on the line because of me."

"Then don't stand by and don't give in." A touch of the pride I've always known my mother to hold gleams in the glance she gives me. "I may not have been baking brownies for your class or braiding your hair, but surely I taught you how to fight."

"I can't." Tears scald my throat and blur my vision. "I've been around and around this, over and over, and I don't see another way. I don't want to give in to his demands, but—"

"Then don't."

"But I have to help Grip. Leaving him there is not an option." My mother's eyes soften some, and her stern mouth relaxes.

"Then let me help you."

CHAPTER 38

B<small>RISTOL</small>

"WHERE ARE YOUR <small>BAGS</small>?" Lust and impatience and arrogance ménage in the glance Parker gives me. "Why aren't you dressed? I thought I was very clear that I'm in a hurry."

Parker stands in my living room, outfitted in power and his Gucci suit.

"I've decided against it." I slump on the love seat, a study in lassitude, wearing distressed denim shorts and my Columbia T-shirt. "You go on without me."

Violence flares in Parker's eyes before he tamps it down. He's one of those careful monsters who won't show his true form until absolutely necessary.

"I'm sure Grip will be sorry to hear that."

"So you do know his name." I grin at him, crossing my legs. "He'll be glad to know. I'll make sure to tell him once he's back home."

"You seem to forget who holds the cards here." Parker thins his already thin lips.

"I started thinking." I study my manicure before looking back to him. "Maybe I gave in too easily. It's a little cocaine. Grip has no previous convictions. We have the best lawyers. Why should I let a few dead ends stop us?"

"Do you have any idea how easy it was to have those drugs planted during your boyfriend's photo shoot?" Laughter lights his glassy blues. "And if you think I only have one judge in my pocket, you sorely underestimate me."

"Is that so?" I ask noncommittally.

At my lackluster response, frustration flares his nostrils, anger mottles his cheeks. The smug smile dissolves into petulant slackness. "Don't make me do it." His voice is practically a hiss. "I'll ruin him. Completely."

My heart tailspins behind my ribs at the certainty his words carry. He could do it. There's no doubt. I just watch him, knowing my stoic silence will provoke him. He feeds off fear, and I've turned over his plate. Even seeing his composure fraying, I'm unprepared when he grabs my arm and jerks me to my feet. He seizes my ass, pressing me into his erection.

"This is how I've felt every time we were in a room together for the last ten years." He narrows his eyes. "I get what I want, and I'm finally going to fuck you again. I'm done waiting."

My mother didn't raise a fool, but I realize in this instant that I have been a fool. I allowed this man to deceive me.

"We didn't have sex." I lean into him, breathing the words over him. "You just said you've been waiting ten years, even though we supposedly slept together that night in Vegas."

That black hole in my memory always felt deeper and darker than a drunken lapse, and I just figured out why.

He blinks, mouth falling open. The prey fights back. He wasn't expecting that.

"You were so determined to get drunk that night." He shrugs. "Adding a little something to one of the Parks' famous martinis was merely expeditious. You would have passed out anyway. I just helped you along, and you bought the story."

I snatch my arm from his grasp, indignation rising in me as I recall my confusion, my frustration, my shame that morning.

"You should have fucked me while I was unconscious." I hurl the words at him. "That was your best shot."

"Really?" He embeds slivers of glass in that one world. "We'll see about that."

He shoves me back onto the couch so hard my head bangs against the armrest, and for a second, the pain is celestial, inspiring stars in front my eyes.

He gathers my wrists above my head, one knee thrust between my legs. His face distorts, florid with his rage. Panic takes flight in my chest, flapping wildly around my heart.

"You thought you could give him what was mine?" The words are projectiles, the force behind them throwing spittle in my face. "Let him have you, fuck you and get away with it?"

He balls the collar of my T-shirt in his hands and jerks, ripping the shirt and exposing the wire taped to my bra. His shock-stretched eyes find mine beneath him.

"Should we add rape to the things you've already confessed to?"

He snatches the wire from my bra and crushes it under his foot. Without a backward glance he rushes across the room. As soon as he hauls the door open, he comes face to face with Greg.

Greg looks past Parker long enough to find me, lifting his brows over anxious eyes, silently asking if I'm okay. I nod, gathering the ripped edges of my T-shirt to cover my breasts. Even though my knees are so weak it feels like they're filled with méringue instead of cartilage.

Parker looks over his shoulder at me, his mouth distorted into a self-assured smile.

"You stupid bitch." He turns his back on Greg, pointing to him over his shoulder. "You think some beat cop can take me down? Even with what you think you have recorded, it won't be enough to keep me. Real power. That's what I have. You have no idea."

"I think I have an idea, son," Aunt Betsy says from the door leading to my bedroom.

All of this was worth it if only to see the consternation and shame briefly flash across Parker's face.

"Mother, what are you doing here?" His eyes flick between Aunt Betsy and me like she caught us playing house or doctor. Like she caught him with his hands down my pants.

"I'm here to do what your father should have done years ago." She hands him a manila envelope, her eyes sad and condemning. "I'm here to stop you."

He doesn't open the envelope immediately, caressing the seal instead.

"Whatever is in here, Mother, cannot touch me."

"Your father is a fool who believes our money makes him invincible and above the law, and he raised you to believe the same. I should have intervened long ago." Aunt Betsy nods her head to the envelope. "I didn't know all the awful things you've done, but I know now, and it's never too late."

Parker's eyes flicker from me to his mother before settling on the envelope still unopened in his hands. I have no idea what's in there. My mother and Aunt Betsy do, though. It's their plan, and since the only alternative involved me baring my nether parts for the world's inspection, I've yielded to their infinite wisdom.

When Parker opens the envelope, he pales, his face a white flag of surrender before he's said one word.

"Where did you get this?" he asks too softly. "Does Dad know you have it?"

"The combination of his safe is our anniversary date." Aunt Betsy's laughter is a peal of sarcasm. "He must have been feeling sentimental that day since this is the only way he's chosen to honor our marriage."

"When Dad finds out—"

"Then what, Charles?" Aunt Betsy draws up to her full height. "You and your father seem to forget half of everything is mine. More than half since the original hotels came from my great-grandfather. Renaming them 'Park' doesn't change where they came from."

"When he hears about this—"

"Oh, he's already heard." Aunt Betsy comes to join me on the love seat. "I believe there's a note from him in there, too. Something about you still not learning your lesson and abusing girls. That one was a very costly mistake. It'd be such a waste of the money he spent covering it up if I were to bring it out myself."

"You could actually leak it through Spotted," I pipe up. "Parker has a guy on standby. He's always got a guy."

"I am deeply sorry I ever thought my son was good enough for you, Bristol." Aunt Betsy brushes the hair back from my face and drops a kiss on my forehead. "I'm glad you've found someone worth your time."

"Worth her time?" Incredulous rage mottles Parker's handsome face. "That thug? That . . . rapper? You would give Bristol to him over me? She humiliated me, and she should pay."

"What am I paying for exactly, Parker?" I cross to stand in front of him, my anger propelling me just inches from his face. "Did I leak pictures of you drunk to the press? Did I drug you and lead you to believe we had sex when I was for all intents and purposes unconscious? Did I coerce you to have public sex to satisfy my own outsized ego? Did I plant drugs on an innocent man and blackmail judges to manipulate his case?"

"You chose him over me," Parker says grimly. "With all I could give you, you wanted some rapper from Compton over me."

"Even if it hadn't been Grip, it would never have been you," I hiss.

"I think this has gone long enough," my mother says from the same entrance Aunt Betsy used. "We have enough to prosecute you, Parker. Not for life, but you'll serve some time. We're only giving Officer James what he has on tape, but we have a never-ending stream of evidence from your father's safe. We'll just keep sending it to Officer James until enough sticks to keep you behind bars."

"You've already given us enough to free Marlon and clear his name." The tears gathered at the corners of Aunt Betsy's eyes leak down her face as she contemplates her only son. "And enough to prosecute you."

My heart breaks for her. I can't imagine how she wrestled with this decision before settling on the right course of action to set an innocent man free. I set all the soft feelings aside, though, to step right into Parker's face, my lips curling with deliberate wrath.

"If you ever, and I mean ever, you cowardly asshole, come near me or Grip again," I say. "More of that information will come out. Call it our insurance policy. If Grip even has a suspicious paper cut, I'm coming after your ass."

"So will I," a deadly soft voice says from behind me.

I look back and almost collapse when I see Ms. James leaning against the doorjamb, arms folded, lips set in stone, eyes lit with fury and indignation.

"My son is a good man." Her eyes drift from Parker for a moment to me. "And Bristol is a good woman. Just try to hurt them again. You find a way to slip from the law, I got some street justice for you. Bet you won't get out of that."

Greg steps into the fray before Ms. James can say anymore about "street justice", whatever that means, and pulls Parker's arms behind his back.

"Charles Parker, you have the right to remain silent . . ."

The Miranda Rights, the other cops streaming into my home, the flurry of activity all fade to the peripheral as I look at the three mothers who made my escape possible.

"Aunt Betsy, I'm so sorry." I pull her into a hug, and she sniffs softly in our embrace. She did what was right, but Parker is still her son. Without the information she took from her husband's safe, none of this would have worked.

"No, I'm sorry." Aunt Betsy pulls back, shaking her head. "The things he's done to other women, to so many people all these years, we failed him somewhere along the way. He has to pay. I just hope he heeds our warning and doesn't come after you again."

"Oh, he won't," my mother interjects. "What he did to Marlon is child's play compared to the things in that safe and the things your husband has covered up for him through the years. We'll make sure he doesn't forget what we have."

"Thank you, Mother." I'm not sure what else to say as our eyes lock and hold and soften. I know everything won't be repaired between us in a day, but today was a big step.

"I do love you, Bristol." Her voice doesn't waver, but her eyes, so like mine, for maybe the first time show me a little of what's in her heart. "I'm sorry Marlon believed that more than you did, but I know I'm to blame."

The flawless red line of her mouth pulls into a grimace.

"I think it's past time you joined your father, Rhyson, and me in sessions with Dr. Ramirez," she continues. "If we ever hope to be a real family, that is."

Her words ripple emotion through me, a tectonic shift in my own heart. I've disciplined my emotions over the last twenty-four hours, held in so much because I knew Marlon's freedom depended on it. The possibility that the relationship I've always wanted with her is something she might want, too, unravels me. The tears that have been bound behind a wall of control trickle down my cheeks. A sob unleashed in my chest takes me by surprise. Before I know it, I'm in my mother's arms. It's still awkward. She pats my back and holds me stiffly, unrelaxed, her walls not fully down, but all that matters is she doesn't let go.

I've always wondered if she'd lavished all her devotion onto my talented brother; if she'd squandered her deepest love on my unfaithful father, and there was nothing left for me. I know what it's like behind that wall. It's cold and lonely. It's barren with no sun. God, I'm so glad I finally let Grip in. And as my mother and I regard each other with new understanding, with new respect, I hope that someday soon, she'll truly let me in, too.

Over her shoulder, I encounter a darkened caramel gaze that's warmed and melted with sympathy, with compassion, maybe with understanding. Through my own tears, I offer Ms. James a tentative smile, and slowly, she returns it.

CHAPTER 39

GRIP

BRISTOL: I'm on my way.

I READ BRISTOL'S text and slip a soft cashmere sweater over my head. Freshly showered, I fall back on the bed and respond.

ME: *I'm home. Upstairs.*

OUR EXCHANGE IS BRIEF, but the air buzzes with anticipation. The last time I saw Bristol, she was on her way to Parker. I wasn't happy with her. I'm sure when I took matters into my own hands and had Ma call Mrs. Gray, Bristol wasn't happy with me. This morning, I woke up in County, ate powdered eggs, and wore jail scrubs that scratched my skin. Tonight, I'm in my luxury loft, wearing a cashmere sweater and chilling a bottle of wine that costs more than I used to pay in rent. An astounding turn of events.

I've never been angry enough to actually kill someone, but if Parker were standing in front of me right now, I might toss him on my rooftop grill and watch the flames consume his carcass. Maybe I would drink my two thousand dollar bottle of wine with the aroma of his charred flesh wafting in the air. There is some base level of my soul that would prefer primitive justice over the legal route we've taken.

We'll have to depend on the bounty of "insurance" Mrs. Parker found in that safe to keep her son on a leash. Though, I hope my conversation with him earlier dissuades him from bothering us, from bothering Bristol, again.

I wrestled with what to do about this menace. Street justice calls for me to use Corpse or any means available to protect myself, to protect my girl. I won't pretend I wasn't tempted to use Corpse. I was, but I wanted a better way. Greg and Mrs. Gray came up with a legal option, for which I'm grateful. If Parker ever tries to hurt Bristol again, directly or through someone she loves, I can't promise them, or myself, that I won't find another means. I wanted to tell him that to his face.

It pays to have a family on the force, connections of my own. Greg managed to get me into the "special" private holding cell where Charles Parker is being kept, separate from general pop, of course.

He was taking a piss when I entered his cell. He studied me warily over his shoulder, and I smelled his fear. It curled around my leg like an anxious cat.

"There are cameras everywhere," he warned. "Hurt me and you'll be caught."

"Just one for this room. It's looping for two minutes. That's all the time I need."

"What do you want?" He managed a sneer, even though I could see the terror in his eyes. "Money? I can give you that."

"You dumb shit bastard," I snapped. "I don't need your money. I have my own money."

"Not as much as I have."

He sounded like a spoiled little boy grasping for a leg up. I glanced down to his tiny dick still hung over his pants.

"Put your dick away." I injected pity in my voice. "How you ever thought that little bit of twig and berries would satisfy my girl, I don't know."

His eyes went reptilian, slitted, and a growl rumbled in his throat. He's used to being the one with all the power. I had a tenuous hold on my temper. The illusion of flippancy cracked the longer I was around that asshole. The longer I had to look into his fucking blue eyes, his entitlement and superiority still bleeding through jail scrubs. I prowled over, crowding him until he was forced to the porce- lain behind him. With a handful of the rough scrubs gathered in my fist, I brought his chest to mine, slamming him into the urinal. His head banged against the wall with a satisfying thud.

"Don't think that all your money and power and fucking hotels will protect you from me if you ever touch her again," I said through my teeth.

The façade of his false calm cracked at the ferocity in my voice, and I saw his fear.

"And you sent me a note asking if Bristol was your queen or mine," I continued. "I came to answer your question."

I ran him through with a look, and slammed the wadded up, half-destroyed note against his chest.

"She's mine."

The sound of the door opening downstairs jars me back to the present and the comfort of my home. I banish all thoughts of Parker, and brace for the rush of seeing Bristol safe and unharmed. I'd like to make a GIF of the moment when she walks into my bedroom. Just replay these few seconds over and over again.

Bristol is wearing almost no makeup. Her hair streams loose down her back, dark and wild and streaked with copper. Her clothes are simple—white tank top, leather jacket, and ripped-knee jeans. She looks so much like the girl I picked up at the airport that day, the one I kissed on top of the world and chased into the tide. In her eyes, though, the color of smelted silver, something tried by fire, I see a woman who would walk through flames for me. Someone who would sacrifice anything to protect me.

I'm seated on the edge of the bed, legs spread and straining against my jeans. Bristol walks over slowly, her eyes holding mine above me. I trace her features with my eyes and imprint her on my heart. The slant of her cheek. The slash of her brows. The full curve of her mouth, now unsteady with emotion.

"Grip." She climbs onto my lap, knees on either side of me, head buried in my neck. "Oh, God. I'm so glad you're okay."

I slide my hands under her jacket, needing her warmth, her flesh and bones.

"Bris." I clench my eyes closed, relief flooding through me. "You're the one I was concerned about. You're okay. He didn't . . . God, if he had . . ."

I can't even finish the sentence, can't even complete the thought.

Today isn't for my rage, and that's all those thoughts lead to.

She pulls back, tear-clumped lashes spiking around her bright eyes.

"It would have killed me to give myself to him."

"I know that, baby." My palms at her back flatten the soft curves of her breasts against my chest.

"But I would have done it if I had to," she whispers. "For you, I would have done it and lived with the consequences."

I know that, too.

"I have something that belongs to you, Bris."

I scoot her back only far enough to reach into the pocket of my jeans and extract a black velvet jewelry bag. She looks from the bag to my face, pressing her lips together, drawing and exhaling a deep breath. I fasten the necklace in the front and turn it until the gold barrel hangs just above her breasts. I flip it over, and for the hundredth time since my mom dropped it off from the jewelry repair shop, read the inscription.

My heart broke loose on the wind.

This necklace affirms what I always knew. Even in our years apart, that day carved itself into her heart. It inhabited her memory as surely as she occupied mine. There isn't a scrap of me she can't have or doesn't already own. And my mother can condemn it, others can question it, but I'm so damn proud to be hers, and so humbled that she is mine. The world can go to hell with their opinions and notions of what fits and what doesn't. My heart is in Bristol's grip, my happiness in her hands.

"Thank you," she whispers shakily.

"My mom got it repaired." She stiffens against my chest.

"She did?" She lowers her lashes, shielding her eyes. "She was at my house when everything went down."

"I know." A laugh forces its way past my lips. "Once she knew the plan, nobody was keeping her away."

"She and I kind of had a moment at my place." A small smile touches Bristol's lips. "It was just a look, but I think it was a good moment. I know it won't happen overnight, but I think maybe she'll come around."

A little laugh slips from her, but I know it hurts her that my mother doesn't want us together. As tough as she wants me to think she is, I know it hurts her that during the scandal with Qwest, so many people came out saying we shouldn't be together.

"Bris, look at me." I wait for her to comply so she's looking into my eyes and I can look into hers. "My mom will come around. She's already starting to, but there's something you should know. Something I want you to believe."

I frame her face between my hands and tenderly run a thumb over her mouth.

"You're the most important thing in my life," I tell her. "I would leave everyone for you."

Her tiny gasp tells me that on some level she didn't realize that. The line of her mouth wavers. Her brows knit and tears slip over her cheeks. She presses her forehead to mine, and her shoulders shake. She folds her arms between us against my chest and surrenders to the emotion she's been fighting, maybe for years. I roll my palms over her arms and back, wanting to send my love through her pores, giving her no choice but to believe down to her bones that she's the most important thing in my life.

"Grip." She sniffs and swipes tears from her cheeks. "No one's ever ... that means the world to me."

She bites her lip to suppress emotion, but it does no good. Emotion suffuses the air around us, reaches inside and clutches my heart. Head lowered, she touches the gold links Parker tried to chain her with, and chews the corner of her lip.

"Grip, if it didn't work, if I'd had to—"

"I would have loved you just as much." I tip her chin up and force her to look into my eyes and see the truth of it. To see the irrevocable nature of my love for her. "I would never have let you go."

She nods, sniffing and smiling.

"I'm still mad at you." With a teary laugh, trying to lighten the moment, she loops her arms over my shoulders and strokes the back of my neck.

"Really?" I frown and cock my head. "You don't look mad to me."

"How do I look?" A grin tips her mouth.

"Like you wanna fuck me."

Her eyes widen and she scoots forward, pressing herself into me. "That, too." She laughs. "But I'm still mad at you for telling my mother and your mother."

"I have a feeling I can persuade you to forgive me."

I fit my hands to her waist, flipping her back onto the bed to brace myself over her. With one finger, she traces my mouth, my cheekbones, my eyebrows.

God, her touch feels so good.

My lips are just shy of hers, and we swap breaths and promises. I study her face like an artist, painting each feature—her eyes, her lips, her cheeks—with love. She leans up, touching her lips to mine, and the stress, anxiety, indignity of the last few days disintegrates. Our love is powerful enough to shrink the world down to this moment, down to a circle no wider than her arms around me. The circumference of her and me. So powerful, but her eyes, if you know what you're looking for, can't hide her secret vulnerability.

Bristol has always watched me. I know because I was watching her, too. I observed her for years like an anthropologist untangling the mysteries of a new tribe. There's something in her eyes when she watches me that isn't there for anyone else. I was never sure what it was. Now I know. It's a passion so wild there are no borders. A limitless, loving fealty beyond what I could deserve. Not my music, not my money, not fame, or anything I dreamed would satisfy comes close to what I feel when she looks at me like that.

She feathers kisses over my lips, down my neck. We start slow and tender, but every touch, every long, lush stroke of our tongues together tosses kindling on this kiss until we're grunting and hungry.

She pulls back, seducing me with her eyes, and reaches down to my waist. Her fingers tease the waistband of my jeans before pushing the sweater over my head. She kisses my neck and shoulders, all the while undoing my belt and sliding my jeans and briefs over my hips.

She peels off her leather jacket and tugs the tank top over her head, sharing herself with me in erotic inches. Her breasts, tipped with plump nipples, come into view.

I ghost my palms over her nipples until they tauten into ripe berries. I squeeze them between my fingers and massage the fullness of her breasts until her breath labors and her head tips back, exposing the column of her throat. I trace the fragile framework of her ribs, gliding my hands down to her hips. I tug the panties down, and palm her center. My fingers tuck into the hot, silky slit, running up and down until she's dripping wet.

"Oh, she missed me." I grin and invade her with two fingers.

Bristol's breath catches in her throat, and she squeezes her top lip between her teeth.

"Did you just personify my pussy?" She laughs in between hitched breaths.

"I *am* a writer." I dot kisses under her chin and any reachable skin. "Take it as a sign of respect."

"I'll take this." She grabs my bone-hard, stretched-out dick. "As a sign of respect."

Her hand clamps and slides over me, thumbing the wet tip. Our eyes connect, and humor falls away, leaving the intensity that always rears between us. I'm working between her legs, and she's working between mine. She drags air in, gasping, churning her hips, fucking my fingers. I suck one berry-tipped breast, watching color blossom over her neck and cheeks.

"Oh, God." Her back arches off the bed, sheets knotted in one fist. "Yes, Grip."

Her hold tightens on me, her fingers dropping to roll my balls in her palms.

"This pretty pussy." I gather her wrists in my hand over her head and ease her knee back to her chest, opening her up. "It's mine, right?"

"Yes. God, yes." With dry sobs, she strains up to my lips, leaving kisses wherever she can. "You know it's yours. Please take it. Just take it."

Her submission, her admission unleashes an unquenchable thirst, an inexhaustible hunger. I need some part of her in my mouth. I bite down on her shoulder and push inside, my breath hissing between my lips at the wet, tight fit. She meets every thrust, and we are fervent, fevered. Pleasure excruciating. Twined together, her heel digging into my ass, my arm hooked under her knee, urging her open to the compulsion of my body pistoning into hers. I cannot possibly in this life be deep enough inside her. I want so much more than her body. She has thieved my soul, and I need to feel the reciprocity, the exchange. To know I've pilfered her and taken everything that she would offer and anything she meant to hold. Because that's what she's done to me.

I loosen her wrists to grab her ass, angling her. Both legs wrap around my back, and she works her hips up, eager to meet every hard thrust. I sit up, bringing her with me, and she hooks her ankles behind me.

"Ride, Bris."

Her eyes, possessive, there's no doubt I'm hers. Her hands, urgent and everywhere at once. Our breaths heave raggedly between our lips. Our bodies are lock and key, and we're transfixed on each other.

Inseparable. Insoluble. I seize her tongue, pulling her in, sucking her, wringing every drop of sweetness from the kiss. She whimpers, her hands clawing at my shoulders, my neck, scraping over my scalp.

"I love you." Her words drop hot in my ear with her breasts flattened to my chest and her thighs clenching at my hips. She tightens her pussy around my cock, a deliberate, hungry grasp and release.

"Bris." My eyes roll back. I'm at the mercy of those muscles. "I love you, too."

She tucks her head into the curve of my neck, her breaths short and sharp as she recites from "Sonnet LXXXI", telling me I'm already hers, to rest with my dream inside her dream, that we are joined by forever itself, and that we'll travel the shadows together. She pants, sitting up straighter, leveraging herself with one arm behind her on the bed, changing the angle, deepening the penetration. In the lamp's light, I see her head flung back in abandon, her muscles straining with the unrelenting ferocity, the rigor of our bodies.

"You alone are my dream," she says, adapting the quote, tears in the eyes she refuses to pull away from me. "And I alone am yours."

It is a pledge of persistence, hidden in the poems I sent her. It's a vow that she won't ever give up on us. Knowing she held the poetry in her heart when she wouldn't even consider me, when I wasn't even sure there was any hope, undoes me.

"Bristol, oh God."

I touch my forehead to hers, twisting my fingers into the damp hair at her neck. Pressed together, our heartbeats ricocheting, the universe tips, a dazzling lurching. A spectacular axis spinning beyond my restraint, just beyond my control. I once threatened to make her come with my words, but as the stars go blindingly bright and then dark behind my eyes, I realize she's the one who did it.

EPILOGUE

Bʀɪsᴛᴏʟ

I HAVE AN eye for the extraordinary.

I can spot something special a mile away. That's how I knew the day I met the man onstage that he was something special. I just had no idea how much he would change my life. Had no idea I would love him this way. I certainly didn't have any idea he would feel the same.

"I think this is the best song he's ever written," Rhyson says to me as Grip sets up "Bruise" for the listening audience.

"You may be right about that." I lean close to the baby cradled to my brother's chest. "What do you think, Aria? Is it his best? Is that god-daddy's best song?"

My niece squeals, and Rhyson and I look at each other with wide eyes in case it disrupts Grip's performance.

"Here." Kai sticks a pacifier into her daughter's little mouth. "Figures you two would get her riled up."

Rhyson holds his daughter in one arm, and pulls Kai close to him with the other. The contentment on his face squeezes my heart in the best possible way. After all the tumult that marked the first part of his journey, private and public, he somehow managed to make a normal life for himself. As normal as being a rock star married to another rock star can be. Though, intercepting the look Rhys and Kai exchange over Aria's dark curly hair, I'm not sure there's anything "normal" about a love that deep.

Glad I'm not the only one drowning. Grip once told me the capacity I have to love could be my greatest strength. Over the last few weeks, I've come to believe him. Especially when that love is for the right man, a man who wouldn't exploit a heart like mine. He never ceases to amaze me with all the ways he proves he's exactly the one for me.

"So you may have seen some footage of me a few months ago during a 'routine' stop," Grip says from stage, a slight smile on those full lips I love so much. "It got just a little bit of coverage."

The audience laughs, but there is an underlying tension in the room. The whole night feels like that, as if it's on the verge of going wrong, though so far everything has gone right. Given Grip's complicated history with LAPD, the organizers of this event weren't sure he'd accept their invitation to perform at the Black and Blue Ball, held to promote better relations between communities of color and law enforcement. Maybe that's why they sent his cousin Greg to ask. With "Bruise" so closely reflecting the message of the event, Grip didn't hesitate to accept.

"I grew up in the part of the world that gave rise to the Watts riots and Rodney King. I was five years old when Rodney King was beaten." He gives a quick laugh. "I barely knew my name, but I knew his. He was a cautionary tale for us, and our mothers made sure we knew."

He grabs a stool and props himself there before going on.

"Even with all that, I thought police officers were dope." He disarms the crowd with a bright smile. "They had flashing blue lights and sirens. What could be cooler than that?"

The crowd laughs a little, some offer smiles. A few expressions remain tense because some people aren't sure where he's headed or what he'll say. Which side of the black/blue line he'll land on, and if he'll come down like a hammer.

"That footage showed me getting stopped in the neighborhood

where I grew up. Some wondered if I would do this show tonight." He looks out at the crowd, eyes dark and earnest. "I'm here because the system needs radical reform. Unarmed men and women are dying. And there are cops who, if they don't do it, see it and remain silent. Do nothing, making them complicit."

He looks out over the crowd.

"And then there are cops like my cousin Greg, who has dedicated his life to actually serving and protecting, not just policing the communities we grew up in. I'm here for him and all the cops who say enough is enough and are ready to do something about it. I want to reimagine the system, rebuild it from the ground up."

Grip clings to the mic as if it's grounding him. He laughs, shaking his head.

"The best way to tear down the walls that divide us is to meet someone, to know someone on the other side of that wall," he says. "Cops were a 'they,' a 'them' until my cousin Greg became one. White people were a 'they,' a 'them' until I went to school with them. Until one of them became my best friend."

Grip turns his head toward stage left where he knows I always stand, his eyes tangling with mine.

"Until I fell in love with one of them," he says softly.

My heart contracts. I blink at the tears he inspires in me all the time. With his words, with his hands, his kisses. He has so many weapons at his disposal to break me down, every one more effective than the last.

I look out over the crowd, faces of every shade and walk of life, and wonder if they'll understand, if they'll hear what I heard from the moment Rhyson played "Bruise" in our meeting months ago. We'll see. Grip signals the drummer to drop the beat.

"This one's called 'Bruise'," he says softly.

Am I all of your fears, wrapped in black skin, Driving something foreign, windows with black tint
    Handcuffed on the side of the road, second home for black men

Like we don't have a home that we trying to get back to when PoPo
pulls me over with no infractions,
Under the speed limit, seat belt even fastened,
Turned on Rosecrans when two cruisers collapsed in Barking orders,
yeah, this that Cali harassment
Guns drawn, neighbors looking from front lawns and windows I know
cops got it hard, don't wanna make a wife a widow
But they act like I ain't paying taxes, like your boy ain't a citizen
They think I'm riding filthy, like I'm guilty pleading innocence.
They say it's 'Protect & Serve', but check my word
Sunny skies, ghetto birds overhead stress your nerves,
They say if you ain't doin' wrong, you got nothin' to fear, But the people
sayin' that, they can't be livin' here . . .
We all BRUISE, It's that black and blue
A dream deferred, Nightmare come true
In another man's shoes, Walk a mile or two
Might learn a couple things I'm no different than you!

You call for the good guys when you meet the bad men,
I'm wearing a blue shield and I still feel the reactions
When I patrol the block, I can sense dissatisfaction
There's distrust, resentment in every interaction,
Whether the beat cop, lieutenant, sergeant or the captain We roll our
sleeves up and we dig our hands in
I joined the force in order to make a difference,
Swore to uphold the law, protect men, women and children,
These life and death situations, we make split-second decisions
All for low pay, budget cutbacks and restrictions
Not just a job—it's a calling, a vocation,
My wife's up late pacin', for my safety—she's praying,
I see what you see on all the cell phones
I'm just a man with a badge trying my best to make it home.

. . .

WE ALL BRUISE, *It's that black and blue*
   A dream deferred, Nightmare come true
   In another man's shoes, Walk a mile or two
   Might learn a couple things
   I'm no different than you!

G_{RIP}

"YOU WERE AMAZING."

Bristol's soft encouragement soothes some of my uncertainty about the performance. Performing "Bruise" in a roomful of cops and community activists is much different than in front of screaming fans.

"She's right." Greg, who is dressed in his uniform, smiles, even though his eyes remain solemn. "We still have a lot of work to do so people feel like we're a part of the community. To protect them, not out to get them. 'Bruise' is exactly the kind of message both sides need to hear."

They're holding a reception for me to meet and greet people. I think I've shaken every hand here tonight. The stream of traffic is finally slowing down some, but I smile when I see my mom walking toward me. I didn't even realize she would be here tonight. The smile freezes on my face when I notice who walks with her. My cousin Jade and my Aunt Celia, who hasn't spoken to Greg in years.

"Hey, Marlon," Ma says softly, reaching up to hug me. "Bristol, Greg."

Greg lowers his eyes to the floor, not meeting my mother's eyes and certainly not his mother's.

"Hey, son," Aunt Celia says, her voice hesitant.

Greg looks up, and suddenly, he isn't the decorated officer. Not the strong man in uniform. In his eyes I see the young man he was all those years ago, wailing on my front yard with his brother dying in his arms. That young man's guilt and pain saturate the air around us. The look he gives his mother seeks something that only she can give him, and she does. She stretches her arms up, and he doesn't hesitate, folding his height in half to burrow into her neck, his tears and hers making peace, forgiving.

"Let's give them a minute," Ma says softly, tilting her head for us to step away.

"It's good to see you, Ms. James," Bristol says once we're a few feet from them. "You, too, Jade."

"Thank you for sending the tickets." Ma says.

Surprised, I look at Bristol, who just nods and tells my mom it was no trouble. I didn't know she sent tickets. Even after Bristol's "moment" with my mom, we haven't talked as much as we should. I've been giving her room to get used to Bristol and me. Maybe she was giving me room to change my mind. I hope she's starting to accept that won't be happening.

"That song 'Bruise,' it is dope," Jade says softly.

"Thanks," I answer. "I still want to get you in the studio writing. For real, Jade, it's past time you put all that talent to use."

"I'm always looking for new talent," Bristol interjects with a hesitant smile. "I won't know if you don't show me anything."

Jade's almond-shaped eyes narrow, like she's ascertaining if we're tricking her. I've never met anyone warier than Jade, but she's had lots of reason in her life to mistrust. She and I finally talked about what happened on that playground all those years ago. I won't say it changed everything overnight, but things have been a little easier between us.

"A'ight," Jade finally says, adjusting the Raiders cap she's never without. "Maybe this week."

"Good." I hook my elbow around her neck and kiss the top of her head, making her squirm and punch my arm. "Rhyson will be in the studio with me Thursday. Why not come ready with something for him to hear?"

Jade's eyes stretch. She may prefer hip-hop to Rhyson's modern rock, but she knows he owns Prodigy. She knows how famous he is, how successful.

"Seriously?" she asks.

"Seriously." I grin and drop another kiss on her head, one she doesn't dodge this time.

"I was hoping to see the baby," Ma says. "Where is Rhyson?"

"They left right after I performed," I say. "They needed to get Aria home."

"Since you're the godfather." Ma laughs. "What's that make me? The grand-godmama?"

"I'm sure they'd love that." I glance at Bristol, who usually gets quiet around my mother. "Bris, that would make your mom the grandmother and the grand-godmama. It's a mouthful."

"True." Bristol smiles stiffly, her fingers tight around mine.

"Guess that'll have to do for me," Ma says. "Till y'all give me some grandbabies of my own."

Bristol and I share a shockwave as my mother's words sink in. It's been a few weeks since that first Sunday dinner, and we haven't gone back. I've seen my mother, of course, but after that first disaster, we haven't been back at her table. I need to be sure it won't happen again, and when we go back, we can make new memories that eclipse the painful ones Bristol has now. Is this my mother signaling that she understands that?

"Um . . ." I'm not sure what to say, but it probably needs to be more than this.

"Marlon tells me you liked my greens, Bristol." Ma interjects, her expression softened, smiling. "I even heard you tried to make them yourself."

I casually mentioned that once to my mother, hoping to show her how sweet and funny Bristol can be. I feel Bristol's irritation reaching out for me. Shit. It might be angry sex for us tonight. No sex is not an option ever.

"Yes, well they didn't turn out very well." Bristol looks at me pointedly. "As I'm sure Grip mentioned."

"They couldn't have been any worse than the first time I tried." Ma cackles, shaking her head. "My mama took one bite and threw them in the trash."

"She did?" Bristol's smile comes a little easier.

"Oh, yeah. They were awful." Ma pauses and offers Bristol a tentative smile. "Why don't you come over a little early on Sunday, and I'll show you how I make them?"

Bristol's mouth drops open a little, and she blinks several times. I elbow her on the sly.

"Um, yeah. Yes. I mean, that would be awesome." Bristol's mouth stretches to its maximum smile capacity. "I'd like that very much."

Ma nods, her smile not as wide but sincere all the same. She turns her eyes to me, and they water. Even when we've spoken recently, this has stood between us. Her inability to accept that I plan to spend the rest of my life with someone she saw as wrong for me and perceived as an insult to the sacrifices she made for me.

"I've missed seeing you on Sundays, Marlon." She offers the words like an olive branch.

"I'll be there this week." I reach down and pull her small frame close. "We'll be there this week. I wouldn't miss you teaching Bristol to cook collard greens for the world."

She laughs against my chest, but her arms tighten around me, and I know she's missed our easy closeness as much as I have. She pulls back, sniffing, but still linking one arm around my waist.

"Bristol, I owe you an apology." Ma never has been one for wasted time and bullshit, so I shouldn't be surprised that she dives right in. "What Marlon said tonight is true. I've treated you like a 'they'. I don't anticipate my son giving you up anytime soon, so it's time we fixed that. Time we get to know each other."

Bristol blinks several times, her eyes filling.

"I used to pray that God would send my son a fighter like me," Ma continues. "A woman like me. I thought she would have to look like me, but that isn't true. When I saw what you would do for my son, I knew God had answered my prayers in you. I'm just a stubborn old woman."

Ma laughs, characteristic sassiness lighting her face.

"Not that old now." She rests a fist on her hip. "Don't get it twisted. Mama still got it."

Only my mother would manage to make even this moment funny.

"But I was nearsighted about you." Ma's laugh fades, but the smile still crinkles the corners of her eyes. "I hope you can forgive me for that."

"Yes, of course," Bristol says softly. "Thank you very much."

"No, thank you." Ma reaches up to kiss my cheek, patting my back before she pulls away. "Come on, Jade. Let's check on your mama and brother. I'll see you both on Sunday. Don't be late."

She takes a few steps before looking back over her shoulder. "Oh, and you can bring my car, too."

We stand there for a second after she's gone, both quiet. An airy laugh from Bristol breaks our silence.

"Did she really say grandbabies?"

I turn her into me, linking my fingers through hers and pressing our temples together so I can whisper in her ear.

"You have a problem with grandbabies? Beautiful, café au lait grandbabies?"

Bristol pulls back, one brow lifted.

"Did you just refer to my future children in terms of beverages? Coffee? Milk? I don't think so."

"Babe, that's what they call kids who—"

"I don't care what 'they' call them." She links her arms around my neck. "Aren't you the one who said no more they?"

That takes my mind back to the performance tonight.

"You think people heard what I was saying?" I don't often show uncertainty when it comes to my music, to my writing, but I can show Bristol every part of me. Even the parts that aren't sure. "I felt like I was performing on eggshells sometimes. Like they expected me to offend them."

"Think about the first time we talked at Mick's that day." Her smile grows reminiscent. "I asked you about people using the N-word."

"Ah, yes, your Twitter," I say, referring to her analogy of things she didn't understand, but made them work.

"Why do you think that conversation worked?" she asks. "Because you had a great rack, and I wanted to impress you?"

"Um . . . try again." She shakes her head and laughs up at me. "We wanted it to. We gave each other the benefit of the doubt. We wanted to understand. That's what 'Bruise' says. Walking in each other's shoes. Seeking to understand so we can change things. They couldn't have missed that."

"I'm the writer, but it seems like you always know what to say to me," I tell her softly.

"Is that so?" She kisses my chin and cups one side of my face. "I think you're just sweet talking me now with all that . . . chocolate charm."

Haven't heard that in a long time. I was a cocky son of a bitch back then. In many ways, I probably still am.

"Oh, no." I turn to kiss the inside of her wrist. "If I was spitting game, I'd say something like this.

A STORM COULD COME, *the winds will blow The rain can wash away*

But what we have will stand forever, to last another day. The world can rail, their weapons clatter

Let them wage their wars

But peace I've found, and all that matters Everything here in your arms."

"Wow," Bristol whispers, eyes wide, mouth softened into a smile. "That isn't Neruda, is it? Who wrote that?"

I tip up her chin and lay my lips against hers. No need to tell her yet that it could be part of my wedding vows.

"Just something I'm working on."

***

Readers are often tempted to stop right here and assume that Still, Book 3

of the Grip Trilogy is an afterthought because this part of Grip & Bristol's story ends happily for now.
NO!
Still is the most emotional chapter of their journey. It's a full-length novel that is the culmination of this epic love.
Tell you a little secret.
It's most readers' favorite part.
It's MY favorite part.
Don't tell the first two books! ;-)

STILL (Grip #3)
http://mybook.to/STILLAmazon

You can grab all 3 Books + Bonus Material
in the BOX SET!
"Future Glimpse" Chapters only in
enhanced Box Set!
FREE IN KU
US: https://amzn.to/2Gh3Rrs
Worldwide: http://mybook.to/TheGripBoxSet

*Audiobooks available for all 3 titles.
Check Audible Escape to listen FREE with subscription!

∾

GRIP/FLOW Spotify Playlist & Pinterest Board

STILL Spotify Playlist

ACKNOWLEDGMENTS

THERE ARE SO many people to thank this time around. There are always lots of people, but especially with this book because I needed so much. I needed perspectives, and you always had them to offer, Teri Lyn, Joanna, Lucy. Your input was invaluable in the early stages. You lived through so many iterations of this book you will probably barely recognize the final product. If there is anything good about it, though, please know you had a hand in it through your constructive honesty and patience with my writer neuroses. Margie, thank you for ALWAYS being in my corner and cheering me on and convincing me that I'm at least a halfway decent writer on days when I feel anything but. Your friendship is so precious to me. Mary Ruth, thank you for bringing so many of my words to life with your designs and all the tireless work you volunteered to do for me. For reading early and giving me wonderful feedback: Shamika, Sheena, Shelley, Michelle. Melissa and Val, thank you for helping with the Rabble Rousers, for giving direction, and making things fun when I can't even. LOL! And thank you to the Rabble Rousers and all the supportive folks in my reader group. You are my safe place. To the authors who supported me, answered my questions, read for me, told me to pull back or to press ahead, you're the bomb. Isabelle Richards, Mandi Beck,

Adriana Locke (#AddyOnTheSide), Corinne Michaels (Boo Biscuit), and Danielle Allen. To Heather of L. Woods PR for enduring my control freak-work-around-the-clockedness. I know I'm a piece of work, and you put up with me wearing a smile . . . and pink hair! LOL! Thank you, love. I could keep going, but this would become interminable, and I really want you to start reading this book! There are too many bloggers, readers, and authors who have impacted and influenced me to name. Thank you for being in my life and a part of what I do. It means the world!

Made in the USA
Columbia, SC
05 July 2025